GINGERBREAD MAN

Michael Shane

LMH Publishing Limited
7-9 Norman Road, Kingston CSO
email: henryles @cwjamaica.com

ISBN 976-610-203-1

Cover and Publication Design by Pamela Paris

Printed by Lightning Print

For Gips, the oldest member of my past…
and for Max, the youngest member of my future.
Love, eh!

Acknowledgments

*Gary, who has read everything I have written
and given me all the right hints.
Pamela, who was the first to really believe,
and the first to edit this monster.
Frank, who was mentor for this first foray into the strange world of
books, and who, unfortunately, is not here to see its final fruition.
To Mike Henry at LMH Publishing, who was willing
to take me to the next level.*

*And, always, there's Googie, who stands beside me,
through everything.*

DENUDED COMPLETELY—*divested of all clothing—devoid of even the tiniest follicle of hair. The skin glowed red; it had been scrubbed to remove any loose dermis. It glistened with a light coating of moisturizing oil. A well-turned body; an athlete's. It was a body not built in the gym, but sculpted in the real world.*

A man's body . . . stout and at least eight inches long, his penis hung in front of him, though he had no scrotum; it and his testicles were tight up close to his body like that of a baby's. Naked, he seemed to lack features, renouncing all personality.

He smiled and a personality occurred.

"How do I look?"

The naked man stood under a light in an otherwise dark room. A man on show. The room smelled sterile. He scratched his newly bald head.

A voice answered from the dark; it came from above, like from—god? "You're going to itch like a son of a bitch when it starts to grow back in."

"It was your idea, you'll have to scratch it." He smiled again; he had a nice smile, and a soft, certainly English accent . . . the naked man still had his charm.

"Yes . . . yes, do go dress yourself, darling." A woman's voice.

1

AT A PLACE where variety came to mingle, on the eve of a not-unlike-tonight kind of night, I met him. Met him by a rock overlooking a bay. A cool calypso voice and graying temples . . . I fell in love moments after we met. He had grown up a child of island aristocracy. It is Thomas' story to tell, so I'll let Thomas tell it.

CHARLESTON. I liked Charleston, I got laid here once. It's like a step back in time for me. I came here for the first time 16 years ago, drove past the historic church towers and got grabbed by the soft southern charm of it all. It was a little like Atlanta, if you know Atlanta, just quieter and by the sea; very important that, being by the sea. A little like home—so I bought some land here.

I heard someone say once that in the South the past is never forgotten. It is very much like that here, you can feel the colonialism; it is palpable in the looks on the faces of dark people you encounter; I have felt this too in other places . . . it is very unlike the feeling of 'Home'. They still live a very colonial lifestyle there, but the atmosphere is . . . one of integration, lacking in the mutual fear. Sometimes I can smell 'Home' . . .

THE TABLE was set with crisp white linen, white white, like an American supermarket eggshell white; and pressed neat. Linen napkins of the same white, circled in silver. Rings polished to sheen. Silverware set formally, fork fork fork on the left, knife knife spoon on the right, spoon fork at the top, bread plate, butter knife on the side; the set had belonged to a great-grandmother and had originally come from Russia. Water was poured from crystal into crystal. The fine Irish lead twinkled in the haphazard light beneath the shade of logwood trees.

Black faces, smiling white, and chattering patois abounded, servile. Going about the business of the table and the breakfast picnic. It was Sunday. A cool breeze freshened the Sunday morning with the sweet fragrance of the logwood blossoms. Around that wafted the scents of breakfast: Frying fish, brewing coffee, Johnny cakes, roasting pigeon and *volaille*, eggs, bread, plantain, green banana; odors of eschaviche for the fish; pepper, raw and hot.

We were at the farm. Friends had come to hunt, fish, eat and relax, and perhaps to drink a few, or a few too many.

I was 10.

"Yu is 'ungry, mas' T., eh, *cher*?" Miss Clarisse and Miss Ida passin' by carrying plates of callalloo and roast breadfruit.

MISS CLARISSE WAS Miss Ida's daughter. She was about 20 then, had worked with us as long as I could remember. She was tall and very dark, long and lean, a body of fine tuned muscle, small of breast and firm of buttocks. She was totally opposite the short stout earth-motherly big-bosomed large-buttocked form of her mother. It was her father she resembled, Mas' Pierre; a past-70 gentleman of stature. A fit handsome man who looked better than many men 50 years his junior. A handsome man of deep mahogany whom I looked up to and feared; he was Grandpa's foreman and my teacher in all things Farm.

"Yes . . ." in final answer to Miss Ida's question, I smiled lovingly at her, mother figure to me.

"Jus' coo a' dat smile eh . . . wha' a 'andsome bwoy 'e d' mek . . . dis one goin' 'ard fe tame, eh, Miss Ida?" Clarisse touched me softly with a cool dark hand.

Brushing me with long fingers that evoked a dry-mouthed remembrance of her nakedness at the side of the river; shining beads of water caressing the ebony length of her flesh. Tall dark and naked, large purple nipples taut and long, dew glistening on the thick curls of her pubic hair. My prepubescent penis stirred, and I blushed.

"True garl, too true, but 'e is beautiful, don't . . . come fe Johnny cake, Sweetness." Miss Ida called me Sweetness.

There was laughter from the house. I glanced over my shoulder; grandma wouldn't like me filling my stomach before breakfast. Clarisse smiled at me and I thought of touching her breast as I had done earlier at bathtime . . . .

I LIKE land. I own a piece in New Mexico, a small piece, south a ways. Outside Vancouver I own an acre. Have two small lots a quarter-mile from the beach in Southern Mexico; it's not much of a beach, and Chetumel isn't much of a town, but I like that. Grandpa left me some bits too, 15 acres in Grenada, 10 acres in Martinique—I had to sell seven—and my favorite piece, five acres near Montpelier in the South of France. Not a house in the lot. I just like the land. Grandpa had liked land. In the end, that was all he had left.

I AM NOT quite a policeman, not quite a private detective. I guess you could call me a freelance investigator. I work for police forces on problem crimes—a troubleshooter, perhaps? A Criminalist. I have degrees in psychology and criminology, diplomas in forensic science and pathology. I am a graduate of Quantico, the F.B.I. school.

I grew up with my grandparents; that spring breakfast under the trees was part of my last full year spent at 'Home'. At ten they sent me off to boarding school in Montpelier, France. Then for my 14th birthday I was transferred to school in Quebec, Canada. A migrant child of island life.

After graduation, I didn't go 'Home'. It is hard to live with people so old, when you are so young. In my heart's memories I love them both still, but then I longed to be away. I went to New York College instead, then got a scholarship to go to Georgetown in my second year.

Studying psychology led by bizarre twist to criminology studies; Forensics was fascinating. Then a most strange turn (I am not a lover of any form of authority), I ran off to Quantico, diplomas in hand. It was 1960-something, they cut my hair and gave me a job.

In 1969 and 1970 I, because of my French I guess, ended up with units of the Fed in Southeast Asia. It was a weird-as-all-fucking-hell world over there in those days; stranger yet to be a cop in a war theater. What we were there to police I will never really be sure, but America was all twisted in those days.

That was the end of my F.B.I. tenure; I blew the fuck out of there the minute I hit Yankee soil. The agency was chock full of fuckheads. It was a microcosm of what was most wrong with America: very straight, very uptight, very self-righteous, egotistical and full of shit.

I grew my hair back and took a job teaching at the University of Florida, professor of Criminology, paid shit but a nicer atmosphere you could never have asked for. It was from there that I got asked to add my expertise to a police case; a pair of murders lacking in evidence. I did well, they were happy, and they liked me . . . best of all, I think, they hadn't had to deal with the F. fucking B. fucking I. as the particular captain had put it. They get in your way, make you fill out all kinds of paperwork and then take all the glory when you solve a case.

An idea gelled, a business developed—slowly, though. It's eight and a half years since that first case, and I still have to lecture and do visiting professorships and write articles to survive.

WELL, that, being my business, brings me around to where I am now. There have been some murders, some brutal killings of some very ordinary people . . . serial-type murders. There had been nine in all, throughout the Southeast, in about twice as many months, when they asked me in. Hardly a clue to go by, and the F.B.I. knocking at the door to be let in. They sent for me instead.

I should have taken that teaching option in Colorado.

THE POLICE forces involved had set up a joint operations center in Atlanta, after Number Six, when it became clear that they were experiencing a regional crime wave. Atlanta is the scene of the latest killing, and also the fourth.

I am not what I seem. I am what you perceive me to be.

Identity is not what you make of yourself, it is how you are seen..
I am perception, 20/20 hindsight- and to you I am a monster.

Why? Indeed? for I am the Master, the king and the Queen. A#1,
Boss, big cheese.

But you can call me Monster.

P.S. Catch as catch can, for I am the gingerbread man.

LOVE YA.

GBM #11.

"HELLO . . ." A drawn-out whisper. *"Hello"*, as she opened the door onto the darkness of her eight p.m. house. It was Sunday. She knew she had imagined it. The alarm called recognition of the open door. The stereo was playing; *"The trains and the boats and the planes will bring you back, back home to me . . ."* Dionne Warwicke. Reaching out she flicked the light switch. Her head snapped up, startled by the image of herself in a long mirror. She was not yet used to the new color of her hair. Keying in her code, heard the distant reply and knew all was ... secure. "Hello," whispered on the wind of the closing door in her mind; it had sounded softly, well ... English. Just house noises.

Picking back up her overnight bag, she smiled at the thought of her weekend with a boy named Bob; a fine body and up-standing penis-ial powers. They had been to Cocoa Beach, Florida. The light in the hall she added for prosperity, "Hello", its glow filtered through to the bedroom. Dropping the bag in-side the door she went straight for the bathroom.

A waterfall of urine echoed in the quiet, unraveling toilet paper following, flush. She hung her panties from the door knob, turned on the light and went to wash her hands. She looked nice in the mirror, scratched the edge of her neat trimmed mons, examined its hairy flow into the valley of her labia. She washed her hands then.

"Tired." She told herself, stretching and sliding open the closet door.

"Hello!"

The voice hadn't then been so very soft, still very English.

Smack! Like in a DC comic the sound registered as a picture, full of color and exclamation, in her brain. And as she fell backward—heading for the floor and unconsciousness—she thought *Christ—he's wearing my favorite dress.* And with that last thought she became victim number 11 .

2

ANOTHER BODY, just like all the other bodies, dead. As you can tell by the note, 11 in all, stacking up, stinking up the morgue. Done to death in some weirdly unalike fastidious fashion. Freaked fucking world: the body bouncing along black-bagged, zippered and tagged. Into the bag, onto the trolley, into the van with the flashing lights and the word CORONER stenciled on the side. Dead girl this time, different size, different shape, different wounds, same pattern: random.

Eleven—almost an even dozen, one about every other month for the past two years. Killed on a Monday night, a Tuesday morning, or maybe Thursday noon; from as far south as Venice, Florida to as far north as Jonesborough, Tennessee, on Highway 11E; the only pattern seemed to be that there was no pattern, so it seemed. Dead people, picked alive, no preference given to age, race, creed, color or sexual orientation. Education, ethnicity, appetites, preferences never seemed to matter. Familiarity found only in the letters that accompanied each body; typewritten, poetic almost, chaotic often, signed each and every: G.B.M., Gingerbread Man ... S.T.U.M.P.E.D.

Forensics and Pathology working day and night, detectives from 11 states; DNA traces and matchups, chemical analyses, tests, fingerprint files, physical evidence, photographic, witness statements, phone calls, Serology screens, blood sample tests, character references, background checks, known associations. Six teams of detectives, from New Orleans in the west, to Miami in the south; Richmond had sent the Virginia contingent. 124 men and women working under them, sorting, matching, correlating, counting, separating, adding, subtracting, calling and following up.

And still nothing but murder.

"SHE BE all free in dar, yu know, if yu wanted to go back in 'eh."

"Nah, not yet . . ." I lit a cigarette, glanced at my watch and realized that I had left it on the hotel bedside. I rubbed through my eyes and pushed my hair back from my face with a grunt.

"'Ow come, man?"

"Tired . . . what time is it?"

"Bout dat time." Detective Leeman was, and I presume still is, a man I found it easy to like. Black as night, short, stocky and very good-natured . . . perhaps the term is, full of fun. He hailed from Haiti, Ay-tee if you heard him say it; Cap Haitien, Northern Haiti, *Ça va?*

I had this wonderful flavor in my mouth; it had been with me all day, I was trying to decipher what it was exactly.

"How you suppose he get it all without makin' no fuck' mess, man?"

We ducked under the yellow tape.

"Evening, boys."

"Hmm," and a nod was the only reply I got; talk much?

"Hey, Tom," detective Dick passing us on the walk, in a hurry; tall, slim and George Bush-like.

"Hi, Dick . . . " Name suited him. "What's the hurry?"

"Bed's unmade, Frenchy wants sperm glow."

"My favorite, checking for cum stains in the dark."

"Don't it, *ami*," Leeman added with that bright white Close-up smile.

The house was cop-full, they were dusting, brushing, dust busting, picking, plotting, photo-ing, tagging, bagging, bullshit-ting. I had been inside earlier for a cursory glance. Now it was like the policeman's ball; boys in blue, plainclothes, lab coats, techs, photo G's, a suit or two and even a couple of guys who looked like they'd just checked in from special ops, or vice maybe.

"Hope we didn't drag y'all off some nice warm pussy, Tom."

"You did, Frenchy . . . but hell, the fucking cat hates me anyway."

"I got this preference for sheep myself, you know." His manner and nature were Southern; he spat snuff now into the cup he always carried. How he got his name I am not quite sure, and never quite rude enough to ask; he wasn't French, didn't seem French. A roly-poly little round-faced dark-haired look-like-an-oriental kind of guy. He had been born in Cambodia, actually; migrated to America at age nine, before *that* war.

"Well hey, Frenchy, why not . . . they say you can't tell the difference . . . ain't that right, Dick?"

"Huh . . .What? . . . sure, Tom, yeah," vacant. We were all leaning around in the living room waiting for the techs to finish with the bedroom.

"Well, Frenchy, you are the boss man . . . I'm ready, do tell."

"Well, son . . ." He handed me some Polaroids. "*Da da* . . . okay, so you were in here at first, right, you saw the layout?"

"Just a glance . . ."

"Well, shit, we jus' go over it again," he spat, wiped some dribble off his chin and smiled brown. A redneck at heart. "They found her in here." Polaroid number 1, he waved his hand at the bedroom, the crime scene unit was still picking up bits and pieces. The floor was mapped in string grids and numbered; it made for easier cataloguing.

There was a large picture on the wall, in black and white: Hemingway on the wall, the bearded man in turtleneck.

"The photographers did a great job." Always the first ones in, the photo boys catalogued the scene before anyone could touch anything, Polaroid for instant gratification, 35 mm. for lasting memories. Then the body could be removed to the pathology lab for forensic examination. The crime scene unit would then go over the scene with a fine-toothed comb, marking and cataloguing. The rest of the house would be given a thorough, if somewhat cursory going over at first, with specific interest given to point of entry, place of crime and point of exit.

"You ready?" He spat the brown ooze into Styrofoam.

I looked down at the Polaroid in my hand and shook my head, "Yep . . . go ahead," looking up where Miss Body had hung, hung upside down, her wrists and ankles tied. Pale big breasts hanging loosely about her chin, nipples erect. She was not an attractive corpse. The dead are usually not much to look at.

"Blunt trauma, hit her . . ." that last word came out "har" . . . "hit har". ". . . B*am*! Square dead center of the forehead . . . a large frying pan, ah . . . hers, of course, seems to have been the weapon of choice. Ah, it were left on the floor by the closet, thar . . ." We didn't enter the room but crowded, six of us, in the doorway like bloodthirsty onlookers. Frenchy spat into his cup.

"Sorry, Frenchy . . ." One arm tight across my chest, the one whose hand held the Polaroid, the fingers of the other hand toyed with the side of my face. Thinking fingers, you know. "Ahm, sorry to interrupt, . . . but, but was she naked before or after the frying pan thing?"

His face lit up like Christmas morning. "Hah . . . I got ya man, read your mind this time . . . A.F.T.E.R., after, except for the panties . . . Um, she seemed to have used the can before an' then hung them panties thar on the door knob."

I had noticed the panties, not yet removed. "Dick . . . can I?" I motioned across the room, he nodded back. I crossed the floor and lifted them from the door, I ran the panties between my fingers, sniffed them . . . to see if they were clean, you know.

"Hmm . . ."

"You are a gross man, sniffin' panties."

"Gross? . . . Look who's talking, the tobacco-spitting red-neck chinaman motherfucker." I smiled and tossed him the panties. "Smell."

"Springtime fresh . . . The panties are fresh." To match his face to the voice almost made me want to laugh.

"Yep . . . somebody took home a trophy."

WEARING her favorite dress, Killer. Killer, tall, lanky, wearing a stocking (not hers, but *like* hers . . . no foreign fibers are found) over the head, stepped out of the closet and set the frying pan down. Killer flexes fingers, latex-gloved fingers, Killer's feet are encased in plastic Glad bags, hers, as shoe coverings. Kneeling beside her, "Hmm . . . lovely." Killer ran a hand slowly up the naked length of her leg, taking her skirt up with the stroke. "Delicious . . . I do hope you're getting all of this . . . Hmm?" Killer glanced back over a shoulder; a small flashing red light gave away a video camera on a tripod, motion-sensored it followed the action. Exposing her, Killer rolled her over, bound her hands and feet, and hoisted her up. "What a lovely face you have . . . porcelain . . . I'm going to drain your blood . . . oh, looky looky, what a pretty little twat, and so nicely shaved."

"UH . . . THE ROPE, the rope came from the garage . . ." Frenchy continued. "I know the question . . . she's a neat freak, everythang had its place, thar's a painted outline in the garage whar the rope should hang . . . that thing in her neck is a curing needle, for ham and the like, you know." He tapped the picture in my hand. "Attached it to a piece of two-inch clear plastic flexi-hose, kind the kids use for bonging beer, 'bout three foot long."

"Anyone making some coffee? Frenchy, what's 'bonging beer'?"

"Leeman, you bring the coffee?"

"*Pas Moi,* man . . . not my day, sir." He smiled; they were friends, spoke their versions of French to one another. I never told them I spoke French; some things you keep to yourself, just in case. "Garcia is the man."

"Well, let's get har done, man . . . I could kill for a cup mahself. I cain't believe that you don't know what fuckin' bonging is . . . funnelling beer? Bonging . . . funnelling beer down a hose, where you been, man?"

"Redneck hell, that's where." The room was immaculate almost, one might say, sterile; they hadn't moved the yellow bucket yet, a yellow pail into which Killer had drained her blood. Once blue in her veins, now Kool-Aid red, with an almost purple undertone; maybe the color of ripe cherries. Something, a fiber from the rope above? A droplet, and wavelets spread outward, rippling the smooth surface of the ocean of blood.

"It's very neat in here," I, making an observation.

"You thinking that that might be the point, eh?"

"Leeman, they always seem to have one . . . yes, a very careful killing."

A very interesting aside about our Killer; never brings anything with him to the party. Everything used in the crime seems to come from among the victim's property. No foreign matter, no foreign fibers, blood, proteins, soil; very clean, very efficient, very professional. If it weren't for the notes left behind we'd have very little except for 11 unsolved murders.

We had put the notes through every possible test, chromatographic analysis, infrared screening . . . graphologists had studied the lettering to come up with the make of typewriter used to type the notes . . . 11 of them to be exact. The paper was a standard letter bond available in any office supply; three letters appeared to have come from the same sheaf, the rest odd. No evidential fingerprints, no fibers, nothing out of place.

"Anything else?" They had moved in vapor lamps to elucidate the room; they made it hot. Black lights were ready for obscure imaging.

"Nothin' so far, Tom . . . if I never knew better I'd a guessed that she hung herself upside down an' drained out her own blood. Damn . . . if this guy ain't good, shit."

"Very good . . . Dick, you boys finished up in here yet, can I light up a smoke?"

"Why not, we ain't findin shee*it*."

"Gimme one too." Frenchy held out two fingers, I offered Leeman too. "What's what on the girl?"

"Jus' the initial age, race, color 'sheeet'." Dick added. "Donovan's on the computey doin' her up real nice now."

"Damn—what *is* this you're smoking?"

"Rubios; a friend brought them from Guatemala for me." A pair of lab techs appeared, they were carrying a stainless steel contraption, a bucket in some kind of cradle . . . a motion carrier of some kind. They were going to try to remove the bucket of blood to the lab intact.

"Captain's coming . . . Captain's coming . . ." Like a telegraph down the line of men to our ears. A whisper through the ranks. Detective Jeremiah, a tall black man with very Arabic features, came with word; he was very handsome, had been a football player in college, now the bearer of bad news. He would have turned pro but bad knees left him flat.

"Jeremiah—couldn't you have stalled him? . . . It's your call, Tom."

Jeremiah was already gone. Using both hands I pushed the hair back from my face; holding it a moment I inhaled deeply on my cigarette. There are many facets to my job: I am hired to organize an investigation, bring into play the proper experts, do an efficiency report on the operation, add my expertise to the case, organize and streamline, set the goals and the parameters and deal with the public relations. This somehow skipped my portfolio but I always got stuck with the job.

"I spoke to him *last* time," whine and pout.

"That's what they pay you all them big bucks for, man."

"Sir Michael . . . *good* to see you," my salesman voice, sing-song and soothing, friendlies oozing. I took his hand. "How are you this evening?" As I met him at the door, moved a hand to his back and walked with him outside.

"Sucking air, Tom . . ." He looked sad, old, his head moved slowly to survey the crowd. "It's 11:35 and I'm out of . . . the house . . . it—it can't be that good . . . what's the story?"

"Breaks the monotony of the nine-to-five, Michael . . . Story's the same, let's walk around back, too many ears and eyes."

"Another 'Letter writer'?" In-house we referred to this as the Letter Writer case.

"Yep."

"Christ . . . in *my* city; her ladyship the commissioner is . . . well, she isn't going to be . . . happy. She kicked my ass all the way over here."

"She with you . . . ?" I looked around nervously; "Her Ladyship" was a real battleaxe. Give her her dues: a strong-willed, efficient woman and a serious fucking battleaxe.

"No, thank god—but, she is . . . she is screaming, says we've been given responsibility . . . as host city . . . doesn't want to look bad in front of her peers . . . you know. How is this one, Tom?"

I was inhaling on a fresh cigarette. "Clean . . . so clean it jumps out at you."

"Shitshit*shit*." Michael Ernesto Fabio Oswaldo and a couple of other things Spanish, Captain; shortish, darkish, once upon a Puerto Rican. He dressed badly, looked at this moment as if he had just walked off a golf course; neon polyester and a wide white belt, white shoes and a bad shirt. Captain had come to Atlanta via New York. Atlanta really isn't Spanish Harlem, too far from Miami; center of the South, a good ol' boy's wet dream. Right now he looked sorry that he'd taken the job.

"You hate me, don't you , Tom." He rubbed the heels of his palms into his eyes. "Aaaargh . . . Nothing? . . . Shitshit*shit*." He ran fingers back through the thick black hair, his face suddenly deeply furrowed, pensive. I imagined I could see his hair graying right there before my eyes; if I listened I might even hear the process.

"The Mayor, she . . . she is even angrier, if that's possible, than the Commissioner—tell me, Tom, please . . . tell me we're making progress . . . *please* . . . We have nothing?" Crestfallen.

"No, not nothing . . . walk . . ." I lit a cigarette, felt the smoke coursing, soothing. We stepped into a sudden light around by the pool in the back yard, a motion detector light; we moved on and it went out. "Not *nothing*, just very little . . ." I smiled, am not sure he felt reassured, "Look, captain, I—I've only been here long enough for the blood to dry but we're working it . . . there are some things here that are very . . . interesting . . ." There was a set of steps at the side of the house entering into the kitchen. I sat. "Look, I've just came back from making my rounds of all the crime scenes . . . I've read all the on-site reports . . . there's stuff here . . ."

"Stuff . . . shitshit*shit* . . . ghost stuff . . . what stuff? Something? What kind of fucking criminal leaves no traces?"

"A smart one in a hard plastic suit."

"Is that a brainstorm?" Grasping straws, his eyes lit up.

"Only if I thought Batman was really doing the killing."

"*Huh*? "

"Never mind, but it's a better explanation than a ghost."

"What, Batman? . . . I—oh, it's a joke, sorry . . . brain lag." He had this habit of speaking in staccato bursts of thought.

"Brainstorms . . . Captain, do me a favor, tell Frenchy that I've gone back to the office . . . tell him to call me when he's through."

"Leaving me? . . . Well, be that way . . . well—what can I tell the Chief, he'll want something to tell the Commissioner?"

"Lie."

"I've been doing that for weeks."

"Good, then you should have perfected it by now." I started away, stopped, patted out another cigarette, paused . . . "Hang tough . . . maybe, just *maybe*."

He smiled then.

Blue cloth, brass badges, flashing lights of all colors, Christmas in hell. I made my way back to the relative quiet of the other side of the yellow line, sneaking out on the side away from the vultures with their press cards. Animals—they seemed to get word directly from god whenever anything horrible happened. They appeared, circling, no matter how quiet you tried to keep things. They were always there scenting death, tasting sorrow, and always lacking . . . sensitivity.

My car, a nondescript American car in police special silver or gray, sat on a lonely street beneath a shedding old oak tree. I glanced at my watch—it was an Omega that I had inherited from Grandpa—and realized that it was still on the bedside at the hotel. Still I guessed it must be past midnight in the dark of a cloudy night. The streetlight above the car was out. I shivered and wished for a warm beach somewhere.

VERY GOVERNMENT, I suppose would be a good way to describe my office at the station. I lit a cigarette; could give a flying fuck for all the no smoking signs posted everywhere, no one seemed to pay them any mind at all. The walls were white, glaring, under the too-bright fluorescents. My desk was one of these standard issue teachers' type, all wood and scratches. The chair at least was nice, a junior executive swivel model, in plush black Naugahyde. It was a big room, 13x17, with lots of wall space and no window; I had put two long tables down the middle, to spread out stuff, and the walls were covered with cork board. Both were covered with papers, pictures, notes, numbers, tid bits . . . a collage of crime, numbered 1-10 . . . with space for more, of course. We are a pessimistic lot.

There was coffee, in the Mister Coffee pot, on a small side table in the corner. I poured a cup, opened the mini fridge below for some milk . . . I believe there ought to be a law against nondairy creamers, there probably ought to be a law against drip coffee makers too and artificial fluorescent sunlight, but hey.

I tasted the coffee. Yuck.

It was there in front of me, there on the wall somewhere, for sure, an inkling. An inkling of a notion, proof of an idea I was getting . . . an itch on my brain, actually. I lit a cigarette with the butt of the last one; the air conditioning was driving me mad. I'm a fresh air kind of guy. Holding back my not-so-golden bangs I studied the wall, not really looking at anything in particular, just drinking in the whole thing. I revolved slowly on my heels; the room was full of death.

"Yes, yes you fuck . . . uh huh . . . I'm getting your vibe now, bitch." Is speaking to yourself the first sign of old age? The hair on my shoulders and the age in my eyes.

I told you that I have two degrees, psychology and criminology, add a dash of forensic sciences; match the crime to the mind, match the mind to the criminal, match the criminal to the evidence, match the evidence to the crime. Sound easy? Yeah, right, but it's what I do. In a nutshell, I catch weird criminals. Blow my own horn: I am one of the best at what I do; the F.B.I. specializes in people like me, and then they stifle them with bureaucracy and mire them down in politics.

You know what they say ... F.B.I., Fucking Bastards & Idiots ... and it is not only their Behavioral Sciences group that could be the best at what they do; yet they often come up short somehow ... the British, Metropolitan police ... Scotland Yard is far better, the Canadian Mounties are a strong and solid force, the French Surete ... it is a matter of jurisdiction and politics more than anything else. U.S. crime fighters suffer from the problem of lack of cross-cooperation ... ATF won't tell DEA what they're doing; NSA and FBI are clueless to one another.

Scotland Yard is a good example of the near perfect type of force; they are the local constabulary, the state police, the federal police, the intelligence community and the secret service all rolled into one ... no boundaries, no holdbacks, no petty conflicts, just good solid police work, from the man on foot patrol to the boys in the "Flying Squads", England's crack rapid deployment police units. Coordination of effort.

If the F.B.I. does one thing well, though, it is producing data; their VICAP unit (Violent Criminal Apprehension Program) has more criminal information on hand than any other police force in the world. For instance, they have over 200 million fingerprints on file at NCIC in Washington.

Anyway, I was saying, there are maybe three other people in this country with my range of qualifications and my years of experience: two work for the F.B.I. and Claire is retired. I am a lot more pleasant to work with than the F.B.I. Jobs come my way, not only on the strength of my work, but also on the fact that the local force isn't trampled all over, they maintain control ... I advise. It is important for them to get their own sense of accomplishment; it is strictly a consultancy that I offer, and I do good work. Still, these crimes were of a trans-state nature, and the F.B.I. usually forced their jurisdiction ... maybe it was my presence, I guess that was supposed to be the idea.

The desk was piled high with files. Paperwork, boy, this fucking job could create paper; photos, photo analyses, hard evidence catalogues, evidence interpretations, DNA traces ... shit, each piece of evidence generated about 10 pieces of evidential attachments. And you had pathology reports, forensics reports, serology reports, graphologist reports, ballistics reports,

crime scene reports, first officer reports, eyewitness reports . . .
hair samples, saliva samples, blood types . . . possibilities, probabilities, hopefuls, matches, similarities, negatories, correlations.
Not here, though, no correlations . . . fucking similarities . . .
bloody notes. (Not blood-covered . . . just a swear word.)

11 crimes, 11 killings; their basic M.O. different, in a sense:
look, the initial methods of death differed, but the notes and the
brutality of the deaths, similar. We've had a straight stabbing
here, a bludgeoning there, here a hanging, there an electrocu-
tion, one gassed, another shot oh, and a drowning with a bludgeoning, yes, and my personal favorite, an entire half of a house
blown up, that was Number Four . . . yes, Number Four, *blown
fucking up*. Different crimes, different victims, graphic forms of
slaughter all tied together by three little letters . . . GBM. Ginger Bread Man.

The notes were top secret, that kept us able to separate copy-
cats from the real thing . . . enabled us to sort the crazy confes-
sors from the perpetrators. The press would have a field day
with the letters, but the letters were our only ace. *Run run as
fast as you can, you can't catch me I'm the Gingerbread Man.*

11 crimes, different crimes, tied together . . . orchestrated?
. . . linked, GBM . . . orchestrator, director. I pulled down one
of the notes.

"Yep, yep, I can smell you now . . . can you hear me
knocking . . ." Note number nine, a copy, of course, on the
same bond with the same type of typewriter. I turned it over in
my fingers, sniffed the bond.

A cockroach watched me from his corner of the room. I say
his corner because he occupied it often.

> Hey where did we go,
> Days when the rain came
> . . . in the misty morning fog,
> With hearts a-thump and you
> My Brown-eyed girl
> The old man with the transistor walking,
> . . . do you remember when we used to sing.
> Even in death she is dead
> GBM #9

P.S. you're falling behind . . .
play catch up
Do you recognize the lyrics?

Sometimes they were verbose and sometimes:

Did you know life is a terminal disease?
—I know, lacking a little in good taste.
Say, are you having any luck yet?
NYAAH NYAAH NYAAH!

GBM #10

I LIT another cigarette—I smoke too much—sat on the corner of the desk and picked up a photo of Number Ten. I would remember Number Ten . . . Number Ten had an odor to it, a nasty odor, vile gaseous intestinal stench. Number Ten had been slit open, gutted like a game animal . . . all the while alive and able to see. The smell, the stench of severed intestines. The smell of burnt flesh.

Smell that smell.

3

YEAH, I MIGHT just say Thomas is handsome, but it's really sexy that I find him. Mr. Average. It's in the way he can look at you, man, the turn of his hands, fingers long, sensual I guess.

A nice smile and lips to match. A quiet cool maybe ... nice legs, too, he said he inherited them from his grandfather, he would pass a smile then ... I think he had only fond memories of the man, you know what I mean. With Thomas what you see is what you get, you know; this alone I think could make him attractive. He likes the beach, Rock and roll and blue jeans.

"It's the smell of it, ... the sea, it's a most ... intoxicating odor ... Cold sea, hot sea, North Sea all the same. Draws you in.

"Rock and Roll, fuck, I don't know ... I guess the first time I heard ... Led Zeppelin, what is this, the fucking Spanish Inquisition? ... "Misty Mountain Hop" I got a hard-on. Like good reggae music makes you high and horny, except Stairway—I never did like that one. Blue jeans ... well, shit, what doesn't go with blue jeans ... I like Elton John too."

Maybe it was the gentlemanly way he had, that was cool. The touches of charm, the poise. That accent might do it, an accent mixed with the world, you couldn't quite place it sometimes. That could do it, huh, nothing like a little accent to water a girl's pussy. Cool, so I said it, I can't quite put my finger on it exactly, 'cept to say that he makes my little southern pussy flutter. Then again maybe it was just his smile.

DROPPING the photo of Number Ten on the desk I picked up the phone, pressed nine... "Dispatch," softly called back down the wire.

"Christie love, *c'est moi.*"

"Ah, Tommy, speak French in my ear ... ohh, it is *so* sexy. How come you didn't stop in to say hello on your way up? ... I saw you sneakin' in, an' you say you love me," she giggled a little. Christie love was a somewhat pretty little thing of a girl; looked "country", 24, brown haired, blue eyed, nice smile, fitted good in cop blues. Two tits, all her teeth and toes.

"Brain overload, sweets, help ... I need *help*. Can you find Frenchy for me, on the radio, ask him to ring me?"

"Sure hon'—you eat yet?"

"Eat? ... it's after midnight."

"Now that don't answer my question, honey ... I'm on a break in five minutes, you want anything?"

"A nice coffee, a latte or cappuccino or something ... oh, and a pastry."

"There's a Cuban place round the corner, 24 hours ... you want a guava thing?"

"*Pasteles de guayaba ... como no.*"

"What?"

"I'd love you if you bring a nice big jug of the coffee ... you want money?"

"Ah ... but would ya take me home ... ?"

"I'd think about it."

"In that case hold onto your money till we done with the negotiations, eh?"

Pace the floor scratching my chin; I had a Marlon Brando habit, scratched my jaw in short strokes with the back of my fingers. Head down, a pace or two, looked at the wall without seeing it. Pushed my eyeglasses back on top of my head. *"In the days of my youth I was told what it means to be a man. now that I've reached that age, I try to do those things the best I can."* Doing the right thing; the right thing, I think, was what first attracted me to the possibilities of the work I do, it is what *should* be that interested me.

I am a man of possibility.

I picked up the phone as it sang its first ring, concentrating myself into a sixth sense frame of mind. "Yeah, Frenchy."

"Uh huh, shit man, you going psychic on me now? . . . damn phone didn't even ring yet." I could hear him spit into his cup . . . yuck.

"Rang this end, man . . . I tried you on the cellular, where are you?"

"Battery went dead but I'm right har still, whar the fuck I don't wanna be." Cambodia sounding farther and farther away. "What you need, sport?" Bet they don't say sport on that side of the Pacific much. Life can really change you: find its cubby-hole and stuff you right in it, or tear you away completely from what you were and fit you into the mold of your environment.

"You coming in?" I ran my finger across the photo: death in Kodak Colorwatch.

"Not if I can help it . . . can it wait till morning? Whar are *you*, by the way?"

"Office . . . I think I might have something." Just then Christie love showed up, with the coffee. "Savior."

"What?"

"Not you Frenchy, Christie just showed up with decent fucking coffee."

"Oh, lucky you . . . tell her I love her, ask her if she'll marry me."

"Frenchy wants to know if you're free for marriage this weekend."

"Yeah, why, is he available for some overtime security duty?" Smiled; she was sexy, a bit of the little girl about her.

"You want sugar, hon?"

"Oh, and she leaves the door wide open . . . no, I am sweet enough as it is. --Frenchy, never mind . . . I'll save it for tomorrow . . . you can fuck off now."

"Kind of you; kiss Christie for me."

"Right." I slumped into the chair; Christie love had taken perch on the desk, her legs dangling a whole foot from the floor.

"So, Christie love, what is all the excitement?" Dipping my lips into creamed coffee, mmmm.

"Heard they had Number 11 tonight, its all over the radio . . . Pretty gruesome?"

"Not at all, actually . . . *mmm*, good coffee, thanks." There was, in this light, a perfectness to her skin.

"Pleasure . . . so, you like this work?" Small talk.

"Hmmm . . ." a slight shrug. "I guess . . . yeah, I really do, god I am *tired*. Shit, Christie, how the hell do you work these hours?"

"Hurumph, I dunno, do it regular-like an' you kinda get used to it . . . like I'll be outta here in an hour, get some sleep an' wake up in time to enjoy the day . . . better than missing all that nice sunlight."

"Yep . . . after this is over I am going to take days off. . ." I studied the creaminess of the Capuchin. I guess at heart I am lazy, liked my life without interference.

"You going to stay around to walk me home?"

"You live close?"

"Near 'nuff."

ONE THING I'VE LEARNED in this work is that America is the sickest and most uptight nation in the so-called first world, or European world anyway. It is, I think, the underscored Quaker mentality of this nation that makes it such a hotbed of violent atrocity; pent up needs, a moral-sexual tension. I am very non-American not to say that I don't like the place, oh, I do—but a more . . . tightass citizenry you couldn't hope to find. So psychologically tense that they are about to pop. Say liberate yourselves, free your minds and your spirits will follow.

Everything is not always about you. Sometimes things are just things.

DO I SOUND oh-too-cool as I tell this story? I'm not, you know. I suppose that sometimes I suffer from this almost British reserve, it is my Island fascia: Evert'ing Cool, Man. It is really more that my brain is working overtime; I can't think and be scared at the same time. This is grisly, gross shit—you have to kind of tune it out or puke your guts every time you walk onto a scene. I . . . it, it gets to you, though, crawls under your skin sometimes, like the urge to go see what happened when you hear the sound of a car crash: bloodlust. I would rather teach, but, vampire-like, the lust for the thrill of death draws me back every time someone whispers its name.

I SPLASHED WATER on my face, ran the wet fingers back through my hair, plastering it to my skull to show off the receding crescents on either temple, gray streaked light brown and red locks. Deep inhale, slow blow of smoke; I watched it curling towards the extremities of the bathroom, attempted to cough up a lung. It was morning already and just a little while ago I swear it had been night.

"So, you been havin' brainwaves, son? . . . come on, what's what?" He stretched and I heard his vertebrae popping. "Man, I did not get enough fuckin sleep last night."

"Hmm . . . " I put my ass up on the basin. "Captain says the F.B.I. called him last night, just checking in . . ."

"Yeah, they're out there . . . like wolves, waiting . . . so, you not telling me anythang."

"Maybe . . ." mischievous smile. "Come, let's go into the squad room, okay?" I stood slowly, coughed, butted out the cigarette. I felt sleepy.

"Bitch, you are giving me a hard-on, and I don't know why."

"Now that, Frenchy, is a strange thing to say to a man in a bathroom."

The situation room was bright lit and full of baggy-eyed cop girls and cop boys. "Well, mornin, y'all . . . every body feelin fine this mornin . . . Carly?"

"Still asleep . . . My ass got here but my brain's still at home in bed."

"Tom." Frenchy, as if introducing me. Everyone suddenly looked at me expectantly; perhaps I looked like lunch.

"Shit . . . ahm, well . . . look some of you by now are probably wondering who wasted their money on me." I took out a cigarette and played with it. "It's been almost three months, since I got here . . . it all takes a while, ahm, I have made some changes in the investigative procedure . . . brought in some experts," it was hard to tell that standing in front of people is my profession. I was nervous. "There are still some facts out there . . .

"Okay look, what all this is leading up to is . . . well, I think it safe to say that our criminal is not working alone. Killer is intelligent, Killer knows the way investigations work, every thing Killer does has a purpose . . . *ergo* . . . Killer is a professional. Ahm, I asked Siggy"— Siggy, Sigmund, is the local lab head, pathologist and lover of women—"I asked Siggy to explore the possibility that the killings are carried out by as many as three people."

I also describe him as lover of women because if I mention Siggy as one I must pronounce him as the other—we are led to understand that although Siggy may be a good pathologist, it is his "minor" calling in life.

"Tom . . . if—and correct me if I am wrong if, as you say, Killer is a pro, an' everything Killer does has a purpose, then what y'all sayin is that, the *victims* have a purpose, and the *crimes* have a purpose." That was why Frenchy was the man; he always asked the right questions and knew the correct answers.

"Yep, I believe that even the letters have a purpose . . . the variety has a purpose . . . I believe Killer is a professional . . . it was Captain that gave it to me last night, lit my brain—he said 'what kind of killer leaves no clues?'"

"I heard that." Sir Michael, Captain of our hearts, full of sudden smiles, was standing in the doorway there, surveying his hope and salvation, his troops. "A breakthrough?" anxious. "I heard you say Killer."

"A possible breakthrough." I glanced for my watch, but it was still on the dresser at the hotel.

"God I hate you . . . hate—you suppose . . . that maybe, just maybe I . . . I could tell the chief . . . well, that we have a breakthrough, a little . . . white lie."

"We'd have to vote on that, sir," Frenchy teased him.

I glanced at my right hand again, no watch, I hated that, felt naked without it . . . no, I'm not left handed, just like to wear my watch on my right hand.

"Well, boys and girls, how do you vote . . . can the Captain lie? All in favor." A show of hands.

"Looks like a vote of confidence, Boss."

"You lie, we cover." Frenchy the cowboy Cambodian.

"Hah— the Commissioner will love me . . . yeah, and the Mayor bitch too."

"Just don't tell the press."

"Thomas . . . god, you can hurt me . . . Christ . . . you can really spoil . . . a good thing. I thought, I thought I paid you to . . . uh, you know, make me . . . feel *good*."

"Uh uh, you pay me to help solve crimes and keep the F.B.I. off your back . . . it's *Frenchy* you pay to stroke ya."

"Frenchy, shoot this man . . . p-p-please." Everybody laughed then. "Oh, and believe me, Tom, the F.B.I., they're there . . . waiting . . . at the door, waiting for a crack."

"Hmm . . . anyway, Captain my captain, please tell Queen Commissioner and Lady Mayor that if they talk to the press *I'll* talk to the press." First rule in criminology, certain silences are golden . . . straight out of the military handbook.

His shoulders hunched just a little, and he turned out the door leaving us here in our world artificial; halogen sun, conditioned air and non-dairy creamers. "Wonder why . . ." I heard him mumble as he walked away.

"Sir?" A hand raised, I couldn't remember his name . . . a guy from Louisiana, with a bad toupee. I raised my eyebrows and tilted my head back in recognition.

"Sir, we've been through every possible connection between these victims, left right and center, back and forth . . . nothin', *rien, nada, nunca, niente*, zip . . . there is no connection, *none*."

"None that we've found . . . look, today is Friday, Frenchy, what do you say we all kinda take the weekend off . . . I want us all to think about this, talk about this, mull it about . . . think it over." I was pacing.

"And you?"

"Frenchy, I am going to go fishing." We had walked to Frenchy's office, his hand was on my shoulder.

"Frenchy . . . we have six teams, right . . . basically two crimes apiece, well, Ten and Eleven are fresh still and won't be out of lab for a couple weeks yet, at least not completely, so set up five teams and use two guys as floaters, get back in to the crimes and start again . . . "

I had of course—well, in a sense anyway— been lying. I lied about fishing . . . it is not my favorite sport, which is a terrible situation for a guy having grown up on an island, surrounded by well, *fish*, really. What I did need was to get away to where I could get a fresh perspective on the situation. I needed to fish for answers where I knew I'd find them. Claire would know.

So I packed a small bag of necessities, jumped into the rented Spirit, tossed the bag on the back seat and set off to the sounds of Bob Marley's "Three little Birds". Out of Atlanta on 20 East, down and out to Columbia, ahm, then north on 26, no, no—south on 26 to Charleston, South Carolina, that is.

4

THOMAS LIKED, when he wasn't working, to be near a beach; to swim, to dive, maybe even play volleyball. I dig volleyball myself, you know. Thomas didn't own a boat, too much stuff to take care of, he always said. He didn't own a house either, but he rented a nice little place a spit away from the sand. The place was a bungalow with five big rooms, a lot of windows, tile floors, old furniture, fresh fabrics and a truly cool stereo system.

Of the five rooms, three were bedrooms, one a living room, the other a kitchen; of course, there were the requisite bathrooms and such. His bedroom was almost—well, it wasn't bachelor. A large, white-comfortered, mahogany four- poster bed filled about half the space. A day chaise, with ornate mahogany backboard, strawberry covered pillows and white canvas upholstery sat against an opposite wall. There was a big Chinese chest at the foot of the bed; it was heavily carved and full of linens. Two large mahogany armoires faced each other across the foot of the bed. It was his grandparents' bedroom, transplanted and bathed in ethereal Florida light through open windows, windows draped, not shaded.

A dark blue Saab 900, hatchback, not new but well kept, cleaned and polished sits in the narrow drive. He also owns a TR4, an English sportscar, you know. He showed me a picture of it once; it's in a garage in New Mexico somewhere, at a friend's house I think. He never got married, has no brothers, sisters or close relatives ... his father was an only child.

"I like myself," he told me once, "and I like books". I often think of Thomas as sort of like

... like Peter Pan on reality.

IT WASN'T really Charleston that I was going to now, but Folly Beach on the just-southern end. I needed to see a man about a horse (something my Grandfather used to say). My man was a woman. My woman was called Claire. Claire long-boned and beautiful.

WE HAD MET first, shit, I dunno, about 10 years ago. She took one of my classes; ongoing F.B.I. upgrade education. A class about sexual psyche and the criminal mind, I think. She is retired now. Claire is 38.

She retired nearly four years ago now, after a nasty shoot-out. She took nine bullets, up close and personal. Claire had been wearing a vest, but 70 percent of the jacketed 9mm rounds got penetration. I had been there. Blood, I saw blood that day. Four F.B.I. agents dead, six more wounded.

A mistake; they called it a miscalculation.

If I am one of the best at what I do, then Claire is the best . . . the very best. But she doesn't do it any more.

Claire is a pleasant thought.

5

CLAIRE'S HOUSE was well off the road, down a track through tall scrub pine, live oak and low bush. The track was pebbled; still, I always missed the entrance. I backed up now and turned in. The drive traveled about a quarter of a crunchy mile through the bush before it broke out into the open. A small orchard in a surround of green grass, and at the center of it all a small house of bright white wood and character.

The back side of the house faced a small sparse wood through which, between the stems of thin trees, you could catch an occasional glimpse of the dark rock coastline and the sea.

I guess Claire was expecting me; she wasn't home. The house was open. The now past-summer air was fresh. I tossed my bag inside the front door and stood for a moment on the low front stoop; the house was very southernish. I lit a cigarette—smokesmokesmoke—up until six months ago I hadn't smoked in . . . shit, what, two years. One night I was having a couple of drinks, something else I rarely do, felt an urge, took a drag and that was all she wrote.

The house is a low, plain rectangle. From the front side three sets of big windows and a low stoop that ran away from you around the corner and down the far side of the house. The roof flowed from its gable down across the stoop, shading the interior. A wide expanse of verandah was wonderful. Inside was just as basic, two bedrooms to the right, a large warm living room right in front of you, all the way back to dutch doors that opened onto the world. On immediate left a hallway led back to the master bedroom, which opened onto the front verandah, the back patio and the kitchen, all through gloriously large wooden doors.

Something about all this fresh air just made me want to . . . piss.

"Well now . . ." I, speaking aloud to myself, the trees shifted and groaned, non- conversational tones. I tucked mr. penis back into his pants and wandered off beachward.

A squirrel, paying me no mind at all, moved from one tree to another, rustling leaves as he went. He paused in his scratching climb to turn and look at me, he adjusted himself so that he was now facing down the tree.

He was sitting on a big dark rock at the base of an anorexic pine tree; the last tree at the edge of a small glade of brown grass. The strip of grass was maybe 10 feet wide; then it met the gray fungal rocks of the shore line. He was sitting Indian-style, tanned, long blonde hair sun bleached, glinting with streaks of red and gold. He had his shirt off, had his jeans on. The light was soft yellow, it seemed to halo his golden tan skin, emanating. Who he was I had no idea.

"Hi!" I called it out, tentatively; he made no answer, didn't move.

"Hi!" I tried again, a little more assertive.

He turned slowly then, as if looking about. He twitched, jerking at seeing me so close. A handsome face, angular, had on RayBan aviators. It was as if the glasses had been designed with just this face in mind. "I am deaf," he says plainly. "I felt you coming, though, I think." He pulled a shirt, tie-dyed blue, green and red swirls, over his head, I noticed he had on a necklace of red, gold and green beads strung on leather . . . Rastafarian colors. Island colors.

"I see."

"Do you . . . Can I have a cigarette? . . . You must be Aunt Claire's friend Thomas, right?" I lit the cigarette for him and he inhaled deeply. "You're a policeman, right?"

"Sort of . . . I guess you read lips."

"Getting better . . . it's hard to be deaf at seventeen . . . a casualty of war." There was a carefulness to the way he formed and spoke his words, a Southernness to his accent.

"War?"

"Hmmm . . ." He smiled. "War games . . . playing with some friends . . . am I talking too loud?"

"No."

"Sorry man . . . but, well . . . it ain't really been too long, you know. About a year ago I got hit in the head with one of them paint pellets; fucked my hearing . . . where'd these cigarettes come from, dude?"

"Guatemala." It was a nice day, especially since it had rained all week in Atlanta; it was good to feel the sun. "You talk pretty good."

"Aunt Claire brought me here for therapy . . . Guatemala? I'm not even sure I know where that is."

"South of Mexico, nice place, nice cigarettes."

"If you say so . . . Aunt Claire went to town to stock up on 'We're having visitors' kind of stuff, you know."

"Honored guest, eh."

He was Michael, Claire's nephew.

MEMORIES . . . I could smell the coffee, feel the quality of a long-ago breeze; F. Scott Fitzgerald in a letter to a friend had put it this way: "The golden bowl is broken, indeed, but . . . it was golden."

The house at the farm sat on a gradual hill at the end of a dirt drive across a dusty tan colored pasture. Through an iron gate into the shady surround of the logwood trees. The yard of the house was verdant green and lush colors, bougainvillea, croton, ginger lily, anthurium. Itself, the house was a rambling scattered wattle and daub structure, 400 years old. The back side of the house, which at one time past had been the front, had double steps leading to a columned entrance.

But it was the view from here, down across a winding valley lush with Guinea grass and distant banana trees, speckled with cattle and horses. We would sit, evenings, on the badminton court and look out, listening to the hum of the world.

Whenever away I would long for that view.

CLAIRE DRIVES a battered piece of shit, a rusty light blue Subaru four-wheel-drive wagon, always in need of a wash and puffing white smoke. Its rattling gait brought me back from my memories as, coughing smoke, it belched from the shadows of the drive into the sunlight, lurched, caught itself and came bravely on. Its engine sounding . . . sounding like the grate of pumice stone on bathroom tile. Claire filled the driver's side, light brown hair tousling, unruly in the breeze. She had cut it since I last saw her, short short.

"Hey."

"Hey back at ya . . . hmmm, you look goodish." She unwound herself from the seat. "Give us a kiss."

"When are you going to buy a new car?"

"Hey, I like my little car."

She stroked the front of my pants, squeezing me fully. "Hello." I looked into nice blue eyes. Light blue eyes. Dark glasses were perched on top of her head.

"Nice to see you too . . . are you by chance horny?"

"I am . . ." she took the glasses off her head. "You gonna help me with the groceries? Hey, shithead." She smiled as she called out to Michael, who was just coming around the corner of the house.

"Hey Claire," he called back.

"Aunt Claire to you, asshole . . . How you doing, pretty boy." She touches his face lovingly. The swear words were an inside thing, I guess.

"Pass a bag then."

"So, Mr. Tom . . ." grabbing a handful of butt and leaning her mons against me. "What's what?" All 5'10" of her. Claire reached me at the nose, tall and wiry, broad shoulders, mannish. "You miss me?"

I kiss her, because I really want to. "Yes."

She licks my cheek. "Me too . . . I love you, you know, sweets." Sweets . . . it was a term my grandfather had always used. I remember you, sport.

I grab two handfuls of groceries.

The inside of the house is very airy, open to the rafters, with interior walls that don't go all the way up. A large kitchen, with big bay windows that illuminate the room with the world out-side. There's a rustic old table there, chipped and dented; it fills the alcove. It is the cultural center of the house. The table is littered with papers, boxes, books, things; pieces of life.

"I'm writing another book . . . well, I started it, anyway."

"You started another one." Scratched my cheek with the back of my fingers.

"See, a fuck like you, Tom . . . how long since I started this book?"

"Shit, I know . . . shoot me . . . I've been busy," I add.

"I know, babes . . . toss me that can of beans, babe . . . right there. Thanks." Michael with the last of the bags. "You two met, I presume."

"Sort of."

"He's Michael . . . Julie's son."

"Yeah, I know."

"Dickhead, put that bag in the bathroom . . . You don't hear so well, do ya, fuckface," she said louder.

"I got the dickhead fuckface part." He turned to me smiling. "Aunt Claire is teaching me to lip read swear words." Like the cat who swallowed the canary. "Right, bitch?"

"Right, cocksucker." They laugh again.

"That stuff goes in the bottom cupboard, no, puss, over to your right—right, yep . . . Julie couldn't deal with him."

"How's Julie?"

"Usual husband crap . . . joys of marriage, you know."

"I can't judge." From behind I wrap my arms around her, kiss her neck.

"Here, this goes on the back of the stove, next to the pa-prika."

"Romantic you."

"We were discussing marriage."

"Well, would you get married again?"

"I'd marry you if I thought I could get you through the church door, puss."

"Marriage tends to screw up a man's psyche."

"You might be an exception. "

Ten years we have been ... dating may be too strong a word; we have been friends since forever, lovers for three years. It is, I think, the Southernness of her that appeals to me.

"SO." Hands out, palms up, fishing compliments. Miles Davis on the radio, "Just Kicking That Doo-Bop Sound", hip hop jazz, cool too. Claire sat amongst the redistributed mess at the table, wine glass in hand.

"Babes, as usual you have outdone yourself, foodwise. . . you missed your calling in life."

"I missed a lot of callings ... missed a lot."

The things I would have liked to have done, the places I never got to see. Life somehow got in the way. I misspent much of my youth and ended up ... I ended up like my father.

I never knew my father or my mother, they died in France two years after I was born. They missed my first tentative steps, my opening arguments. But that was by choice. Shortly after I was born, the war now over, they returned to France and left me behind with Nana and Papa. They died in a car accident, drove off the road in the stupor of an opium high. They were party animals, I was their burden of joy.

There were many things I suppose I could have been, but I like what I have become. I like Claire. I like the memories of 'Home', the thoughts of grandpa, I like the challenges of my job; I like my life and I am not sure that I would change too much of it. Except maybe my eyes, I find them too small.

Claire, queen of my evening, summoned me. "Bring on the case files, puss ... and fill my glass of wine, please," and I obeyed. She was settling down to go over my crimes, confer on · and confirm my questions, my guesses.

"*Just a little bit ... just a little bit ... ooooh, kisses sweeter than honey, whooop.*" Aretha!

6

JUST A MAN coming home late from work of a night, about eight. It felt like relief after a piss of a day at work to finally walk through the apartment door, home! He'd been working a will for the Memphis family Robinson; the dead father was probably turning over in his grave at the shit that was going on; first wife and children battling step-mother and her son for who should get what . . . everything had been left to the children, with the second wife as executor, no funds to be released till all children were of legality. That meant that the two in their 20's had to wait till the baby came of age to get their hands on daddy's money. So home was a relief when he arrived, aaaaah.

The briefcase was dropped at the door, taking off the jacket he tossed it in the general direction of the couch as he passed on the way to the kitchen. A kitchen chair was given the added decoration of his paisley tie. He bent at the waist to get a closer, more personal look at the fridge, chose a beer, not like there was much choice. Pop the tab, guzzleguzzle, set the can down on the counter and belch . . . aaaaah, relief.

His belt he dropped on the counter next to the beer, and headed for the bedroom on the other side of the apartment; he paused to take off a sock, turned the corner at the end of the hall . . . *Snick*—a sword, long and straight, plunged through his throat and out the other side, severing the Adam's apple and the windpipe and coming out through the nerve center at the nape of the neck. His body sagged under its own weight and he went straight down, like a loose pair of pants, onto his knees. He tried to reach out for the haft of the sword, but his fingers couldn't quite seem to find it, he rasped a breath.

Killer walked a slow circle, examining the aesthetics of the sword strike; the blade was found to be surprisingly clean, really it was completely clean, shiny silver, winking in the light. Blood was just starting to trickle down the man's shirt, front and back, tie dye in death. And he fell forward, his last thought before becoming statistic number one . . .   this guy walks like a fucking *woman.*

The fall drove the sword through the neck, twisting it till it tore free, slicing through flesh and spraying blood, sending bits of this and that about the hallway. The head lay at an awkward angle, held on the neck by a small torn piece of flesh.

Killer rolled over the head.

"*Yo yo yo* . . ."   reached in the mouth and cut out the tongue. Probably took it home and sauteed it up, served it with a nice brown poivrade sauce and asparagus in cream garlic, mmmm.

The note had been laid neatly on the chest of the victim, the white of the paper matching the pallor of his skin.

"**PUMP IT,** *pump it up, shake your body, you gotta move this* . . . *shake your body for me.*" Technotronics doing Revlon. I leaned in the doorway to the kitchen watching Claire as she sifted through the material in Number One's case file. I watched a moment of her; she was concentrated intensity in half-glasses, scribbling something on the notepad beside her, right hand hovering with the glass of wine as she wrote. Sipping, she seemed to ponder what she had just written. Claire is a woman, no doubt; all grown up to perfection. A strong mind, a strong body, a strong soul.

Number One engrosses her, catches her from the very first turning of the page, the first taste of a glimpse at the first Polaroid. Fuck. A hell of a way to start a crime wave it bloody well was. The victim was an average guy, about my height, about my weight, same general hair color, almost anyway . . . I mean, well, you know, nothing special. He was a lawyer, recently divorced, long-time separated, who lived alone except for the occasional weekend when the two children came to visit. He had a girl and a boy, one nine, the other twelve. He was about my age, was.

I lit a cigarette, it was cool here and now on the back stoop , you could smell the sea, hear it slapping on the rock shore in the distance. Yeah, fuck. Standing, I stretched, old bones creaked and popped. I walked off into the night. The sky was full of stars, brilliant shining, the moon wasn't up yet, but shadows still danced between the trees of the grove; I looked up to the sky. Stars, millions of shining beacons to other worlds. The smoke from my cigarette spiraled upward, illuminated briefly. What was I really here for, what questions had I really come to answer?

Moving shadows in the night, a quadraphonic cacophony of sounds never present in the daylight, my senses seemed alive. Star lit and lapping at the shore, the sea was placid beauty. Feet came to rest at the edge of the grove of trees, right there where the sea, the trees, the sky and the salt burned grass all came together, where worlds came to meet. I looked out at Carolina's sea and felt peace . . . some sort anyhow, I am confused. I thought back to Claire, and that took me back to killing number one.

NUMBER ONE had been found only about 11 hours after his death, when the maid came to clean the apartment. She had become hysterical, later suffered a nervous breakdown. Two years after, she still wakes up with vomiting, screaming fits. A lot of blood had spilled into the carpet, enough to stain the concrete below. The body, when they got there, was deformed, pale and bloating on top, flushed and puffy where the blood had pooled under the skin on the back side.

The mobile crime lab boys had wrapped plastic bags around the hands and feet of the victim after, of course, snapping the requisite pictures from the possible angles. They made a careful study, on sight, of the letter and its placement. They were able to perform a lot of tests on the spot: litmus tests, dye tests, fingerprint dusts. The few blood spots were analyzed for typing and cross-correlation to the victim. Infrared screening was done to determine if any hidden (that is, non-visible) water spots, stains or foreign matter were present on the paper.

His head was askew on its severed neck, facing in the right direction, but at a quaint angle. It was noted that the head had been moved; also that the killer had used a pair of scissors to cut out the tongue. These were left with the sword beside the body. It was a beautiful sword, had belonged to some cavalry officer great great uncle, or something a "Johnny Reb." The scissors were of the standard bright plastic-handled variety.

The body, too, had been moved, turned over, that was evident from the blood patterns. That the victim had been standing when struck was also evident from spray patterns and the indications of the tearing in the wound. All these factors were determined before ever moving the body. All possible tests were done on-site, this lent less possibility to certain mistakes. The tech specialists could see the scene as they made their . . . estimations. They had a good frame of reference.

This scene had good integrity, since the Memphis team was very professional, and able to do much of the forensic pathology in place. Still, nothing; that was the sum total of their findings. All fibers were either of non-specific origin or local to the crime scene. No foreign blood, skin or hair, no telltale spittle or semen as is sometimes the case. They found clear evidence that the killer had used hand and footwear protection so that no fingerprints or foot impressions were left. Entry had been gained through the back door, exit had been the same.

The apartment was one of six in an old converted house, with access through the front door, as well as by back stairs built up the side of the old house to a stoop at the back. There were no signs of forced entry, a good lockpick or key could have been used. No eyewitnesses reported seeing anything out of the ordinary; no strange faces, no noises were heard. There was no theft, nothing displaced except for the sword, which had come from the victim's study where it normally hung on the wall, and the scissors from the kitchen.

And the scissors from the kitchen, that about says it. In the hall with the sword from the study and the scissors from the kitchen. Nothing.

I SAW THE MOON begin to peek over the horizon, sending a line of light across the Carolina sea toward me, and I exhaled smoke.

"Hello."

"Shit!" I jumped, throwing my arms, cigarette flying . . . "*Fuck*ing hell, whoof, *Jesus* you scared me."

The voice had come from "The" rock; where he had sat earlier, she now took her place. She being young and fresh, her now moonlit face sharp-featured, pleasant, surrounded by a golden curly wheat mane of hair. She sat yogasized, long legs tucked up in front of her, jeans-clad. A plain white T-shirt glowed against the swell of her breasts; simplicity made . . . yes, beautiful.

"I'm sorry." She smiled a perfect smile, white, in spreading symmetry beneath a slightly hawkish nose.

"Is . . . is there something special, ahm, about this rock?" Still a little edged.

"What?"

"I found Michael here this morning."

"Ah, you're Claire's friend, aren't you . . . "

"Seems I have been expected, and you . . . are?"

"Margaret . . . but my friends call me Bugsy."

"Why?" I breathed deeply through my nose . . . new air.

"Habit, I guess." A shrug with a smile attached.

"Ahh . . . well then, hello, Bugsy, nice to meet you . . ." I came closer for the first time, offering a hand. When she took it hers was warm, soft and electric. "I'm Thomas."

"Yes, you are." Closer now and I could see her youth, she was about twenty, all smooth and tight. Without letting go my hand she shifted over on the rock. "Join me."

And I did.

7

YOU *know, in the very beginning of this . . . story, I introduced you all to Thomas, and here we are meeting . . . that is, well, like cool, you know. Here where the varieties of a world joined, so we too have come to meet. I felt like I already knew him.*

"Well?"

"Well what?"

"How does the rock feel?"

"The same way it felt this morning . . . strangely comfortable . . . why do I feel so awkward all of a sudden?"

"My youthful beauty is flustering you." *I said it to him deadpan, Thomas stared at me flatly for a moment.* "I'm joking."

"Hmm, yes . . . " *he laughed,* "but I think you're right . . . you are . . ." *He didn't look at me, just stared off to sea as if thinking of something else as he spoke to me* " . . . Beautiful."

"Ah, Claire said you were too sweet." *He had a nice smile that lit up his whole face, wrinkled his eyes.*

"Claire talks too much . . . you are Bugsy the writer, daughter of SanDra the other writer, SanDra writes political novels about color, you write wonderfully full novels of character and life . . . dig this, I get the gossip too." *A big cute smile.*

"You're quite handsome, you know. What, no answer?"

He had a wonderful voice.

"HELP . . ." It was all I could think of to attach to my smile.

"Sorry, you'll . . . um, have to excuse me . . . mother dearest always says that I'm, well you know, like a little too forward." Every word she spoke seemed carefully chosen, spoken with clarity, enunciated with thought.

"Yes."

Quick change of subject. "You're a policeman."

"No not really, ahm, sort of . . . I mean, well—I don't carry a gun or a badge or anything . . . I'm sort of a criminalist."

"You don't carry a gun even?"

"No." I was looking down at the grass, leaning across my Indian-style crossed legs. I shook my head.

"What, you don't like guns?" She liked to stroke the flesh of her neck, just to the back at the hair's edge.

"Oh, yes, I . . . yeah I guess I do . . . I think it's better actually if policemen don't carry weapons."

An owl made his presence known; a low hoot.

"An owl. Anyone ever tell you your accent is, like, really cool?"

"Not this week . . . that's your house up through the trees, huh?" There were several deep yellow glows scattered through the silhouettes of the trees.

"Yeah. You worked with Claire at the F.B.I." I guess it was the inquisitive writer's nature in her, she seemed to want to get to the fathoms of my being.

"Yeah . . . you're well informed."

"Yeah, what can I say?" Rolling eyes and a grimace, as if to say, sorry. "Sorry, um, Claire and I are very close . . . she is a very, well, you know, interesting woman . . . why no guns?" As if the question were perfectly contiguous.

"Shit . . . attitudes, I guess, it has a lot to do with attitudes. Perceptions, talk first . . . if I am not perceived as a threat we can talk . . . it's a perpetuating thing—it's better without guns, I mean where possible."

"Okay."

"You have an accent yourself."

"Finishing school in Switzerland . . . You were born in Martinique." She said the last part in French, I answered in English.

"Ah, you speak French."

"A bit . . . I am, intrigued, Mr. Tom."

Laugh. "How so?"

She toyed with herself then, there, for a moment, sensual, sexy . . . a finger in her hair, touched her own cheek, stroked her throat as she looked skyward. My c o c k hardened.

"I think that I'll take the Fifth."

"Am I making you . . . nervous?" Playing the game, I turned slowly on my elbow to look up at her sideways.

"No . . . aware . . . *very* aware." She smiled fully sweet then, nibbled her thumb; "It was something Claire told me about you."

"I don't think I'll ask."

"Do you find me attractive?"

"Yes . . . "

She had stood, rising above me on the rock. She balanced on one foot for a moment, poised. "You'll be staying a few days?"

"Yes."

"Good, then . . . um, I will see you . . . tomorrow, huh . . . I'm going to go now, before . . . before I get myself in trouble. I like the accent, Mr. Tom . . . keep it."

The forwardness, in her, was not out of place . . . it was not sluttishness, just coy, genuine unselfconscious fun. Bugsy was in touch with herself. I was set somewhat aback by Bugsy. Claire had spoken to me of Bugsy, often, like she did to others of me; so I felt that I already knew Bugsy, sort of.

There at the edge of the woods, where a dim path led up through the trees to her house, she turned back to wave. I stood for a moment not knowing what really to do with myself. I realized that I had a serious erection.

The sky was so full of stars; it had been a long time since I had seen the stars alive like this.

CLAIRE WAS STILL deeply engrossed; the file was spread about in front of her, papers far flung, her eyeglasses were perched precariously at the edge of her forehead, the glass of wine just below her open lips. I leant quietly in the doorway until she noticed me. We smiled at each other then and she went back to her absorption, with two words:

"Wine, please." Holding her glass above head level.

"Interesting?"

"Hmm . . . very." She lifted the glass to stop the flow. "Thank you," turned and kissed my crotch. "Hello . . . ooh, you are tempting me."

"Mr. cock's dying to say hello to miss pussy." Sometimes we are really a pathetic race of people, the things we say.

"Go make your coffee . . . I won't be long . . . I love you."

"Yes . . ." as I had started away I stopped. "Pleasure."

"What?"

"What you give me . . . pleasure."

"Nice."

"I met Bugsy."

Claire looked down at her watch, "On the rock I bet, cool. . . look, let me finish this shit up and we'll . . . heh, we'll talk about it, hmm?"

"Hmmh."

In the doorway I paused, turned back again, she was looking at me smiling. "I can still taste your cunt . . . " I laughed, "Christ, what a hell of a memory." Shaking my head.

THE LIVING ROOM, rustic, was furnished in the well-worn, the soft-cushioned, the aged, the rugged and the comfortable; a nice room that lived up to its name. I sunk my aging ass into a soft-cushioned, wooden framed, Navajo fabric-ed sofa . . . boy, what a fucking mouthful . . . a hundred other aging asses had molded the seat cushions to perfection. I put my feet up on an age-worn oak coffee table and opened the closest magazine; I rather like Elle.

Fashion, fabrics, color and style hold some fascination for me. I guess some might say that I have a blossoming feminine side; cooking, decorating, designing, shopping . . . especially with women. I have a thing for women, think I always have . . . I can remember fondling Miss Clarisse's breasts as a boy, recall their firmness, the length of the nipples. I was five then but had been studying her and others' nakedness; there was always an attraction for me in the female form · . . . and not through the camouflage of clothing; I liked to see the nakedness. And Claire's nakedness was always my favorite.

Claire, she enjoyed wonderful things, color and texture were a passion for her, clothes she loved, she was a fucking joy to shop with . . . she also was known to like to fuck in the changing rooms from time to time.

Claire liked being feminine, liked to look . . . well, beautiful . . . although, that never seemed her direct intention, she just liked nice things and had a flair for putting them together to suit her beauty. Not that she was magazine beautiful, not really at all, still more than simply pleasant to look at.

Strength also helped make Claire attractive, strength of presence. Claire was a professional, in control of her mind and her life, strong, intelligent, ambitious . . . a very smart girl, *very* . . . and fun too. It is hard for me to explain her without perhaps sounding condescending; suffice it to say she is a woman, in a man's world, being the type of woman a woman would want to be. Confused? Me too.

My brain played on Bugsy just then. She was a different type of woman in a similar sort of way. Young, beautiful, confident, assertive, full of herself and her abilities. I had not told her earlier, but I had actually read one of her books . . . I want to say neat, as in cool, but I'm not sure that word works anymore. Her writing has edge. She in herself is neither timid nor submissive; beautiful Bugsy bookwriter . . . her characters carry that with them. Characters with edge, maybe Robin Williams does Norman Mailer, maybe . . . maybe not. Mailer just doesn't quite have the good looks.

Intelligence is such an attractive trait in a person, especially when used to its fullest extent.

Please do not brand me a Liberal; it is not quite so simple for me. I am not an American, either by birth or by assimilation. Therefore I don't search for the pigeon holes to fit each individual into, everyone's specific mold. I am somewhat a child of the world, tempered by education and mellowed by cultural diversity. My morals and my politics are as such, varied: knowledge is king, knowledge has made me tolerant of all points of view; some I hold more dear, others are not to my taste, but none do I ever discard.

I am not religious, but am thoughtful of a god; I find the practices of most churches sacrilegious, but the belief in a god comforting; the religious embodiment of a spiritual state of mind. But I believe in the theory of evolution; my mind does not allow me to discount it, or Darwin. I believe in destiny, and maybe astrological science; yes, I am an enigma, but that is because I am human, because I have a mind which I have tried to allow to range freely, not tying it to any linear thought or specific, shielded, ideology.

If you have difficulty following this, then you'll understand why I am good at my job, and you . . . well, you aren't. You have to let your mind free to do this job. Claire, too, is good at this job, very good, and you . . . well, you are *still* not. It is what brings us close, the way our minds work, I like her mind. I saw some of that in Bugsy too, a glimmer in the way she used her banter.

The magazine I set aside, I lit a cigarette . . . inhaling deeply, headed kitchenward.

"Hey sport," she, stretching, spoke to me in smiles.

"I feel . . . lonely . . ." My bare feet paddled the floor, shuffling. I turned a chair backward and sat down.

"I'm nearly done, sweets, . . . can I have a cigarette?"

"I thought you quit."

"Yep . . . can I have a cigarette?"

"Can I kiss your pussy . . . ?" Spoken around exhaling smoke, slowly, looking deeply soulful.

She . . . lifted her skirt. "No panties . . ." Eyebrows arched and smiling wickedly, just in the way she whispered the words at me.

I could hear Claire flipping through the papers in the other room; me, I was just watching the fan turn lazily above me. I sat up, lit a cigarette, took a gulp of my coffee, NBC's Forest Sawyer was talking at me from the television . . . Forrest Sawyer, Wolf Blitzer, newsman names, manly names . . . should I think of naming my first born son Savage Killer, Lion Tamer, Tibetan Monk?

I could smell the night on the soft breeze that lilted rhythmically through the wide open doors that spread across the entire posterior wall of the living room.

"I got some tapes for you." The hollow echo of Claire's voice from the kitchen.

"What you get?"

"A great one called Captain Ron."

"That's a great one."

"You seen it?"

"Of course." I am, I guess, a movie fanatic, never really get to go to the theater much, but rent a lot of tapes, belong to a video club thing too, through a dealer friend in Orlando, who does video and music exports.

"I should have known—is there *anything* you haven't seen?"

"Yeah, there was this one called Secret Games, I haven't seen that yet," with a smile at myself.

She was moving on to Number Two.

Flapflapflap, the sound of the fan like tires on wet pavement. My thoughts carry me back to somewhere else actually. It was raining that night when I flew into Venice from Memphis; Venice is a small, sandy town about halfway up the west coast of Florida, just out south from Sarasota. I couldn't see the sand for the dark and the pissing rain. The front wheel drive on the otherwise shitty Sprint they had waiting for me handled the weather ... well ...

8

SQUINTING, perchance to see a sign, I was lost; each of the squat concrete block, slab-roofed, louver-windowed Florida boxes looked the same; turn it on a different angle and call it a pool home, son! They all looked like shit to me.

2346, that's my number. There was the house, white like all the rest, distinguishable only by the mango tree that loomed tall and fat over the carport. I wondered if this was the future town Mr. P.T. Barnum had envisioned when he made Venice the home of his circus.

2346 was the home of the police chief, chief . . . shit, I have a terrible head for names, something Slavic . . . -vich, -tov, -off, -escu, some similar ending. The chief was expecting me. He was drunk by the time I found his mailbox, and made it to his front door.

In his age-grayed undershirt, with his stubbled jowls, and protruding belly, he looked every bit the movie version of the jaded southern cop. There was a distinct but undeterminable stain on his shirt front, right at that first curve where drooping breast meets bulging stomach.

"Thomas?"

"Chief."

"You can call me Harold . . . well dang, boy, come on in."

The house was . . . well, the house was gold lamé and silver mirror wall paper, mustard carpet, the kind that is plush in spots and tight weave in others, patches that are supposed to be a design. The furniture was Formica and velour; curtains were dark green plush with gold brocade trim, lampshades that even a drunk would avoid. Mirrored walls and gold lamé—this was 1972 chic, minus the lava lamps, of course.

"So, son . . . want a little drink?"

I was wet, and tired, I thought a drink might just go down quite well. "Yeah, a rum."

"Bourbon do ya?"

"Bourbon, on the rocks."

"Shit yeah, my kinda kid." He kept calling me boy, son or kid, even though maybe barely 10 years stood between us. "So, boy, you're the genius they gone an' got to do the crime solvin'. Whar you from, Miamuh? Shit, boy, what you waitin' for take a seat, pull up a chair, they all comfortable." I was out of words for the moment; what could you say.

"Well, boy," he handed me my bourbon, I could smell him, even at arm's length.

"Sir?"

He began then to talk jubilantly to me, as if we were long time acquaintances; me, I listened, didn't have shit to say.

"Don't talk much, do ya . . . tired?"

"Yeah, a little . . . "I sipped the bourbon. "Nice . . . smooth."

"Special fuckin' stock, son . . . I got me a cousin up in Tennessee . . . works at the JD distillery, yeah . . . so you really a professional Sherlock?"

"Professional might be too strong a word."

"Well . . . you know, when they done called me, they told me they was sending down a professional, they done faxed me your pictures and credentials . . . yeah." He nodded heavily. "A professional, they said . . . they said to make sure I afforded you every courtesy . . . yes boy, that's what they said . . . yes sir, a *professional*."

"Yes sir, a professional."

"So where you staying?"

"Motel out by the Barnum house." The Barnum house was a red brick two story place that just kind of stuck up, awkwardly, in a circle of green grass on the southern end of town at the side of Highway 41. It was an oddly out-of-place structure.

"Ah."

"But, you know I just thought that I should, well, check in with you ... you know on a personal level, ahm, before tomorrow."

"Uh huh ... nice, it's damn good to get to know who you're workin' with, yes sir ... damn straight, boy."

"You have a nice house here sir." Small talk.

"Yeah, yeah I guess it ... well it's kinda big for me now ... wife ... uh, my wife died last, last year." And then I understood ... he was terribly alone. "We were married 31 years." His eyes had glazed, it was worse than I had thought. Alone— he rattled the ice in his bourbon, staring at the golden liquid.

"You were married a long time."

He didn't answer.

VENICE WAS the second stop on my misshapen circle journey, traveling the crime road, running the gamut of murder. I followed the trail of the killings from town to city in order of occurrence. The second had occurred here in Venice. Across the bridge, actually, on the north side of the city.

At the Atlanta headquarters there was a detective from each of the cities where a killing had taken place. It wasn't quite the same though, you know, as getting the direct flavor of the crime, the texture of the surroundings, the feeling of the space where the death took place. The walls can talk volumes. Sometimes you need to get up close.

The trail here was about two years old, cold, memories clouded but the trail was still here. Secrets still in the minds of neighbors, first impressions stamped on the memories of cops on the scene. The scene would speak its own gospel. Be the crime.

This was, like most Florida towns, an artificial village with no seeming reason for being. *"Sugar Sugar, aw Honey honey .. . you are my candy girl ... an' you got me wanting you ... danananana ... you are my candy girl ... when I kissed you girl ... I knew how sweet a kiss could be."* The radio beat forth the Archies, memories, fuck ... good music.

No reason for being except for sand and sun. Engineers had to rescue land from the sea, subdue the sand, import the grass and the trees, kill the mosquitoes, invent industry, and pump in fresh water . . . build it and they will come. As out of place as the raw-fleshed snowbirds that blistered winterlong on the city's beaches.

I opened the doors and the windows; there was a mustiness in the house, and you could still smell the taint of death. I opened all the doors onto the Florida room, fresh; I lit a cigarette. Harold had sent an officer with me, he was sitting outside in the shade; I could hear him sniffling in the distance. The house was intact, as if it had just been vacated for a few days, closed for the summer. Except for the dust piling up it was hard to tell that the owner was dead and never to return.

Because the crime was still unsolved, and the case remained open and active, the police had logged the house as evidence. As such it was maintained in its proper state by the city, the air conditioning still ran, the yard was mowed once a month, lights left burning, much like that night . . .

I would like to make an introduction at this time.

You don't know me, but you will know me, well, before long and wish you hadn't... perhaps. Not, of course, that I am not a personable soul; I think myself that. Just, perhaps, I am a little bit crude for some tastes.

Before you lies a body, horribly done in death. It is my doing, and certainly, there will be more.

I have a name, but, well, it is personal. So, just for courtesy's sake I shall give you another to work with.

You may continue to call me, amongst other things, Gingerbread Man.

So work fast, run fast, for you can't catch me I'm . . .

YOURS TRULY
GBM #2.

THAT NIGHT the doors had been open too, it was a rather still night, warm, the beginnings of summer already in the air, though it was still only April. He had turned up the lights; at 56 he just wasn't seeing as well as he used to.

The canvas was vibrant color, animated shapes of animals among tropical verdance. Beasts which were elongated of shape, non-proportional, and walking in their midst were tall black men and black women, primitive and naked . . . as was the art itself, primitive and full of naked emotion. The artist had originally hailed from Haiti, a tall, elegant, coffee cream-colored man, who wore clothes on a model frame. A man who had grown only more handsome with age.

That night he wore, as usual, linen. Trousers stained with paint. The coffee cream that was the flesh of his fingers was ingrained with tincture; he loved his art.

Hand poised, he was about to enliven the sketch of a thatch-hut village drawn at the right side of the half finished canvas. "The Village of the Sun" he had named this piece, which at sale would fetch several thousand dollars.

That night his brush hovered over the canvas, imagining the stroke. Outside, Killer cut the screen of the Florida room with three quick slashes of a knife. Killer entered the house; Killer was dressed in clothes that looked surprisingly like they had been taken from the drying line outside. Killer looked quite good in khaki linen.

He made his first stroke of color. Killer paused to put on gloves, tucking the shirt sleeves into the top of the blue high-risk latex. Killer added foot coverings.

Texture, shape, a hut just gathering life. Killer walked up behind him and deftly, deftly, snapped his fucking neck. *Pop!* I say deftly, because although the neck was broken, the victim was left alive; that takes a certain . . . touch.

Killer slashed the victim's wrists using a paint knife, letting his blood run out. Paralyzed and unable to move, he died of an empty heart.

That night his blood had been used, in a strangely fitting way, as paint spread on canvas; art of the grotesque. The body itself Killer had propped up, seated, in position to view the gallery of horror. A smile painted onto his face, his eyes darkened with charcoal, he himself had become canvas. That night his blood drained from his body and spilled to the floor, spreading outward to stain the sisal rug in a large mosaic of black and deep maroon.

I WALKED around the room, weaving in and out of the naked easels and spot pins, long pins with colored flags that the crime scene boys used to mark evidence. Each flag was denoted in the file. A desk was in the far corner, an old rolltop which I would have liked to carry home with me.

Flicking at the papers and pulling on drawers, I wasn't really looking for anything in particular, just looking, getting the feel. Along the side wall of the studio was a day bed—or a psychiatrist's couch for those who, like me, often can't picture what the fuck a day bed is supposed to look like. It was button leather, dark burgundy colored; maybe I could fit it and the desk in the rental car. Patting the pockets of my pants I felt for the photographs by reaction, pulled them out, 20 of them.

Leafing through the Polaroids I walked back toward the bedroom; there was a picture that he hadn't painted on one wall, full of marlins and bright blue color. "Nice linens." I took note because I love linens, was then wearing a pair of linen trousers, loose and comfortable.

The bed had not been made. I sat on it and opened the drawer of the night stand; condoms, a camera, a book, some papers, photos, a watch; I glanced at my wrist—shit, I'd left my watch in the hotel bathroom. I picked up the condoms, non-lubricated Trojans; I tore one off and put it in my pocket.

It was a comfortable bed. I rolled across it and looked in the other night table: a pack of playing cards, an old ashtray, shells imbedded in poly with sand epoxied to the bottom. It still gave off the odor of marijuana, the artist had been a weed man, inspirational smoke; he had, it seemed, also a small habit with heroin; his heart showed evidence of endocarditis, caused by infusion of bacteria into the blood stream with dirty needles.

There were closets on either side of the hall to the bathroom. Clothes, shirts and slacks, all cottons and linens on one side, suits and jackets on the other. The suits were all very nice and very tailored; he had some by John L. Smith, an old time Miami tailor that all the West Indian who's who's had once used. Nice stuff. The shoes were all first rate, Clarke's for comfort on one side and Florsheims for dress on the other. Even a couple of well pressed tuxedos, but no jeans—now what kind of guy doesn't own a pair of jeans?

At the dining table I sat and scribbled some notes on the case file. Lit a cigarette and walked back into the studio, sat my ass down on the psych couch, it squeaked under me. I started spreading out the Polaroids on the floor in front of me, glancing around the room as I dropped each one to get the bearing of it.

There was a gruesomeness to this killing as with all the others, gruesomeness with purpose. Polaroids of the canvases were the last in the stack; I stood to put them on their prospective easels. I lit another cigarette. The ghosts in the room weren't talking to me.

And then I noticed it.

There on the floor, as I stared at the photos, a space in the stain. An almost-circle, right there on the floor between the two center easels. Bending over the Polaroids, I squinted, took my glasses out of my top pocket, put them on and looked again. Polaroids are for shit. Back on the dining table the case file had the quality lab photos. And there it was, clear as day . . . I checked the scene notes, the forensics reports: no mention of the somewhat circle, clear as day in the blood.

> I feel in a mood tonight. Emotion, could it be?
> Elation, joy, happiness?
> Anger, pain, sadness?
> Is there a difference, does it make one? I am in
> a mood tonight; or maybe I just have gas.
> -Ooops, what a horrible place to leave a dead body.
> Arrest me!
>
> GBM #3

COFFEE is my life.

"Hey babes," walking into the kitchen to put on the kettle. The TV was still on, muted models mouthed the words to George Michael's "Freedom". All beautiful.

"I like this tune." Finding the remote, I turned it up.

"How can you watch this drivel? . . . you're too old for MTV."

"Yeah, and you can kiss my wrinkly sagging butt."

"Threats and promises . . . so, what's what?"

I pouted. "Thomas lonely . . . Thomas need friend, talk to friend . . . me Thomas."

"You are such a fucking ass . . . and cute too. I can leave this till tomorrow; you got a cigarette?" There is a touch of the rich hippie in Claire. She wore an elephant hair bracelet and another of leather on her right wrist. One had come from Africa, the other, Peru.

"How about a coffee and . . . a joint?"

"Texas bud . . . good smoke, very good. Put on a little music, eh."

"*Como no* . . . what you want to hear?" Sniffing, I eyed the end of the jay; the pungent smell always titillated me, but I didn't smoke myself.

"How 'bout one of them tapes that you brought me last time?" I have a friend. He a Trinidadian boy, who DeeJayed at West Indian clubs and parties in Miami; Dougy. Twice a year or so Dougy sent me a tape, or two with the latest sounds: Reggae and Calypso. "*. . . Brother was hungry . . . hungry . . . hungry. Two white women traveling to Africa find demselves in the hands of a Cannibal headhunter . . .*" the song had a lively soca beat, Sparrow. "*. . . He cook up one an' he eat one raw . . . they taste so good he wanted moooore . . . me want more . . . I envy the congo man, I wish it were me, I wanna shake he han' . . . he eat till he stomach upset, an I never eat a white woman yet.*" Truly . . . Calypso at its best, like Sparrow, is bawdy fun . . . to rass, no. Mek dem white gal loose dem inhibitions an' dem draws. He eat she raw.

"Dance with me." She liked black and white. Tonight she was wearing both, black jeans and a white shirt. The joint was out. I paused to light it for her.

"No guurl, yu mus' be sayin . . . cum baby mek we de jump up—" It had been a couple . . . well, a while since I had been into my deep patois accent, it sounded funny to my ear. "So how far you get?"

"Just getting through the lab nonsense on Number Two, briefing it really, fuck—this jay is out again."

"Good bud." I produced a match and lit her up. The Calypso gave way to an old Ska style tune, "Stay a little bit longer". Ska is the predecessor to reggae; it's where Bob Marley started.

"A lot of information in the files . . . a lot of bits to put together . . . but—"

"But nothing of consequence . . . It is basically like that all the way through; I can't wait till you get a little further . . ." Toke toke, sniff sniff.

"Hmmm, that's it, dance, big boy." A little smile, she tried on a West Indian accent.

"Fustly guurl, ees big bwoy, win' up yuself big bwoy . . . yu mus seh, me nevva see a bwoy coudda win' imself up su . . . seen."

"Fuck, it's a cute accent, babe . . . you can make me wet just talking," her arms were around my neck. "You love me, don't ya?"

"Yes babes, you know I do."

"Tell me so I can hear."

"I love you."

"Yes . . . you want to go make some love . . . quietly?"

"Can we leave the music on out here?"

"I'd like that . . . " She kissed my cheek, slipped a hand down to take mine. Closely we walked to the bedroom. As we walked down the hallway the music changed, "Inner Circle" started to pulse . . . *"Girl I wanna make you sweat"*. I couldn't have planned the musical entrée any better . . . hmmm.

"Uuuuurgh." Dutch doors were open, letting the night in. I could hear the sound of the sea in the distance, the wind rustling the leaves of the grove. We lay crossways on the bed, she on her back, breezing, me on my front, looking out to the night. I could count the stars between high cirrus clouds.

"What are you moaning about, puss?"

"I feel good," I answered; up on an elbow I touched her. The feel of her made me—hmm, what is the word I'm looking for— Claire made me feel . . . satisfied. Not, now, in the sexual sense; just content all around.

"So you met Bugsy."

"Hmmm, yes . . ." I rolled unto my back, brought my legs up, my left hand played along the top of her thigh.

"Nice girl, eh?"

"Fresh, forward, intelligent . . . had a nice smell to her, but the light was a little dim. She looked pretty good."

"Oh, she's beautiful, trust me. I told you about her writing, right?"

"You sent me one of her books."

"She's a really good writer, she'll far surpass her mother in time, I think." Claire looked back from the bathroom door as she said the last word. "Her characters are absolutely brilliant." Her voice had that hollow, I'm talking to you from the bathroom, kind of resonance ". . . She's looking for an interesting character to head up her new book, a male character . . ." Stream of urine, splash, flush. She leant for a moment in the doorway, upside down. I rolled over to look at her. Claire was tall, longlonglong. Strong and sinewy of body, muscular, almost mannish, small bre—you know, maybe, if she wants you to know what she looks like *she'll* tell you. "You are beautiful," I sat up, stretched to unkink my back . . . "I can still smell your cunt on my face."

"It seems to be making you hard again." Stalking me, she came forward, a cat unwinding. "You love me, don't you?"

"True." She stroked mr. penis. I lit a cigarette for us to smoke. "Nice cock." Kissed it. "So, Bugsy? . . . what do ya think?"

"What, what?"

"I think she'd find you interesting."

"As what . . .?" I lay back onto the bed, a pillow behind my head.

"As a character . . . and perhaps . . . well who knows . . ." A flick of the tongue— " . . . she's sexy . . . different from me, curvaceous, busty . . . young and soft," husky voice, a smile again. Then she laughed. "How come when I try to shock you I can't? Do you feel jealous?"

"Everyone feels some jealousy," I smiled. "You are the love of my life. Jealousy wouldn't be real . . . it has no place, doesn't . . . doesn't *fit*, you know?" We lay together, quietly; she nestled in my shoulder. " . . . I've slept around, yeah . . . dated, dicked, toyed with, fucked and fondled . . . licked," tongue snaked out; performance art. "I've sucked and kissed a lot of women . . . a hundred . . . fuck . . . but babes, no really, this part is true, *true*." I smiled, playing at the truth. Sat up and lit a cigarette, smoke my brains out. ". . . The last few years with you I can, well, it's been nice . . . you know, me and you, I don't know, guess you'd call it an affinity, sexually and emotionally, and a really nice social friendship too, that's—fuck, man, that's hard to beat, really . . . "

"Oooh, kiss me . . . but you can talk the fucking talk, eh, man . . ."

"So what are we going to do?"

"You give me pleasure . . . it would be nice for the both of you."

"I have no answer to that."

"I love you, you know."

"Yes, I know . . . I need coffee."

"Enjoy you too . . ." she was talking, her back was to the room, sitting in the doorway, her feet out on the patio, knees up, arms wrapped around them. I got up, headed for the kitchen. "Would you like to come live with me, Tommy?" I stopped a moment in the hallway. I smelled of sex.

"You getting to feel lonely in your old age?" My voice echoed back toward her, bouncing off the walls; bank shot answer.

"Yes." She raised the volume of her voice.

"Are you good with your tongue?" And a laugh.

THERE IS something a little edgy about cooking naked. I poured boiling water into the cup; careful as I was, I could feel little splashes. There was my reflection in the large glass pane.

"Well, since we are up, you want to go over Number Three with me, huh?"

Claire lounged into the room; she had pulled on a shirt, to ward off the cold . . . it was open entirely, her flesh beneath was tan, a beautifully sculptured navel and a mons trimmed. . . just so.

"What time is it?" I glanced at my wrist. I'd left the damn watch on the bedside table.

"Middle of the damn night . . . so shall we?"

"You want coffee?"

"I'd love a wine, really."

"Just give me your version, with or without the file." I chose the file; it was a legal size, reinforced tab and file fasteners on each leaf. Plain tan. I opened it in front of me. The crime scene reports, photos, victim information, eyewitness accounts, all this initial information was on the left side of the folder. The right side held the forensics and medical lab reports; ballistics, pathology, photos and recordings of the coroner's examination.

There's always something that relates one other sense to a memory . . . it was the smell of maleleuca blossoms that always reminded me of South Florida; a sickly cloying odor.

THE TREES lined the highways everywhere. A cousin of the eucalyptus, some people called it the paper tree because its bark was papyrus-like. Imported from Australia to help suck up all the fucking swamp water that is all over the goddamn state. The tree turned out to be a bloody nuisance; now I hear they're planning to import a bug to eat the goddamn tree.

It happened in Delray Beach; that's like halfway between Boca Raton, and Palm Beach, horse country. The house is . . . is just kinda off 441, south of the Atlantic Avenue exit at the turnpike . . . a development of all three to five-acre lots.

A ranch style . . . western, you know . . . all dark oiled wood siding, shingle roof, low front porch, high eaves kind of deal with the railings interspersed with wagon wheels . . . real cowboy shit.

It was at the end of a cul-de-sac, kind of took up the whole end arch; house on the left, grass in the center, stables and riding ring on the right. A five-horse stable, but I only ever saw two horses. I like horses. One was a bay mare, the other a dappled gray . . . like Clint Eastwood's horse in all his westerns, you know.

The house itself was large, five bedrooms . . . yes, separated across the house by a wide, I mean huge living room. This living room you would have to see, there were these two chairs in it, wild, made of long horns and leather. Probably give a cowboy a hard-on just to sit in it . . . longhorns and leather, imagine, shee*iiit*.

Look, the best way I can think of, to give you an overview is this . . . The body belonged to a female, Caucasian, 46. Big buxom redneck bitch, tits and ass and big fat pussy all shoved tight-packed into wrangler jeans and Lucchese snakeskin boots, the best. She had long brown and gray hair, wore a plaid shirt— think of Janis Joplin at 40 plus and you got a good idea. Picture it?

Now let's just say that baby is an NRA wet fucking dream— she's got so many fucking guns that she has a room for them: in cases, on the walls, lying around on tables, display boxes . . . some very nice pieces. Including a Boss & Co. .28 gauge, a shotgun; it's worth about $30,000.

Anyhow it's the middle of the day, high fucking noon . . . read it if you think I'm lying . . . high noon, baby walks into the fucking house.

It's hot outside, she's thirsty, it's lunch time, whatever . . . she walks into the house.

Boom.

Bullet traveling faster than the speed of sound, 1200 feet per second. Out the end of the barrel and across the room in shit, about 2/10ths of a second. The flat smack of contact, like when you drop a steak on the floor, is lost under the echoing reverberation of the discharge, making ears ring in the tight confines of the house. There is an instant smell of powder burning.

Killer had positioned himself in the doorway of her gun room, laid a table with weapons across the opening. It was a nice selection of firearms. He didn't try to kill her with the first shot, from a Weatherby .375 Magnum . . . damage and pain.

Now get this, they use this fucking Weatherby to hunt elephants, right? She takes it in the right hip . . . flying flesh and bone . . . pins her back into the door frame, *bam!*, impact splits her forehead over the left eye and down across her cheek, breaking her lip and two teeth.

But she's packing—bounces off the wall, draws down, and as she comes around gets off a shot—it's wide. Killer jams her twice more, at this range nearly tearing off her right arm. Tough bitch, she never lets her weapon go. Fuck, what a mess, see the pictures here.

Anyhow, dig this, half blown apart, bleeding like a stuck pig . . . enough fucking trauma to kill a lion, but she drops for the ground and draws a Smith .380 auto that she's got pigeoned in her boot, with her left hand, she rolls and gets off three shots.

She gets off three shots, yep, and *hits* her fucking target. I shook my head, amazement, admiration, you choose a word. Yeah, she hits her target, because what? Because we find no slugs, no holes, no .380 debris at all.

Killer picks up two .45 ACP's —the two guns were once used on the set of "Miami Vice", 11 rounds each—and he riddles her. Then Killer walks across the room, stands over her and shoots her three times, twice to the chest with an old 44-40 . . . you know, I had an uncle once who had an old 44-40 Winchester; it was a saddle gun, with lever action, I always liked that gun.

The last shot, *coup de grâce*, was from a Desert Eagle .44 auto mag., to the head.

All right, so she fired three rounds from a .380, hitting a target across the room, hits her fucking target . . . but, there is no blood pattern across the room, or anywhere else that doesn't belong to her . . . no teardrop blood spills from a moving target, actually, no blood other than hers, and a lot of fucking bullets flying around the goddamn place.

"Bulletproof vest, Kevlar body armor."

"Obviously, maybe . . . but there's usually fiber expulsion on impact . . . no fibers found, none . . . *nada*."

"Was the room cleaned?"

"Not according to the white coats; good integrity, fresh scene . . . the hail of bullets finally alerted neighbors—seems that they all get together from time to time to cap off a few rounds around the neighborhood, rich rednecks—so at first the firing meant nothing."

"Hmmm . . . so what else?"

"No in and out . . . neighbors are alerted by the noise, but they see no one come or go from the house . . . 11 minutes to first police presence . . . neighbors' guns all a-drawn all over God's green goddamn acres, no perp . . . poof—gone and fucking vanished."

"Blue uniform?"

"News man?"

"Neighbor?"

"Oh yeah, except for the note . . . right there on her body, a Remington piece weighting it down."

"What caliber?"

"No—Remington the Western artist, pewter carvings, paintings and such."

"Not my bag . . . Blue uniform . . . the first response in 11 minutes—neighbors' time, or cops' time?"

"From police log sheets."

"Did you ask the neighbors when you went on your tour?"

I smiled then, Cheshire cat; opened the file to my notes at the back . . . neighbor stated that he believed that the police car, lights flashing, appeared sooner, say about three minutes at the most after his call . . . he said that he placed the call at 12:05; police files indicate that 911 didn't receive the call till 12:08.

"Five minutes isn't much of a difference, watches differ . . . I mean, what does yours say right now, babes? Doctors differ, patients die."

Still I smiled, "I know . . . and it wouldn't matter except for the presence of a police car in that five minutes . . . and that the car with two men in it removed themselves to, in the words of the neighbor, set up a perimeter and direct traffic."

"Ballistics reports?"

"Only tell us what she was hit with—all her own weapons, too."

"Well planned . . . anything else? Hematology?"

"As I said, only her blood showed up; fiber analysis turned up nothing unusual. . ." I was pensive a moment, a fist, thumb end against my lip , the other hand wrapping it tightly, twisting.

"Who did the lab work on this?" Naked and businesslike.

"Miami and Palm Beach . . . and Jacksonville, I think, as well as their own on-site teams . . . nothing unusual, Palm Beach has the best forensic pathologist around, Miami's ballistic boys are hot . . . and Jacksonville's got that hot shit Chem lab that they just paid a fucking fortune for."

"And of course any strange samples would have been analyzed through the F.B.I. NCIC computer link up."

"The Forensics reports seem to indicate that everything was well, all done according to protocol."

"Let me see."

I pushed the file across the table, to where she sat in the alcove of the breakfast nook. Claire examined the lab report analyses carefully; the very first item on this side of the file was the very first item in every file; the document analysis and graphologist's report . . . there was chromatographic and infrared analysis, paper typing and sourcing through watermark. The typewriter was matched for make and print style. A different typewriter had been used in each case; this time it was a Brother.

She flipped to the next page.

Hair samples from the scene were compared to samples from the victim, and from other prospective matchups through neutron activation. A fair amount of horse hair was found—mostly matched the horses she owned. Fiber analyses were categorized through refractive and dye properties, photomicrographs using fluorescent microscopes were used, broken down into categories and checked against fibers that one could expect to find in or around the victim's home or life. No find in or around the victim's home or life. No mention of poly-scrim weave fibers . . . bulletproof vest casing.

The ballistics reports covered six handwritten pages and two typed summaries; included were the results of test firings; casings from the scene and test rounds were compared . . . riflings, calibers, EDX—x-ray diffraction tests to compare residue samples . . . it all added together to prove that the bullets were all fired from weapons found on the scene, that no unaccounted-for rounds were in place on the scene. As well, that all the weapons fired were shown to have been purchased by the victim, or been given to the victim; no strange weapons were introduced to the crime scene.

Fingerprint cards and proofing followed in the file . . . latent prints were lifted with Kromekote cards from the victim's flesh, but she turned out not to have been touched by the killer. They had used laser illumination to identify the prints . . . they turned out to be the victim's own. Hard surfaces were dusted, ninhydrin spray, silver nitrate used on the wooden surfaces. The conclusion was one single large typed word: NOTHING.

The fact that only about two percent of all crimes are solved by fingerprints should at least make us feel better after all that work.

The medical examiner's notes were next, including a small audio cassette tape; a step by step of the procedure. The notes began with the generalities of the subject, height, weight . . . sex. Identifying the location of all the wounds, entry and exit, followed, for the clueless graphic photographs were included. Some of the wounds were small, some ballooned by the bow wave of a heavier caliber; some wounds were round, those where the bullet entered at an angle more oval . . . there were 40-plus wounds on the body, entry and exit . . . descriptions of the weight and physical characteristics of the victim's organs; her liver, for instance, had the yellowing signs of heavy alcohol consumption.

The body was cut from each shoulder, in a slow arch meeting at the sternum, then vertically down the length of the abdomen.

Once opened up, the chest lifted off like a car hood, the medical examiner removed all the organs, weighing and measuring them, taking tissue and blood samples. Probing inside the body cavity, feeling the organs, he searched for any slugs that may have lodged themselves in the body.

Using a circular-blade bone saw, the doctor cut open the back of the skull level with the posterior slope of the head and removed the brain . . . in the case of this victim, the killing shots had done severe damage to the skull and the brain, but he catalogued and weighed it, noting what percentage had been destroyed by the action of the bullet.

Following this were the general statistics of the examination, the lab reports on the blood and tissue samples. And a final concise sentence relating to the determined cause of death: listed as gunshot trauma to the right side of the skull above the ear toward the posterior of the skull, into the parietal lobe.

It was all there as it should have been and it all added up to *shit*.

And then there was this last section, added after I had arrived. It included my own notes and a few new evaluations.

There were reports from private diagnostic labs, like one in Maryland which specialized in blood and DNA testing, and another in Chicago that has had much past success with hair samples; because of the body damage on Number Four, I had asked for advice from a forensic anthropologist, renowned in his field, from University of Florida. Special firearm, explosives and toolmark reports were filed by independent contractors, to cross check the file reportings.

Claire was looking at the ceiling, her throat stretched out. "So where are the three bullets?"

"In the bullet proof vest."

Her neck straightened slowly and she gave me a look. I smiled, wolfish. It was not a popcorn ceiling, I hate popcorn ceilings.

"And where is the bullet proof vest?"

"It was in her closet, on the back rack where it came from." I smiled bigger, broader.

"You are a bad boy, Charlie Brown . . . bad, bad, *bad* . . ." that winning smile again, around squinting eyes. "I'm tired. . ." She left me then; I was tired too, but wanted to pause a moment.

A SAM Peckinpah-directed, Technicolor violence in slow motion; I must have fallen asleep. I woke sweaty, on the couch; the morning came cool, calling on a soft mist through the open doors. There was a not-quite-yet dawn grayness outside, dampdamp . . . you could taste the morning, fresh and fragrant . . . birds.

Claire was entangled with the sheet, the mist seemed to emanate from the very room. Her back, each vertebra, broad shoulders, sinewy muscles and olive tan tone was exposed all the way down to the first slope of her ass.

Coffee. I pulled on a pair of khakis, cool against my naked skin.

The skin on my hand is so delineated, I think of the plates of an alligator's hide, each scale joining others in a tenacious geometrical haphazardry. The palm full of lines of life, love, luck, and the protruding butt of a cigarette.

I waited for the coffee to express. Claire was a coffee—well, maybe connoisseur is the wrong word . . . I mean she knew a lot about it, learned it from her grandfather who had worked in Guatemala, Costa Rica and Brazil in the 30s and 40s . . . She had a large picture of him, dressed in his khakis, opening a new well head in some far-off now unremembered place. The old adventurer—maybe it was his spirit she inherited; there was definitely a family resemblance, especially around the eyes.

I wandered out into the freshness of the morning, cool, nice against the nakedness of my chest. I set the coffee mug down among the dew on the porch rail and lit a cigarette. There was a jaundice to the day. The smoke I exhaled seemed thicker than usual.

Taking the path through the grove toward the sea, leaves rustled, birds warbled, life called out hello. A cat sat quietly in the bushes, black and white. Patches was his name.

Naturally.

I am, I suppose, a somewhat introspective fucker, nature of the beast and all that.

I am reliving my crimes in my head, I call them that . . . these killings that I am working on.

Tired. I wanted a life.

9

BACK TO MY coffee, in real time, and a cigarette to wash it down with. My feet were bare and the dew was cool, wet. I walked the distinct trail through the orchard to the shore, leaves rustled, birds warbled, life called out hello.

"Well well, good morning. What . . . did you like sleep here or what?" Bugsy appeared, steaming mug of tea held close to her chest; she paused to blow on it. She had hung a loose knit cotton sweater on her body, moving to an outline with each step, it gave a hint of naked. The look of early morning was on her face. Her legs were long, brown and bare. So were her feet.

"Morning morning . . . " A wonderful smile, squinting around tired eyes, big brown eyes. "God it's so . . . beautiful out here in the morning . . . the sea and all, you know . . . sleep well?" The sun was pale yellow and the sea was dark blue.

I scooted over on the rock. "Warmed a spot for you . . . slept great, short though, we were up pissing around with my files till the wee hours, but shit, when I'm here I always sleep like a baby."

"Holiday sleep . . . " She blew the steam off the tea. "I sleep like that when . . . when I go to my uncle's . . . in Arizona . . . you know, like you leave the world behind, do some of my best writing when . . . I'm there too, I love the mornings."

"Me too; unfortunately I kind of like nighttime too . . . shit, in college days I never used to sleep, sometimes for days."

"Where'd you go to college?"

"Guelph and NYU."

"Boring town, Toronto." Sometimes she seemed a much older woman. "I . . . have never managed to like it."

"Either, that's why I went to NYU . . . Toronto always had such a—a *fucked* way about it."

She stretched her legs out full in front of her, put her hands on her knees a moment, looked out to sea. You could see forever in all directions, and there was nothing out there. She had two earrings in her right ear, the left had three, two in the lobe and one half way up . . . it was in the shape of a little gun.

"I hope I didn't . . . I was kinda weird last night . . ."

"Nope . . . you know what, you are . . ."

"What?"

"Prettier in the daylight." Add to that the Mr. Smooth smile.

"Yeah, right." And laugh.

"No, really."

"*Et vous etes vraiment charmant.*"

"That's French, right?"

"Wait, I thought you spoke—"

"Joke . . ." Happy happy, joy joy . . . She had the most enlivening smile, she patted her knees and then drew them up, the sweater down between her thighs, I had an urge to stand and casually walk to the sea, so that when I turned back I would be able to see her . . . you know, tell if she were naked. she wasn't just prettier in the daylight, she was fresh, young, sensual, and she was definitely naked under the sweater, *definitely.*

I heard Neil Diamond singing "*Once in a while*" somewhere in the back of my head, god knows why. But it is a nice song.

"So . . . did you guys . . . solve any mysteries last night?"

"No." I turned back from the shore, but she had crossed her legs Indian style. A smile. She had silver rings on her fingers, and one on her toe.

". . . Cute toe ring." I was getting . . . hard.

"You like?"

"Uh huh, I'm the MTV generation." I made a face, pointing at myself with two fingers from opposite hands. 'Who could have known that we would have flown, like two birds to another place, another space . . ."

"Psychological misfit . . . that's what my new book is about . . . Claire said you'd be good to talk to, get an angle . . . do any good drugs lately?" She played with the ring on her pointing finger, it was a Northwestern Indian design, Snoquami or something, representations of birds and whales ... quite pretty.

"Your book is about reggae?"

"No, a psychological misfit ... he could, perhaps, like reggae ... drugs?"

"Coffee and cigarettes ..." I smiled, "why?"

"My hero is a drug addict ... heroin."

"That doesn't sound very heroic."

"That's the idea ... it's the flaw that makes the character more ... well, lifelike ... I guess, huh. What's *your* flaw?" She took on a different self when speaking about her work; it was the older woman side of her again.

"I'm afraid of heights."

"Done in too many stories ... how old are you, Thomas?" My name sounded good.

"Well over 40."

She had stood up and was circling the top of the rock. "23 here, shit, man ... when I'm like 60 you'll be ... dead."

Her legs were tan, the color of honey, calves that were turned just so, like they had been molded on a lathe; she was a somewhat dancer, I'd heard.

"You have nice legs."

"Ain't that the truth ... " Bugsy looked down at them, looked up and smiled, "Thanks ... I always worry that they're losing their tone ... I dance, you know; take classes in Charleston, but since we moved out here to boony land I don't go as often ... you know ... What kind of books do you read?" She was studying the tea leaves at the bottom of her cup, rolling them slowly about.

"Historical stuff, adventures in the wilds ... but I really like stories with historical significance—ooh, that was a big word sentence ... where are my cigarettes?"

She laughed at me. "Sometimes it's hard to get you ... you're supposed to be the kind of pro ... that lives by his right brain."

"What kind of books do *you* like?"

"Promise that you won't like laugh, right ... "

"Hmmm ...?"

"Harlequins, I love trashy books, you know, like with Fabio on the cover, I think Fabio . . . is just a *god*, so cute." The girl came rushing out of her, it was a joy to see.

"Fabio as god . . . My grandmother used to love romance novels . . . I remember that when she was sick, dying, grandpa would sit by her bed all day reading them to her . . . "

"So you grew up with your grandparents."

"Yes." I got a clear—as if he were standing in front of me—picture of the old man . . . *yeah, stay cool boss man* . . . and it was as if he smiled at me.

"So your new book, it's about a druggie sycophant."

"Who likes reggae . . ." she kicked out at me playfully.

"You wearing panties under there?"

She blushed, I smiled. "Am I blushing? you got me . . . yes, I am."

"Sorry, but it was bugging the hell out of me."

"You are fearless, aren't you—Claire said you were."

"No way, not fearless . . . I just compensate for my shyness."

"Overcompensate maybe . . . I like you, Thomas, me and you are . . . gonna get along, straight up."

"I'm in over my head . . . Jesus, Fabio is god." Laugh.

We walked back toward the house, playing with words back and forth. Conversation with half the calories. She was good on her tongue, worked well with words.

She took a seat on the step to the patio; her sweater rode up and I could see the white of her panties; her lips parted moist, I looked into her face framed in hair that was morning mad and I wanted to climb inside her cunt.

"Morning, guys." Claire came to stand in the doorway, leaning against the door jamb between the bedroom and the patio. She was wearing a white robe, a cup of coffee in her hands and a sweet smile on her face. She looked that morning lovely disheveled perfectness.

"Morning . . ." Bugsy bounced up and kissed Claire on the lips, wetly. "You look . . . refreshed." Eyebrows raised, for emphasis.

"Tommy, I look *refreshed*." All smiles.

"Oh girl, you look lovely, my pleasure puss."

"Mmmm."

Bugsy bounded into the house calling over her shoulder. "Where's Michael?"

"He called to say he'll be here later; bet he'll look *refreshed* too."

Laughter was the answer. Then, "Coffee, guys," reverberating through the halls.

"Yes," in unison.

"You look . . . "

"Beautiful," helping me out, "ravishing, maybe."

"Took the words right out of my mouth . . . better than beautiful." Claire had come to sit beside me on the steps, tossed her legs over me, the robe opened to reveal knees. My turn to kiss; a little dry and tasting of coffee, toothpaste. "Tastier than ravishing."

"Mmmmorning."

"Hello . . . " She kissed me back. "So you two met again . . . on the rock of ages?"

"Is that what you call it?"

"Yep."

"She's nice. Come, give us a kiss." Tongue to tongue, lips warm, mouths wet, taste sweet, taste . . . sex. My hand ran onto her thigh; she opened her legs just a little.

10

THOMAS, WHEN *he touches, is soft sweetness. I see it when he brushes elegant fingers across Claire's cheek. He has love, and the fear of love, beating against one another for rule of his soul; but it is love that he seems to choose. He has tenderness, he has warmth. There is kindness, all pure in his smile. He has a smile, that boy does, a light-you-up, butter your muffin kinda smile; eyes that send electricity straight through your pupils down to your clitoris.*

BUGSY WAS at the table deep into the file on Number Two when we walked in; the kettle was rattling away on the stove.

"Do you mind?" she looked up, eyes wide with hope, a tentative smile.

"Not at all ... I guess I do the coffee."

"Hmmm." Was all the answer we got out of her.

"I'd love some, sweets, you want me to do it for you?"

"Nope ... Bugs, you want tea or coffee?"

"Tea please ... this is the Atlanta Weekly thing, right?"

"Yep."

"Too cool ... shit ... what's for breakfast?"

"T. makes the most divine French toast," she slid into the nook around the table with Bugsy. "*World* fucking famous," and she kissed Bugsy's cheek; she turned and smiled at Claire, touched her hand softly.

"I'm up for that." They kissed softly, bussing lips.

"I am gone to bathe ... you okay, babes?" Referring to me.

"Yep yep, under control . . . " I was already working on the ingredients for food. "Copetotious."

That was something my uncle Ray always used to say; it was his version of 'copacetic'. Uncle Ray had lived on another island . . . Grandma and Grandpa had moved there when I was seven, a lush green mountainous place, an English place . . . Uncle Ray was a tall slim man, I remember him being very tall, and very slim, but mostly very small. He had strawberry blonde hair, which he always slicked back with an oil that darkened it. A pencil-thin mustache, and the most elegant hands that were no wider than his wrist, with long slim fingers . . . Uncle Ray was a beautiful man in his white slacks and buck leather shoes.

West Indian men are different from those you may know; they still live in a deeply patriarchal society, Lord of the manor and master over the dark of skin. Breakfast at the men's club, lunch at the cricket club, dinner after drinks at the yacht club— or any combination of the three. You could carry your girlfriend to either of the first two, but not the third: wives were *non plus* at those, *de rigeur* at the third, oh, and you called them mistress.

You could carry neither to Bird Bush; the gun club was strictly men's territory. West Indian men are never homosexual. Uncle Ray certainly was.

It is a strange world I was born to. A world that when I was young was testing its sovereignty, looking for its independence. Later the need for independence would develop into a zealousness for non-dependence. Non-dependence was a freefall collapse, the result of which was furtive overdependence. Uncle Ray was going through those very same motions himself, I suppose. I remember his smile—that and his height. He killed himself one night; got blood all over those nice white pants he was always so fond of.

He was Grandpa's younger brother, by nearly 20 years. He had a nice farm. He left it for Grandpa. We moved there full time then; Grandpa had said that it was prettier there, we grew bananas . . . the farm back home was a dairy, Grandpa had kept that one too.

I could hear Claire's shower. Bugsy was engrossed in her reading. I took the phone and went into the other room.

"THIS IS *so* interesting." Bugsy was leaning back, long legs up on the edge of the table. Golden brown flesh and white cotton-crotch panties. I was sitting on the cook's island watching the bread brown.

Claire came out, fresh washed, a long white shirt, crisply ironed, made her look all the brighter. She ran fingers back through water-slicked hair. Looking down the length of one of the legs that lifted her to her 5"10" height.

"Shave me later, babe?"

"All of you."

"All of me." The big smile; lifting the shirt she showed off the stubble at the edge of some very brief panties. The bones of her pelvis stood out; the darkness of her pubis hinted through the delicate lace. I always enjoyed shaving her.

"Claire, this stuff is so interesting . . . I have never seen one of these before . . . really, really cool."

"Which one are you reading?" She had walked through to the living room.

Bugsy flipped over the file to look. "Number Two."

"Yeah, I just finished that one yesterday . . . Music, music," she turned on the stereo.

"What do you think?" I asked. I was holding the spatula like it was a fly swatter. Claire laid out the Polaroids for her to see.

"Fuck!" I'd never heard Bugsy use the word before. "Fuck, shitshit, *god*." She touched each photo, lightly, her fingers brushing the images as if to feel the horror.

Claire laid a hand softly on her leg. The comfort of the real. "So what do you think?"

"Think how?"

"Impressions, what impressions do you get from what you've seen . . . you know, and read."

"The killer has a very high opinion of herself."

"Say again."

"The killer has a high opinion of herself." Head to the side, she played with the skin at the nape of her neck.

"You said *her*self, why?"

"Yeah, why?" Claire, too, wanted to know.

"A feeling . . . I don't know, the words she used in the letters . . . I don't know, why are you guys looking at me like I'm weird, what, did I like say something mistakenly intelligent?"

"Women don't kill like this." Claire was the one who said it. "Every F.B.I. identikit will tell you that the chances of it being a woman are 100 to 1."

"So what do *you* think, puss?" I egged Claire a little.

"I think she's . . . look, there's a sense of something weird here, really . . . when, when I'm finished I'll give you an answer . . . but it's weird, all right."

"Hey hey you you get off of my cloud . . . *the telephone is ringing* . . . *it's three a.m there's too much noise."*

"Women don't kill?"

"Oh, women kill . . . just . . ." the thought kind of petered out in my head.

Developing bond between us. Breakfast and banter, coffee and colloquy.

"How's it taste?"

"Fishing for compliments." Claire smiled around her wit.

"Always."

"This is good . . . I should call mom."

"You should." There was a hint of Claire's nipples against the crisp cotton.

"She's writing . . . hates to be bugged when she's writing."

"Talking of that, you wanted to write about a 'psychophant' . . . this, now *this* is the real thing." I stabbed home the point with my fork.

"True. This crime fighting thing is hard, huh?"

"Babes, do you find writing hard?" Claire asked back.

"No, not really, kinda comes natural, you know." I watched the banter, from the other side of the table, like a tennis spectator.

"Right . . . for me it's my aptitude . . . it comes sort of easy." Claire wasn't being conceited.

I got up, taking the plates away, setting them down and looked for a cigarette. "Me, I find them both difficult."

"You lying bastard—don't listen to him, babes, this fart, ha— Tommy is one of those guys who find everything easy. You can light me one too, pretty please."

"After you called me a fart?"

"Oh, but with the *deepest* respect, darling." Add the smile.

"I'll have one too, please."

"Shit—don't any of you buy?"

"We only smoke occasionally . . . like the occasions when *you* buy."

Claire was doing the dishes. A light was filtering into the house, enchanting the particles of dust in the air; they glowed as they floated by on the soft breeze that seemed to seep through from all directions. It was getting on in the day.

Bugsy had wandered off somewhere; I had my feet up, reading and smoking. I flicked the ashes on the floor. Laying the Cosmo flat on the table I sat up. *"Q. I'm easily excited during foreplay, so much so that several men have told me they've never seen a woman get so aroused. My current boyfriend seems to like it, but is such excessive lubrication normal?"* . . . Problem? . . . I sometimes enjoy a little read of Cosmo, certainly, though not for the enlightenment it lends me. "Is a horoscope the same for men as for women of the same sign?"

"What?"

"Is—"

"I heard you, babes . . . Tommy, that is a good one . . . I don't know—*Bugsy.*" She yelled that out.

"*Yo.*" Yelled back.

"What—"

"Is—"

"Yeah, I heard the question. What kind of question is that? That's the question from hell . . . you guys are weird, you know?"

She wandered back off into the other room. "Weird," she called out. Then: "—I'll get it."

"Get what?"

"The doorbell," Claire said. I hadn't heard it.

"Who is it, Bugs?"

"Margo," echoed back.

"Ohhh."

"Did I miss something, I didn't hear the door—what's going on?"

"A car's coming down the drive ... it's Margo."

"Margo?"

"Wait for it."

11

BOOM!
–GBM #4

.

THERE WAS a house on a wooded street; it sat on a small hump in the middle of manicured green lawn. It was white and brick led up to it; the garden around it was perennial perfect. Perfect.

Frenchy pulled the car in at the bottom of a long drive that ran from the corner of the lot to the garage at the other side.

"Nice."

"Half million, son."

"Shitting me."

"I shit you not."

"Pity."

"Hmm."

We walked across the soft green of the grass, trimmed to golf green specifications. The lawn service still came twice a week. We walked up the neatly bordered brick path to the front door. It was posted, *police crime scene keep out,* hard to read on the red paper. It was open.

Frenchy pushed it, I walked on in.

"*Shit!*" The back of the house was torn open onto the world. "Shit," I said again.

What had been the rear of the house was now scattered across what had been the back lawn.

"Wow ..."

"Uh huh . . . they found the note pinned to the front door when the fire department arrived."

Frenchy held out the file to me: Number Four.

"Yeah." I opened it, the note was the first item on the left. " 'Boom'— how eloquent, eh?" He spat.

I slipped my trigger finger between the two sections of the file, marking my spot as I walked with it closed. You had to pick your way through bits of the house that were . . . well, just a tad out of place.

The pool was green and full of shit; I stood at the living room's edge and looked out, imagined for a moment what the view would have looked like.

"Wow." I touched the yellow crime scene tape that hung waist high . . . a fluorescent barrier where a wall had once stood.

"Two propane tanks . . . you know, the kind you use for the barbecue . . ."

"What did they use to set them off?"

He took the file from me a moment.

I used my free hands to light a cigarette.

"Ah, see it here, there weren't much left of the fucking thing . . . a timer and . . . well, some sort of plastic containment . . . here, see." Passed me back the file. I looked at the technician's report—Greek to me.

"Where?"

"In the bedroom back there."

I looked, expecting to see a door leading somewhere; there was none. Just open space.

"Well, I mean, shit, where the bedroom *used* to be."

"Ah." There was no sign of burning, no charred marks—I had never been on a bomb scene before; I had expected there to be, well, you know, fire marks. "No fire marks."

"No fire . . . Explosion, son."

"Yeah, but . . . "

"Don't be asking me . . . this is my first bomb . . . you're the pro."

"My first fucking bomb too, man."

"Well, ain't we just a pair of losers today."

We uprighted two white wooden lawn chairs beneath the oaks in the back yard and settled into the lunch that we had picked on Plantation; sourdough French bread and goodies.

I poured the coffees. We put our feet up.

"Nice spot." The sunshine laid warm patterns of light on the shaded lawn.

"Yep." There was a bird house built like a barn hanging from a near limb; a blue jay bounced about from perch to limb, limb to perch, unsure of himself.

"This fucking crime fighting is a real bitch, eh, son."

"Hmmm." I couldn't speak around my mouthful of bread.

"What about this accomplice thing with the relay intercept?" I had the coffee cup almost to my mouth. "How do you do a relay intercept?"

"Hook into the phone lines at the main trunk . . . you know, like you see in the movies . . . like that Sneakers movie; you take the outgoing call at the junction box, if you've got the proper equipment it reads the number dialed, the number called from, whole shit . . . phone company stuff . . . "

"Okay, yes . . ." I did actually have some inkling of what he was talking about; we had all been through tech courses, and many follow-ups afterward, but I was still probably a good five years rusty; when I had last followed up you would need a large truck to accomplish what he had just described. I presumed with advances in digital technology and laptop computer power that we were now talking about a small truck . . . but still you had to have the capability of cellular microwave snatching and the like, which when I started out, hadn't been applicable . . . I mean, that is, if you were covering all alternatives, and if we were dealing with professionals then they were covering all bases . . . "Yes, but can you do that all with just one accomplice?"

"You think I'm wrong."

"That's not what I said—do you think, perhaps now, that they could cover all bases with just two people?"

"Presuming that they are professionals."

"Well, if they're intercepting calls, then they are professionals."

"What if we're just assholes barking up the wrong tree . . . and that it really was just a fucking mixup with time—could happen, eh, son?"

"Could happen . . . see, we're still dark on this shit."

"Hmm . . . you got more that coffee? . . . Now correct me if I'm wrong, Tom, but you said something 'bout video tape."

"Something." He was slapping mustard on his sandwich with a plastic knife. They are awkward instruments. "On that Number Three, did anyone see a service van?"

"Nothing in the report nothing, frankly, in any of the reports."

"Means shit . . . service vans don't stand out, fucking people never notice the damn things."

"Shit, son . . . shit . . . What you think?"

"I think that I'm more confused than when we began—when I began."

Frenchy took off his jacket and laid it across the arm of the chair; the butt of the automatic he carried flopped around. It was a Smith & Wesson model 52, .38 special automatic, they had this unique design, pleasing; a dinosaur of a gun, but good.

"Where in hell did you get that old piece?"

"What?"

"The .38."

"You spotted it . . . not many people get it . . . I thought you didn't carry a gun."

"I don't, but that doesn't mean I don't know them . . . can I see?"

He handed it to me sideways; the first thing I did was eject the magazine, and then empty the chamber, making sure the weapon was unarmed.

"Five down and one in . . . the weight of it is great, though."

"Yeah . . . an' you don't carry?"

"Well, I have a gun, two really, that I travel with . . . I, you know, I just don't carry them, I've got a .380 H&K P7 and a model 36 Smith."

"Ah, the five-shot .38." He lifted up his pant leg smiling. "Me too . . . man, if you got a likin' for guns you should have seen the arsenal that came out of that lady's house you just come from, in Delray, you know . . . she was loaded, paramilitary stuff and all."

"Oh, I did, man, I did . . . nothing went missing?"

"Nothing . . . that we know of, but she an' all had stuff there that was definitely not catalogued anyhow . . . we talking 1928 Thompsons, .45 caliber, with the rotating mag, she had an 82A Barrett, a 50 caliber military thing . . . " I didn't know it, Frenchy was obviously familiar. AAR-15's, M-16's, Franchl and Mossberg shotguns, H&K 91s and A3s, two Uzis and a MAC-10, all fully auto, handguns out the ass, a goddamn *arsenal*, shit yeah."

"I was looking at the rifles; if I thought I could get away with it I would have taken the fucking H&K .308 sniper rifle she had, well shit, and maybe some of them 1800's Colts that she had . . . those I really liked, and the Boss."

"True enough, yes."

We didn't bother to walk back through the house, but took the scenic route instead; the paradox between front and rear began about halfway up the wall of what had been a guest bedroom at the back left of the house, opposite the master suite.

I paused to catch the scent of a double red rose. The juxtaposition between the red and the bright yellow of the police tape was, at least, pleasing to the eye.

She was leaning against the hood of the car, and she was tall. Long legs dressed in white linen that traveled almost four feet from the ground to slim hips.

But it wasn't the height of her as she unlimbered from her perch to reach about six feet into the sky. It wasn't the beauty of her face, which was sculpted in cream-smooth flesh. It wasn't the elegance of an obviously well-toned body . . . no, it wasn't that.

Baby was bald.

She ran her hand back in a gesture that would normally have swept away flowing locks. But there were none.

"Hallo." She smiled and perfect teeth showed white against the dull pink of her lipstick. "Are you the Realtors?" She waved her hand at the sign that was akilter on the edge of the lawn.

Blankly, like ... idiots? we both looked at her.

Her bald head was perfect symmetry and the same color as her skin.

Her eyes were green, glowing.

Tits.

This woman was sexy. Was her pussy as clean shaven as her head? She wasn't, on closer inspection, quite beautiful. She was good looking.

"Are you selling the house?"

"Ahm, no ... ahm—"

"Tongue tied," I heard Frenchy mumble under his breath while looking down at his small feet.

"There's been an explosion." She had no eyebrows either. I looked at my wrist.

"Explosion?" Maybe she was sick but she looked so very, very healthy ... very. "I don't see any damage."

"Try around back ... " Frenchy took out his badge and opened it with a flourish. "I'm a detective with Atlanta Metro..." She stepped forward to look, unflustered.

Then to me with a smile, "And you are ... ?"

"I am Tom, but everybody just calls me Tom." Try a little smile with the wit.

"No badge, Tom?"

"No cop."

"Ah, no cop ... "

"And you are, ma'am?" Frenchy the cop.

"Obviously *not* going to buy this house ..." *Bam!* Slam the door shut on Frenchy's questions. She looked at me and offered her hand. "My name is Valerie." She took her hand back and flashed a smile at Frenchy. "Officer." She sashayed away—no, she sauntered away, fuck knows, but she went, all bounce and sex and verve. Fuck—and I said as much. "Fuck!"

"Uhhmmm ... Son, I never thought that you'd hear me say this, but that there is a bald sexy bitch if ever I seen one."

"Sexy *bad*."

"I think she wanted to eat you up, Tommy."

"Yeah, in my dreams."

"Heh— 'but everybody just calls me Tom' ... too smooth, son ..." He was speaking to me across the roof of the car, hand on the open door, his eyes trailed off in the direction she had gone. "Fuck, where'd she go?"

I stepped my foot back out of the car and turned slowly. "Poof—gone and vanished ... hey man, easy come, easy go."

BALD. Both of them were bald, and tall. He was bald, she was bald. He not quite as bald as she; a stubble was growing on his face as well as his head. He was tall, a good six foot two or three inches, she must have been 5' 10", or maybe 11. He had an angular face that was definitely on the handsome side, and Peter O'Toole eyes of the most wonderful blue. He was sitting on the trunk of a BMW 325is, the blue of which matched the Polo shirt he was wearing; his jeans were pressed neat and his fingernails were manicured. He wore a stainless Rolex Oyster Perpetual Datejust watch on his left wrist and a pair of rubber-soled black leather shoes on his feet. He was immaculate. He was a god.

She was the long-legged Valerie.

"Do you think that was wise?" A soft English bass, words all clearly enunciated. He scratched the top of his head with two middle fingers, like people like to do when they think.

"I wanted to get a sense of him ... the adversary." She held each side of her head softly, close to the back of the skull, almost as if she were massaging it.

It was a nice day, all light breeze and sunshine, just a hint of coming fall in the air. Valerie sipped on a diet Coke through a straw.

"Want some?"

"Never touch it ... health kick, you know."

"Hmm ... says mister cigar man."

"Arnold Schwartzenegger smokes cigars ... they're not quite like cigarettes at all, you don't inhale them ..." When he spoke he often sucked his mouth as if he was smoking a cigar. He pulled a silver cigar case out of his pocket. "Come smell this, they're absolutely wonderful."

"Darling, I quite believe you. Really I do, promise." She had a mischievous smile and this lilt to her voice. Valerie had come originally from Hungary. "Are you going to smoke one now?"

"*Nicht, miene herr.*"

"Your German is atrocious." Valerie had been through "education" in East Germany in the late 70's.

"The bald thing looks good on you."

"So what are we doing?"

"Waiting."

"I know that, silly, what are we waiting *for*?"

"Word from above."

"God?"

"Exactly. I'm going to smoke one of those cigars now, shall we go and get an herb tea?" He was, of course, joking; he hated herb tea.

"You are a *most* funny man, darling."

Waiting; they always waited between jobs, "wet work," they called it. They were the advance team, moving into an area ahead of the main force . . . setting up Ops centers: weapons, supplies, communications, computers, security, housing and transportation. Once they had secured a perimeter of operations, the rest of the team would follow.

WHILE THE hairless crowd was setting up their operations for Number Ten, I was delivering some evidence from Number Four to a friend of mine. He was an explosives expert stationed at Forces Command HQ, Fort McPherson, Lakewood District, Atlanta, Georgia.

Frenchy was sitting on the hood of the car, back against the windshield, hands around the back of his head. He was looking at the sky. The day had gotten gray.

"Was he thar?"

"No, but I left it for him . . . with a note." My hands were in my coat pocket, shoulders hunched. My shoes were brown. I looked up at Frenchy.

"He's good?"

"Best I can think of."

"Good . . . it were a sad thing, that bombing . . . the first that I'd ever seen one, first hand anyway . . . a sad thing . . . she was on the bed, I guess, an' he was coming out of the bathroom . . . " He sort of snickered. "You know, he still had the light switch in his fingers when they found him yeah, like his finger tips just clamped up on it, weird . . . weird, son, weird, had the fucking light switch in his fingers. His body was it was flaccid, there was stuff oozing out of every fucking orifice, blood, mucus, brains, shit . . . the blast had kind of sucked the fucking life out of him, from the inside out. His wife was different, though . . . she'd been closer to the bomb . . . on the bed . . . it was the wall that killed her." His black hair was thick, long on top and parted in the middle. He was holding clumps of it in two hands.

"It were a sad thing, Tommy . . . shit like that shouldn't go unpunished, man . . . The woman, his wife . . . and the wall were outside on the lawn. Her body seemed . . . well, you know, normal, it was the side of her head, where she'd hit the wall . . . you see, son, in a bomb blast the force moves outward from the epicenter; he got torn up by flying debris and the blast wave sucked his insides out, but . . . she, she—" He moved to the side of the hood, legs dangling. "I had an interview with their daughter, a nice, good woman. I did ask her about the gas cylinders . . . know what she said, son? She said that barbecue was her father's passion . . . a retired man . . . he used to barbecue every night . . . he always kept spare cylinders in the garage . . . she loved him . . . So, he's good?"

"The army thinks so . . . so, where are we—you want to get some ice cream?"

"Where we gonna find ice cream?"

"It's your town, man, I feel for ice cream . . . sorry."

"Yeah, yeah, ice cream it is, you buying? . . . .You know, I'm more confused than ever . . . We have possible professionals probably killing what may be ordinary people which might or might not be on video . . . yes?"

"Sounds like it."

"So what next, son? . . . 'cause we still got nothing."

"Yeah . . . but suppose, just *suppose* we do."

"Well, son, if we did, then we'd definitely have to check all the victims again . . . if these are professionals . . . and I do mean *if*, son . . . if they are pros, then there's a reason for the killing, damn straight."

"Damn straight." I lit a cigarette, inhaling deeply; I gritted my teeth, exhaled through the nose.

"We done been through these people with a fine-toothed comb already . . . the initial agencies' reports, then the task force did their own, then again when you come on board . . . nothing."

"So what then?"

"So I assign Danny and Ingrid first thing . . . they're both damn good at data, give them a guideline to work and they'll find it . . . Just give me the parameters."

"Parameters . . . arrgh."

"You're the man."

"Parameters . . . how long do I have? . . Look, I'll work it out, I'll set the parameters by tomorrow . . . now where's my ice cream?"

"When you leaving for Mississippi?"

"M-I-SS-I-SS-I-PP-I . . . soon . . . sooner the better . . . I want to get these fucking prelims out of the way; only really two more to do . . . Number Ten's still too fresh, I went there, so don't have to go back; seven-eight, that was where we first met—do you remember where we first met? I don't have to go there either."

NUMBER Nine had occurred just after I took office. I was in Tallahassee when it happened; I had other work to do. It was only 45 minutes after the fact when they called me. Well, I called them, actually, to tell them I was arriving back from Number Three.

"We've had another one," Frenchy'd said.

"Shit." It was 40 days after Seven and Eight.

"Exactly . . . we're all getting on a plane right now; you want to meet us?"

"Yes."

"By the time I'm back they should have in all the toxicology reports and everything on the last one, right?"

"Toxicology should be in by Monday, Serology by Thursday . . . yeah, by the time you get back . . . look, I've got to go to Memphis myself; I'm to pick up some evidence and do conference with the big boys . . . let them know what's what."

"Thought that was the liaison's job."

"He's got to be in Miami same time."

"A lot of sucking up."

"So who'll be running the office?"

"Danny, but I'll only be gone for the day anyhow . . . Just call Christie love and tell her what you want, son; she'll make all the arrangements, drive, fly or walk . . . Christie'll take care of you. And you got my numbers, I'll be on cellular if you really need me . . . I think we're getting somewhere, Tommy . . . I think so."

12

I WAS IN HELL, and the Devil was a redneck.

"No, man, the greatest country album's gotta be David Allan Coe's "For the Record."

"You crazy, Dan—Waylon Jennings' Greatest Hits."   Yeah! And then spit into that Styrofoam cup.

"Fuck that shit. George Jones . . ."

Crime had taken a back seat to Trivial Pursuit, the Good Ol' Boy Edition.   *"Mama sells eggs at the grocery store, my older sister is a first-rate whore; she's been to hell since Junior went to jail, and tires for sale for a dollar or two cash . . . if that ain't country, I'll kiss your ass."*

"Wait, wait, 'You never even call me by my name', even I did know dat," Leeman, all white teeth and flaring nostrils. He raised his eyebrows: "Eh, eh?"

"Damn good choice, son . . . best song, what you be sayin, Danny?"

"Frenchy, most guys would say 'Mama, don't let your babies grow up to be cowboys,' but man, I am gonna go with Tammy Wynette, 'Stand By Your Man'".

"Bocephus' version of 'The Ride'".   Christie love had appeared in the doorway, pert and cute as a button. They all turned to look at her; they paused for a moment, chewing their cuds, mulling it.

"Hmmm . . . .. okay, okay, the funniest country song."

"Party song? Bellamy Brothers, 'If I said you had a beautiful body . . .'"

"No, Danny, I can't give you that one, son; close, though. I say, 'Longhaired Redneck.'"

"Tough one, Frenchy, tough."

"Johnny Cash's Cadillac song."   She was pert but tough. They had to look at her again, thoughtfully.

"Girl, you are tough."

"Redneck heaven . . . so, when does the South rise again?"

"You don't like country music, son?"

"Sure—doesn't everybody?" I smiled.

"Smartass . . . . your friend from over at MacPherson called; said he got the package." Frenchy came and put his arm over my shoulder; we walked out into the bustle of the main room.   It reminded me of the city room of a major newspaper.   "He said we should give him about four days, maybe a little less.   He asked a few questions, I gave him the answers that I had—He's good, right?"

"He's good, Frenchy."

"Good . . ."

"My choice is   'Amanda'", the Waylon version, not the original."

"Christie," he turned, "Christie, give back that prize.   I think our boy here done got the winner.   He says 'Amanda'", the Waylon Jennings version."

"*Shit* . . ." She stamped her feet. "Man."   I gather it was a consensus: my long hair just can't cover up my red neck.

We went down into the basement.   Remember chem lab at school?   It had that look and that smell.

Sigmund—Siggy—was the team's chief of forensics; he oversaw the crime lab, including the pathology from the medical examiner.   Siggy was a graduate of MIT and Harvard Med School; Siggy spoke four languages, had played pro golf, and was a top-notch chef; Siggy was an M.D. and also had a Master's in chemistry; he had been published in the Journal of Medicine—twice.   Siggy was six foot four, athlete-fit, brown hair, blue-gray eyes, perfect teeth.   Siggy had a warm sense of humor, the kind of personality men liked and women lusted after. Siggy was Adonis.   Siggy was a god.

We found him sucking on a lollipop, watching as a titration changed color.   He held up a hand for quiet: the solution changed, blue, then purple, then red, and back to white. Siggy made a note.

"Well, hello, gentlemen, what brings you to the bowels of the earth?"

"We were looking for Dr. Frankenstein." Frenchy.

"That's *Fronken*steen, and he's in the next lab, with Dr Jekyll."

"How's the golf coming, son?"

"Managed to knock another stroke off the handicap at the last tournament; getting better." He made a swing with the lollipop.

"I hate golf." I looked around the room full of mica counters, stainless sinks, Bunsen burners, Petri dishes, test tubes, electrical shit out the yazoo; stuff I know nothing about, chromatographs, spectrographs, autoclaves, centrifuges, Kodak analyzers. I am confused.

"What kind of man hates golf?"

I put on my glasses. I hardly ever wear them. "I hate football, too."

"Blasphemer. Baseball?"

"Yeah, and Mom, and apple pie."

"Ohhh, you are a bad boy . . . you really hate baseball?"

I took my glasses off. "I like cricket."

"Ah, Frenchy, now we get it: it's the English snob thing."

"You're right—there are no sports but English sports." We laughed together.

"Guys, we did the whole bit: thin layer chromatography, liquid chromatography, tested the retention time of the residues. We did debris searches . . . there were no accelerants used; no fire, just a blast. By the crater, we determined the blast site was the back of the bed . . . residue analysis confirmed it was a propane bomb; we found shards of the tank in the husband's body. One tank valve was completely intact; it was embedded in a tree outside, it had plastic and tape still attached to it . . . actually, it was a milk bottle used as a trap for the gas; we couldn't find what the trigger mechanism was, though, possibly it was wired from the light switch—uh, the husband was still holding the switch . . . We found no embedded pieces of trigger, pressure-sensitive or otherwise; what they used is a mystery. That's about it, you know . . . ."

"What about the victims?"

"Well, he was a bit difficult, he'd been scrambled by the blast . . . a rag doll, really. She was intact, but there was nothing there to indicate anything; she had traces of Recombivax in her system; it's a hepatitis vaccine—we called in her medical records and found that she'd gone on a trip to Costa Rica last month so her doctor had given her that vaccine as well as one for cholera, as there've been breakouts in Jamaica and Belize recently . . ."

"Vaccines . . . Frenchy, any of the other victims take trips lately?"

"We graspin' at straws now, son? We cross-checked all that —especially since the vaccine was so prominent in the report; not a one had gone anywheres near Costa Rica, the closest was Panama, and that was two weeks previous . . . and hardly a one had even been to Central America. Number Six ain't never been anywhere that we can figure . . . Two was a regular traveler, the mister in this duo hardly went anywheres either. He liked Florida though, it seems."

"Zero. . . what the fuck is this, ahm, thin-layer chromatography, using a liquid transport silica gel separator—Greek." I tapped my copy of the file with the backs of my fingers.

"Vaporized samples, for instance, the propane, all went boom on exploding . . . we take samples of fiber and so on, and we run this test: propane would show up as a residue in liquid separation, get it?"

"Frenchy?"

"Fuck no, son —fuck, no."

"CLAIRE, DARLING . . . where are you? . . . Mmmm, something smells good." A warm deep sexy-sounding voice. Tall, tanned and muscular.

A wolf in sheep's clothing: Margo was a man, slouch socks and all. "Ooops—and who is this?"

"Margo, this is Tommy."

I stood, offering a hand. She was taller than I. "Margo." He . . . ahm, *she* was dressed stylishly, feminine fresh. Looked damn good, tall. A summer tunic dress, with a crisp white T-shirt under, slouch socks and white Keds . . . nice honey wheat hair, cut short. A soft smooth face, pretty eyes and nice legs—if I hadn't known I wouldn't have.

"Hello . . . you'll have to excuse the way I look . . . I'm not quite finished yet." Margo still had her penis. There was none of the overtly homosexual stereotype about him; he was no Ru Paul, no fawning femininity.

"So I see." I smiled warmly.

"Not shocked."

"Hasn't quite sunk in yet, I suppose."

Laugh. "Well, yes . . . you've been rather the talk around town lately. Obviously Claire kinda likes you, I can see why . . . Don't start fretting now, Tom, I'm not gay, just built that way." He had a nicely soft-spoken southernese to his voice. "Hey, isn't anybody going to offer me a fucking cup of coffee? . . . Ooops, did that just come out a little mannish, or is it just me?"

"Mannish," was agreed.

"Guess the damn hormones ain't all kicked in yet . . . anyway, I've got a whole 'nother nine months to practice. What's for breakfast?"

"Tommy makes a divine French toast." Bugsy hopped up on the island.

"God, you are a sexy bitch, Bugsy." Margo looked down at his growing breasts. "Hmph... I could use your tits . . . Claire, sweetie, what fucking blend of coffee are you testing on us this week?" There was this flirtatious manliness in her yet; Margo liked women.

"Kenyan - Jamaican."

"Mmm, it's not bad smelling."

"It should be a good blend of body and aroma . . . the Jamaican coffee is renowned for its aroma . . ." she was fishing in a drawer and brought out a silver spoon that looked much like a large measure. "This is a Goute-Cafe, it's what professional tasters use to test coffee . . . I saw it once when I was young, grandpa took me to a tasting in Costa Rica . . . It was the smell, you couldn't believe the wonderful smell, beautiful."

"Oh, girl, you've sold me, I'll take another cup." Me.

"Tommy, we need a new opinion here . . . We, that is all of us, have been debating whether Margo should lose the Southernese."

"Southernese makes for a sexy chick, Margo; I like it, keep it in its subtle way."

"Ta da . . . I win, Claire, cough up, you owe me five bucks."

"You know, if men were my thing, you'd be it."

"Stupid question: if men aren't your thing, then why?"

"Change of pace, baby . . . Look, I'd been an accountant for twelve years . . . boring job, boring life . . . hell, I just felt like, you know, maybe it was . . . well, time for a drastic change." Deadpan serious suddenly broke into a smile. "Joking . . . Really, I don't know—maybe it's just a chemical thing, maybe it's what I was meant to be, maybe . . . I just felt really drawn to being a woman . . . even when I was young I always wanted to grow up to be a lesbian.

"You know, Tom," she continued. "Most people . . . I mean when they ask that question, they always seem to have, well this . . . deep sound of condemnation in their voices . . . Thank you, you . . . well, thank you. You know, I never cross-dressed, never had any homosexual tendencies, straight arrow hetero . . . But I just wanted to be a woman . . . hear me roar."

"Be the best that you can be." Claire called over her shoulder, her head buried in the arctic regions of the freezer.

"A big step . . ."

"Margo lifted his feet. "You ought to try it in these shoes."

"So what are we doing?" Bugsy was fishing in my shirt pocket for the cigarettes. Pack in one hand she cupped a flame and lit up. Deep inhale, exhale to the sky.

"Girls just wanna have fun, sweetie."

"Charleston?"

Everyone looked at me—Master, do you hold the key.

"I like Charleston." I shrugged, spoke around my cigarette; Bugsy lit me.

EVER SEE the inside of a prison? It's a grim fucking place, smells like a hospital gone bad. You feel locked up the minute you see the front gate. Dread and fear come cold calling. She's in one now, six years she's been inside already, only got 150 to go before first chance at parole. Annie, born Angelina Carmen whatever.

Annie kidnapped and killed 10 teenage boys. She raped them. She tortured them. She cut off their genitals and she fucking sewed them into their mouths and left them to die.

When we busted down her door we found a stack of bodies in her basement, all in various stages of decay. She sprinkled them with white lime to keep down the stench.

How would you picture her?

Well she wasn't at all like that. She wasn't at all butch. She wasn't at all ugly, not even plain; 5'8", slim-waisted, well busted, nice ass, long legs, blue eyes, soft blondy-brown hair, cut to shoulder, bobbed, sexy . . . she could have had men anyway.

It was in the eyes though; nothing. Cold, like fish fucking eyes. I saw her again, last year. There was a missing boy case in Seattle, a seven year old case, they asked me to go and see her, see if maybe it was one of hers. I flew to Arizona.

She wasn't in general population. They had her in isolation. Annie had severely injured another inmate and maimed the guard who rushed to break up the fight; she bit his bottom lip off. She plucked out his eye, crushed one of his testicles. They Tasered her.

She ate the eye.

She was sitting alone in a small yard, reading a book and sucking on a Marlboro. She still looked stunning, sitting there in all that Arizona sunlight. "Annie."

She looked up from her book, and a smile lit up her face. She set the book down, and flicked away the Marlboro. "Well, surprise the shit out of me . . . they said sum-un was comin' to see me, but weren't expectin' you."

"Well, I was in the neighborhood."

"Yeah, bullshit . . . how's the right hook?" She pushed out the bridge holding her two front teeth, smiling witchlike around it.

I was the last one through the door that day, and the first one in her way to freedom. She popped up from behind a chair and tried to cut my heart out on the way to the door. I feel proud of myself; I broke her arm and knocked out her two front teeth.

"Haven't used it in a while." Added the smile.

"You be a strange one, Tommy T. . . . I can still remembah you thar, smilin down at me, softly, when I come to . . . you woulda thunk I was your date wakin up from a fucking faintin' spell." She leaned forward and put her hands on the chain link fence between us. "If there weren't no fence between us I'd probably kiss you. . . with tongue."

"I could think of worse things." I lit a cigarette, leaned forward and passed it through the fence.

"Thanks . . . so what brings you?"

"Seattle; they asked me to come down and ask about a missing boy there, he went missing about the time of your thing."

"I was there . . . drove up with some friends." She sniffed, wriggling her nose.

"Did you do anybody?"

"Hah . . ." A big beautiful smile, fuck, what a face—an angel fucking face with the devil's fucking eyes. "Now what kinda fucking question is that to ask a lady . . ." Then she looked serious a moment. ". . . A boy named David, 17 years old, brown hair, brown eyes . . . a good fuck . . . he used to do this cute thing with his eyebrow. . . I did him. Do you need a written?"

"Nope . . . Just want to know where he is."

She hesitated. Precedent was that she could ask for some privilege.

"Ranier, about three mile down from the 3333 Lodge, left hand side of the road heading uphill . . . I couldn't be exact, but round bout there, maybe 20 yards off the road . . . I guess.

"Fuck —Tommy, do you realize I haven't had a good fuck in six years? Best I can do is get my pussy sucked by some bitch. Christ, I would kill for a nice hard fuckin' cock right now."

"No pun intended."

"No . . . sorry . . . how about you T., you free? Huh? I could give you a fuck that you'd talk about for the rest of your life."

"Be kind of hard through this fence."

"Too bad, huh . . . ?"

"Was it worth it, Annie?"

"Now no . . . then, oh yes . . . it was my drug, man, I got a serious sexual thrill out of it. It got me off, the power of it, I owned them punks.

"I ain't sick, T., don't think that . . . it were something I couldn't help . . . you know, like wanting to suck your cock *right now*." She squirmed in her seat, flexing her thighs. "Mmmm, the want's there in your eyes too, I can see it . . . they all had that look, T.—even when they was scared they wanted me. It was power. Do you want me, Tommy?" She ran her hands across her breasts, pulling two buttons open.

"You're very beautiful, Annie—who wouldn't want you?"

"Yeah . . . look at my body, Tommy . . . still good, curved just right, perfect tits, my cunt tastes like sweet sex."

"I bet it does."

"It's wet now, my little pussy."

"You getting yourself off?"

"Trying to get *you* to get me off . . . come on, T. . . I want it, look." She eased her leg up and pulled the prison shorts aside. Her pussy was there, naked pink, fleshy, glinting in moisture, sex syrup. "Just look at that, you'd like that . . . mmmm, wrapped around your cock."

She was drawing me in, and I knew it.

"T., you want, I want. We all want together . . . suck me, fuck me, eat me, beat me . . . touch me, love me . . . give it to me in the ass."

I squirmed. Her fingers were tracing her vagina. I was hard, horny, mesmerized.

"Come on, I'm all wet. I can see the sex in your eyes . . . you'n me naked, T., cock in cunt . . . fucking, humping like wild fucking animals, hmmm?" She slipped two fingers inside her cunt. She was looking at me through eyes slightly glazed.

"Can you see it, my finger is your hard cock. Picture it . . . pussy wet, dripping around you, sweat, sexy sweat, smell of cunt, taste of lips, oh god . . . . come on, fuck me, hard fast, I want you in me, in my cunt, in my mouth, I want you in my ass, T., in my ass, fucking me in my ass . . . mmm*mmgh* . . . ." She removed her fingers slowly, looked at me and tasted them. I could see the moisture. Across the divide I could smell her. I could feel the moisture of my own secretions.

I was . . . uncomfortable, sweat-soaked, hard, dry-mouthed. I was on edge. She smiled at me.

She hadn't put her pussy up yet; she used it as a . . . as a hammer, to drive home her edge. "I'll show them where the body is . . . that's what you wanted, isn't it?"

"That's why they sent me."

"Hmmmm . . . ." and she smiled again, that sweet smile that lied "innocence." "I always liked you, fuckface."

13

"**NICE STORY**— nice chick; so what does it have to do with anything?" Some sarcasm.

"Well, you two wanted to know about women who kill . . . Look, Bugs, women who kill are a rare breed, relatively. Women serial killers are even rarer . . . and those, to date, anyhow, are for the most part like Annie . . . you know, with a sexual trigger. You see what I'm getting at."

"Yes, that what I said earlier about it being a woman—is wrong."

"Likely."

"Yet your Atlanta Killer seems to be a woman, I mean." Margo checking her lipstick, looking down into the rear view mirror. He . . . she was standing in the jeep.

"Ohhh, Margo, that's good," I studied the end of my cigarette. "I'm impressed."

"Well try this on . . . suppose that the averages prove right, then statistically speaking, it probably ain't no woman. Then, then someone is sending you a, um, what's that they call it . . . a—oh, yeah, a red herring."

The wind was up. The day had lost some of its beauty. There was the portent of winter in the air.

My chin was down on the hood of the jeep. The weather had started to cool off rapidly as the day vanished; dipping to cool from the lukewarm it had been a few hours before. The sky was gloom. I bent my head sideways.

Claire was sitting ass-down between two pieces of driftwood, benchlike, on a rock at the edge of the shore. The sea was just over there. The beach was wide and sandy here. She was deep into file number four. Bugsy was sitting on the hood sipping on a Pickney Cafe Espresso to go. Margo stood in the jeep, leaning over the windscreen, holding her green Styrofoam cup in both hands. She brushed her hair back, tucking it behind her ear in a gesture that was so feminine . . . . I took a big drag, turned my back to the jeep, and exhaled in a long cloud.

Bugsy bent at the waist, placing her hands flat on the hood in front of her, between her feet. "It's almost as if the killer knows what solving crime is all about, eh? . . . Check this, as a writer that's what I would do, you know . . . I mean, if I were writing a crime story, what better criminal, you know, like one that knows how not to get caught . . . Killer in the know . . . dig, and I'm going to paraphrase here, ooh, big word, Thomas, write it down . . . You said in your beginning notes that Killer brings nothing to the crime scene . . . you getting it?"

"Vibes." I could look between where Bugsy was sitting and Margo leaning, manlike, and see Claire. She was looking at the sky, shaking the file. Inspiration, I could presume. "From heaven."

"What?"

"Just mumbling to myself, Bugs."

"Fuck—so what did we decide? Is it a woman or isn't it? I am con-fucking-fused."

"Penis and pumps—I would be, too."

"Yippy Ki Ay, motherfucker."

"The world is confused, Margo."

"But what's your opinion?"

"Bugsy baby, I'm not sure . . . really . . . But Claire will know, when Claire is done she'll know . . . you see, girls, I've worked every angle of this fucker . . . I think I've found all the missing evidence . . . I have some suppositions . . . Claire will look it all over and she'll have the answer; Claire will be right."

"You have this very . . . childlike quality about you."

I was warming my hands on the hood of the jeep. "What makes?"

"If you don't believe me, ask Bugsy."

"It's a lack of seriousness; Margo is right."

"I saw a werewolf, drinking Pina Coladas at Trader Vic's . . . his hair was perfect." I wanted more coffee, no, no—I *needed* more coffee.

"What, what?" They looked at me strangely, as if I was loathsome, perhaps.

"Guys, what's going?" Claire came to join the trio; we were quadruplet.

"We are, sweets."

"Thomas was being childlike, we decided."

"Nice, isn't he? . . . and very very good at his job." She held up the file. "Tommy, this is really . . . really . . ."

These were my personal files. I always developed my own set; having taken copies of the originals, I would produce my own data in my own way. They were always accessible to me. They were full of my own notes and observations, scribbled across the pages . . . these were the basis of the final notes that I would forward to Frenchy to have put in the Crime unit's working files.

I really wanted coffee.

"You have an opinion yet?"

"Two more and I'll start talking."

"You said that two ago."

"I lied . . ." She kissed me on the lips, holding my chin in the fingers of one hand. ". . . How about we go and get some videos and go home. Is SanDra home?"

"Supposed to be, I think."

SanDra is Bugsy's mother. I come to the dim realization—by the way, I'm letting you in on this early.

"Sandra?" I am, as yet, unclued.

"SanDra, Bugsy's mom . . . you know."

"Hmmm." I guess I was supposed to remember something forgotten. Lost out all around, really. U2's "Who's gonna ride wild horses" was playing on the radio, and for some reason at that moment I thought how much Margo looked like "the Edge".

"God, I really love this song, it is so happening . . . Bono is *so*—you know." Sometimes the woman just completely left her and the girl took over. Bugsy was beautiful.

We drove 17, ocean highway, back townward from Mt. Pleasant. Spun around the "Battery", along the bayfront, million dollar row; very Georgian . . . I think it's Georgian, well, very Southern anyway. White wooden columns and white wooden siding on palmetto-lined boulevards overlooking a sapphire blue bay. Many of the houses were turned sideways; their porches, wide and shaded, ran down the side length of the house . . . something to do with early land taxes, like how the Dutch used to build up instead of out . . . it was the Dutch, wasn't it?

Turn here and a twist there and up on Church Street, the spire of St. Phillip's Episcopal pointed to a cool crisp icicle-blue sky; the coolness was deepening to chill and the clouds had gone. The day was afternoon. The spire is a Charleston landmark. 146 Church Street.

Southern hospitality and all that, one felt a relaxed warmth here.

Warmth was not in the temperature; summer in all its glory had passed to waves of Autumn. I was looking for the Pickney cafe. I wanted coffee.

"Turn here, T."

"Did I tell you, Bugs, that Tommy's got a piece of land here? . . . nice spot, you want to go show them, T.?"

"No, babes, fuck it, let's just go get a couple of movies, some coffee and piss off home."

Memorial Bridge to Ashley Bridge to 171 south. You rode high above the sound; on a clear day you could see the rivers run, Ashley and Cooper. Old Charleston on its spit of land. Drum Island, a large sea of blowing dry grass. Crossing the Ashley you could look back and see the Citadel. Here at the confluence, nature was alive, and man had built his city in the perfect place to enjoy it.

171 south, going not quite into Folly Beach, at least not exactly; I'm not sure the exact name, but it's close enough to call it home.

Michael was hanging upside down from the limbs of a peach tree as we eased down the drive. It was 4:12 p.m. I know not because I had remembered my watch, but because I asked. I was driving, Margo was standing in the back, feeling the breeze in her hair.

"God how I love this . . . Tom, you ever think of becoming a woman?"

"Not yet."

"It really gives you a completely different perspective on life . . . what is Michael doing?"

"I'm getting a different perspective." Michael's words.

"No, it couldn't be . . . you know, if the little fucker weren't deaf . . . I swear."

"So, guys . . ." he swung legs down, put his feet firmly on the ground. "What's hanging?"

"Heh, you're all smiles . . . are you feeling . . . refreshed?" Bugsy bounded to the ground and bounced past Michael, all flash of hair and smile.

"What . . . what?"

"Re Freshed." Bugsy around a smile.

"Refreshed . . . why are you all smiling? . . . I'm missing something, come on, guys clue me . . . what am I missing?"

"Your virginity, maybe."

"Virility?"

"Virginity." Claire mouthed the word, not actually saying it aloud.

"Ah . . . fuck you all . . . and I mean that in the Bud Bundy way it sounds . . . what movies you guys get?"

"Some artsy shit that you won't like, although it is European and probably full of tits." Claire spoke the last part over her shoulder as she turned for the house. How he caught the word tits I'll never know. But adolescent-like, he homed right in on it. "Tits—did I see you say tits?"

"For a deaf boy you hear all the right parts." Margo patted him on the shoulder. "—So Diedre giving you any?"

"Yeah, grief maybe . . . pussy no."

"It's a sin . . . if I had my pussy I'd give you some."

"Margo, you are a true saint."

"Bugsy baby, ain't I just, though?"

"So when you getting the nip and tuck?" Okay, so I'm inquisitive, or would nosy be a better word?

"Hormone treatments first, baby . . ." he looked sad a moment, then the usual joy sprang back into her face. "Soon . . . soon."

Margo smoked, I smoked, both of us in manly fashion. Michael had gone to pick up Diedre. Claire and Bugsy were in the kitchen. Margo dropped into one of the chairs, took a big swig of coffee.

"I know, I know, I need attitude adjustment."

"Poised and graceful, poised and graceful."

"Words to live by."

"More coffee, guys." Beautiful Bugsy Baby stuck her head out the kitchen window.

"Fuck no, I'm wired . . . almost drink time, isn't it?"

"Must be fucking six o'clock *somewhere*," Margo added. "Drinks, Claire darling, we want drinks."

Claire stepped through the window with a pitcher of Martinis in hand.

"*Ta da* . . . I am so far ahead of you guys it is a sin."

"You finish reading through Number Four?"

"Oh yes."

I write, I dance, I sing, I kill and then I write again. It's a cycle. Now isn't that special. You work, you ponder, you sort, you question. Isn't life unfair . . . life's a bitch, and so am I..

Anyhow I hate to gloat; I hate in general.

TA TA.

May we meet when the song is over.

                        –GBM #5

CISSY FROM Mississippi sat next to me on the flight to Jackson. I read my file; she slept.

"I read it too." Bugsy was animated, she stood and hand-talked her description of what she had read.

"Jesus!" Margo belched.

"Jesus, Margo, you are definitely no God's delicate creature," Claire.

"Speaking from experience, eh Pusskins?" I had to tease.

"Oooh, Claire, that hurt . . . *Rrrrr*, cat scratch."

"That's right, Bugsy, you stand up for me . . ."

"What's for dinner, guys?" Margo tucked a stray strand behind her ear.

"Margo, darling, you eat like a fucking man . . . remember, girls are always on a diet, sweets."

"Fuck that, food is *life*—Claire . . . Chinese?"

"Pizza?"

"I love pizza."

"Me too," Michael piped up from nowhere.

"Michael sweets, why don't you go see if Diedre would like to come for pizza and shitty movies with lots of tits . . . hmm?"

"Aunty C," he smiled broadly, a handsome boy really.

"Well?"

"Call her for me, then." He smiled his perfect-in-every-way smile.

We drank coffee, smoked cigarettes, told small exaggerations and maybe the odd blatant lie. We laughed and joked at the short stories of our long lives. We bonded, fell in like with one another.

It was a sweet-scented southern night, the taste of sea in the air, and we took coffee in a deep dusk. I heard the ballad of Lucy Jordan: . . . "at the age of 37, she realized she'd never ride through Paris in a sports car, with the warm wind in her hair". I liked Margo.

"Where's SanDra?"

"She should be right back—Betty said that she just went to the village to get some Comtrex."

"You know what I am really going to miss?"

"Pissing standing up." It is probably the greatest single thing about being a man that I can think of.

"No . . . Cigars, I love a good cigar, a good Macanudo or when you can afford it, a Davidoff . . . in lieu of Cuban, of course."

"Women can smoke cigars . . . shit—I'd smoke a cigar," Bugsy said before digging into her Martini.

Claire came to sit on my lap, kissed my forehead and edged back against my shoulder, her arm around me. She took the cigarette out of my mouth and sucked on it.

"Love you." I said it quietly into her ear, she exhaled slowly over my head. and smiled.

Sweet-tongued soft-lipped smooth . . . "I'm glad you're here, babes." Claire kissed my lips sweetly and I realized why I had come here—really.

Appleton Vx in a short glass, lots of ice. Rum on the rocks, a cigarette and some soft music. The rum was rich gold, scotch smooth. I felt it going down, warm, all the way to my feets. I like a nice drink. The lawn was cool between my toes.

I had tried to reach Frenchy; he was not on cellular, so I left a message with Leeman; who had said. "We maybe did got a liccle sometin . . . Frenchy, me sure will tell yu when him come in, ah."

"Thomas . . ." she called it out . . . Frenchified; it played nicely off the tympanic membrane, tremulo'd against the stapes, tittered into the inner ear. Bugsy came to stand next to me. "Nice evening, huh."

"Yep—what time is it?"

"Time to buy a watch."

"So funny, Bugsy, you're so funny."

"Sarcasm will get you everywhere . . . six-ish . . ." Jeans and a colored T-shirt, wide belt and a pair of boots, cool. Brown eyed Bugsy baby, beautiful.

"I feel strangely at peace here."

"Strangely?"

"Bad choice of words."

"So stay . . . I mean you didn't just come here . . . for . . . your case, right?"

"Astute beyond her years."

"Cool, huh . . . I'm really good at reading that stuff . . . so?"

"Yep."

"Yep . . . what kind of answer is that? —Hey, come on over to mom with me . . . she might need the extra . . . coaxing, she's probably working on some . . . paper or the other."

"Okay . . . does—" I glanced back over my shoulder; under the light Claire and Margo were miming something that closer up would have been conversation. Michael had gone off for Diedre.

"I told Claire I was dragging you." As if on cue Claire and Margo looked up and waved, smiling.

14

THOMAS IS tall enough not to be short. He is wealthy enough not to be poor. He has read and so is not stupid. There is age in his eyes and hair on his shoulders. He reminds me of French men from the movies—those older men that women always fall in love with, you know. His eyes are plain brown. His ears are perfectly shaped from the flesh that god had left over. And there is this really cool European overcoat that he has a habit of wearing. He has wonderfully expressive eyes. And when I see his hands, the grace of his fingers—I am his piano . . . waiting.

WE HELD hands as she led the way through the wooded path up to her house. It was really a guiding grasp rather than a lover's clutch. Though . . . it, it felt warm and nice.

A black and white hairy, floppy-eared pooch guarded the porch in his sloth. He never barked. He did lift his head, tongue out, tail wagging, for a hello pat.

"Hello Pugsley." An Addams fan, she patted the dog.

It must be Jazz, because somewhere inside Sinatra was singing "Fly me to the moon," at volume. *"In other words, I love you . . . Fill my heart with song, Let me sing for evermore . . ."*

The house was early South; wood sided, shingle roofed, wide porched upstairs and down. The patio's boards were painted gray; they creaked with every step. The slatted shutters were the same palette, as were the posts that supported the

white picket railing around the porch. Window boxes held perennials, now in bloom, autumn flowers.

There was a swing seat at the north end. It moved of its own
volition.

"Mom . . . yo, Ma." Bugsy called out as we stepped in
through open four-piece doors, Dutch doors I think they're
called. The floors were deep polished dark hardwood. A stair-
case, steps grooved in the center from years of use, climbed right
in front of us. Nat King Cole was singing . . . *"Are you warm,
are you real, Mona Lisa, or just a cold and lonely, lovely work of
art?"* His voice was molasses syrup. At a landing the stairs
turned back overhead.

"Mom . . . Mom, yo, I have Claire's friend Thomas with me."

I wandered to the edge of the drawing room. Fully stuffed
chairs, floral in Brunswig *et Fils*. Blackout curtains looked to be
Stroheim & Romann, a long writing table by the window looked
like a Grange piece . . . okay, okay, so I know a bit about interior
design, lick me.

"What . . . I can't hear you, come on up." A distant voice.

"You decent? . . . I have company." And then to me. "Ladies only house, we like to prance around naked, you know."

"Who?" came the call back. We were on the landing, with an
African figure, tall with an oddly protruding belly and exagger-
ated penis, carved out of wood.

"Thomas, Claire's friend."

"Oh, come on up then." I could only call it recognition in her
voice, I was the long unseen cousin being welcomed.

I patted the wooden African on the head. Nina Simone was
singing. A Beatles tune.

Surprise my eyes. SanDra was . . . a high color woman, coffee
cream complexion. She was wearing a large shirt, and, my
guess, nothing else. Tall she was, statuesque. Her brown eyes
were very dark and stood out against her paleness. Her features
were sharp, aquiline; North African, softened. She didn't have
that hawklike gauntness of an Iman. One could never have
looked at Bugsy and known that her heritage was, in part at
least, African.

SanDra offered up a long-fingered hand and a warm lovely smile in a pretty face. She was not the academian cliché.

"Well, hello, Thomas . . . I am pleased to finally be able to put a face to the stories." She was Sade-like, her accent had that touch of Europe to it. I was to learn that she had spent years in Paris. A beatnik student of love.

"The pleasure is all mine . . . I would call you mum, but that . . . that would seem a tad strange, huh."

"Call me SanDra . . . let me go slap myself together. Why don't you show Thomas the house eh, *cherie*?"

"Where's mom from?"

"Mississippi."

"Shitting me."

"Am not . . . she spent twenty years in Paris, though . . . that's where she met my Dad."

"Where's he?"

"He departed during childbirth."

"Oh."

"*Et voila* . . . this is my room."

Wow . . . it was large. She did her sleeping and writing here. A long low table, scuffed and nicked, sat in an alcove with windows on three sides; there was a bay seat in the window. The windows looked out onto the woods and parkland lawn. The desk was strewn with paper, books and an Apple Mac computer; patches of an old Persian design blanket showed through the clutter. The bed was a large and fluffy, a French carved mahogany four-poster with a white down comforter. There was an old Navajo blanket draped across the foot. Three chairs, comfortable and old smelling, were grouped around a book-littered table and a TV in the very corner. It was a room you could live in.

The TV and computer were the only things of this century; even her phone was an old-fashioned bell and horn model. "Wow . . . Nice . . ." I stood and turned myself to face me, came to lay my eyes on a painting that caught my interest.

"It's something by Alice Ravenel Huger Smith, she's from Charleston." She's a mouthful.

I sat down on the slip covered couch that faced the bed, smelt the odor of the fireplace behind me. I could live in this room.

"Great room."

"Cool, huh . . . you really like?" She, Bugsy she, was such a lovely contrast of worldly woman and loquacious lass; at moments the published author, astute, knowing . . . then the naïve. She fascinated me.

Fuck, she made me hard.

"I DO this sometimes, drive down from Miami—it isn't that I expect her, the ferry doesn't run anymore, but it happens sometimes. I see a boat offshore, and something goes faster in me— hope, I guess. What the hell, Fidel Castro was on the Jack Paar show, so anything can happen.

"I even read the newspapers now, not just looking for the points spread or the odds; human interest . . . I'm doing okay these days, way ahead . . . but it's not the same, I sit with my back to the wall . . . you never know who's going to walk in, somebody blown off course. This is hurricane country, you know."

The ending of "Havana", with Robert Redford, played out on TV to the sounds of Earl Thomas Connelly singing, "The Chance of Loving You" which was playing from somewhere else in the house. I liked this movie, the ending was particularly poignant; an essay on what it is to have been in love at the wrong time in the wrong place—with a woman who you know is the right one. The words played on my soul.

You see, I know how he felt.

Me and my memories, looking out over saccharine sand onto a Ty-D-Bol sea. The scent of the coffee in my hand.

Film maker Mira Nair once said: "You don't have to orchestrate life in the third world. It's going on all around you". That is intensified on an island. Islands are lovely, confining places, limited by space and time . . . hardly big enough for dreams. Drawn still, though, to the smells of the sea, the flavors of the food, the vibrancy of the colors, everything quite so acute. On an island, life is so concentrated you can taste it in your very soul. I had loved on an island once.

Myself and Michael sat, outcasted as men, outside in the crisp night. The women were entrenched, fully, around the table in the kitchen. Margo had them in stitches.

I could hear SanDra's full, hearty, sea lion laugh. She was a striking woman. SanDra well and tall, long legs and hair thick and straight, a touch of silver at her temples. My age. Her complexion was cappuccino pretty . . . she was lovely, not beautiful. Maybe her nose was too large, not broad, but round, she had high cheekbones, her neck was perhaps too long. But still she had that, that—thatness?

Diedre, Michael's girlfriend, was a petite thing. Slim and short, small in all proportion. She had almost carrot-red hair, gone awry by maybe two shades of brown. Her eyes were green, like peas, kinda, almost, nearly. Her teeth were not petite; Bugs Bunny fullbigwhiteperfectpearly teeth. There was youth on her face.

Claire stood and poured the wine: She was tall, like SanDra, but broad-shouldered and lean, muscular, slim. Thirty-something. Her brown hair cut short, and her breasts were small.

Bugsy's breasts were large. Her flesh was pale, pure. Honey wheat curls, long and fluffy to her shoulder. A medium-sized girl, fit and full of all the right curves. And eyes of brown just like mother used to make.

Margo laughed deeply, he was surprisingly woman-like; the shape of the body, the swell of the breasts. Her face was soft, pretty blue eyes and a wonderful smile that animated the whole face. Broad at the shoulders, slim in the waist, long in the legs. Margo was really a woman . . . a woman with a spare penis.

I sat and sipped my third rum of the night, smoked my 24th cigarette of the day and thought my one thousandth un-original thought. It was a thought of the diversity of beauty, the variety of attraction, the rainbow of possibilities. Myself and Michael didn't speak, we just enjoyed the night. He helped himself to one of my cigarettes; and once when I put down my drink he picked it up and took a taste.

Claire had asked me earlier about the final bombing report for Number Four, it had not been included in my file . . . frankly, I had forgotten the damn sheet of paper on the desk at my office . . . I would have asked Frenchy to fax me a copy, but he was off till tomorrow. I made a note to myself to give Richard a call . . . Captain Richard T. "Boom Boom" etc. etc. we all used to call him Boom Boom. He was my friend from Forces Command, the explosives expert.

In the shadows of the trees, hiding from the night, I ran a warm, rum-wet finger around the edge of the glass and listened to the crystal sing. I set the tumbler in the crook of my arm and lit a cigarette, Zippo cupped against the cool. I should call Boom Boom and thank him again.

RICHARD HAS been a soldier f— excuse me, a *Marine* for 31 years. He should be about 48 now, I think; just had a birthday. We were, in our youths, living different realities in the same city: New York. When off base he was dating a girl I knew; she was from Dawson Creek, British Columbia. I can remember that, but I can't remember her name . . . she is long forgotten, but he and I have remained friends.

We met again, he and I, when I passed through Vietnam.

I remember that he smelled of death, or like death, that day. He had walked out of a low mist into a base camp in some fuck-ass jungle corner with a French name in an Indo-Chinese nation on the other side of a different world. His hair was plastered to his skull. Exposed flesh was tarnished by the scum of a dozen bathless sorties. His eyes were jaded, glazed by the tension.

He'd been out arming and disarming ordnance that at a moment's notice could leave you one limb short of a full body. I remember that he was gray.

"T.," he had smiled a nice smile. "What you doing here, man?" His voice was a whisper with a growl at the bottom of each word.

"Fucking the dog, Rich . . . F.B.I.'s got me on the job in the war zone . . . who the fuck knows."

"Hey . . . voices carry, man, walk with me." Even here in the well, safety might be too strong a word . . . perimeter of the camp his eyes never stopped moving. His ears were pricked, listening. He was killer elite. "F.B.I . . . Police in country—Fuck."

"It's a weird fucking world, Charlie Brown."

"No shit, Dick Tracy." We spoke in cartoons.

"So what's up, doc?"

"War, man."

"Yes."

"What you policing?"

"Just checking up . . . no one wants to get left out of the only violent thing going, I suppose."

"How you feel about it?"

"Tell you what, man . . . when I get home I am taking a walk . . . too much bullshit for me."

"Yeah, Corps never going to be the same after this . . . War's never going to be the same. How long you staying?"

"Long enough for us to get drunk together; any more patrols?"

"Nope . . . I'll follow you back to the peace tomorrow. I've got two weeks out of the zone."

"Heh, better yet."

Those two weeks, I think, sealed our bond It's good to have friends.

I remember one Indo-Chinese night he had suddenly blurted out, around the fragrance of a dozen scotches. "You remember Anne from Dawson Creek?" I remembered her then, with a clarity with which now I don't. Dawson Creek is an insignificant dot about halfway to nowhere on the border between Alberta and British Columbia. In the days when Yukon was a big name in gold, Dawson Creek was a big name in towns. "Yes."

"Was she pretty?"

"Very."

"I can't remember her face . . . the color of her hair, her eyes . . . I can't remember her.. . The smell of her, yes . . . her scent, her fragrance, that   yes . . . You know, if she were to walk past my closed eyes right now, I would know her. But—I can't remember her smile . . . So she *was* pretty."

"Yes."

"I have died here, T."

"Yes, yes—we all have."

THE WOMEN were framed in silent pantomime. I imagined a zoo display with tag: "Humans in 20th Century Kitchen". Hands moved in all directions, a soundless spastic oratory. I stirred my rum with my index finger, sucked it . . . I thought, for a moment, perhaps it might be nice to get drunk and . . . and fuck them all. Maybe even Margo . . . I tried to picture them all naked.

TURN OUT the lights, the party's over. A good time was had by all . . . in a little while. I can't resist that smile . . . turn out the lights and close that door . . . maybe we can make a little bit of heaven. Claire's bed was big, king size, polished oak framed the box spring. The bed head a solid piece of hill shaped oak.

Her palms were flat against it now.

Her face was in the pillow, her ass in the air . . . thrusting . . . back at me, her back arched . . . as to make entry easier.

Epileptically . . . I thrust into her. There is something supra-sensation-ful about anal sex . . . Even in the cool of the night we were sweat-slick, wet. Tension was building. The liquor had dulled orgasmic senses, heightened sexuality. We were Palsy and Twitch as the anticipation built in our bodies.

CLAIRE sponged me off with a warm rag. I watched. She was beautiful, naked; muscular, slim, wiry.

"What are you looking at?" She smiled, she now had my semi-soft cock in her hands, bathing it. The smile was terrific.

"I want coffee."

"At this time of night?"

"Yep, and some music."

"Am I having another sleepless night, puss?"

Fat white man doing the Bogle.

Up all night—and now it was morning. I tried on the focus of my red-stained eyes. Splashed water on my face, slicked back my morning hair. Water, cool, down the slope of my neck; *aaaargh*, a growl where my voice had been.

Claire had Number Five scattered all over the table. She was fast asleep on the cushions of the window bench, a leg up on the window sill. Cool land, warm sea, and there was a soft morning mist . . . just call me weatherman. My eyes were dry.

I was watching coffee drip into the bowl. Tired. Did I tell you we had been up all night? I coughed, jiggled up a piece of chest.

"What's the story with these explosives?" Claire called out loudly, in her sleep.

I could have given her the answer off the top of my head anyway. Boom Boom had basically confirmed Siggy's affirmations. Propane barbecue tanks, milk bottle . . . but he had isolated the detonator as . . . "an automatic light timer, on/off switch like people have for when they go away on vacation . . . they send the current down the line on time, a spark bridges the gap between two now live wires, the tank valves are open, the milk carton works as a detonating chamber, keeping the gas in an accessible environment and still maintaining the pressure needed for an explosion. It's easy and its cool, T., real cool . . . takes a brain to do this . . . regular people don't think of shit like this; I've seen it done before . . . spook shit—Professional."

"Spook, professional, you mean like in spies?"

"Not necessarily, man, just spook shit; anybody's professional, shit . . . it can slip by if you need it to, you know . . . come off like an accident, you dig? . . . real pro stuff."

"Oh, I dig."

"Good, here . . ." he handed me a sheet of paper, his report. "Don't lose that, I didn't make a copy . . . and I didn't keep the shit you brought either, I torched it . . ."His eyes were always moving as he spoke, his ears perked . . . he was still in the jungle. Our jungle was Piedmont Park. ". . . I don't like this professional shit, you understand me." We walked slowly through the Botanical Gardens.

"Oh, I understand you . . . crystal."

"Good . . . I say no more."

15

FRENCHY WASN'T yet in from his suck-up tour when I arrived back from Jackson. I called from the airport, spoke to Christie love.

"You always on duty?"

"Seems so, doesn't it . . . you want a car?"

"No . . . no I'll just take the MARTA." The south line ran from the airport right to five points station by Atlanta Underground, city center really . . . they were putting me up in the Suite Underground Hotel. I would go to Mick's Underground for some food.

"How was Jackson?"

"Hey babe, the capitol is great, Capitol Green is beautiful, city hall is this great Greek revival building, the Mississippi archives building . . . the town is full of wonderful fucking history."

"Sucked, huh?"

"Had to deal with Elmer Fudd."

" I *like* Elmer Fudd."

THERE WAS a knock on the door at 6:30. It was Frenchy. "Rise and shine, it's a beautiful day . . . get your sweater, son, it is cool." He slipped off his raincoat as he came through the door.

"Shit . . . I hope you bought coffee." Scratched my ass, walking.

"Oh yes, oh yes—and nice things to eat too . . . fuck, son, go brush your teeth—I can smell you from here."

I saw myself in the bathroom mirror; my hair was gone awry, my eyes had packed luggage for the trip.

"I hear Jackson sucked."

I was shaving, trying to see myself in steamed glass. "Yep—but hey, there's always the Davis planetarium, biggest in the Southeast . . ."

"Didn't get along with Buford."

"Buford is an idiot." I still had morning in my throat.

"Yes . . . but his staff is good." Frenchy was sipping coffee, room service had rushed. A pot sat waiting on the table.

"Sure, they put out a strong report, but Christ—with an asshole like that overseeing operations . . . Jesus, man . . . he's got the carpet in custody, and the walls."

"He cut out the *walls?*"

"Uhhuh."

"Well, did you get anything, at least?"

"Aggravated . . . yes, yes, I got . . ." I paused to wash the razor. "Yes, I got his DayTimer."

"From the police."

"From his secretary." I could smell the paleness of the coffee. "How was Memphis?"

"I brought back some information for you, son . . . they think they found something—well, they done isolated something anyhow, a piece of metal and plastic that they found; it was entwined round a carpet fiber, they found it only because of a piece of the sword that had chipped off . . . so small they near and almost missed it . . . took a lot of work to actually get a reading on it."

"You're a rambling man."

"Uh huh . . . it was machined aluminum, elliptical, with plastic—like they use in . . . video cameras . . . well at least, the combinations are present in video cameras, as well as 10 or 12 or 20 other items . . . but that thar strengthens our possibility."

This work is not an exact science, it is often based on probabilities . . . the probability that a fiber and a semen sample, for instance, can occur in the same place at the same time; this either proves or denies the theory of reasonable doubt. Danny Rawlings, the Gainesville murderer, is a good example of this theory at work . . . Police cannot tell you, definitely, that he was the killer, but the forensics evidence pointed to him, beyond a reasonable doubt, being the killer.

"There's something else too . . . you want to hear?"

I, towel wrapped around me, wet half still, was looking for a shirt to wear.

"Well, son, there was a some sort of disturbance in the phone systems at the time of the murder . . . Memphis just done and finished a full update of their systems, modernization, son. And the computers registered a disturbance, an interruption . . . there weren't no complaint to follow, so it just kinda slides on by . . . but I was there, and curious. I had them check . . . it originated a block away at a main trunk, and it was a rotating disturbance on a random pulse, so that it disrupted several lines at any one time—but only momentarily . . . almost like a mistake, a shiver in the system, it would have gone on if I hadn't mentioned it . . . pro stuff."

"Shit, so we check all the systems then." I poured myself a cup of coffee. It was dishwater dirty in color, like Chinese tea; even the milk didn't add body.

"Done already, I done put Santiago on that, son."

"So this pulse . . . this disturbance . . ."

"Would disconnect calls, disrupt them, each line every couple of seconds for three minutes."

"Long enough for the killing to take place."

"Correct . . . in which time, boom . . . no one could make calls, some citizens would get disconnected, but . . . but nothing so long-lasting as to cause . . . consternation. Like that word, son?"

"Good word."

"How long?"

"We gonna need some court orders and such, some phone offices are . . . well, you know, it's good to be king."

"Five days?"

"Sounds good . . . nothing before its time—son, I don't like that shirt."

"You're right."

WE HAD a conference, Siggy, Frenchy, Leeman, Dick and myself. We took our meeting at the Auburn Avenue Rib Shack. It's in Sweet Auburn . . . Leeman was on fucking terms with one of the girls. It was a small place, lacking in tables, but full of the fragrance of good food and the memories of better times. Three booths and a Formica counter. We were early. It was 9:30.

I ordered some chicken.

"So . . ." the neighborhood was black affluence. "Where do we stand . . . what are we looking at . . . what progress we done made . . . ?"

Here's how the breakdown looks; Leeman was in charge of the office. Dickhead Dan was in charge of the crime scene units. Siggy was chief of Forensics, Frenchy was big cheese, and I was like the roving safety on a football team. The traveling I was doing now, they had all done in part, before me. In each man's team there were representatives from all the crime scenes. But, these were the boys with the oil.

"So we believe that the killer has accomplices . . . we believe that the killer is filming the scenes . . ."

"Professionals?" Danny asked; he was sipping a Coke.

"Maybe . . . it would seem so son . . . anyhow, we do have a possible correlation on the camera from Memphis."

"Could more than one be doing the killings, maybe?" Siggy.

"It would explain a thing or two." He added after a pause.

"What? Siggy, you think more than one person is doing the killing?"

"There are some discrepancies in methodology that might indicate that . . . I stress *might* . . ." it was my turn to be smart.

"How did you come up with that, Tom?" Siggy wanted to know. God, he was a good-looking man.

"I read the files, I asked the questions . . ." I smiled. "It's my job to think of these things."

"Well, I did put Santi on dat telephone ting dis morning, an' . . ." Leeman was biting a toothpick inch by inch, his third for the morning. "Danny and Ingrid be going back into tings, looking deeper . . ."

"The telephone shouldn't be a problem; Captain our Captain spoke to AT&T, and they said they would liaison for us, with just one court order, issued from Atlanta, somebody is on that already."

"I'm hungry . . . smell that barbecue, man . . ." I smoked, Siggy adjusted his chair to get away from my fumes.

"Tommy sent the samples from the bombing to McPherson, we expect a report, tomorrow, maybe . . . feels we might learn something there."

"Well, I've been redoing all the crime scenes; you know I visited them all . . ." Danny holding the Coke in both hands, staring into it perhaps for inspiration. "But mostly just pictures to work from . . . the scenes were good, mostly professional work by the individual forces . . . we've got as strong evidence as possible to work with . . . if we're lacking anything, it's due to the professionalism of Killer and not our fucking up . . . yeah."

"I'm getting an idea . . ."

"What?"

"Not yet . . . let me think it out."

A plurality of pluralism passed us by on the street outside. I watched them from time to time, distracted.

Picking rib from between his teeth, Dan. "So what's the plan then?"

The potato salad was homemade.

"Fuck the surface thing . . . there is definitely a connection, and we got to find it, son . . . we want to go back over all our work to date and dig in, deep."

Leeman was destroying a plate of pork.

"Rework the whole fucking case?"

"If that's what it takes, Danny, yeah . . . and hope we get somewhere before the next one, eh, son . . . man, these greens are good . . . Lissette, we gonna need some more sweet potato, darlin' . . . Siggy, you dig this?"

"Man, I haven't eaten like this in years . . . Homestyle . . ."

I belched.

"I NEED TO GO to church." Frenchy put a pinch of snuff between his teeth and gum. Tamped it with his tongue, sucked, spat.

"Only a Catholic would think of church at a time like this."

"That's me . . . I'm a Catholic, son."

"Call it prejudice, but I thought all rednecks were Baptists."

"Not this one—You don't have to pray, just sit and wait."

The others had gone back to the office. I'm not very good at church.

"I'm not very good at church . . . I mean, not that I don't believe in a god . . . just, well . . . I don't feel comfortable about church. They have church on Wednesdays?"

"Every day . . . I need a confession, and you could pray for a clue to the outcome of this mess."

"I'd try it if I thought it would work."

"You never know, son."

The Shrine of The Immaculate Conception, a conspicuous Catholic Church-y looking place across from Underground.

IT WAS SUNDAY at Claire's, but we weren't preparing for church. Did I tell you we'd been up all night?

"Number five . . . what's this . . ." A big, deep yawn. "What's this all about . . . I just can't read, I'm too tired."

"Dead guy, found in his office building, he was killed the night previously, while working late . . . found by his secretary the next day . . . nothing missing, nothing stolen."

"Read me the note . . . oh, shit." Claire spoke the last words through a yawn. "Is that coffee made yet?"

"Almost."

"Sleep . . . okay, read it to me . . . I feel like shit . . . 'I write, I dance, I sing' . . . what the fuck is that ?. . . Oh, god, I am going to yawn my head off . . . 'may we meet when the song is over?' This is all too weird, you know . . . sometimes you feel like you're reading a riddle . . . Tommy darling, give me coffee or give me death. God, what kind of name is Clark . . ."

She'd gone back to reading, coffee cup in hand.

"Cause of death was the final blow to the skull?"

"No . . . no, latest evidence shows that he was already dead; Killer removed the victim's shoe, and then struck the final blow to the head."

"I was about to ask you about that shoe."

"Ahm, from the position of the foot, and the marks on his face   he had bruises on his nose that were not caused by the bat—it was . . . well, it was only evident during autopsy . . . but he never put his hands out when he fell the last time . . . ahm, from the settling of blood, he must have been dead three or four minutes before he was moved, for Killer to take off the shoe . . . then the final blow was struck."

"What was Killer doing for three minutes?"

Claire turned to the hair and fiber analyses pages: "A lot of fibers in the bat."

"A lot of smacking around."

"Hmm . . . I need a shower . . . I'll finish this later."

I am a mouse.
A mouse in a jungle of lions, but I am
an attack trained killer mouse and I eat fucking lions
for breakfast.
Are you a lion? This poor dead bastard was one. Poor
baby.
Now, unfortunately he is, well, dead, oh and cold. Have
you felt his toes?
It's been a pleasure pissing you off.
In time, by the light of the silvery moon.

DREAM ON
GBM #6

POLICE WORK has changed much. "To protect and serve" is a motto of the past. Police have become Public Relations with attitude, simply because they cannot cope. The average police officer is not prepared for the mortal combat he has to face on the streets. The average policeman is unable to compete or keep up with the high tech para-militarism that is crime today . . . the thieves and killers are better funded and far better equipped.

Detective rooms across the country are filled with people who take notes and pictures. If a crime in America is not solved in the first six hours, it is likely never to be . . . The guy with the smoking gun did it.

So we were working against the odds . . . that is, if the killer never killed again. The race was on to find some evidence that would give us a head start on the next crime. You see, that six-hour window changes in multiple killings, serial crimes . . . the more killings, the more chance of a correlation. We needed a fresh killing to test our theories. Kind of horrible to hope for a killing, isn't it? I was on my way to the next stone-cold scene on my elliptical tour—see America by death—and basically we had semi-correlated a lot of nothing positive and a bunch of maybe on the side.

Frenchy had left a taste of god in my brain. Have you ever seen god, felt him, tasted of his flesh, drank of his blood? I never have. I have considered him, though, pondered his existence, thought of his probability . . . the one thing I do know in my business is that evil in its ultimate does exist . . . and if this evil exists, then goodness in its purest form must also coincide.

To wit, that a god is the epitome of that goodness, then surely a god must exist. Whose god, now becomes the question, eh! This is where the argument turns to war.

And so I am not very good with church. I will believe in a god, worshipped in whatever form you choose, in how many idolatrous quantities, but I will not believe in a church. Church perpetuates the sin of intolerance . . . because if Jesus is the only savior, then Muslims are heathens . . . if Allah be the only god, then Jews shall burn in hell. Christianity, or the lack thereof, was an excuse for slavery; Catholicism the catalyst for the Inquisition. I am uncomfortable with church.

Evil exists in all of us. A story goes like this: they were on a shooting trip in Colombia, some time in the late sixties. Four friends from a good life. They had hunted the world. On this trip they were attacked by banditos, and the friends shot the banditos dead. They then buried them at the bottom of a hillside, caving in dirt and rocks on top of the three bodies. Later, they would refer to it, and they always laughed when they did, "yeah man, we took them to a rock festival . . ."

"The Rock Festival".

I am tired right now; the pressure is killing me. I am to go on to Jonesborough, Tennessee. Go on to Number Six. But I am tired. It is my job to get in the mind of Killer, to visit the scene and feel what Killer felt . . . to see what Killer saw. If I can imagine the path of Killer's mind, then it can lead me somewhere. Sometimes I get a good vibe . . . sometimes only interference. I didn't like Jackson, Mississippi: it gave me no vibe.

So instead of going straight to Jonesborough I decided to go home, to take my files with me, reread and relax. I would catch the morning flight to Ft. Lauderdale.

IT MAY HAVE been cooling off in the rest of the country, but it was still hot in Ft. Lauderdale. The runway ran north-south, a windsock of faded orange blowing toward the southwest. There was a small open airy building at the end of the road by a circle that held a solitary and disheveled little tree.

A highway and a wide open space. And just in front of a sign that said STOP, No Taxiing, the plane was neon green and azure. The engine revved, and slowed to a steady beat. The plane was four feet long, with a wingspan of five. No Spectators Beyond this Point, and the plane's owner were sitting on a low fence. He had the remote control in his hands. There was 150 yards of runway, but the plane only needed maybe three. Enya played on my radio . . . "And the sky above is Caribbean blue . . . before the dream was you". God, what a beautiful fucking harmoniously haunting daunting melody.

And the sky was.

The plane did loops and the plane did rolls and I watched.

I saw a bumper sticker that said "Commit Random Acts of Kindness". There is consummate good in the world. A story goes like this: The New York Post published a Christmas piece, as I believe it does every year; about a child too sick to survive, too poor to live. In need of a transplanted liver and the means to proliferate. And people commit random kindness, willing to part with their wealth, their organs, their blood . . . by the thousands. It happens every day.

I really like it here, the warmth that the place exudes. Some people say it's hot. There are blue skies, wide expansive skies. There is blue sea. They rave about our neighbor to the south, Miami . . . Miami is the third world. Miami always feels like peasants with money . . . .this is better. You sit for evening drinks at the poolside bar of Marriott Riverwatch, lunch at Seawatch or the Cove, dinner at Panama Hattie's . . . Fishing from the Pompano Pier, the Guy Harvey marlin at the 17th Street causeway bridge, the beach at Atlantic Avenue and A1A, equestrian weekends at Wellington . . . .

This is less put on. This is more real. This is better.

Beauty is a difficult commodity to explain, but once seen it is immediately evident. I found this a beautiful place. It is not in the aesthetics, for surely it is a featureless place; very unlike my island home, which is full of verdant mountains, vibrant foliage and saccharine sands. There is no ramshackle oddity.

I came here to stay, following the dim whit of romantic novelty. And I have settled.

You know, I have reveled in the progression of my life. I have really enjoyed, truly, each changing turn of age. I look forward to the difference that each new day, new night, new year can bring. Experience and experiences are the fuel of life; food, music, sight, sound, flavor. Things and people that you have loved, places that you encounter . . . life. For all its . . . problems . . . it is wonderful. Every day is different, even the drudgery evolves. Each day is newly seen through changing eyes.

Like I love Paris . . . you know Paris . . . Paris was different for me at 14 than it was to me at 20. When I was 30 it seemed a place of infinitely more sophistication than it had ever been before . . . I went back last year and Paris was full of new tastes, new sights, new sounds; the women were ultimately more beautiful, the food truly more flavorful . . . it was as if I were visiting the city for the first time. I was Thomas at almost 50; Paris herself had remained the same.

These words all lead me into a thought; my life, a thing of my own making, which I have enjoyed. Look—you see this exciting, full of fun, somewhat-biography, and it is only because I leave out the shit parts. I have lived in my car. I have suffered lack of money, lost a few hands of poker. I've had my heart kicked in the balls, broken and crushed a time or two. I have been a drunk, a loser and a long lost fucking soul . . . but—and here is the chewy part—I always knew when to call up god and laugh . . . hey man, I ain't giving it up. I have always enjoyed this life, it is the shit experiences that give the good ones their level of intensity. And besides, I would really miss the occasional piece of pussy.

The sun is shining and it is—a lovely day. It is only five Celsius in Vancouver. I lit a cigarette; Fort Lauderdale is warm. The little plane went into a barrel roll. The files were beside me, but I was reading a book. The files were producing nothing, and it was frustrating. The book was interesting. I let out a deep sigh of a breath.

She was sitting on the low fence, the one with the "No Spectators" sign. Longlonglong . . . and bald. She looked at me a moment, unfurled herself and walked over to the car.

"You know . . . I know you . . . ever since you are pulled up I keep saying to myself, God I know that man . . . I do know you, don't I?"

She is erotic. "Yes . . . we met . . . in Atlanta, a few days ago." There was peach fuzz on her perfect head. I realized that she would be a blonde.

"Ah yes . . . you're right . . . that house, yes. Well this is a big coincidence , isn't it? . . . Wow."

She is exotic.

"Really . . . I'm sorry, I forgot your name." I pushed the door of the Saab open; she backed up to let me out.

"Valerie—and you were Tom, right?"

"Right."

"So what brings you here . . . to this, um, this coincidence."

I found myself imagining the sight of her cunt covered in that same soft yellow down as her head. "The planes . . . I really love the planes . . . and you?"

"Thinking . . . I came to think and ran into the planes by accident."

"There's not many people out today . . . but sometimes, especially on a Sunday when they have a meet, it is really quite beautiful, and exciting." Her eyes had a twinkle, it was . . . truth.

I put my ass against the fender, crossing my ankles; if I didn't smoke I wouldn't have known what to do with my hands.

"So . . . what do you do that gives you the freedom for all this coincidence . . . Atlanta, now Fort Lauderdale?"

"I work for Paramount in their video sell through . . . I was just in town with Blockbuster . . . their rep said that I should come out this way to have a look at their new entertainment complex, 595 and 136th Avenue . . . I heard the planes."

"Oh . . . Paramount, that must be exciting."

"It's a job—and you?"

"I'm a criminologist . . ."

"What?"

Her eyes are enchanting. But it was the fucking baldness that excites me. Her eyes are green.   "A criminologist . . . ahm . . . you ever see that movie 'Manhunter'?"

"'Manhunter '. . . oh with . . . oh Christ, um, oh god, I can see clearly his face, he was in 'Hard Promises' with Sissy Spacek . . . I saw it on HBO the other day . . . yeah, anyhow, I do know who you mean . . . yeah."

"That's what I do . . . I track killers."

"Wow . . . were you tracking a killer that day, then?"

"Sort of, not really; we were looking at a scene."

"But there'd been a killing."

"Yes."

"Wow . . . now that's a great job . . . where you from, Tom? I detect an accent, is it Irish?"

"No, no, I'm West Indian . . . I was born in the islands."

"Nice accent." Her chin rising in a nod.

I CAME TO live in South Florida, a little over eight years ago, followed the smell of the sea. Many of the first times I came to Florida were by sea.

Once, I remember, I was crewing the Newport to St. Georges yacht race and we had to sail a boat, the "Tambourin" . . . which was registered in New Hampshire but had wintered in the Grenadines . . . to Port Everglades to be outfitted before taking her north for the race start. That was sometime in the early sixties.

In 1958 some friends and I had brought a 52' Princess up from St. Johns to Miami to refit the engines before doing a trans-Atlantic run: Bermuda, Azores, Portsmouth. I remember 1958, because we stopped in Cuba on the way, in Barracoa on the Eastern edge. A sandy little town of washed out colors, wood buildings and Mambo music. Cuba was such an interesting place then . . . I got laid there that night.

You have never seen sea so blue as through the Bahamas. A blue so alive and fragrant that you almost want to taste it. Yes. . . we dawdled up the islands in 1957. One afternoon we swam ashore where what looked like a tropical clubhouse sat on a bluff. Like the house in the opening lines of Hemingway's "Islands in The Stream"; it was solitary, on a narrow tongue of land, painted white as to be cool, and with windows that opened onto the sea.

It was indeed a clubhouse, stocked with liquor and beer, snack food and water. It was empty. A sign behind the mahogany bar indicated what was available and at what price. You helped yourself, and were expected to pay. Everybody did.

We got drunk beneath the tin roof of a ramshackle bar in Andros. Drank overproof rum with warm milk and slept on the beach. Sheltered from a storm in Bimini harbor. The ship rolled heavily at anchor, and I puked my guts out.

The Gulf Stream moves up the Florida Straits at 22 mph. A miscalculation, and we made landfall at the Hillsboro inlet almost half a degree off course. We got drunk at the Crabhouse that night; there was nothing much else for miles, just a lot of sand, and flies . . . sand flies.

It all looks very different today. All very functional. And I have come here to settle. It is something I often thought that I might never do.

I wanted to fuck this woman. I wanted to bury my face in her almost hairless fuzzy little twat.

My leg was bouncing, tapping as if it were listening to some definitely *passé* little disco beat. I was looking at her, she was telling me a story. I didn't hear a fucking word that she said; I could only hear Rod Stewart screaming "Hot Legs" in my head.

"What are you looking at behind those glasses?"

I could only smile.

"Man, you are bad . . . you are either going to have to take off those glasses or wipe that grin off your face." She was holding imaginary hair back from her face. She was lovely.

"You are . . . lovely . . . it's the bald thing really . . . can I smoke now?"

"You are blushing." And she was not.

"Yes, yes I am . . ."

"Oooh, what is happening here, Mr. Tom?" She was no more than 25 or 26.

"I . . . I think we should go find a place to drink some coffee . . . do you drink coffee?"

"No . . . but I would kill for a mineral water . . . do you have a place in mind?"

"Not yet."

"*. . . I love ya honey . . .*"

We never got to fuck. She left me after the coffee was cold. "Maybe we'll suffer another coincidence soon, huh?" She had a lovely voice and a sexy smile.

I could only hope.

16

I TOOK MYSELF and my file to a somewhat-cafe on Las Olas. Poor coffee and not-quite-European style pastry; god, I longed for an apple bread and cafe au lait from Croissants de Paris, Truman & Duval streets, Key West. This was a velvet painting: A poor imitation of the real thing. Italian take out and coffee bar. It smelt plastic. There was no resounding continentalism, and the coffee sucked.

Number Six, I took another coffee and lit a cigarette. Number Six was already two days old by the time they found the body. He had been killed on a Saturday night, and had not been found till Monday morning. He was a male, Hispanic, 52 years old, brown on brown. Single, never married, heterosexual—yes, that was in there too. 5'11", 171 lbs., no visible scars. His dental records were there, and his medical charts. He suffered from cavities, probably due to a calcium deficiency in his youth. His occupation was listed as Veterinarian. The address of his lab was the same as his home.

And that is where they found him.

I leafed through the scene report, glancing at the photographs to get a feel for the layout. A bone saw had been used to cut the hands . . . I looked at the photos . . . Miss Jeannie had been right: the scene almost seemed artificial, staged, put-on performance art.

The hands laid out just so. The whole thing had a feel of a real serial scene. "Serial" killers often have an aesthetic image of their scene; they like body placement, and the art of the kill—it is what gives them that almost sexual thrill that most experience.

I needed to see the scene. I needed to go. It was an urge that came to me—maybe it was because the coffee was so bad. I lit me a cigarette and went in search of a phone. I made a call to Christie love in Atlanta, and she made the arrangements. I drove to the airport and got on the late flight north to Raleigh-Durham, a commuter to Winston-Salem, and a pond hopper to Jonesborough.

This is Pioneer country. Jonesborough is Tennessee's oldest town. It lies about 50 or 60 miles from Knoxville, out toward the North Carolina/Virginia border; a scenic trip through rolling hills, woodlands and farms that seem to have changed little since the 1700s. You can feel Davy Crockett, visualize the slave plantations, hear the battles of the Revolution and the Civil War. This is history country. It just doesn't seem like America out here, but I guess this really is America . . . It's the cities, that we all know, that are the artifice.

It smells like America. It is still dark, damp and cool when I arrive in Jonesborough. It is not quite yet morning, although my watch says 6:00 a.m. It smells fresh, like forest and wet leaves, there is a tinge of domestic livestock. I like the way it smells; it would go nicely around the aroma of a good cup of coffee. I presume Christie love has told the locals that I am on my way, but there isn't a soul around to meet me. The light is on, but the small terminal is all but deserted. There are two black people cleaning quietly, a he and a she in gray coveralls. They are not Americans; I hear by their accents that they are Haitians, I think. This must be America.

There is a lone taxi outside; the other two people that arrived with me have been picked up, so the cab is mine.

Even in the gloom of early dawning you can see the age of the town, its in its brick and wooden fretwork, the antebellum church that we pass, the not-quite-symmetry of the lay of the lands . . . the individuality. It is nice, I smell wood smoke, a light mist lies close to the road. The taxi driver came originally from Delhi, in India. Ah, America!

"Where be you going, sar?"

"Police station."

"Police station, sar?"

"Yes . . . can I smoke?"

"I . . . I am not . . . oh, you are wanting the cigarette, most certainly sar, I too do smoke." We smoked.

It was a red brick and boring building, all square and heavy in its lines. It had a date stamped in the marble above the entrance, 1804 . . . it had been a school once, or so I heard. It sat obtrusively in its own surround, but like it didn't really belong there, out of place. Windows shone with light on two floors. Dawn was graying the sky.

"Thank you." Paying the cabbie I stepped out. I felt awkward with my briefcase and overnight bag. I hate briefcases and jackets and ties. I hate sensible shoes and waistcoats and shaving to go out. I lit a cigarette, cigarettes I love. A Ford LTD, plain, dark and police-ish, pulled into the lot with a screech. The door opened.

Clint Eastwood stepped out. And he smiled at me.

"I guess you're my out-of-town pro." He was tall—lanky, the Louis L'Amour word of the day—in two strides he crossed the distance to me, his hand out. He smiled and his creased face deepened to valleys, his eyes glowed.

He shook hands with enthusiasm. "You can call me Dixie, everybody else does . . . I'm the big guy around here, chief of police and all that shit . . . I think they said your name was Tom."

"Yes sir." His personality filled the open space, he was live and in person.

"Sir . . . that's what you call my father; Dixie will do . . . sorry I missed you at the airport, just couldn't drag my ass out of bed, we were out on a hunt last night . . . you hunt, Tom?" His voice was gravel.

I sort of smiled. "Only people . . . they make good sport."

"Damn right . . . but hell, I'm a redneck and rednecks hunt."

"Don't fret . . . I like a little hunt from time to time . . . eat what you kill . . . the primal thing."

"Primal . . . yeah . . . so you come to see our little crime scene . . . it was quite a thing . . . shit, give me your bag, let's go inside and do coffee some justice, put our feet up a little, then when the light improves we'll go out to the clinic . . . oh shit, I was saying, yeah, it was quite a thing, that killing, a hell of a thing, Jonesborough had never seen a thing like it . . . used to work in Knoxville, been through F.B.I. special services training, still, it was something . . . I've seen some shit . . . I bet you've seen some shit . . . hey, what do you take in your coffee, Tom?"

He moved on long strides, his cowboy boots falling silently. He was a cat and he noticed everything. He spoke in a most jovial way. His hair was gray mostly, his eyes still nicely blue.

He had Eastwood's smile.

And he had nice hands. I don't mean that in the way it sounds, but he had nice hands. President Clinton has nice hands. But his nails weren't manicured.

"So Tom . . . I smoke cigars, you don't mind, do you . . ." I don't think he wanted an answer, he took out and lit up. ". . . Mmmm, damn good—you like cigars?"

I coughed on my cigarette, feeling the softness in my throat. "No . . . I'm a cigarette guy, hooked in the gills."

"Yeah . . . smoke one once in awhile myself . . . what the fuck, Tom, if you can't enjoy life might as well be dead . . . cheers." He raised his coffee cup.

His office was clutter and commendations. I had a feeling that his house would be much the same way. He was married and had been for twenty-two years to a fine woman named Jean. There was a leather sofa over against the wall; I moved some papers and found a soft spot to put my ass.

My coffee cup had Yosemite scrolled across it on pastel background. The inside was blue. I wondered if Dixie had actually been there. I have a cup, it says Denali, with a picture of mountains on it. I had never been there.

"Oh, the doctor was a fine man . . . very civic . . . he was very involved in the community, well respected by the farmers and always his small animal clients—the housewives, you know." He added the last almost like an afterthought.

"Did he fuck around?"

"Boy, you *do* ask the hard questions. . . look, he was a single man, a doctor, not too terribly bad-looking, and certainly a joy to talk to . . . there was gossip, and well, several girls cried heavily at his funeral, and yes—some of them well, shall we say, are attached. But that ain't what killed him, I am sure. Look, Tom, the boys around here . . . if they wanted to do a guy, well, they're the kind that would take him out on a hunting trip and shoot him accidentally, run him off a road, or crash his dirt bike off a cliff, that kind of thing . . . this guy was really murdered in an on-show kind of way. . ."

"Don't worry, I'm quite sure he wasn't killed for fucking around . . . was just trying to get a feel for the guy . . . this last lady that left the evening, late, after the assistants were gone, the lady with the sick poodle . . ." The cigarette paused on its way to my mouth, I tamped it on the pack again. ". . . He was fucking her."

"Would seem so, yes."

"Just checking."

"Good eye."

"I try . . . damn good coffee."

"Isn't it . . . I send for good coffee, comes from the Starbucks catalogue . . . it is good, isn't it?" He paused to light up his cigar, puffing trainlike, spewing exhaust into the atmosphere. "You want to hear what killed him . . . you want to know what we saw, what we smelled? . . . We fucking smelled death out there—Death put on show.

"Look . . . we got there sometime about nine on Monday morning . . . the crime scene unit from Knoxville was coming in by chopper, but hadn't gotten there yet . . . I have some good boys here, but well, guy, this was some shit . . . really . . . It was like a scene from a Dick Francis I read one time . . . His ankles and wrists were harnessed with padded leather cuffs, designed to handle horses . . . the doc'd been injected with an animal tranquilizer, Bute, um, butorphanol tartrate; to kill—excuse me for laughing, guy, yeah, to kill pain . . . the pain he would have felt as the killer cut off his hands . . . So see, we weren't quite equipped, so I sent for the state boys.

"We pulled in round nine, I set roadblocks at one mile, closed off the side of the road the house was on . . . I'd already radio'd ahead to close the scene and not to use the drive or anything . . .

"His blood was all over the large stainless steel operating table—all over the goddamn floor too . . . they think he was very aware and that he had screamed . . . horribly . . . Something to do with the color of his larynx . . . The house is away from the neighbors, and the lab is secure, soundproofed, sterile . . .

"No one heard him, guy . . . probably died of fright . . . look as I've said, I've seen things, this . . . this I never seen . . . never—" He was rummaging in his top drawer, wrapped a rubber band around his hand. Stim-U-Dent, interdental cleaners, clove flavored, by Johnson & Johnson . . . toothpicks in a matchbook packet. He took one out. It was orange. He offered me one too.

"His last patient out, uh . . . Cindy . . . who shall, at this time, otherwise remain nameless . . . to protect the innocent so to speak . . . dig, she left his office less than an hour before the probable time of death. She has seen nothing . . .

"My supposition was that the killer had come in across the fields to the back and had left via the graveled drive in the front . . . there were dirt prints where he had walked into the sterile environment wearing outside boots, big green English Wellingtons, same boots used by all the staff . . . He was wearing the doctor's own gown, we found it at the door . . . and those long long gloves that vets use . . . although we didn't find those . . .

"He used a long electric prod, HD, high power. It was chromed steel with a bright red handle and two evil-looking prongs at the other end. It had enough of a jolt to it to lay the vet out, Taser like . . . We found where the vet's body had twitched on the floor, the current darting across the synapses of his nerve cells . . .

"The killer used a needle that was long and broad, animal size, it was driven into the jugular at his neck.

"Guess is what guess is . . . that his eyes would have opened wide, he probably screamed, real loud . . . the Bute would have burnt like a fire in his blood . . . can you imagine fire in your blood . . . fuck . . . I think he shook, violently . . . he was helpless . . . frothed at the mouth.

"His veins scorched and his heart scalded. Less than 10 minutes and he would have felt a growing peace, light, painlessness.

"I'm sure that it was probably too wild to click until the second hand came off . . . the Doc would have stared at his own hands, his ring . . . the index finger of the right hand twitching. His blood pumping, arterial blood spraying, blue hued.

"Then euphoria would have set in. And he would die."

KILLER sat down in a comfortable chair and put his feet up. It was a heavy duty steel and vinyl swivel job. It creaked loudly as he leaned back.

"Doctor, Doctor, bleeding bright, in his dark lab tonight . . . Doc, hey doc, you feeling like shit . . . eh, doc? Doc—you looking a little pale, Doc . . . *Doc*?"

"YOU DID your homework, Dixie . . . Did he live out there alone?"

"Oh, yes . . . Oh, we did our homework, my friend, big time; worked this one over . . . Hey, after all I am running for mayor, gotta do the job right . . . yeah, he lived alone, a nice place too, with an up to date operating theater, convalescence barns, outpatient facilities, padded drugging room, cableway system to move the large animals . . . he even had a mobile operating room in a semi that he could carry out in emergencies . . . did a hell of a business. Man, would you look at that, it is a glorious morning outside, can you smell that . . . life, Tom, the world is *alive*, that's why I moved back here from Knoxville . . . hey . . . 8:30, you want to go out there now, or do ya feel like some good breakfast first? . . and I do mean good."

"Breakfast . . . yes."

"Good, a man needs a good breakfast in him . . . did I tell you I am running for mayor next year . . . ?" He tapped the poster on the back of his door, it was full of dart holes. "I throw darts at it when I'm bored . . . shit."

I thought that if this man were to run for president he would win on sure presence alone. Magnanimous . . . is that a word I could use here?

.

THE GRASS was tan, the trees gold and green, the morning fresh. We drove 15 minutes through rolling pasture land and the occasional wood along the line of a stream, or run, as they like to call it. Came around a corner and there it was: White fences, hedgerowed drive, stone barns, gabled roof . . . it was England in Tennessee . . . I was in—fuck, I wished it was *mine*, is what.

"Wow!"

"Yes . . ."

The hospital was not an addition to the house, but was built into what had been the kitchens in the old days. We pulled into the large circle of gravel at the edge of a not-too-steep ramp that led up to a pair of wide blue doors. The circle of gravel was 40 feet wide. There was a horse box trailer off on the grass, a six-horse unit, a 4 Star, built in Oklahoma, according to the tag on the front quarter.

The fencing looked so white in the paddocks close at hand.

"You noticing the fences?"

"Yes . . ."

"They're not wood . . . they're plastic . . . he uses them in the convalescence paddocks, they flex unlike wood, you know—for when the horses try to scratch themselves."

"Ah."

"The report says that according to soil samples he . . . the killer came in across the pasture there, right?"

"Yes . . . muddy footprints in the blood . . . but there were no tire tracks . . . no one noticed any cars . . . nothing."

"Yep." This, at least, was as usual.

Dixie leaned back on the hood and poured himself a cup of coffee, it steamed heavily in the cool of morning. I wished I'd brought some rubber boots, there was clay here and it was sticky. I walked out past the hospital to a back paddock . . . the fence here was real wood. I climbed up and took a sit.

There was a small rise in the pasture. My breath was vapor, I lit a smoke. Jumping down off the fence I walked up the rise to get a better look at the lay of the land. The pasture sloped away in all directions, the grass, dew-soaked in the early morning, was camel-colored, unlike the fertilized green of the front paddocks.

There were a dozen cows off to my left at a water trough in the corner; one looked stupidly over its shoulder at me, mouth moving lazily, ruminating its cud. There was a line of trees in the near distance, across in another paddock; it led in a slow arc across the property coming close to hand on the other side of the house. Then it turned away toward that corner we had come around in the road. I went back.

"Drive me."

"Where?" He had a small smile on his face, he blew on the coffee and bummed a cigarette.

"Back to the corner."

"See something?"

"Don't know . . . Could you drop me off and go back . . . I want to see something . . . oh, and please park right where you were before."

There was a stream and alongside it a trail along the line of the trees. I hoofed it. Although you couldn't tell from the house, there was a hill in the wood. It lay at such a point along the path as to provide a clear view of the entire property, the entrance to the hospital and the driveway . . . Once at the bottom of the rise you were shielded from view from the house by the stone stables.

I could see Dixie and the car. He was looking for me.

Walking in circles I looked at the ground, but months had gone by. Yet—just the mere presence of this rise, and the fact that Killer had approached through the pasture land, showed a thing or two . . . Killer, being a stranger to the area, had obviously done some serious reconnoitering, one; two, he had chosen a covered approach with a military sort of thinking; and there was likely, because of the spot chosen, a backup, who had kept watch. For the hundred and fifty yards to the house Killer would have been unable to see any changes in his objective; this was not like him. It seemed likely, therefore, that there was at least one other person on the scene.

When I appeared around the barn Dixie didn't look at all startled. I was somewhat out of breath; too many cigarettes.

"You found the rise . . . there were no tire tracks leading in there . . . the only foot prints were his boots, one pair of tracks onto the rise, one pair off, his boots or ones identical . . . all of which are just what the doctor ordered, so to speak. You have a good eye."

"So do you, obviously—but he didn't return that way?"

"No . . . and there were no prints walking out either. We tented the area and worked it with a fine tooth comb, took plaster casts of the prints for comparisons . . . hey, we thought that there might have been an accomplice . . . why choose the rise and then give up the advantage of line of sight? . . . but then we decided that maybe he had just used it as a vantage point . . . when he was satisfied that there was no one left at the house, he went on down and did his killing."

"Stream."

"They used the stream?"

"Yes."

"How?"

"Rope . . . they padded it of course . . . I think I found a scar mark on a tree on the creek bank."

"We missed that."

"It was high up . . . and only a possible—but then again you could be right, maybe he was alone . . . but the killer walked out the drive, which means that he was sure no one was coming down it . . . was there any report of telephone outage?"

"Your office in Atlanta sent in that request already, I believe, but no, I don't think so."

"Service trucks . . . did anyone report service trucks?"

"No . . . no work's been going on . . . except maybe for the tree work over nearer to Telford, State trucks though."

"But he still walked off up the drive." We did a walk around the hospital. "You want to feed me lunch, Dixie?"

"Sure, man, sure."

IT IS ALL confusion. What is real seems false, what is false seems real. The crime scenes twist the possibilities, deny the probabilities all in one breath and then boom! give them all back to you in their proper proportions. Every clue is misleading. You see, we are trained on statistics and probabilities . . . it is the basis of behavioral sciences, criminology and forensics. The abstract hardly factors in.

I knew here that I would need help.

I turned the pictures of Doctor dead over in my fingers; blood the color of the day.

I HAVE KILLED a man twice. He wasn't the first man I killed, nor the last, but he was the only one that I ever had to kill more than one time.

I was young then, working the FBI beat. We were on a man-hunt for some bad boys—and we had found them. They were holding fort in a house in a small New Mexican town called Vaughn. Vaughn, the crossroads of the Southwest: A one-horse settlement smack dab in the center of the state. I remember that we drove for miles from our jump-off spot of Roswell. Miles of nothing but gray scrub brush and yellow sand. There was a something that looked like a gas station on the west side of the road one time . . . it had those 1950s pumps and the station building was twisted.

Then we came over a bump in the road and had to brake hard or we would have passed right through the town. The sign said: "Welcome to Vaughn, pop. 610." A road ran off to the right; there was a trailer and a Quonset hut just down there. The road led to Santa Rosa. Most of the town bordered the highway on our left. Motels lined the right; behind them was where the Indios lived, the *chiberos*.

An agent, a guy named Dorsey, was there to meet us. He said the bad boys were up the road in a house that belonged to a guy named Sanchez. It was a stone house, with a protruding front stoop that was shaded by a steep A roof, built in the 40's I would guess. It was dull and green in color.

We were hot wired and ready when we broke down the door. It was 3 a.m.; everybody was asleep. Adrenaline pumping, I came through a door round back; I was second through, Colt .357 held at port.

A guy went for a gun in the dim light of my flashlight and I shot him, top dead center—two rounds and he went down.

It went to hell then . . . the dark house was strobe lit in exploding cordite, gunfire the bass beat. Bullets and screams. I could smell the death and I was wild. A partner dropped and I picked up his sidearm and killed again, this time at close range, and the blood sprayed across my face. I was reloading when a shadow came at me. I dropped the empty, hot-barreled gun and drew my combat knife.

I was alive and laughing. The shadow was a man, blood flowing down his chin. It was the man I had first shot for dead. I stepped in close and the knife went to work like a piston; my arm drove the blade into the soft of his belly over and over. The gunfight was a distant echo in my head. Then grabbing his arm I spun him, brought the knife up and slit his throat. Warm and salt his blood splashed on my face, I tasted it, dropped him; relieving him of his gun I turned, looking to kill something more. The violence had left the room, moved outside . . . FBI bodies were on the floor. I was drenched in blood and it was flowing on the floor.

It looked like these pictures.

On the northern edge of town on the right side of the road, just before you got to the post office, there was a small restaurant. I can't remember its name now, but it served the best *carne asado con salsa verde, frijoles negros y pan Mejicana*. I remember the flavor still.

17

IT WAS about noon the next day when I got back to Fort Lauderdale. I drove North up US 1 to pick up a Heineken; I was thirsty.

Home is where your harp is. I have one, tall and wooden, painted white; it is leaning against the back wall of the living room. I pass it every now and again and strum the strings. It makes an angelic noise, but I can't play the fucking thing. It's a small house that I live in, and rather empty of furniture. The harp holds a prominent place.

You enter from the back, I guess; the front faces out to sea. My study is on your right, it shares a bathroom with the guest bedroom, which is the other side of the house. The back wall of the study is the back wall of the living room, the harp's wall. The walls are not bare of art; there are several small pieces, that scene of home. Master bedroom on the left, guest room and kitchen on the right. The living room's outside wall is all doors, open so you can see the sea. It is airy, the floors are tile, only the harp and a sectional sofa fill the living room. There's no TV out here, only in the bedrooms.

The patio wasn't on the house when I first moved in, I had it added. Nice to sit and sip a coffee and look out to the sea. It runs straight from north to south, then at the south end the takes a smooth outward curve, the dining room bulges out into the world, the curved wall all windows. The dining room is bright. The walls are sea foam green. Open to the rafters, the shingles washed white.

The beach outside is Hillsboro beach, just north of Pompano pier. Today it's full of tourists. There's some Miller in the fridge, Genuine Draft, I take one and go change into some shorts. My legs are white; it's been weeks since I've been in the sun. Air out my toes. I sit on one of the planters chairs I inherited and smoke and drink. My grandfather would call it blasphemy, but I have painted his fine mahogany chairs white.

It is a day made in heaven, 81 degrees, breezy and cool, humidity is 30 percent, wind from the northeast at 11 miles, bays and inland waters a moderate chop, seas 3-4 feet, swelling higher in places, small boaters should use caution. I look at my watch. I have left it in the bathroom, but it's probably about 2:30.

FROM WHERE she sat on her high window perch, ass on a peeling paint sill, feet out on the mossy slope of the shingle roof, Bugsy could see the world filtered, now and again, through the tall pines, cottonwoods and the low woody scrub. Way up there the morning had an altogether different thing; you could feel the peace that just was possible in this weird-as-fuck world we live in.

There was a crispness to the day. SanDra was playing some country in her studio.

She was working on something quite . . . wonderful, I am sure. As Bugsy says; "SanDra mom is like a brilliant writer, with . . . with this thing for language, the . . . the imagery of her words you know, an imagery that . . . well, I am kind of biased . . . but she plays with genius, like V.S. Naipaul."

Mr. Naipaul has been called by some the greatest writer of our time . . . he, like Derrick Walcott, is very important to the Caribbean psyche, I suppose.

"SanDra mom has that gift, she writes quiet stories about African sisters and their struggles against the prejudices that affect their abilities to be . . . to be only Human". Bugsy often said out loud that she wished she had her mother's genius . . . But I think that neither is more brilliant than the other. It is that the inspirations, the visions they have come from different angles. She is a black sister from a time of struggle, Bugsy is a white chick child of a yuppie-mad world, the African in her subdued by years of dilution and the genes of a white French father. SanDra works with how the words sound off the mind, Bugsy and her PC beat out words that sound real, that roll off the tongue . . . look, you may not get the difference, but it's simple: words written for the way they flow through your brain sound strangely unfamiliar if rolled off the tongue . . . you know, for ears to listen . . . It is why Shakespeare sounds so good aloud, but the written beauty of Ondatje's "The English Patient" plays like an untuned serenade.

They are different. Yet we are the same.

"Rapunzel, Rapunzel, let down your hair."

"God, Thomas, what are you doing down there?" She closed her book on her lap.

"Feeling good . . . I am not so . . . so tense as I was when I got here." Hands in pockets I looked down, then up. We were holding our conversation at volume.

"Ahh."

"I was very tense when I was working alone . . . maybe being alone made me tense."

"I don't like being alone . . . are you coming in?"

"I thought actually that . . . well, the day is wonderful and I · don't mind talking at volume; did you sleep well?"

"I did . . . you look . . . nice."

I was dressed. Khaki trousers neat pressed, a dress blue shirt, long sleeved, brown and very English shoes. Even socks and a belt.

"I like to dress on a Sunday."

There was a swing seat under the trees that afforded a view of her. Relaxed and sitting on her high perch, she was lovely, I thought. It was all so like a dream. I think perhaps that my solitary life had become sad for me. Or maybe I had become too sad for it.

I sat, crossed my legs just so. It was a self-contained swing with two benches facing one another in a frame. They followed each other as you swung.

"Where's Claire?"

"Files files and more files."

"That was really . . . interesting . . . that stuff, you know . . . I'd like to read some more one day . . . I mean, if I could, you know."

"Yes . . . I have copies of several cases that I've worked on, bits and pieces that I've kept, a lot of the stuff I should have turned back in . . ." A cat, this one a ginger gray color, paused, two feet lifted. In transit. It looked at me, then up to Bugsy. Bored with us, it moved on.

"So what's Claire reading now?"

"The sixth one." I toyed with a cigarette a moment, then lit it.

"Are there . . . going to be . . . more?"

"Weirdly enough . . . I hope so . . . need some more clues . . . Do you write poetry?"

"Yes . . . why?"

"Don't know . . . I used to write poetry when I was younger—impress the chicks, you know. I was never very good at it though."

"I have a . . . a small book published of just poetry . . . it doesn't sell, though—what, Mom? . . . no Ma . . . sorry, Thomas, Mom was asking something . . . I like poetry ; for a writer it's instant . . . gratification, you know, what was it, I heard someone say once, Poetry is your soul in words . . . something like that, and it's . . . true . . . what was it like growing up in the islands . . . is it very different from here?"

"Yeah . . . very —" And my mind drifted off to another time and another place.

18

THOMAS has mischief and fire . . . passion. At six foot tall it's not like he's really imposing or anything. He has this habit of raising an eyebrow while he scratches his jawline with the back of a finger. Lasciviousness on his lips, often attached to a smile. I suppose that he could turn quite easily to violence. I think that Thomas would like violence.

I shake all fucking over at the thought of violence, passion and fire. He could raise my skirt and grab a handful of me. I could just die at the thought.

He seems so young today.

A SWIMMING pool among the ruins. The building's original purpose was by then long forgotten. It sat next to the cattle dip, under the shade of grand trees that were a few days older than dirt. I suppose it was the warmth of the sun and the play of the shadows that brought it rushing back . . . I can hear the sounds of laughter, blond boys and blonde girls splashing in artificial blue. Two tall gangly dark boys are leaning through a ruined window, watchers. A mother or two, cotton-frocked and put together, are brushing flies away from sandwiches laid on a table at the far end. There is a solid wall there.

"Redmond, pass de baaal, man." A blond boy calls out to a dark boy, their language the same. Redmond was not as old as the oldest swimmer. His, though, was a life of work.

The walls of the ruin, once probably white, were gray now, tinged with moss. Both black and green. Ferns, like ornaments, adorn the limestone walls growing between the cracks. I imagined a Roman bath. There is the sound of the men driving cows into the dip.

The dip is a hole in the ground under a narrow shed; sloping serrated concrete ramps lead down into the hole, which is ten feet long and three and a half feet wide and filled with a deep Ty-D-Bol blue and antiseptic-smelling liquid. It gets rid of ticks. They dip the cows' teats in much the same stuff at milking time.

The "Great" house sits atop a tall hill about one mile away. The shaded drive under whose trees I had once remembered a breakfast faced the other way, south. I drank lemonade—not that pale first world lemonade, but tan in color, sweetened with brown sugar. Raw brown sugar, flavorful, not bleached, processed, refined and fucked. I am unused to the flavors of process and package.

I am a product of my nativity.

I have something to say: your heritage is not your ethnicity, it is your inheritance. I am not what my ancestors were.

A matinee of memories, a rustle of wind in trees, trees either here or 3,000 miles and 40 years away. I am here now.

"WHERE'D YOU go to just then?"

"Dreamland . . . I was thinking about a life more golden . . . more youthful." I smiled. I find that I am not so subdued here, I am feeling more alive.

"So tell me about it."

"Oh . . . it was a life filled with infinite sunshine and vibrance, at least I remember it that way . . . you know what . . ."

"What?"

"'*That behind this smile I'm lonely, a fool can tell . . . .Well I need some sweet affection, Take my hand and hold me close . . . Sweet love, that look on my face is sorrow . . . sweet love, that memory fades behind you . . .*' a group called "View from the Hill", a sweet song. A good Sunday song.

I heard the song as I was crossing the lawn. There was a tent down on the lawn; Michael and Diedre had camped the night out.

"Hello." Claire long and tall. Jeans on. A long-sleeve white shirt was unbuttoned. Her stomach was flat and brown, her bra was white and lace. The kitchen smelled of Lysol.

"I'm cleaning."

"You want some help?"

"Maybe . . . where's Bugsy?"

"Perched in her window . . . you feel like cutting some hair?"

"Yours? . . . Why not, we can talk, I finished Number Six. You look tired."

"You look beautiful."

"Don't I just though . . . you know I looked at myself in the mirror this morning . . . and hell, I thought, Claire darling, you just get better looking every day."

"Hah . . . give me some sugar."

"Any time . . . did I tell you this morning that I love you? Can I have a smoke?"

The windows are open wide, the day is inside with us. A high backed chair on the hardwood living room floor. The light was yellow, Claire aglow . . . *"I can see clearly now—the rain is gone"* . . . The angle of her body, the blouse is open, she is straddling my leg, fingers in my hair, the muscles of her stomach . . . *"I think I can make it now, the pain is gone"* . . . Fingers, flesh, touch, tingle, at the nape of the neck the scissors sing. She is behind me suddenly—a brush of skin, fingers trace my shoulder, I am in my undershirt . . . *"Here is that rainbow I've been praying for"* . . . I see her face in periphery, feel her breath. I can smell her. She touches me. She steps over my leg. Fabric is friction. Songs change. The shirt comes off. She is concentration . . . *"Stir it up, little darling . . ."* . . . lifting the hair, she strokes it over my ears. I can count the freckles on her left breast. A gentle touch to raise my chin.

I am hers.

"Looks even . . . you want any more off?"

"You can cut my hair anytime."

"I notice you mention that Killer left by walking up the driveway."

"Yes."

"You think that he knew no one would be coming down? You think he knew he would be safe?"

"Yes."

"No one noticed any unusual traffic, right? But there were, um, where is it . . . state tree trimming crews on the road, yes?"

"Yes . . . but no specific mention of any by possible witnesses."

"I'm going to have a beer, you want one?"

"Why not . . . did you read the tool mark report?"

"Oh yes, the blade was—" a kitchen echo changed pitch as she looked back into the room, one beer in hand. "—Fresh, the blade on the saw was not the only blade used during the killing, yes . . . interesting, I'm not sure that I get any significance though . . . you didn't happen to find the other blade, did ya?"

"No."

"You liked the police chief . . . what was his name, Dixie?"

"Dixie, right? Yes . . . very competent guy."

"Yes . . . they tented the look-out spot . . ." She was wearing half glasses, the cigarette hanging from the corner of her mouth as she held the file down for inspection. "These are the pictures—they did some good work." She held up two pictures showing the plaster casts that were made of the footprints. "Paris or dental cement?"

"Plaster."

"Better . . . You notice the breadth of some of the footsteps?"

"Breadth?"

"Yes . . . how wide they are, you can see it from the pictures."

"Big feet, slippery mud, carrying someone on your back . . . maybe?"

"Yes, no, maybe so."

"Anything else strike you?"

"The beauty of the goddamn place—it was fabulous."

"No phone interruption reported."

"No, but their system isn't fancy update stuff either."

"Hmm, so, come, tell me, babes . . . what do you think?"

"'*Do you come from a land down under . . . where the women blow and the men chunder.*'"

"What?"

"Lunacy . . . You read my primary report file, right? . . . I'm not sure, but those are the theories; basically what it boils down to, for me anyway, is more than one killer . . . what do you think?"

"I think it's confusing . . . what is true is false . . . yes, yes."

Claire had gone to change the music; I was looking at the autopsy report. There was a picture, the victim's chest opened up like the hood of a sports car. Claire had the audio tape already in the recorder. One of the mortuary dieners was talking as he went through the indications of rigor mortis, livor mortis and algor mortis. These readings at autopsy were compared to the original readings taken *in situ*. The comparison was used to get a further correlation of time and conditions of death. His tone was bland; it is surprising how little sorrow people really feel for the dead. The medical examiner's voice came back on.

I leafed to the VICAP report. The FBI keeps a file of crime scenes from across the country and occasionally around the world; they've been putting it all on computer since 1985. The idea is that the computer can track similarities between crime scenes, see perhaps if your killer has killed before. So you tap into VICAP and look up your crime; well, really you let the computer do the work for you. Of course there were some cross-correlations, mentions of previous vets killed in their offices. One mention of "Bute" having been used before, that was a killing at a race track in Florida—squabble over a drugged horse and somebody was stabbed with a syringe several times. It was much the same stuff that had appeared in VICAP reports from the other files; a lot of nothing.

The FBI was being very helpful, but—surprisingly—not really interfering. Well, maybe if we take into consideration the little visit I got in Fort Lauderdale just before I went back to Atlanta, just after Number Six.

I had stayed home another day. To rest, I suppose.

IT TURNED to a nice day. It had rained all morning; not a heavy rain. The sun was out now and the world smelled fresh, full of evaporating rain. The Saab wanted a wash. I wanted to wash it, so drove it up onto the front lawn.

ESPN had a rerun of the "King of the Beach" volleyball tournament . . . A guy named Karch was set to defend his title. I like volleyball, play when I can, watch when it's on. I ran the TV from the bedroom out onto the porch. Karch, now that's a good beach name.

It was down to Karch and a young Brazilian, Jose whoever. Hot hot hot on Daytona Beach. I could clean the Saab, but couldn't get around the scratches and dings of 112,000 miles and six years. The match looked to be going to Jose whoever and his teammate . . . Karch and his partner Dodd were both old men of the sport; 110 degrees on the sand was telling on them. People say that the Saab sucks; mine has been a dream—a wet dream.

The leather inside is still supple, Armor All just brings out the luster. I sat in the passenger seat looking at a Karch service point.

"Hello."

I held up a hand behind me. It was a good play point.

"I'll be right with you . . ."

" . . . Damn! Now would you look at that . . . hello," I stood up and looked over the roof. "Suits . . . Hello . . . so, which agency you boys belong to?" Butt and Fuck in their cheap plain grays, white shirts and dull ties, shoes polished just so.

They held up badges, the short one opened his mouth. "I'm Agent Edward . . ."

"Hold on, hold on . . . come here, closer . . . may I see your shield please . . ." I reached across the roof. It said Federal Bureau of Investigation. It was real, besides they looked too . . . is bland a good word? . . . not only bland, but they had this, this I-am-an-asshole demeanor about them . . . that demeanor that seems to be oh-so-prevalent amongst government officiators. I wished I were in Provence; I like it in Provence, I got laid there once.

"Agent Edward," I held the high ground, and I hate these guys; I know them and so I hate them; I know what they are capable of and so I hate them; I know what they do and how they do it . . . and so I hate them. I know who they work for . . . I know these guys.

I slid the badge back across the roof of the car to Agent Ed, cast an eye at his partner, I wasn't interested in them. I am afraid that my blatant distaste showed on my face.

"What?" Curt—'cause just looking at them made me angry.

"We . . . we, we, uh, came to talk to you about the Letter Writer case."

"Isn't that nice? . . . do you have a warrant, a subpoena, a writ . . . a fucking *clue*?"

"Excuse me?" Agent Ed's partner forwarded up himself, he seemed . . . very angry.

"Which one are you . . . Butt or Fuck? come come now, don't look at me with that face . . . I . . . look boys, I have nothing to talk to the F.B.I. about; boys, look, nothing personal, I just don't like you guys . . . so guess what."

"You can't—" Ed's partner looked like he wanted to draw his weapon and pistol whip me with it.

"I can't what? . . . Eh, you were going to say something . . . I can't *what*, dickhead?" I mumbled the last word.

I would like to explain my animosity, but it wouldn't make any difference. I have done some things in the name of government that would chill you. You cannot imagine, and if you all could—it would start a revolution.

They looked at me as they sat for a moment in their stealth car, taking notes. Wanting to remember exactly how my sacrilege went. Wanting to take me into custody and abuse my rights. They do that, you know.

I opened a Martinique natural spring water and took a long cool drink. "Go Natural With Martinique". Fuck them.

CLAIRE came back from changing the music.

"So?"

"So what?"

"So do you love me, or what?"

"Claire, darling, I love what you do when you do what you do."

"What?"

"Yes."

"We done with Number Six?"

"Done, finished, *kaput*, over, history, *fin*."

"You want to tell me about Number Seven?"

"With a surprise gift too . . . you look tasty, kisses." She came to me, crotch at face level, I kissed the denim frame of her vagina.

19

RIGHTEOUS INDIGNATION‼
—GBM #7

Is that frustration I smell, or did one of us
forget to bathe?
I have missed you in my dreams.
So many dead bodies, so little time.
My dance card still isn't complete, play a song
that we can both dance to.
—GBM #8

THE DOG was big; as a house. It was a kind of gray color . . . and dappled. It looked like a Great Dane. Only . . . this dog was sleeker, taller and looked infinitely more . . . evil. A Rhodesian Ridgeback—as big as a Honda. The owner stood next to him, diminutive still, despite his girth; he had a round, fat head around the edges of which gray hair grew sparsely. He wore a cloth Roo golf cap. He looked like a New York cabbie. The little man and his giant dog stood on my sidewalk looking out to sea. The sun was setting at their backs and casting an orange shadow over the world.

I had just hung up from Frenchy. I was still in Florida.

"The Feds called," he had said.

"Oh."

"Oh yes, Mr. Courtesy . . . they called, most upset, son." I heard him spit. "—Yeah, most upset . . . I seem to remember the word fuck about, hell, 'bout six times . . . the F.B.I. don't usually use the word fuck, son."

"They make me angry . . . they like to demand things, like I just must speak to them . . . I'm afraid that I didn't give them much of a chance . . ."

"No . . . not much . . . they wanted to talk to you about the case?"

"So they said."

" . . . Why?"

"Fuck 'em."

"I . . . yes . . . oh, that guy that you asked me to look up . . . quietly, uh. . . Neathersole—what the hell kind of name is Neathersole? anyway, son, I got back the line, and it's a hell of a long one; his sheet looks damn interesting . . . they got a file on him over at state too . . . a professional killer . . . a friend of yours?"

"We've been known to know one another from time to time—no big deal."

"Yeah, right . . . he's a professional killer."

"Was . . . Not since someone shot him in the head . . . it's a long story, I'll tell you when I see ya . . . do me a favor and just drop it on the fax to me . . . it have his current address and everything."

"Yep, and I confirmed it too, he's there, definite."

"You're the best man."

"Wouldn't know what to do without me, right?"

The Army is so polite. After I spoke to Frenchy I made a call to Fort McPherson, looking for Boom Boom; the Captain is not due back on base till 20:00 hours . . . sorry sir, 8 o'clock sir. Sir, shall I leave a message for him, sir? . . . Sir, yes sir, does he have your number sir . . . thank you sir.

Back on my front porch perch, the Mini man and his Cadillac dog had ambled off . . . I wondered what he fed the beast, probably live human sacrifice . . . I heard the kettle whistling. The dining room's arc of doors open out onto the porch; I walked through to the kitchen in the back. The dining room table is large, it had belonged to Uncle Ray. My kitchen is big enough that I could fit a breakfast nook in the back corner.

The window at the back looks down the side wall of the guest bedroom. From the window facing south, if you lean back just so and contort to your left, you might just catch a glimpse of the sea. Yet still it is a comfortable little place to sit and contemplate food. I shuffled the two African violets in their Chinese porcelain and sat with my back in the corner between the two windows. Coffee and literature; I was reading "Meditations", philosophy by Marcus Aurelius. Why, I have no fucking idea.

"But I who have seen the nature of the good, that it is beautiful and the bad that it is ugly" . . . I have told you that I am a somewhat introspective fucker. Yes, I suppose.

Now the fax from Frenchy begins to arrive.

"OKAY . . . Okay . . . here she is coming . . ." he is devoid of all hair. He is patting the top of a computer monitor in the plush interior of a giant motor home . . . it is bigger than a house, bigger than the dog. Nice. It is plain tan in color.

"God, I do love this technology." He is black, he is an ugly man—his nose is awfully broad, his lips overly large, his eyes are sunken, forehead protruding. He is very neolithic and his skin is polished ebony. He is blackest.

The fax that was spitting out on my fax machine was spitting out of his computer system simultaneously. He of blackest skin picked up a set of head phones. Then the door to this patio home on wheels opened and Valerie the bald stepped up.

She smiled. "You got it."

"We got it." Teeth that seemed snowlike against the blackness of his flesh.

"Good." she picked up the end of the fax, reading it as the printer regurgitated the rest. "What the hell kind of name is Neathersole?""

"Are you not supposed to be in New Orleans?"

"Joseph, no, I am supposed to be right here . . . I'm the one who first smelled our friend coming; I get the job of keeping an eye on him . . . I asked for you, to come ahead of me, your special talent, eh." She held up the fax. "You are a fucking African genius." She bent and kissed his large purple lips. "Now . . . smile for the cameras." She waved at the camera in the corner. They recorded everything—security precautions.

Valerie was wearing a Rolex. She glanced at it, 7:30, Jeopardy time. She never missed it if she could help it. The night was perfect—but she went back into the trailer and turned on the television. Along the back end of the RV was a sofa sectional, around a coffee table. The aisle ran up the middle and on either side were entertainment centers. Facing forward the stereo system, all Denon, was on the left. On the right the 42" Sony and VCR, DVD, surround sound amplifier were fixed in place. The whole RV cried *money well spent.*

She put her cowboy-booted feet up on the table. Long denim legs. She unbuckled her belt and undid the top button of her pants. She was drinking cold Coke, from the bottle, hated the taste a can gave it. She stroked her hands back across the sides of her hairless head. A habit from hairier days. She interlocked her fingers at the back of her head. Relaxed. She straightened back up, and reached under her shirt . . . drew out a model 6690 S&W stainless auto . . . no hammer, 12 shot, 9 mm., only seven inches long overall. She ejected the magazine with a motion so practiced it wasn't noticed, pulled back the slide and cleared the chamber. She looked at the weapon for a moment. She brought it up to her face and she smelled it. There is a smell that each weapon has. She replaced the round into the magazine, replaced the magazine into the weapon. She fired the slide release and the weapon made that metallic slap, sliding a round home. Left thumb to the de-cocking lever and the hammer dropped harmlessly. She set the weapon beside her on the couch. She touched it lightly with loving fingers.

The computer was humming away. Joseph had gone to get groceries. One small part of the machine was collecting information on a man named Neathersole. Large reel to reel tape decks, voice activated, four of them in a bank, lined a high shelf. There was a computer switchboard that was tracking phone calls in and out of the neighborhood . . . a red light would flash if a call was en route to 2615. The roof was an array of antennae: parabolic, directional and dish, cellular and radio, satellite uplinks, downlinks, intake and output all linked into the four computer terminals and computer processors inside. Enough megahertz to power Wall Street. God bless America.

ANYHOW, anyhow, let me tell you about Number Seven . . . well—it comes as a package, actually . . . Seven and Eight are listed together; they were found together. Same time, same place. The bodies only yards apart. It was a dump site; they were killed elsewhere and brought there for disposal. The dump site was just outside Columbia, South Carolina, out off of, ahm, Route 26, near Lake Murray.

Each had been shot once in the right temple through the parietal lobe; the concussion fracturing the orbit bone behind the eye, causing the eye to bulge out from its socket. The bullet shatters, normally, against the far side of the skull, scattering fragments through the parietal lobe. In the case of Number Seven, a major fragment had careened off and lodged at the base of his skull, in the occipital lobe; because of some weird trauma caused by the bullet's path, his arm now stuck straight out from his prone body. Number Eight was found face down.

They had been killed elsewhere, a day apart, but dumped simultaneously. . .

HAVING FINISHED my recital I tossed the file down on Claire's table. I was standing, with one foot in the chair; she was lounging against the wall, a cushion behind her head.

"Woof—that was a mouthful . . . are you tired, babes? I am fucking exhausted . . ."

"Yep, drained, really."

"I'm going to take this and go lie down . . . god, it's so nice and quiet." The sun was out and the day was perfect, only a hint of the coolness that was morning still in the air. Out on the horizon, gray clouds were brewing, heralding the afternoon of gloom, but right now god was alive and walking the earth in all his splendor. "You want to lie down with me?"

"Sure." It had a real Sunday feel to it.

"Maybe something will come to mind."

20

I FOUND my Sole in West Virginia. He, Neathersole, was living near a town called Mt. Jackson. See, you take Route 66 from Washington DC, all the way out to the western edge of Virginia, turn south on Route 11 or highway 81. Mt. Jackson is a quiet town, and small. It looks like it was all built back in the forties, all wood and old, dull, in green, maroon or black trim. Small porches, plain two story rectangles. The people you pass all look like they were built in the forties too; at least they were young then. They are old now. The card shop has gift items in there that look to have been around for more than 30 years.

A nice elderly lady runs the shop. She seems a little vacant to the world. She talked to me about the people in the county— seemed to know them all, by name at least. It was a horrid day, rainy and gray, but at least the rain had taken the edge off the cold. This is the Shenandoah valley.

There's a Seven-Eleven at Vista and Main; I used the phone there, you know, to call ahead. I was to go straight through town and out the other side, past the block factory on your right, past the race track on the left and then I would see a covered bridge on my right, just down the road, off to the side.

God, this was beautiful countryside, rolling hills, raging run streams, tall trees, their red and bronze leaves littering the ground. Shrouded hills, misty valleys, the first men and women here must have cried with joy on finding it; even now deer roamed the open pastures.

It was the Memms bridge that I was to cross; I later found out that it is the oldest bridge of its kind still in use in the United States . . . Mr. Memms had built it across the run so as to be able to reach all his pastures at all times of year. I was to take the bridge road across the bridge, up the hill, a sharp corner to the right. Watch out for it 'cause sometimes tractors are coming down the other way, fast. Then you go about two miles along and there's a big white gate with an arch over it, on the right, turn in there, wait at the gate and someone will meet you. Those were the instructions.

I followed them to a "T".

I stopped at the bridge to take a picture or two . . . I've now got this great collection of closeups of interlocking shingles and hewn rafters, brilliant fartography.

They say that everybody has a twin. I haven't met mine yet, but I hear about him everywhere I go; he even dated an ex-girlfriend of mine once. I hear he has a better lifestyle too; last I heard he was traveling south down US 1 with a beautiful blonde in an XJ-12 Jaguar sportscar; she was driving. Did I mention she was beautiful?

(And if Christian Slater were here with me now he'd say . . . "Fuck me, hey . . . does that guy look just like me or what?" . . . "Naw, well maybe just, well a little" . . . "Fuck me;" . . . "Ah, you're sexy and all that, man, but not my type.")

Neathersole used to be a killer. Now he's a blind ex-killer who looks like Christian Slater. A bullet through the temple can do that to you, you know. At close range. It had severed his optic nerves, but left him otherwise unscathed. Neathersole was the luckiest unlucky man I ever knew.

"Hey Sole . . . how you doing, man."

"Familiar voice, got a cop kinda calypso sound to it . . ." ("Shit, he even has the Nicholsonesque, can you fuckin' believe it" . . .) "What you sayin', Tommy fuck."

He smiled whitely; the four front teeth were artificial, the originals were knocked out by a gun butt.

"Come come, my friend . . . where the hell are you, let me hug ya." He stood stiffly; his right knee had been badly damaged by a deflected blow from a baseball bat . . . the guy was aiming for his head and tripped. "Well fuck me silly—how are ya?"

"Fine."

"What?"

"Sorry, wrong ear—I'm fine man, how you been doing? You still got all your toes."

"All ten of them . . ." It was our inside joke. "The ears healed up nicely too." A dog had almost bit his ear off. His own dog. His seeing eye dog. "Got a new dog . . . not as good as the last one, but she's got a better temperament."

"Where is she?"

"Outside, I hope . . . I asked Jackson to let her out . . . well, shit, it is good to hear your voice, man . . . shit, this blind thing is really a fucking drag, I would love to see your ugly face . . . Hey, I got a new girl, she thinks I look like Christian Slater . . . I gather that's good, right?"

"Yep, that's good . . . he's a movie star . . . what you drinking—is that coffee? it smells good."

"With a touch of the Irish in it, man . . . you want?"

"I'd love . . . so tell me about the new lady."

"She has all her parts." He sniffed the air; ever since the bullet he often smelt gunpowder. "You smell something burning?"

"So you don't love me anymore, or what? Man, I haven't heard from you in over a year—I had to get the cops to run a trace on you."

"I've been hiding out . . . kind of busy . . ." Sole flexed his right elbow. The arm wouldn't straighten fully. Badly broken in a car accident; he'd been run off the road. The car had rolled six times and plummeted 25 feet. He had broken five ribs and punctured a lung so badly that they had to remove a piece of it.

"So—you buying lunch, Calypso?" One would never guess that his life had been cold-blooded death.

"Where?"

"DC . . . there ain't nowhere out here to eat."

"I just drove from DC."

"Beautiful drive, isn't it? I still remember it from my seeing days . . . beautiful drive . . . You've got a rental, right?"

"Yes."

"Good, then leave it; Jackson will take care of it. We'll fly to DC . . . the Jet Ranger is standing by outside. The Red Sage is really good, we can sit by the kitchen, watch them prepare the food, I hear it is quite fascinating to watch . . . they have a fuck wonderful jerk sausage, Jamaican style, mahn . . . well, you watch, I'll listen."

"Helicopter?"

"Yes . . . so why the drive, right?"

"Precautions?" Would be my guess. "Well, at least your girlfriend dresses you nicely." He was suited, nicely in midnight blue, a dark shirt, no tie, soft leather shoes, the kind with rubber walking soles.

"I'm glad, 'cause you know how much I always loved clothes . . ."

"How about precautions, you never used to like those."

"My world's kinda dark now man . . . I can't see shit for myself, so I take precautions, can't really protect myself any other way . . . you know what I mean, man."

"That's why the blind address in Georgetown, and the phone tag."

"Yep . . . you've gone to a lot of trouble to catch up with me; it must be something pretty fucking important, man."

"Yeah, I need an ear."

"Good . . . 'cause I've only got one." He smiled broadly. "I made a fucking funny."

"I left it wide open."

"Yes you did. Even with all this technology they can't make these goddamn things quiet inside . . . you like my helicopter? It was a gift from a friend."

"Obviously a very *happy* friend."

"Oh yeah . . . definitely happy . . . is Miami still as . . . as fucking blue, as it used to be? I . . . I remember the *blueness* of it—a beautiful blue, man, beautiful."

"Yes . . . yes it is, you know, man, I don't think I've ever heard anyone describe it that way though . . . Blue Miami."

We were above it all, moving at speed. It—the world, Virginia looked so . . . so *clean* from up here, perfect, unblemished. You missed the imperfections traveling on a galloping horse. It was . . . awesome.

"It's good to see you again, Tommy . . . damn good . . . Chicks in Jack boots, you know, um, Doc Martens, right . . . I think that must look real sexy. I miss fashion."

"It looks very sexy . . . very." We spoke in spurts of shit, over the noise of the short flight. Smoke filled up the interior, made the pilot cough. I always wanted to learn to fly one of these things.

"I always wanted to learn to fly one of these things."

"Yeah, but not right now . . . Christ."

"Passionate kisses, passionate kisses, passionate kisses" from . . . Mary Chapin Carpenter. Don't you just love music? I cannot imagine the soundless void of deafness.

"You like my fucking stereo, man? . . . good tunes, eh . . . thank god I'm not stone deaf—hey look, we're there, there's Watergate."

"Cool . . . where're we landing?"

"In this thing, anywhere we please . . . heh."

The Red Sage, it's Southwestern, it's Santa Fe. The Jamaican barbecue chicken with fruit sauce and jerk sausage is fucking great, fucking. We sat downstairs at the kitchen bar, watching the chefs do dinner. I watched, Neathersole listened. The clientele looked lawyer.

"So that's your story, Tommy?"

"Yes . . . I need an ear . . . I think this may be a pro job . . . you're the man, if it's one of your people involved, you'll hear something . . . at least I'm hoping you'll hear."

"It'll take time . . . I'll put the word out . . . but, but—damn, the food smells great, hmmm, . . . Is there a woman cooking? I smell . . . Pussy, pussy in Chanel."

"Yeah, she's cooking."

"Is she pretty?"

"She's pretty."

"Good, good, I like pretty women, used to love to stare at them . . . yeah, I'll put out the word. It'll take a week or two."

Later we drank Grappa. Like Hemingway heroes. Lonely men in a dim bar. One a blind victim of manly war, one the sorry soul, the remnant of a wealthy man. I had all the trappings of once and previous prosperity. We smoked. We were alone with the Mahogany.

"That was a great dinner . . . great."

"Yes, interesting food isn't it, matching flavors . . . What is this you've given me to smoke?"

"Craven 'A' . . . Jamaican cigarettes . . . strong, aren't they?"

"Hmmm . . . Tommy . . . it's, it's good to be with you." He looked at the end of the cigarette, like a seeing man he contemplated it. Then put it to his lips and drew deeply on it . . . he exhaled and blind eyes followed the trail of the smoke skyward. It was a play of old habit. The cigarette had a very short tan filter.

He sniffed the pungent rotten champagne odor of the drink. Etter Suisse we were imbibing . . . 'cause we weren't just drinking, we were absorbing . . . two glasses and one bottle, chilled. "These cigarettes are harsh, man, it's like smoking Turkish shit—goes well with the drink though, eh . . . Grappa was better in the old days though . . . like moonshine. We drank it in France after the war, do you remember . . . Montpelier?"

I smoked, the cloud filling the room. Adding atmosphere. "Yes yes, yes I do remember . . . Montpelier."

WE HAD BEEN there separately together. He was a recent veteran of Special Forces, me a recent runaway from the Feebies. It was 1970-something. We were looking for memories to kill.

He heard my accent one day in a small cafe.

"You ain't French, but you speak the language . . . you're one of them Colonialists from Indo China, Vietnam, Laos, Cambodia . . . I've just come from there, met a few the ones that were still alive, if you know what I mean?"

"No . . . no, I'm not, you're American, huh? You've got Army written all over you."

"Special Forces, yes, just got out . . ." He tapped the walking stick hanging on the chair next to him. "Bullet with my name on it . . . My name's Neathersole." He could see then, of course.

"Neathersole . . . hmmm, my name is Tom . . . what kind of name is Neathersole? Kinda long to put on a bullet."

"Don't know, Scottish background, I believe . . . you . . . ?" His question faded off.

"No . . . no, I've been. Did two short tours, with the Fed, FBI."

"They're there . . . the FBI, why?"

"It's the only real war thing happening in the world today, man."

"Will you join me? I'm drinking Grappa; it's a manly drink . . . I am planning to get *very* fucking drunk."

The day was warmth. Two cats were outside making love like savages; Banshees wail in passion. I lit myself a Gauloise. The dark tobacco was pungent, sweet and strong. It burnt heavily, emitting much smoke.

"Drunk sounds like a damn good idea." He was drinking from a tall glass, poured me one to match. It was strong, burned going down, smelled like . . . like, like linseed oil; I used to use linseed oil as a young boy to oil my cricket bat . . . no it didn't smell like linseed, but—but I'd smelled that smell before.

"I've taken a house here; where are you staying?"

"Well actually, well—my grandfather left me a piece of land near here . . . but there's no house . . . I, I didn't want to be in America."

We drank that day away.

"I'm a professional killer, you know, man . . . That's why I'm here . . . I didn't get invalided in the fucking jungle, man . . . got invalided here, fuck yeah . . . there's Ho Chi's all over this fucking country. They sent me to kill a few . . . you know, the money collectors.

"I lost my partner, my spotter, he was a good man . . . the slopes got him, the chin's bad ass body guards . . . I killed the fuck though, blew his head apart, he won't be collecting no fucking money for the cause no more . . ." He was comfortably numb. I was drunk.

The cafe's owner brought bread and cheese, with a slab of sausage . . .

"You ever lose your partner?" There was a pungent pause. "Your friend?" Turning the glass he studied it, set it down on the table; he repositioned it, searching for the aesthete in its plainness.

"I lost a woman once."

We remember the men in our lives by the drinks we have drunk together; the women we remember for the quality of their cunts.

Is that strange?

We drank that week away.

"YES, MY FRIEND, I remember Montpelier—fuck yeah—but I especially remember the hangover, the hangover was a *bitch*. God, I hope I don't have that same hangover tomorrow."

"So, Tommy T., while I'm still half fucking sober you gonna fill me in some more on your killer? . . . what's the M.O.. . . . how does this particular fuck do the deeds?"

"It's a long story."

"Hey, I've got one ear."

"SO, YOU BELIEVE then that, ah, this's the work of a team?"

"More than one person maybe, team I don't know . . . professional, possibly . . . I'm grasping straws . . . feeling the wind . . . think you can help me?"

"I can try; the MO doesn't sound at all familiar . . . it is strange, almost like a dis-information campaign, you know . . . throw out a bunch of conflicting scenarios . . . you're in deep shit, my friend."

"I like deep shit, I guess . . . it's where I seem to always find myself, huh? . . . If there was one place in the world you could be right now, where'd that be?"

"Now that's a segue . . . anywhere, right now? . . . right now . . . shit, I know, I know, fuck, I haven't been since I could see . . . god, yes . . ." He sniffed. "Is something burning?"

"No. You were saying?"

"Yes, yes, I'd go to New Zealand, yes, it is the wildest, most beautiful place on god's green fucking earth . . . It's beautiful like an England gone wild, exotic, that's it, exotic . . . Shit—I am getting to be one drunk motherfucker."

"Hmmm." It was about all I could say. My lips were numb.

AN HOUR earlier a C-130 transport plane had landed at Washington National and coughed up a lovely RV, resplendent in its array of antennae and equipped with a hairless Valerie and a state-of-the-art bald African genius.

21

"FUCK!" I sat bolt upright in the bed suddenly. Jumping awake. Claire was already sitting up.

"Shit, you scared me," her hand over her heart.

"Scared myself . . . whoa—" I blinked, rubbed my eyes, scratched my scalp . . . vigorously. "Burn the witch, burn the witch."

"Were you having a nightmare?" She rested a hand softly on my chest.

"No . . . it just, it just came to mind . . . so, so did the—" I sat up, sniffled, coughed. "My head is still full of cotton balls . . . but I think I got it, on Seven and Eight. . . while I was sleeping."

"Sorry, sorry babes . . . but you got something, I got something too, it woke me up, so, I went back to the file."

"Phone calls?" I asked.

"Yep, sweets, phone calls, yeah . . . they weren't killed at the dump site, they weren't killed at home, no fucking struggle . . ."

"So, so they went freely to where they were killed, they were *summoned*, right . . . called anyhow." Our brains were working in sync.

"But the guns—the guns weren't reported stolen, so they carried the guns with them . . ."

"Yeah—it could have been a call about gun value or some bullshit . . ."

"But a call, can your guys get the incoming call log to these numbers?"

"Yes . . ." I smiled, "we're gods —we can get anything . . . look, here's how it goes:"

HIS LIFE IS shit these days, the wife and the kids gone. She didn't want the fucking house, so at least he still has his kills, his animal heads, his trophies . . . guy is a shooter. He's drinking a beer, there's shit on the TV. The phone rings.

"Hello sir, this is so and so, Mr. Bullshit, I'm informed through a search of files that you own a .38 Smith and Wesson 4" police special CTG, vintage 1937 . . . do you still have this weapon, sir ?"

He, being a cautious man, of course, wouldn't want to answer the question.

" . . . Oh, sir, please, this isn't a police interrogation; it's just been found out that due to discrepancies in the factory line, your weapon is a rarity, if it is still functional and in original condition . . . You see, there is a series of ten weapons that by freak of factory have turned out to be extra-accurate, one, and by that same freak of factory only seven of the weapons turned out in that run were without detrimental faults . . . your weapon is one of seven in that specific run . . . the only vintage .38's from 1937 that are still in existence . . . your weapon could be worth as much as $10,000 if I could authenticate it."

He's a shooter, our boy is, he reads all the trades too, loves his guns, he's heard of this sort of thing happening before, weapons with a twist of fate. Now it's not that the money is important, it's the gun that's the thing, because he's a shooter and always dreamed of owning "the gun" . . . if he could afford a vintage Purdy or a Holland and Holland in .300 magnum, that had been to Vietnam, something special. He's not a great shooter, but he fancies himself. So he scratches his balls and says, "Go on."

"Well, that's it, really, we need to meet, I've got a guy in Savannah to see too . . . say, can you travel? I mean do you have time, could you say, come to Columbia, that's where I am? We could meet in the middle, so to speak . . ."

"HAVE YOU GOT a map, Claire, of the state . . . where would he kill them . . . you got a map?"

"Coming, coming . . . I've got one somewhere . . . hold on."

"Okay . . . here we go, sweet pea . . . they were found between White Rock and Chapin, Lake Murray watershed district. So what do you do. . ." We laid the map out on the breakfast table, leaning over it . . . vultures hovering, looking down for the scene of death.

Okay, so you're the killer and you want to meet, you've set your dump site, you're about to bait your hook and set your line. The shores of Lake Murray—it's been used as a dump site before; three times in the last year it has been in the news. Every thing you do is opposite, right?. . . opposites attract.

"Yes, sir, can we meet in the middle . . . there is another gentleman I need to see in Eastover, that's southeast of Columbia, and don't forget to bring the gun with you, I'll be at this number —call me when you get in, if I'm not in then leave a message at the desk . . ."

"That's the swamp, the Congaree swamp area, secluded, out of the way . . . kill them in the swamp, right . . . of course he wouldn't be staying at the number . . . it would be a blind."

"So what number are we looking for then . . . something in 803? . . . no, they wouldn't do that, would they, something outside of 803 . . . something not terribly obvious . . . shit—you should go to Eastover . . . you think?"

"Well, let's run the number check tomorrow and see."

"You want to move on to Number Nine?"

"No, let's take it easy a little . . . I'll call Frenchy in a while."

I STOOD in the bed. Despite the trim, my hair was still long; I held it up. "I feel good."

"What?" Claire, her voice was outside. She was on the porch watering flowers. It took a moment, then she appeared in the wide doorway.

"What are you doing?"

"Standing in the bed."

"I can see that . . . the question, darling, is why—*why* are you standing in the bed?"

"I feel good . . . I don't fucking know, baby, I just feel good, I haven't felt this good in ages, I don't feel stale, I feel . . . alive. Do you love me?"

"You're an asshole."

"Usually, but do you love me?"

"You know I do . . . I'm wasting water, shit." She dropped the hose.

I walked outside to meet her. Leaving my bed top pose behind.

"Just look at this." I held my arms out, palms up. It was a beautiful afternoon—the kind of sky blue day where you can see forever. Cool blue, and you could pick up radio stations that you don't normally get. Very rarely does god cough up a day so perfectly wonderful. Clapton is god.

Nicholson is the devil.

Heston is Moses.

"Tommy T., you are my man . . . look at you . . . god, but you make my pussy twitch." She laughed out the words.

22

Hey where did we go,
Days when the rain came,
. . . in the misty morning fog,
With hearts a-thump and you
my Brown-eyed girl.
The old man with the transistor walking.
. . . Do you remember when we used to sing . . .
—Even in Death she is dead.

GBM #9

PS. you're falling behind . . . play catch up.
Do you recognize the lyrics?

I REMEMBER that I lit a cigarette . . . looking at a picture of a woman.

Victim.

Naked in a bathtub. Dark rosewood nipples. Very erect. Very erect they were, large. I was fixated by them, looking at them from every angle. Even now the image is very strong in my brain.

"Frenchy man . . . yu . . ." Leeman was looking at the woman, tilting his head this side and that. ". . . yu ever see nipples dat . . . Dat—"

"Large?"

"Good word, man . . . yeah, *large*?"

"Beautiful, isn't she." I lowered the photo. I was on the other side of the old-fashioned tub, which in strange manner sat in the very middle of the bathroom floor.

"We're in the way, I'm going outside for a smoke."

"Might as well, son."

"What you smoking today?"

"American, always good to come back to a nice Virginia Marlboro red."

"You hear the Marlboro man had cancer, son."

"Sure . . . you want one?" I pushed one up with my thumb.

"Yeah . . ." he patted his jacket. "Forgot my goddamn snuff in the rush . . ." He puffed up a cloud, then inhaled deeply. "Mmmm, a sippin whiskey, JD on the rocks would go good right now, son . . . So what do ya think?"

"I love the smell of napalm in the morning . . . what time is it?"

"1:30 a.m., the middle of the night."

"I think . . . I think that this is a strange case, girl naked in a bathtub lets someone in to push the stereo into her tub without making a fuss . . . two men carry their guns several hundred miles to be shot with them . . . these people know too much about their victims, they have to be getting this information from somewhere . . . a deep source . . . I don't know what the fuck am I rambling about . . . fuck . . . we get an ID on her?"

"No torture, no pain, no horribleness . . . ID . . . eh, where the fuck is my radio?" It was a Kenwood, with short wave frequencies and cellular phone built into a radio that was about seven inches tall and about three inches deep, compact. "Ah, here . . . Dick, Dick—this is Frenchy, do you read? Over."

"Yes yes, I read . . ." It was crackle and pop, I never understood voices over the radio. There seemed to be an art to deciphering radio garble. "Over."

"Do we have an ID on the body? . . . over."

"Uh . . . —shit, hold a minute Frenchy, let me confirm . . . stand by . . . Santiago, do we have an ID on the deadite?"

"Who, bathing beauty? . . ." Dick had the mike open for all to hear. "Who needs to know?"

"Frenchy."

"I'll check, *momento no.*"

"Frenchy, Frenchy, you there."

"Yeah, yeah . . . what's what?"

"Santi has gone to confirm . . . Chanice, Chantrice or something I'm pretty sure . . . you know, man, one of them black-sounding names." What a dickhead, he really was. Our body was, shall we say, complected.

"One in every crowd, son." Frenchy shook his head, he rubbed the slant out of his eyes, when he removed his hands it came back. "I am tired . . . this one is different, isn't it, Thomas?"

He had never called me Thomas before.

"You know, I read something the other day . . . about Antarctica, you know, there's this river that flows backwards to a lake that's fresh water on top and salt water below . . . and there's, there's this mummified seal that's over 100 years old on its shore, they even showed a picture . . . desolate . . . desolate and fucking beautiful."

THAT WAS THEN and this is later. I had left my Sole in Washington DC and headed back to Atlanta. My tour was really, well pretty much anyway, over. But Frenchy said that we would go together to Columbia and Mobile to do the follow up and the suck up. See where the last two investigations had turned. I could fill him in on the friends I had made, the places I'd been and the things I had seen.

But it was Mobile that I was most interested to get back to. I had never been there before the killing . . . actually I had driven through once on my way from New Mexico . . . but I had seen nothing but a sawmill and a Denny's. So Mobile interested me. It was a lovely city; as are most of the old cities of the South. It is much like New Orleans in its flavor and architecture; it was once the capitol of the French Colonial Empire prior to New Orleans. If I'd had time I would have taken the Mansion tour.

I had once met a guy who was from Mobile; a fellow named Robert, he pronounced it *Ro Bare*. We had met in some far off place in my traveling youth. He was off in search of his fortune. He had himself all packed up in an old Ford pickup and headed South through the Americas. It was Puntarenas, if memory serves me, Costa Rica's west coast. Over copious amounts of coffee, stewed in a pot over an open fire and sweetened heavily, he told me stories of September Celebrations in Bienville square, of tree lined boulevards, of Azalea festivals, dinners at La Louisiana and the Pillars, Gulf State park, the East coast of Mobile bay. Of Fairhope and other small very Victorian towns. It was the third world. It was 1963. It was reassuring to talk of civilization.

THE NEXT day Frenchy and I were walking down the long steps of city hall. A long black car, a new Lincoln Town Car, windows tinted black, pulled to the curb. Clint Eastwood stepped out and he smiled at me. "Well shit, looky what we got here . . . Tommy, Frenchy, how you boys doing?"

Dixie! He took the steps two at a time with his long strides and then he was there in front of us shaking hands.

"Don't look so stunned boys, Carl—Carl's the chief here, he's a friend of mine from way back, he asked me to come on down have a look-see . . . he here yet? . . . Don't smell him." In that whiskey voice.

"No, he showed earlier, then went with the mayor to parlay with the governor . . . the governor's down from Montgomery— I think he's running for re-election soon—son, you still planning on running for mayor?"

"Shit, Frenchy, if this thing goes as good as I think it will . . . I—I'm gonna run for *President*."

"You feel good about it?"

"Look at this fellow next to you . . . see him, Frenchy? . . . Look at our friend Thomas closely now, this boy has a *brain* . . . he may be the quietist thinking pessimistic genius fucker I've ever met . . . bet he's almost got it already—I'm not embarrassing you, am I, Tommy? Give me a light please." He puffed and his cigar belched smoke. "You don't know it yet but he's already got this fucker half figured . . . and me, I'm gonna be governor. Heh, can you believe it . . . yeah Frenchy, believe it.

"Hell, I'm a bit late, aren't I?" He looked down at his right wrist; he was left-handed. "What time you got? . . . Carl's gone off with the Governor eh—shit, that'll be a day and a half . . . heh, them two old boys can gab it up something awful . . . so what you boys doing?"

"We were planning on going down to the cop shop and see what was turning over on our little girl."

"Ah, grease work, huh . . . well, well . . . mind if I tag along?" The cigar was the small kind, slim and sweet smelling. "Oh Christ, I almost forgot . . . where do I ha—here it is." He was patting the pocket of his western shirt, wide collared, tablecloth thick and trimmed with what I suppose was meant to be rope. He had the cowboy hat on his head, it was the slim-brimmed, short peaked version that southern cops fancy. A car passed us on the street below; the sound of "Layla" unplugged, playing loudly.

"Don't know why the hell I brought it, must've been a . . . premonition . . . but I did." It was an envelope, white with the state police seal in the left corner and his jurisdiction's address.

"We got y'all a little something—nearly missed it, too." He held it out, then pulled it back in as he went on to explain.

" . . . The boys over at county road works came to a realization last week that one of their trucks which had been set aside for maintenance was missing . . . so they called it in as a theft—they've got 42 identical units there, you know, exactly alike . . . anyhow, they found the thing before our officer got on the scene; it was just parked somewhere it shouldn't have been, it was overlooked anyway, I'm making a short story long, aren't I?

"So, it would have gone in the bullshit pile, but I remembered Thomas' thing about a service truck . . . County is usually good about their maintenance shit, efficient, you know . . . So, so I got a warrant and laid claim to the truck; my boys are just into it now, but this here is a copy of the E-mail that was sent to your office in Atlanta this morning tag coded for the update to that file . . . anyhow I made a hard copy, and here it is. We—we don't have anything further yet . . . I *am* good, aren't I?" He smiled. Remember that word—magnanimous! His face was joyfully lined; weathered, the Louis L'Amour word for this day. "Here, it's yours."

THEY ALL smelled the same, like local meat shop flavored with just a hint of your favorite hospital wardroom. Stainless steel tables seen through safety glass. Cutting and sewing implements, computers and analyzers; blood and otherwise. As they all were, it was quiet down here, a hospital-in-the-middle-of-the-night quiet. Even our padded footfalls echoed loudly. Through a window you could see a job in progress—we stopped to watch; a pathologist, a bright light, a tape recorder and a dead body: Doctor vs. DOA.

"I saw your mommy and your mommy's dead
I saw her lyin in a pool of red
- and she doesn't know how to swim
I think it's the greatest thing I'll ever see . . ."

Like spectators of a sport we lined out at the window, hands behind our backs. Why the words of Suicidal Tendencies came to mind I may never know. The brain works in its own graphic way.

WE WERE WALKING the halls of death in a basement down Mobile way, and Valerie the bald was taking a call in Washington DC.

"What have you got?" it was a woman's voice over the line, the distance interfering, still authoritative.

"Little."

"Valerie darling, I have Mr. Neathersole's file here in front of me . . . do you see him as a threat?"

"No." She cupped the rear bulge of her skull.

"Then wrap it up and bring the vehicle to New Orleans, we're about ready to go to work."

Joseph the fucking African genius was lounging on the couch; he made a jerking off motion. They smiled at one another.

"Or would you prefer to stay there a little longer on this one, Valerie? . . . If you feel that it might warrant some attention . . . Hmmm?"

"That might perhaps be of a good idea . . . what is . . ." she left the question to trail off, without asking it.

"Would you like me to send old blue eyes out to keep you company ? . . . We will of course need that fucking African genius of yours back in New Orleans . . . we have the surveillance to finish setting up yet before the job . . . the DIP equipment needs to go in . . . shall I send him out?"

DIP, Digital Image Processing; it was first used as a way of mapping fingerprints, but developed rapidly. A computer, using a laser, an existing picture that is unclear, or a video signature, maps the surface that is visible. By using specialized mathematical algorithms and spatial and temporal averages, the computer calculates the missing parts and fills them in according to the symmetry of what is visible. So you can take a blurred picture and make it clear, you can take an image seen behind a blind and make it a person, you can take a heat signature behind a wall and determine sex.

"If you don't need him, I could use the backup—you don't need us on the job?"

"No . . . not yet . . . take care of the problem though, huh? . . . make sure it doesn't develop . . . let Joseph set up some stuff for you, yes." Her tone was motherly in a real way.

"Yes."

THE DOOR WAS marked CID Laboratory Division. And there was nobody inside.

"Quiet, eh?" Dixie looked around; walked down the length of a table, his finger running along the edge until he reached the back of the room. "Halloo."

His voice died almost instantly on leaving his mouth; there was no echo, and the silence was oppressive.

"Fuck, quiet."

I tried on a little humor. "Yeah, maybe *too* quiet."

23

THOMAS CAN think; he feels that he thinks too much, prefers to play the fool rather than the scholar. There is this great soulfulness in his eyes, depth and warmth. I could bathe in the warm moisture of his eyes. But they hold a sadness.

Thomas said once that he sometimes wondered what life would hold for him had he been born under a different star. Was he destined for this path through life, or could just one small change have sent him off on a completely different tangent? . . . something about the seminal disorder of natality.

What if I had never met this man, hadn't known the feel of his touch, seen the warmth of his eyes, kissed the joy of his lips, been in the glow of his smile? If I had been born under a different star, would Thomas touch me the way he does now, deep in the depths of all that is my being?

God—I am so wet just thinking about him.

"SOMETHING interesting." Claire was eating a banana.

"What interesting." I could hear her brain go whir.

"Number Nine, don't you see it." Legs crossed at the ankles, she was sitting on the floor; I was lying on the well-worn couch, a Navajo pillow clutched to my chest, a cigarette doing its own thing in my mouth.

"Maybe . . . what don't I see?" I sat up.

"If you don't see it, I'm not telling you."

"You promised."

"I lied . . ."

"So what about Number Nine?"

"Lack of violence—just a dead girl . . . different again . . ."

"And . . . "

"A feeling . . . what have you got left to come in on it?"

"Pretty much cleaned up . . . no further evidence as yet . . . just that one little inquiry. Just a dead girl killed nicely."

JUST A DEAD GIRL killed nicely. Dixie hopped up on the long table, picked up a Bunsen burner to examine the intricacies. Standing near to him Frenchy's shortness was evident.

"Well, son, what you think?" He tamped his snuff, took a pinch, tucked it in with his tongue.

And then she appeared: Dr. Death.

"Sorry, sorry, gentlemen . . . I had an op to do, sorry." She was a blur of movement on short legs. Thick long curly brown hair was tucked up into itself in a haphazard French knot at the back of her head. Strands fell at will all over the shoulders of her green scrubs . . . she seemed more like a pediatrician on uppers.

"Please, please . . . introduce yourselves, I must wash my hands." We did, and she did, then she donned a white lab coat. "Well, I am glad to see that we are all on a first name basis heah... my name is Clarissa." She smiled and somehow became attractive. "Why, Mr. Dixie, you are a tall drink of water, are you not?" Southernese, and her features were uneventful. She offered Dixie a hand, turned one way, then the other, to smile at the rest of us. "Mr. Frenchy, it is good to put a face to the voice— I was unfortunately unable to make your acquaintance on previous visits . . . I must, however, thank you for that *splendid* man you sent in your stead, simply a breath of magnolia blossom." She was an effulgent effervescent overabundance of the Southernness in blatant stereotype.

She had fucked Siggy, that was obvious from the husk of her voice. That she would fuck Dixie was there, too, in the open. She hadn't yet let go of his hand.

And then she did. Clapping hers together at her lips. "Well well—I do suppose that you've come to see what's new in the land of your crimes . . ." She dropped into a seat in front of her computer, swiveled and crossed her legs. They were short but nicely turned at the calf. "The computer knows all . . . we were running independent tests on the bath water . . . the FBI came to call, you know, sent a rather handsome pair of boys. I had sent samples to their Mobile office for correlative tests. They came to ask . . . courtesy questions, or so they said. Well—they seemed a tad more interested in the investigation as a whole, rather than this crime as a specific . . . they feel a little shut out, I guess, you know what I mean.

"I am tired, what I need is a nice hot bath and a man with good hands . . ." she smiled at Dixie, *Come hither, come hither.*

"Let us see heah, boys." The blue screen split into windows, then the windows gave way to the blue screen filled with writing. "It's heah . . . of course this has all gone down the line to Atlanta . . . some of the water tests are still not in yet, we are looking for any blood, semen or skin samples, a lot of skin tends to flake off during a nice bath . . . friction."

"You think someone else might have been in the tub?" Me me me me.

"I think someone might have been in the tub, yes."

"That's not in the report . . ."

"It is just a supposition." She spoke to Frenchy but had eyes only for Dixie.

"Somebody else in the tub—now wouldn't that be interesting, and what about the boyfriend, very very interesting, *very*." He held up a beaker, looked at me through the twist of the glass.

"You won't find any semen."

"Oh son, do tell." Melissa swiveled her chair, Dixie lowered the beaker.

"She would have been in the tub with another woman."

"Frenchy, I told you Thomas has the brain for this . . . come come, let us in all the way, boy."

"Several things: No contraceptives: no foams, no gels, no pills, no condoms, no diaphragm . . . an invitation to a place called "Flicks" I think it was . . . art books with nudes of women, several books on women's issues, some on gay issues, human sexuality . . . I thought at first that they were the guy's, but just twigged that they were hers, it fits her patterns . . . it fits the things in her bedside drawer."

We went out together onto the town. Dixie had forgotten the chief, he had the chief forensic pathologist. Frenchy was sight-seeing. A little red Subaru car, looked like a Yugo, kept appearing. Rolling by on its tiny tires with wide rims and 50 series rubber. Kaminari ground effects, Thrush exhaust, windows tinted, and Eric Clapton blaring from a dance-hall powered sound system only fractionally louder than the throaty growl that the exhaust developed from the normally sopranic engine. It was the same car that had earlier serenaded us on the court-house steps with "Layla". Cruising to be cool. I was reminded of the seventies graffiti I had seen in London and Paris: "Clapton is god".

"CLAPTON is god" written on tin walls around building construction; the words like sunshine on those cold-ass English days. I remember "Wonderful Tonight" cruisin' in a Ford Courier, 1977. The place was . . . Tumbridge Wells, in Kent. And in 1977 it was an open, airy, grassy place full of wide open "Commons", chestnut trees, and a fragrance of hay, all within commuting distance of London. She was blonde, and I had more hair. Her name was Fiona. She was a dancer. They used to call her Fee. I have thought of her often over the years . . . I remember "Lay Down Sally" *sur la Bois de Boulogne, seizieme arrondisement, Paris, avec une chick qui etait passant sa temps la, a l"université. Elle s'appela Marguerite. Fut la . . . la plus belle, avec des cheveux chatain . . . chatain roux, et des yeux qui etait d'une couleur si bleu, si bleu comme une mer caraibe. Elle etait jeune la . . . dix-huit ans. Avec des jambes la laitier atoucher, du bronzage avec couleur du miel. Miel comme le gout de sa sex. Sa vagin entourer a roux, une vagin laquelle put faire les, les choses . . . ah, les choses qui n'etait pas quelconque . . .*

When I was a boy at school I often used to go to England on holiday. We would pick the horse chestnuts and make them into "Bonkers", that is, we used to tie a string to them and play a game where you would smash your nut against someone else's; the nut to break was the loser, naturally.

Europe was a lot different then than in 1977. There were still scars from the war, although it had been over more than ten years. But in 1977, that was ancient history, except to old biddies who still used their tea bags three times out of years of wartime habit. Anybody over 65 had lived through both world wars. I had been to Vietnam; like all soldiers there I was a tourist, so to speak. Even the wiliest special forces spooks only saw the kind of action in his tour that can be counted in hours. Some of these old biddies had seen years of bombs and gunfire.

In 1977, though, the world was alive to the sounds of its own freedom, and Clapton was god.

NOW GOD IS dead. Technology killed him stone. And we are four, sitting on a patio in the rapidly cooling Mobile afternoon, praying for a miracle to a being we killed back in 1962. The world we live in is death and its not a pleasant place to dwell. I've been there a long time and believe me, god ain't there—he isn't in the eyes of the dead. On the night of September 29th he was absent when we lifted that girl, cool and dead, out of her tub. He wasn't there, and if he had been, he left no clue.

"She was with a girl, you think . . . why, my how progressive. I, unfortunately, am not so brave . . ." She was sipping a Coke.

"Tommy . . . the girl, if there was one in the tub, is she the killer?"

"Maybe."

"Maybe . . . maybe a girl was in the tub and maybe she was the killer, and maybe our little miss had to meet the maybe lady somewhere, maybe."

"Sometimes I hate you, son."

"No you don't, you love me, you want to marry me."

The little red Subaru passes by again; the music has changed, I don't recognize it right away. The driver is tall but I cannot see him clearly through the dark tint.

THE FBI loves acronyms. The FBI loves image. The SAC, special agent in charge, of the Atlanta OF, field office, sat at his desk. On his desk was a blue covered booklet; every week the FBI director gets one just like this, the bigger version. The SAC leafed through, noting that the entire office was occupied with just one project. There were no light green sheets of paper in the booklet, it was all confidential, highest level security, SAC Director-OPS eyes only.

The operation was being handled out of SIOC in Washington DC, his job just to liaise and assist. The Strategic Information Center had sent in extra SOG's and SSG's from the DC office and the Dallas office. Special Operations Groups and their special support groups all bouncing around the South, running what technically was an illegal COINTELPRO, dropping Creds, showing the Roast Beef to anyone that got in the way, Title III was out the door. They were running widespread surveillance. A CART team had come down with the MEGAHUT crowd from FBI/NSA co-ordinations and were floating in and out of cities throughout Dixie, running wire taps and computer transmission thefts.

The teams had set up their own communications system, using DECT, voice-encrypted stuff, on a European digital system, for their ground communications, with RPT-1 capability, so that each radio acted like a repeater expanding the available area of coverage. Incoming and outgoing communications were run through a MC-TDMA exchange and linked to the outside of the surveillance system through VSAT on spread spectrum modulation. Very Small Aperture Terminal communications is military hardware; the whole system was virtually closed to outside interception, the secrecy of the operation was obviously of the utmost.

The SAC tapped the file absently; even he was half out of the loop, he felt helpless.

"The most effective weapon against crime is cooperation—"

Cooperation. It was Hoover's epitaph. Overwhelm them with numbers.

VALERIE the bald delivered the RV to Washington International, the C-130 brought a passenger, took the RV. Blue eyes walked, confident in stride down the ramp onto the weather-blown Tarmac; it was cold, a wind blowing in off the sound. He was dressed for it in a wool greatcoat, his hands were gloved. The BMW followed him down the ramp.

"What's with the car?" Valerie yelled over the noise of the engines.

"I like the car, we need transportation," he smiled. His face was perfect. His hair was still just a stubble.

"You need a shave."

"Yes . . . all of me." It was surprisingly quiet inside the warm interior of the BMW, but their voices were still raised. "Ooops, that was a bit loud, no?"

"Quite . . . so, what have we got?"

She had a manila envelope, that plain yellow-brown color, she handed it to him. He took off the gloves and blew on his fingers, which were still cold. He felt the stubble on his head, it made him smile, the feel of it, a little boy pleasure.

"What kind of bloody name is Neathersole, god . . . so what do we do?"

"Kill him, I suppose."

"Ah," he had put a cigar in his mouth, but not lit it. The end of it was cold on his tongue.

"Why not let the others take care of him . . . he isn't on our charter?"

"He is peripheral, collateral damage control."

"You sound like U.S. military—you sure you went to the East Berlin school for advanced spying?"

"Graduated with honors . . . it's good to see you." There was an edge of unexpected softness in her voice. These were people to whom emotions were fatal.

24

Did you know that life is a terminal disease?
I know, I know, lacking a little in good taste.
Say—are you having any luck yet?
           NYAHH NYAHH NYAHH
                    —GBM #10

I EAT MY pussy and enjoy it.

Claire had come to stand there, her pants not yet done up after taking a pee. I could see the top of her panties.

"Hey, those look sexy, let me see." It was the sight of her bush, just a shade against the fabric. And I am hard.

"Hmmm, I want to eat you—can I eat you?"

"Oh . . ." She flushed instantly. "You can eat me any time."

"Run then."

The jeans were around her ankles, panties halfway there, legs in the air and I was buried up to my ears in cunt that was already . . . lubricious, wet with anticipation. It had little taste, only smelt like sex in its sick-sweet nectar kind of way.

It was a mango, dripping sweet ripe to be devoured, sucking licking chewing gulping, juice on your chin, hair in your teeth, skin peeled back, succulent flesh exposed, ripe ripe ripe, to the taste, to the touch, fingers wrapped around the meat, lips wet with juice, mouth filled with flesh, tongue and teeth searching— for that sweetness at the seed. The closer to the bone.

I AM GETTING old. I see myself in the mirror, having just rinsed the smell of pussy from my face. There are lines around my eyes. I didn't shave this morning: the bristle shows shades of gray around the mouth. Thank god I am not naked. I run fingers back through the long hair, wet, they press it into a place. There are only thin streaks of gray.

The medicine cabinet is on my left. It has double doors that open outward. It does not have a mirror. I have an urge for aspirin; there is ibuprofen, I take two. What doesn't kill, fattens. My shirt is a shambles, it looks as if I have eaten pussy in it.

"Baby," she calls.

Just a head around the jamb. "Hmmm?"

"I need water . . . that was nice." She hasn't pulled up her pants, instead she has pulled them off of one foot, she has pulled the blanket over herself. She is beautiful.

"You are beautiful."

"I look like a boy."

"Yes, a beautiful boy . . ." I was already on my way to the kitchen, I stop and turn back. The doorway as leaning post. I raise my hand to speak. There's a thought. But it's not clear.

"Nothing—I'll get the water . . . but you are beautiful."

In love . . . one should not rush anything. In murder, I suppose the same applies.

We drank Pellegrino in bed, she underneath the blanket, me on top. Music played elsewhere in the house. Its melody only a memory on reaching our ears, it is merely sound and rhythm. The day has turned to shit, the leading edge of a cold front.

It is raining and gray, a wet coolness. Claire touches me, her fingers are warm and dry. I remember the first time I ate pussy. . .

SHE WAS black and shiny and smelled like wood smoke. I was barely tanned and smelled like anticipation. Her breasts were small, nipples large, her mons matted with coarse stiff pubic hair. I was bald and small, only just seeing the first signs of my pubescence. But I was beautiful... more beautiful than she. Her labia were a dull purple, in sharp contrast to the bright pinkness of her inner flesh. There was a slight pungency to her and a taste of salt.

"Oh das it, oh yes, mas' Tommy"—it came out as always, *Tummy*— "Oh, yu does got it bwoy . . . lik de ting, eat de pussy . . . yes, eat de pussy lik fe yu love it." Her voice was unfamiliar. My little penis was harder than it had ever been.

My grandparents, had they known, would have been mortified. It was the way of the society that had nothing to do with blackness, but with the strictures of class decorum. Grandpa's parents were both French, but Grandma was an island woman; that is, her people had in part or parcel been there for some time . . . she had the blood of many ethnic generations in her. She was riddled with her blackness.

Grandma was a beautiful woman. She was of the right kind of family. She had good hair.

Good hair: it is an important level of social distinction.

CLAIRE HAS good hair. I look down on her, she swivels her eyes to look up.

"I can see right up your nose."

"Isn't that special."

"Are we going to run through Number Ten quickly before the girls get back from church? . . . We're supposed to go over to Margo's and see the new sculpture later."

That bit about the boring life of accountancy! . . . No, Margo is an *artiste*, once a man, now . . . well soon, a woman. I understand there is talent in those size 12 shoes. "Number Ten . . . yes, I—I suppose . . . I—"

I had hoped to avoid any more, really. I was feeling the strain again, as I had when I paused in Miami. Crime like this is difficult on the system. It is why we joke when on scene, it alleviates the, the—I want to say tension, but tension is the wrong fucking word—but I can't think of one. Remembering the scenes is almost as difficult as being there. Death is not nice: the smells, the colors, sometimes just the looks on the victim's face. The jokes and the innuendo help to remove you from the turgid putrescence.

You don't want to remember death.

It is the smell of Number Ten that I try most not to remember. The smell of ruptured intestines and burnt flesh. Flesh which oddly smells like roast pork, until you realize what you are smelling . . . then the odor takes on a certain repugnance.

AN ARCHED carriageway. An inset double gate, in wrought iron. The work is as intricate as the fan of a peacock's tail. The gate is square, the arch filled with fixed iron work; stars in squares and stars in circles. It was the gateway below a Garconniere, the "Bachelor's" quarters common in many old New Orleans houses. The carriageway led into an open garden courtyard; the main house is almost 80 feet away. It was empty at this time of the year; only the Garconniere was normally occupied.

One walked into an old world after passing through those ornate gates: the outside world could be shut out by closing heavy wooden doors, which lay now against the damp stone walls of the tunnel. Dark green was their color. It was a jungle world of ferns, palms, ornamental ginger under the shading of a large oak tree; itself a host for myriad ferns, bromeliads and old man's beard. Walkways of brick meandered amongst the growth, clay pots outlining the path at interval. Orchids, themselves in clay pots, decorated a low brick wall around the base of the oak. At opposite corner a brick walled pond below a bronze fountain, atop, the customary "boy pissing". A wrought table and chairs in black and intricacies. The table too is littered with orchids. Two are blooming, beautiful in pink and white, a spray of color. It was a 19th century world.

It was filled with 20th century technology.

The RV is parked across the front of the carriageway. The road is narrow. The RV door opens. The fucking African genius steps out. He pauses to look both way along the sidewalk before closing the door. He is dressed loosely. He walks straight down the carriageway. Another de-capilliarated man, tall and indistinctly featured, white, lounged in the cool damp shadows. He shifts his weight and the bulge of his gun suddenly becomes evident. He smiles. He has nice teeth.

In the garden a recessed stairway that curves up to the balcony of the Garconniere. A wall of doors are open onto the garden view. It is a long room. A room of computers and communications. It was basically a repeat of the technology in the RV.

A VSAT downlink terminal is in the room, the dish having been mounted on the roof. A CTA in its aluminum watertight briefcase is on a separate table, wires run into it. A computer analyzer, it kept its ears open for "bugs". The room had been made "Safe": cigarette-pack-sized single transducer ultrasonic emitters in each corner pulse out high frequency interference on non-specific frequencies at random intervals . . . thus making it virtually impossible for active or passive eavesdropping on conversations within the room. The walls have been lined with reflecting insulation, aluminum faced, these disrupt inward-aimed digital imaging technology which could use heat and motion sensing to map the interior of the room. All incoming and outgoing computer communications were done via VSAT, code-encrypted. Ground communications through a voice encrypted ICOM system further isolated, through spread spectrum modulation.

A petite woman, who might have been attractive with hair, is tapping away at one of the four computer terminals. The systems checks are running. There is an off-white push button phone on the table next to her, the one concession to the world of mass communication's outdated technology. Doug uses it to order three pizzas. Doug, a very stout man, all upper body musculature on small but well-defined legs. He has a Sergeant Rock jawline.

"Yes, yes, yes—three larges, yes—Doug . . . yes . . . 555-6306. Thank you." Even in paradise there is Domino's.

Baldness makes Doug's nose look too broad, his features freakish. It suits the fucking African genius, a certain wild flair.

Across the garden the main house is now occupied. A not-too-tall dark skinned woman, a red dot, Hindu decoration, on the bridge of her forehead between her eyes, stepped through French doors onto the opposite portico. Her eyes penetrated the distance. The fucking African genius felt the gaze, turned. She was standing against the railing, arms wide braced, hands wrapped around the dark green wood. He felt a chill and thought "this is the scariest fucking bitch I ever met." Even in his head "fucking" came pictured as "focking". Her alopecic head shone bronze in the oak filtered sunlight.

Her mouth barely moved, but he heard her clearly. "How is it coming?"

"We are finished—just are running de systems checks now—Doug has ordered some pizzas."

"Pizzas, hmmm, how very nice." The London School of Economics was evidenced in her accent. "Find Valerie for me, please . . . see if she is still in Washington."

The two cats, one rust, the other an almost-purple, that belong to the house, have come to spy on them. They lie like leopards, tails moving . . . slowly . . . taut.

25

THE SAC Atlanta ran fingers over the cool blue cover of the folder on his desk; the weekly report. He hadn't looked at it yet, but, the signs were already evident. The patterns had been developed. The Hostage-Terrorist boys from New York, SWAT, had boarded their plane this morning in Atlanta for Moisant Field.

New Orleans was being saturated with talent—The MEGAHUT boys had been there for two weeks already, four more SOG teams had left Atlanta yesterday. It was happening again.

The F.B.I. is a team game. And he—he was part of the team. That he didn't like the situation was unimportant. The individual was inconsequential. The interest of the team paramount. This team belongs to the U.S. government; the president—is head coach.

VALERIE WAS sitting in Booeymonger, eating an extravagant sandwich and reading a book about an old lady's life. Blue eyes was on the street down the block, comfortable in the warmth of the BMW, across from The Lantern, Bryn Mawr bookstore, O street, Georgetown. There were no children in the small playground on his side of the street. Too fucking cold. Neathersole's townhouse was on the Bryn Mawr side of the street, halfway down the next block. Valerie the bald had a clear view of his door from where she sat . . . Her hairless head wrapped in a wonderful scarf that had come from Amsterdam, in some far off, almost foreign time.

She felt her pager vibrate.

"We . . . well, we're getting rather close now, what is your situation?" There was that warmth that the phone line exuded whenever Valerie spoke to her.

"It hasn't changed . . . strictly surveillance . . ."

"Is he tracking us?"

"Has an ear to the ground, but it doesn't seem to be leading anywhere."

"Do you want to kill him, Valerie?"

"Not yet . . . you have need of us in New Orleans?"

"Within a day or two . . . shall I arrange an independent team to run the surveillance?"

"That might be a good idea, yes, I think so . . . we—we will—will you send the plane for us then?"

"Yes, day after tomorrow—no—you are both under control?"

"Yes . . . yes, it is very nice here at this time of year, Washington is quite so beautiful, eh."

She hung up the phone; a red light on the unit went out. The system looked much like a small fax machine. Leaning back her head she pressed the heels of her palms into her temples, the fingertips massaged the top of her skull. Her watch was thin and elegant; she wore it on her left wrist. She glanced at it now. She was dressed for ease of movement; a collarless linen shirt in natural color, the hem squared off. Her pants were khaki. Shoes with soft rubber soles and leather uppers.

The fucking African genius was standing by.

"Joseph."

"Hmm?"

"Time."

"Hmm."

"Put the RV into position; Doug and Bertrand will run the ground work . . . do we have all the clothes ready, is everything in order?"

"Yes . . . yes, pretty much, we are in order."

"Good . . . Doug, you will take the blue 280 C in the garage; Bertrand will take the black." They had new Mercedes C classes to drive; the mission was certainly not on a budget. "Dee, are the radios all charged up and ready?"

"All a go-go, boss." Dee, too, was an African—a white one perhaps, but an African. She had grown up in Rhodesia when it was called by that name. So when she said boss, she said "bass". Her eyes were mush; there was little attractive about her.

"Good, good . . . All right then, Doug, off you go, Bertrand will be on station . . . if you need backup we can be on spot in 3.5 minutes . . . Any questions? . . . Valerie and baby blue eyes will be back day after tomorrow, we are at this time a go in five days . . . all clear."

"All clear."

THEY WERE there in the shadows of the night. Like seven angels heralding Armageddon—"Come hither; I will shew unto thee the judgement of the great whore;" Rev: 17, 1. Beautiful-blue-eyed "Claud" and Valerie, Doug and Bertrand, Joseph and Dee, and she . . . she, as in "the cat's mother."

The RV was parked half a mile from the killing ground, halfway from the Garconniere, GHQ.

Joseph, the H&K PSG .308 caliber with Starlite scope, image-intensifying night vision in green glow, sandbagged in front of him. He could traverse and cover all approaches to both the RV and the killing ground; lay down suppressing fire.

Bertrand was to the west, up the street. He sat in the driver's seat of an armor-reinforced 500 S-class Mercedes Benz, black as night and clean to any trace. He was the emergency getaway. Valerie and Claud were at street level, lost in the darkness just doors away; H&K 9mm AP's held at ready, night vision goggles perched on their heads.

It was Doug's killing tonight.

She was in the Garconniere, video linked. Each participant was wired for sound and picture: the miniatures of modern technology. Her fingers made a steeple, booted feet were up, her eyes were scanning the monitors. Dee was doing the same. Testing, tuning. They were five minutes from a go.

It was late in the evening. That time of the night when most of the whores and all of the taxis are only taking calls for cash. The night held jazz.

She watched as one of the cats took flight to the table, prowled the smell of the technology. The other watched her from the floor, insolent. The rust cat stopped to eye her as it passed by, feet soundless on the hard wood of the table top. I could shoot it, she thought. The room seemed to have given it-self up to be soundless.

Doug is calm. He stands motionless. As he has for more than half an hour. He is part of the night. Part of the giant banana trees that lord over the courtyard—that is not dissimilar to the one that he has earlier left . . . more tropical perhaps, without the oak. Smaller and more dense, definitely. He can smell honey-suckle. The faded blue wood shutters are open against stained ochre walls. There is an ornamental apple in a rusty and white cast iron pot against one wall. The doors that the shutters would normally cover were open too. The heavy steel gate was sup-posed to keep the wild things out.

Doug moves for the first time, touching fingers to cool water that fills the moss greened clay of a Provencal olive jar. It is cool; he rubs it across his hairless scalp. It's fresh against the just-shaved flesh. He hears a voice in his ear.

Claud follows the shadows and enters the courtyard. He touches the microphone that is attached at his throat. Valerie, taking to different darkness, occupies an opposite doorway.

Dee, with the depression of an enter button, disrupts the phone service on this exchange. An intermittent pulse is sent down the line by a pin-sized emitter/receiver embedded in the line outside. Later, at the press of a button the minute transmit-ter will flame out in the smallest way, leaving little trace of a once-existence, existentialismical?

Bertrand starts the car. He fondles the Sig Sauer automatic pistol on the seat next to him. Blue steel and bullet-filled death.

Joseph releases the safety on his weapon. He is the all-seeing god from above now.

Dee turns over mission control to she in the Garconniere, and turns her attention to monitoring the killing ground. Active surveillance; sound-activated directional microphones. Motion sensitive detectors, heat signature image intensifiers with digital imaging. The RV is alive with the enhanced sounds and animated pictures of the night.

In the house next door two men are fucking in blue; they are bright white and gray heat impressions. Their grunts are . . . acoustical. A dog ambles down an alleyway, even the scratch of his toenails audible.

She calls a go and Doug moves, shedding his shadow. He flicks the water from his fingertips and heads straight for the house. He is a soundless spirit.

Dee trains the technology attached to three screens on the house. There are the sounds of sleep, a heat signature at the left rear of the house. Doug's signature is marked by the computer; it has a designation, it is moving. Claud's signature has entered the edge of the garden, he moves close to the wall. The image from Doug's mini-cam comes live and in living color.

He crosses a creaking floor past toile curtains and old cypress bookcases. Two gondola chairs, rounded at the back, stand either side of a doorway. In the bedroom an Empire mahogany bed, its mosquito net, hooped and tied, hangs from the ceiling above, pendulous, precipitous, furled. A motionless body, on its back, fills the center of the bed. It is a woman, naked, the sheet covering the knees and one thigh; a foot is exposed. Her breasts are large, sprawling across her chest. Her belly is wide. Her pubic hair is a dark thick heavy carpet at her mons; she is 50ish . . .

26

WE CAME IN by seaplane. Flew south across the shores of Al-
giers, banked steeply to come around for an approach upriver.
The "Old Miss" was muddy waters; my view was straight
down. Even from up here the river was vast. We were under the
gray, watery clouds now, and the ride had smoothed out . . . I
had never flown on a seaplane before. I could see the river
flowing away from us as we approached. We were moving
faster, catching it up. The plane bounced hard, twice, then you
could feel when the river took hold, called it all in and sucked
the plane to her bosom. I felt a somewhat sense of relief.

The plane used the Canal Street ferry dock at the World
Trade Center. It was 3:15 p.m., more than 12 hours after the
killing.

Her name is Jack. She was short, black and stout. She wore a
long blue greatcoat, which seemed to shorten her further, gray
slacks and sensible shoes. The coat was tucked behind her holster, revealing the stainless steel weapon and a badge in polished brass . . . a girl who knows how to accessorize. The gun
bulging at her hip, a Ruger Blackhawk, in .357 magnum, was
bigger than she. She was not pretty; long plaited locks, large
purple lips. She was not ugly; big big brown eyes . . . she was
good. Like the Mounties, Jack always got her man . . . always.

She had a better than 95 percent closure on her cases. *A boom she boom!*

"The smoke's just cleared—you boys are right on time . . . the CID team just walked into the house half an hour ago . . . how many of you are there?" She went up on tiptoes to look past Frenchy's shoulder, past me.

"Four . . . right now."

"Okay, okay, then we can all fit in my car . . . Emile, my partner, is still at the scene . . . Frenchy, we know each other; hi, Thomas, nice to see you again."

"Jack." We exchange small smiles. She is in her efficiency mode.

"Jack . . . this is Dan and behind him . . . ah there she is, that's Carly, they're part of my permanent team . . . Dan is our chief crime scene investigator . . . Carly will run team liaison . . . if that is okay with you, ah, Sigmund . . . the forensics team leader may be in later today, or one of his techs, to assist at the autopsy . . . but, right now this is all you get, eh."

"Good, good, then we . . . go, yes."

I remember feeling very tired while watching the back of Jack's haphazard somewhat dreadlocks-ed head. There was an air of the 70's about her; her hair, her dress, her manner. That had been her time, I suppose.

It was raining.

We were headed uptown along the edge of the "Quarter" on Canal Street. This town always made me feel uneasy; too many ghosts. I'd never been laid here, not even once. We turned on Burgundy and the buildings were old, the streets were quiet. It felt like the backlot of a movie studio: all alone with unreality.

Then we saw the fire engines.

"The water boys made a mess of the scene fighting the fire— hosed the place down, tore out walls, floors and doors . . . it wasn't till half hour into their thing that they found the body—it was fused to the mattress springs in the back bedroom. Christ— and we're only about two blocks from the police station . . . fire and water, we're screwed, never find a solid clue."

Yes, the fucking smell.

I came to sit across the street. The sidewalk was wet; that I felt the cold dampness was almost a relief. It was raining still, well, not so much rain as that the clouds had come to settle around us, close to the ground. I lit a cigarette and drew deeply; a knee was drawn up, the other cast aside carelessly. I was staring, seeing nothing.

My left eye was twitching; I rubbed it with the back of my right hand . . . a hand that was black with soot.

The smell, I couldn't get the fucking smell out of my head; it was caught up in the hairs of my nose, the cilia in my throat. It had penetrated my dermis. The sight of tortured flesh had embedded itself in my retinas.

I swallowed heavily, and smoked some more.

The eye twitched again and it came to me that I was hyperventilating, my mouth open, eyes wide. My smoking hand was shaking, not badly . . . yet it was shaking. I saw Frenchy coming. He was slow motion, and white was his color. His coat was flapping in the breeze, arms limp at his sides, the grayness of the day seemed to swirl around him; the colors of the firemen and the police; blues and yellows, the reds . . . in movement and rest . . . like some Technicolor battle.

I half expected to see a lone white stallion, blood-stained with the remnants of life, on a battlefield filled with the leftovers of death.

They had found some clues . . . "Goopher dust", the dirt from a fresh-turned grave, had been poured on the floor, encircling the bed. The symbol singed into the door had been painted in blood and crematory ashes—human ashes; the blood was hers. The cross also . . . it is a powerful symbol, where the lines meet is the place where magic is strongest . . . when you do the voodoo that you do. An apple had been stuffed in her mouth.

"You have another cigarette, son?"

"Seen a ghost."

"I don't want to talk about it . . ."

"Yes."

He put his back against the wall. We watched the action across the street; like a line of army ants stripping a tree, there was a constant movement of burdened people moving in and out of the house.

The house was, from the outside, a semblance of order . . . except that one noticed lifeless windows and two broad black marks of fire along a white wall.

"It was horrible." I am not so sure he was talking to me. But he had lain an arm on the brick wall, his forehead was on that arm. He looked down at the cigarette poised for smoking.

"I don't know why but I thought of my child . . . my daughter . . . she's six . . . you don't have children, do you, son?"

"No."

"Tell me . . . will we catch them, these fucks, will we catch them?"

DEATH IS more often subtle, but almost never without incidence. When I was, oh, about 12 or 13, I came upon a friend of my grandfather's, a man named Etienne. A grand man when he was well, large and booming . . . it was a sucked dry skeleton whose bed I sat next to on balmy afternoons in June.

He had been a merchant sailor and a trader in goods brought, along with great tales of feuding warlords, jungles thick green and moist, mountains that were so tall they touched the sky, and silk the colors of a rainbow—only twice as bright — from *La Indochine*; Thailand, Malaysia, Cambodia, China.

I kept his company while he ailed and he taught me how to read palms.

A house in black and white on a small rise, large windows and doors always open for the four winds blowing across wide patios, filling the house with their semblance of coolness. His mahogany bed was massive, the wood almost black with its age. But, he did not sleep in it; a hospital bed had been brought to the room and it sat opposite.

Etienne's wife had been dead almost 10 years and he was alone. He had married late and had no children . . . his friends kept him company. Comfort, in his pain, until he died. He looked green to me, as if he had already begun to rot, but his teeth were still white and the eyes still blue.

"This, right here in the middle of the hand . . . if it makes an 'M' . . . yes, right there, you will be wealthy . . . see, you have an 'M'. The left hand is the money you were born with; the right hand is the money that you will earn . . . you will do well, Thomas ah, and here, running along the base of your thumb is your life line . . ." He laughed then. His hand was dry and brittle as he held mine. The tip of his finger, as he traced my lines, was ice. "Yours runs off your hand, see . . . you will live long, long— ahhh, life." With a little smile. "It is good, yes." He still had the Belgium of his youth in his accent. He was frail; his voice was wet sandpaper on pumice. "I have enjoyed a life oh, *cher* Thomas, you must travel, you must see the world . . . it is grand, it is beautiful, it is of such variety . . ." He tilted his head back slightly and closed his eyes. " . . . A man is not complete in his knowledge until he has experienced of the world, Thomas . . . it is a classroom that the neighborhood cannot provide, no, no, no oh, and the women, Thomas, yes the women . . . brown ones, yellow ones, white ones of all the shades . . . I have loved these women, Thomas, I have loved many women . . . oh yes, you can hate a man for the shade of his skin, or the color of his religion, but never a woman, Thomas, never a woman—that kind of love knows no prejudice, ah—I have loved many women, and now I am dead . . . and now I am *dead*."

He did not die just then, but later, as he slept. I sat reading an old book of short stories he had; Jonathan Cape, London, first published 1928. He suddenly opened his eyes and sneezed, made a fist, then opened his hand to look at it, sighed audibly and died. Stone fucking cold dead, just like that—not what I had expected at all. But I knew he was dead.

When I called the maid, she cried out and wailed. I sent the gardener to the village for a doctor and a constable.

I STILL HAVE the book. It has this wonderful smell about it, and the pages are always cool to the touch; I think if pressed I would say that it smells like burnt cane from a distance on a cool evening after a rain.

But I am reading another book now, feet up in the soft couch as I wait for Claire. I am rooting, and the couch envelops me. The book is good. I can enjoy reading.

I can enjoy my reading. The sun is shining again, but only in spurts of weakness through a broken ceiling of gray. Music is playing, and in the distance I can hear an undercurrent of Claire; she sings *"Don't let me down."* ... She done me good.

"He who waits loves", I heard that once somewhere, or maybe it was "He who loves waits"; anyway, I wait now in comfort and in joy, comfort and joy. I am, I think, content ... today.

"Water, I need water . . . this blowdrying is making me thirsty; whatcha doing?"

"Reading." Well actually, now I was up and walking. To the kitchen, to the kitchen. "What you want . . . mineral or seltzer?"

"What?"

My head had been in the refrigerator, I pulled it out and tried again.

"Mineral or Seltzer?"

"Seltzer."

"Okay."

"What?"

"Nothing." At higher volume. I poured two.

I walked back into the bedroom. "You call Frenchy yet?"

"No, sweets, he . . . where is my watch?"

"On the bedside."

"I could have sworn I had it on, you know . . . what time is it? . . . he's playing golf . . . I'll call him later." My cigarettes were on the bedside table too; I lit one. The dryer was blaring. Off, and Claire leaned around the door. "I'd love one."

I sat on the bathroom countertop, feet up, and handed her her smoke.

"Show me what's under that shirt."

"Ain't nothin on but my skin."

"Tease."

"Yep . . . show you some butt for a dollar." She lifted an edge, showed me some skin. Nakedness makes me hard. " . . . and you can't have none."

"I'm drained."

"Good."

" . . . I think I have some ideas—are you going to stay around?"

"I might ship out for a few days tomorrow; I'll wait to speak to Frenchy . . . later, but I won't be gone long . . . ahmm, ahm, what would you say, I mean we talked about it, yes, but what would you say, I mean if I broke my lease and—and moved closer to you?"

"Closer . . . closer, why not in—with me . . . We have talked about it." She was playing with the hair in the brush.

"In love you can't rush anything." Have I said that before? I was playing with my toes.

"You're a chicken."

"Yes I am . . ."

"I'd love you to move closer." She touched my face, jumped up on the counter with me, we heard it creak. "Yes, I'd like that—yes." She smoked like a woman.

Michael was watching *futbol* on the TV when I came back to the living room. He looked up and smiled. "AJAX vs. NEC." He said *Ayax*, that's how it's pronounced. Dutch football. FA cup semi-finals. I nodded. NEC was up by two goals to one; the announcer was English, I can never recall his fucking name.

"Diedre's gone home, she'll be back."

"Hmmm." He wasn't looking at me so I couldn't talk to him.

"You have another cigarette?" Still watching the TV he reached out a hand.

"Definitely your aunt's nephew."

"Yes . . . oh thanks, man; hey good, you're smoking normal cigarettes."

IN A BATH of blood red and steam she lay, head back, long neck extended, smooth and sinuous. Her eyes were closed and her head was bald. Valerie. But she was on California time. Arms, graceful long, sounded from the depths of the massive tub, breaking the surface, eruptive, carrying a wash rag with them. She dropped it across her face. There was a soft moan of comfortable pleasures.

"Arrgh, I don't want to get out." A muffled mumble. But then she removed the rag and sat up. Her breasts were pink. There was a gurgle as she pulled the plug. She stood, model tall, her vagina was a pedophilic fantasy; hairless, the labia evident— it was so, so fleshy.

Toweled and semi-dressed; there was a message on her secure line. She turned on the computer, booted up and ran the message through the encryption.

. . . subject on the move . . . been looking for you for two days now . . . we have lost contact with subject . . . please advise . . . O.S.

Things were coming apart at the edges—they were already having to make moves against certain holes, chinks in the armor. There were people "in house" who seemed unhappy with procedure; clean up had begun, clean and consolidate, run on maximum interference . . . The COINTELPRO teams were saturating Atlanta.

She would have to go to Atlanta . . . Claud and his blue eyes were already there.

If Neathersole had slipped the hounds then he had found something—imagine losing a blind man—shit. The game was getting difficult. She thought that she shouldn't have left the operations area, but she needed a break. She would have to call in, bring the bloodhounds out. She should have killed Neathersole earlier on, but that might have caused a complication, deviations from the task at hand. He was supposed to have been contained and controlled. Shitshitshit.

Too many cooks.

And only one week left. The advance team had already moved on to Miami this morning. Who had dreamed up this fucking operation? They should have just brought in all 12 and eliminated them quickly and quietly. What was it she had heard someone say . . . there's nothing quieter than an unsolved serial killing . . . one of the Federales had said that, no doubt.

Fucking idiots.

And she had hoped, Number 11 just freshly over and done with, that she could rest awhile . . . enjoy the California pace . . .

Fucking idiots.

27

AND THEN it dawned on Claire. The feeling she had inside became suddenly tangible. It was the middle of the night, but she made the call.

"You're up?"

"You know me, love, never could sleep worth a shit."

"I have a question for you."

"I bet you do . . ."

"Has there been any—ah—unusual activity in-house lately?"

"Oh yes . . . things have been wild here at home, the kids are driving me up the wall, job's a nut house."

"I see." And she did; she realized that he couldn't, or wouldn't, talk on the home phone.

"How's life been with you? . . . oh shit—Jenny is up, love, I am going to have to call you back." He rung off.

But she knew that within the next day he would call back. Claire had felt the weight in his voice, the tension. She had been right. And he—he knew about it all; he was on the inside, and he didn't like it. They had been friends for years. She knew him well. He would call her back and spill his burden . . . because he could talk to her. She would understand.

A MILLION miles away in another galaxy I sit in my Atlanta hotel room, unsleepable. There is a fuckfest movie on the box and my cock is hard. I begin to stroke it, cupping my balls, squeezing the shaft, stroking the glans; the tip is purple with rage. The vein pliant beneath my palm. There's a warmth to the head. Stroking,

pulling, pumping, squeezing. The head became alive and between my shoulders I felt a . . . a tickling sensation. A wave
spread through my brain from the base of my skull to my eyes.
And at the last moment before I cum, pale yellow and viscous,
there's a clarity to my perception; I can almost hear god, my skin
is alive, and I can see through walls of lead.

If orgasm were an injectable drug!

Only the perception of my flesh was less than fleeting.

And I realized that I suddenly knew everything, everything
that pertained to nothing.

I am a missing man, lonely old soul. I've got a black dog
hanging around my days and he's as big as Mr. Churchill could
have imagined him . . . I never thought that I would suffer these
kind of feelings . . . of loss, again. But, yeah but I miss them,
Claire and Bugsy, miss them... I thought I'd left those feelings
behind a long time ago, in faster days, me as the peripatetic
man. But here they are, looming out of the semi-darkness of my
room.

I am alone and I don't like it.

I have just gotten in and it's the middle of an Atlanta Monday night. The world is asleep and I don't know what to do with
myself; the weight of my emotions is unbalanced, I am unevenly
laden. About six hours till dawn and sleep avoids me. I have
picked up the phone 10 times to call, but don't know who I want
to speak to . . . I find myself wishing that my grandmother were
still alive. We could have talked about pain.

I don't want to think about crimes, and luckily they don't
invade my head . . . which is a jumble of women . . . in various
shades of pink.

Tomorrow, tomorrow I will deal with crime . . . I had spoken
to Frenchy earlier this morning; the truck from Jonesborough
public works had almost definitely been used during the crime
on Number Six, but was clean of discernible evidence.

The lesbian lover angle on Number Nine had pulled in three
names. Three names which led to nothing solid—but a fourth
name, which belonged to a Melissa who was on vacation in
Europe till Tuesday night.

A team had left today on its way to Eastover, the Congaree swamp, to follow up on Claire's theory of the killing site for Seven/Eight. Frenchy and I would go to Mobile to interview Melissa.

Neathersole came sprinting through my brain on hobbled knees, and I wondered where he had disappeared to; I had thought that he would have had something for me by now, from his large book of contacts. If this wasn't a set of crimes committed by professionals I would eat my fucking hat.

He was followed closely by Bugsy baby; dressed in the sweater of that first morning she walked into the room of my imagination on slow feet; sauntered up and took hold of my thoughts. I could almost hear the timbre of her voice. Her odor followed her. I sat on the edge of the unhomelike bed and smoked a cigarette, I was naked from the waist down, my penis now flaccid and small.

It is the impersonality of the room that is often depressing; no wonder they seal the windows. Many a man was probably driven to suicide by the color of the bedspread at his Holiday Inn. I was at the Underground Suites Hotel . . . a more-comfortable-in-its-ugliness version, a doorman in top hat at the lobby door, liveried.

If I had a gun I might shoot the chair in the corner and put it out of its misery. The fabric was agony.

28

THOMAS HAS walked through his life alone for 40 years. He has loved and been loved, a thousand souls passing briefly within earshot. Thomas has come to feel his loneliness . . . to recognize his desires. He came to America in search of the dream. Only now he finds that the importance of things lies in family and culture, in kinship . . . propinquity.

He plays at the piano, not well though . . . likes Jimmy Buffet tunes. There is still so much of the islands in him, though he has been gone for half his life. A cool Calypso voice, deep and foreign even now. The way he smells, fresh, before that first cigarette, plain and odorless, skin so soft, only lightly golden.

Only lightly golden. I dream skin only lightly golden.

"FRENCHY DARLING—are ya happy to see me?" as I slump through the door of his office, feeling the weight of my sleeplessness.

He looked like death warmed over; a hint of hair at his chin, he was drinking a giant cup of coffee. "Drank myself into the bottom of a quart of Cuervo last night son, with some friends," his voice is gravel.

"Christ, where's your voice?"

"Bottom of the bottle with the fucking worm . . . or did I eat the fucking worm? God, son, I *hurt*." He opened the drawer, rummaging. "Aspirin, I need aspirin—Leeman . . . yo, yes you, man... You got aspirin?"

I think that the strain is beginning to tell on us all. My weekend hasn't helped except to cloud my brain further; other issues.

"Don't you know never to drink on a Monday night? . . . fuck, especially when you gotta work on a Tuesday morning."

"Aaargh . . . seemed like a good idea at the time, son, that damn worm were just calling my name. Leeman . . . Aspirin: let me spell it for you son, A S P E R I N . . ." He did a thing with his fingers, lips moving, silent, like counting. "Did I spell that right? whatever . . . shit."

He covered his eyes, squeezed his face between both hands. "Aaaah . . . oh—forgot . . . message." Eyes still covered, he holds out a piece of pink paper. It is in hieroglyphics.

"What does this say?"

"Can't you read it?"

"Can *you*? Did you write this?" I handed it back.

"Yes."

"So what does it say then?"

"Uhh . . ."

"We're fucked now."

"Oh, oh . . . it says, um . . . you can find me at Humpty Dumpty's . . . from . . . what is that word, oh yeah, it's from a guy called Arnold Ten Toes . . . must be an Indian."

"Neathersole . . . no number, huh?"

"Uh? No."

"Neathersole . . . I was wondering where he had gotten to— when did the message come in?"

"Friday, it looks like, after you left . . . I forgot all about it."

"That's cool . . . I'm going to need a D&D on Humpty Dumpty Herman."

"You're kidding?"

"Not really." I wrote Herman's real name and three aliases on a piece of paper and passed it to Frenchy. He looked at it like he wasn't seeing it; his eyes were bloodshot, the color of blood-filled urine.

"Who is he?"

"An Estonian Jew who came to America when he was 10."

"I'm sure, but dat ain't what I meant."

"Contractor."

"Killer?"

"No . . . he only contracts specials, doesn't do any of the killing himself."

"You want fe narrow de search a bit."

"Well . . . where do all old Jews go eventually?"

"And Haitians."

"Florida?"

"Try Fort Lauderdale."

"Hey."

"Hey."

"Are we going to Mobile tomorrow?"

"No."

"Why?"

" 'Cause she's coming here, son."

"Ohhh, that's convenient."

"Ain't it just though, son . . . she's gonna be on tomorrow night's flight, with your friend Dixie."

"Dixie . . . doesn't he just get around."

"Do you want a coffee, man?"

"What I want is a new head, son . . . coffee might be nice . . . do we gotta drink that drip shit? . . . what we need is a decent coffee and some beignets. I could send Santi."

"You could send Santi . . . I'm gone next door to the killing room . . . we have any updates on Eleven yet?"

"Sure . . . I'll set up the coffee, son, then meet y'all next door—we can go over stuff. Aspirins are setting in . . . what time is it?" Rhetorical, because he is looking at his watch.

It looked just as I had left it on Friday; the cockroach was in hiding . . . maybe he'd gone to cockroach work.

War room, walls cluttered with killing. I went to the beginning: —Number One, too cold . . . the piece of plastic that may or may not have been from a camera, a piece of blade. Number Two, an expatriate Haitian artist spread all around his studio and what may have been a tripod mark in the blood that covered his sisal. Full of holes in Number Three, shot full of holes . . . full of holes, fuck . . .

"Interrupt."

"You can walk?"

"I can hobble . . . we just got in those phone records on Seven and Eight."

"Call me impressed."

"Damn right, you should be, son . . . now, what are we going to do with them?"

"We're going to look at them."

"You and me?"

"Do we have to?"

"Ain't no one else available, son."

A knock at the half-open door, a girl in blues and brown hair, I'd not seen her before. She isn't very pretty. "They sent this up for you." She had a phone sex voice, and then I was drawn to her eyes, which were a pretty blue; in almost any woman a man can discover the attractive.

"Who did?"

"Lab, sir."

"Thank you . . ." Frenchy reached backward without getting up. "Darling, do me a favor and get some more coffee up here, get one of the detectives to go get a pot or something . . . do you know Santiago?"

"Yes sir."

"Good . . . give him the message for me, okay?"

"Yes sir."

"Thank you."

"She has nice eyes."

"I hear her blow job is something special." Men talk.

"Why, who's had her?"

"Nobody's had her . . . but she'll suck a cock at the drop of a hat, likes the flavor . . . good for her complexion."

"She doesn't fuck?"

"Nobody's been able to separate her from her drawers yet, son."

"But she'll suck dick."

"She'll suck dick . . . looks like we've got the initial report on our bloodless babes from Number 11 here . . . yeah man, even Leeman at a party a few months ago, says she nearly sucked the black off the fucking thing, devoured it like it was lunch; shit, son, sorry I ain't had the pleasure."

"I bet . . . it sounds like a worthwhile pursuit . . . nothing here but blood work, positive ID . . . first stage autopsy . . . a recent abortion. Do we know who she was seeing?"

"No . . . no we don't, not yet . . . but she was just coming in from a weekend trip, we've narrowed that down, and trying to find the boyfriend through hotel receipts." He leafed through the file . . . "Nope, nothing in yet . . . uh, the Q & A with workers and family, neighbors, Ignacius has that file, he's transcribing now, I think."

"Not today."

"You gonna tell me about the weekend's revelations."

"Nothing to tell yet really . . . I left my files with Claire . . . so it's all just what I told ya so far . . . Congaree and that shit, this phone stuff ."

"Should we look at them?"

"Already did."

"Couldn't have."

"But I did."

"When, I didn't see you . . . well, what then?"

"What what?"

"Son, my head is still a few sheaves off of plumb, so if you fuck with me I'll just shoot ya."

"A few sheaves off of plumb? Shoot me? . . . Better tell you then, huh . . . can you keep a secret? . . . they both got the call, number, . . . ahm, Number Seven got the call twice from 615."

"615 . . . 615, where the hell is 615?"

"Phone book, look in the phone book." We both glanced around the room; volumes on murder but no phone books.

"Help."

"You go get one."

"Too lazy . . . where's the phone, son? . . . Leeman's extension is 106, dial him."

Phone. "Hello . . ." Into the phone. "615's Tennessee . . ." To me, mouthpiece covered. " What? . . . good idea, Leeman . . . Tommy, where are the numbers? Hold a second, Leeman . . . which one, T.? Okay, okay I got it, Leeman, you ready son? . . .

Okay, here it is, 615-555-2121. Cool, son, call me back . . . He's going to check back the phone company and get a location on that phone." He had the phone poised over the receiver.

"Do you realize that ten years ago we never could have got this done, not like this, man."

"That's what I was just sayin' son, a minute ago when you weren't listening."

"Oh."

Phone. "Hello . . . yes, yes, yes, yes, yes, do it . . . he's arranging a team from Tennessee state police."

5'6", 110 pounds, brown hair, brown eyes, blood type O+. Her blood in a bucket; evidenced traces of 2-butoyethanol, ammonia, trisodium phosphate, diethanolamide; scrapings from the bucket naturally indicated that these were dissolved cleaning agents common to the container and not prior present in the blood . . . T-Cell counts, white cell counts, hemoglobin, blood sugar, glucose factors, aminos . . . 36-22-34. Baby had tits.

Number Eleven.

Frenchy was fixing two coffees.

I looked at my watch. And despite the company, a shadow of the "missing" man crossed my path. Forehead on the table, I light a cigarette with the butt of the one I am not finished smoking. Nikes to speed my feet. I must look like a Gap commercial; I had neglected to shave this morning, stubbled; "Man in the Rugged". Lonely old man in the rugged.

Lonely: *adj.:* Solitary, companionless, isolated, infrequented. I am the infrequented man. My forehead laying table, I watch the smoke curl away from the cigarette. I don't hear Frenchy's voice on the phone. I am infrequented and insensitive to harmony. Deep drag, exhale through my nose, and somewhere in the back of my head I hear the letters F.B.I.

29

THE GOVERNMENT can do anything.

"Checks and balances" is bullshit. There are no controls at the top.

Power corrupts; absolute power corrupts absolutely.

Most of us in America are so far away from the base of power, completely removed from the people who make policy. But those close to the power know that the power is absolute.

Example: an American owns a large tourist property on a large Caribbean island; the property is financed by Citibank. In the 1970s the island goes Socialist, the American lets the property payments lapse. Citibank offers the property for the cost of the loan; the island's government takes over the loan and the property. In the 1980's the island revives and prospers. Socialism is dead—the American wants his property back. The island government then politely asks him to fuck himself. The American calls a friend, a Texas representative on the committee that handles Third World loan money. The committee holds up the island's loan money till the government agrees to give the American back his legally foreclosed property.

Example: an American gets caught with drugs in a foreign country, on the edge of Europe. He is a prominent son. He is an idiot. He is a drug runner. The jail is horrible. His father, saddened, talks to friends on the Hill. The word runs around the Hill. An operation is mounted. A man in a pale blue seersucker suit, dark hair and ordinary features, carries $60,000 of American taxpayer money and arranges a jailbreak. The escape via train to safer hands. I met the seersucker man many years later in another place under another acronym: Agricultural Attache.

I use these small examples as illustration. If the government's full power can be wielded quite so easily for the handling of the personal foibles of the friends of power, imagine what can be done when government feels its tentative grasp of power threatened—from inside or out.

The FBI is the single most powerful government organization in America. The FBI can do anything . . . *anything*.

FRENCHY is still on the phone and my brain is running a wild gamut, hurdling over preposterous possibility, chasing that ganoid probability at the end of the dark tunnel. I stand and wave to him; he holds up a questioning hand, overturned; I shrug, add a thumb signal, indication of outside, I mouth something without real meaning, he understands.

Outside it's gray, raining. I sniffle, fumble a cigarette, wishing I were near a beach.

The possibility of my being right suddenly scares the shit out of me . . . "Whatever's left, no matter how improbable, is the truth." . . . it's a saying, or something like that. I feel the urge to glance over my shoulder, I hurry and cross the street to nowhere. I find a phone and call upstairs.

"Frenchy . . . me . . . look . . . I'm feeling fucked, I'm taking off, I'll call in a little while, see if Leeman found Humpty . . . you didn't need me, did ya?".

I wanted to call Claire . . . bullshit, I wanted to catch a fucking plane to something sunny and south of the border . . . If my wild imaginings were even half correct . . . how do you protect yourself, protect your friends, against the power of a government that can do anything? . . They can destroy the world; how well would I fare?

I have seen it happen. I have been there when they created their Panamas, their Iraqs. I have smelt the scent of sanctioned killings.

Do you have sympathy for the devil?

DREAD HAS spread over me . . . Neathersole had gone to ground, leaving crypted messages . . . an investigation so twisted away from reality that it had dropped over the edge into the fucking twilight zone, evidence that led nowhere, suppositions that pointed one way, probabilities that belied . . . professionals. I was right, I knew I was fucking right.

Down into Underground. My hair is wet, I slick it back. I— am glazed over, wandering aimlessly almost. I look around, I am not alone. I want to scream . . . HELP!, instead I smoke.

Everything smells of fish. It is in the rain, as if the moisture was sucked from the depths of some stagnant sea. Back against a damp wall I am looking down on Coca-Cola, behind me, over my . . . my left shoulder is CNN . . . I wonder what they would do with this story . . . story, hah—fuck, all I've got is wild imagination . . . but who else could pull off such perfect crimes, and with all the tools evidently brought to this game? Who could plan a crime to avoid some of the best detecting mechanisms available in the world ? . . . Yeah, fuck, the guys who *own* the fucking mechanisms.

Everything smells of fish.

Why, though? and the *why* is very important . . . the motive. What fucking motive could there possibly be? We found no link at all between any of the people . . . they were far removed from one another, not a single real common characteristic. 11 completely different people.

My brain was working faster than my fear; then the fear found a fast gear. The cigarettes are not helping at all, but I smoke them like there is no tomorrow . . . which there may not fucking well be . . . I am cold, and tired. 11 different people? . . . spies? . . . fuck, C.I.A. —I can only hope that I am wrong, I can pray . . . god yes, I can pray, I needed to call Claire. C. I. fucking A., shit, help. Spies—I must be going over the edge.

SHE IS STILL close to bald and standing in the high domed lobby at Hartsfield. It is Tuesday. Nobody is coming to meet her; they are waiting for her to arrive, a car has been left for her. Valerie feels like she should be wearing sunglasses. She picks up the key from the Avis desk—it is a LeBaron. She would have preferred the new Mustang, but the weather is too shitty to enjoy the convertible anyhow.

Blue-eyed Claud had arrived two days ago, the rest of the team had already moved on to Miami; so the other men waiting for her call were freelance operatives used on previous occasions.

They had some mop-up work to do.

Washington was involved with the trace on Neathersole, big time efforts brought to bear . . . she had been given the go . . . calls had been made and received, leaks were possible if certain holes weren't plugged, suppositions were being made in certain offices.

The SAC Atlanta was a possible problem . . . there had been a call monitored to his home that had indications . . . the woman in Charleston, Claire . . . a friend of the detective . . . Thomas. She remembered his hands . . . strange how it all ties in . . . she had met the adversary . . . Blue-eyed Claud had asked her why she had taken the chance: "Do you think that was wise?" he had asked . . . yes, yes you had to see the adversary's eyes to feel his danger. Thomas had smiled at her, devoid of danger . . . sex appeal was what she felt. The second time in Fort Lauderdale, watching the planes, it was there too—sex, not danger: *oooh, I could fuck this man*, she had thought.

Even now as she thought of him there was a sense of sex; she felt a warmth in her twat . . . how would she kill him? She had the James Bond dream of seducing the adversary over to your side, sex them into submission, to your will. Then live happily as lovers.

SATURDAY was Guy Fawkes day . . . why I thought of that I have no idea—my brain is a jumble. There is a line from Seder prayers, " . . . All that is human is deceptive . . ." or something like that, I have probably taken it completely out of context. I am not

Jewish. But, I do know things. I suppose that that is the crux of my job, or at least my skill at my job . . . I must know things; I don't know the Hebrew translation.

I do know that I must work fast on some corroboration; I cannot go further without it. I don't know if I should tell Frenchy my suppositions, especially without further information; I know I must reach Claire, I have tried twice already, once at Bugsy's house. No one home. I left messages, I don't know which way to turn to avoid my anxiousness—I need to find Neathersole, that I do know.

Did I mention my anxiousness . . . ? It's a better word than fear.

I hang up the phone, and lean back against the wall of the MARTA station; I have wandered downtown Atlanta for an hour, aimless. " . . . *I'm a spaaace cowboy, I'm sure that you know where it's at, yeah yeah yeah . . .*". Claire is still not found. I want to call Frenchy; have they traced Humpty Dumpty?

I have a piece of turtle shell, shaped like a fang, on a long silver chain around my neck. I fondle it . . . Obeah . . . it keeps me safe from evil intent; makes vampires find my blood hepatic, bad to taste . . . bad dogs tame at the sight of my smile, bullets go astray . . . the phone next to me rings and I nearly jump out of my skin.

A young black woman takes one large step and slide past me—looked like a dance move—and picks it up; she's in red jeans with a bright yellow shirt and shoes to match. Her hair was ornate and streaked with orange; it was piled in licorice marzipan layers and swirls above a prominent three-teeth-in-gold smile. She herself was as ornate as her hair, bedecked in gold rings and chains; she jingled and glinted as she spoke in a language I didn't really understand, but was sure wasn't English. She stops talking to check her beeper.

Looking at her I feel my age, because her dress and language don't indicate her blackness, but her age . . . I am separated by two generations and a common language. I feel tired. I look at my watch, happy that I have remembered to put it on this morning, fuck. It is too wet, cold and crazy . . . I find myself drifting back to what Boom Boom had said to me:

" . . . It's easy and it's cool, T., real cool . . . takes a brain to do this . . . regular people don't think of shit like this . . . I've seen it done before . . . spook shit . . . professional." He had seen it done before, he had said, I hadn't asked him where . . . I needed to ask him where.

I took the MARTA from downtown on the airport line out to Fort McPherson. I hadn't called ahead. I am anxious to speak to Boom Boom.

Traveling by train. Spellman College station, and I overlooked a parking lot; I am still several stops away from destination. Below I could see two lovers . . . She, a woman 40ish, not at all tall, hair a browner shade of wheat; slim, medium and dark haired, he was about the same age. They were too clasping for it to have been anything other than a clandestine meeting—she hugged him too closely at parting, then he got into his van and she into her LTD and each went their separate ways.

Suddenly I got up and went out the door. On the station platform I lit a cigarette, inhaled deeply. The train pulled away without me . . . I didn't care. I am feeling much better now. I think that it is anger that has begun to set in . . . Fuck them.

The rain has ebbed, but the air is still heavy with moisture, and cool, not cold, definitely gray. Turns in the weather, like the fickleness of friends, changes in the wind . . . life is a moveable feast, no? Full of fluctuations, tides.

Somewhere there is a heavy heavy bass beat, " . . . *level de vibes, we a level de vibe, Reggae music played all right . . . one for all, all for one, level de vibe . . .*".

The bass is pulsing, vibrating the very air that I was breathing, I could feel it in my chest. I wanted to follow the rhythm, feeling suddenly very good; it is the music that I crave, like the children of Hamlin I am drawn to the music. But the music is sweet.

The music reminds me of times at 'Home' . . . Actually it reminded me of a Rebecca who I once loved when I was very very young. I hardly remember her now—just a pink dress and soft honey curls, skin to match . . . eyes, yes, she had big brown eyes. I ran into her many years later when we were old enough to fuck. We didn't fuck . . . we didn't even remember each other.

It is a weird life we live, I have known a lot of Rebeccas. Why she would choose to invade my now-in-turmoil memory, I don't know.

"You're in my heart, you're in my soul, you'll be my breath should I grow old . . ." Music is just bouncing around my head. I am empty otherwise. Too confused to have linear thought. Weighted, I think might be a good description, burdened . . . I look for a phone to try Claire again . . . Number Five, a man beaten to death, a joke killing, with his own softball bat. The sixth . . . dead doctor, hands cut off, the saw blade taken. It all seemed too strange. One wonders if my supposition could really be correct. Yet, it is the peripheries that hold the indications. Bizarreness of crimes—meant to throw you off the scent.

Claire's phone rang without a human answer; automated, she asked me to leave a message and promised to get back to me as soon as mechanically possible. I think area codes . . . 615, Frenchy, they probably had the number in Tennessee isolated by now; had they found out anything in the Congaree area? The train is coming, I will take it to Fort McPherson now.

Buzz cut and khaki clad, he walks erect, a statue in motion. His age does not show on the body of discipline. Then the hardened face breaks into a smile.

"Fuck you."

"Fuck you too."

"How are ya, T.?"

"Boom Boom, I am feeling fucked . . . am I allowed to smoke in here?" His handshake is a chiropractic alignment.

"No the brass would throw a fit, new fucking Pentagon rules came down the line last week, you smokers can suck shit and die now."

"Ah, it's the compassion I love."

"Well this can't be a friendly fucking visit, it's still during business hours . . . so what do you want?"

"I used the word compassion a moment ago, didn't I?"

"Sure did, man, what, you look that up this morning? . . . now it's time to see how many fucking sentences you can put it into."

"I should have shot you that night in Saigon."

"Oh you mean that night over that slant bitch . . . drunk we were, fucking A, shoot me   hah, I'm made of fucking steel, man . . . so what's the business?"

"The thing you don't want to talk about."

"Well, if I don't want to talk about it, then why you asking me?"

" 'Cause I need to know."

"Not much of an excuse, man . . . what do you need to know?"

"Last time, when we spoke . . . you said something about my mechanism, well . . . well you said you'd seen it done before."

"Fuck, man, you listen too good sometimes." He rubbed his stubbly hair and his eyes took in the world. "Walk . . . Yeah, that is what I said . . . you want to know where, right?"

"Right."

"That's kind of touchy there, boy . . . Kinda fucking touchy. You're my friend, right? but dig, I have a duty too, and that's fucking *important* to me."

"Our government or theirs?"

"Theirs."

"You know names?"

"Faces, son, I know faces, these were my counterparts."

"You know faces . . . you know faces."

"I know faces."

"Fuck—you've *seen* a face . . . you son of a bitch . . . here in Atlanta?" The lighter never quite reached the cigarette.

"You know, Atlanta is very nice in the fall; a lot of people come and go."

"But you saw a *face*."   I removed the cigarette, used it for pointed emphasis.

"Features. This face had no hair."

"No hair, bald . . . but still you know . . . I mean you ID'd the face."

"We're out of time, my friend, I have a briefing to give some students on disposals . . . sorry man, you understand."

"I am crystal on this, *crystal* . . . thank you . . . thank you, man."

"Watch your step . . . keep your fucking back to the wall, the face wasn't the only bald one in the crowd."

"**YOU CAN'T** *always get what you want . . . but sometimes, you get what you need.*"

Fuck, yeah!

"Frenchy—it's me, what ya got?" the office had rung busy, but I finally caught him on the cellular.

He wanted to know what had gotten into me.

"Nothing man, really . . . look we'll talk about it later . . . I'm fucked up that's all . . . tell me what you got."

Where was I? He wanted to know.

"What is this, twenty questions? I'm on the road, why?" What he told me next I didn't want to hear.

30

THE POLICE station was on smoke; I saw no fire . . . thick and dark gray, noxious. It looked as if all the fire trucks in the city were parked in the street and that they had been joined by every policeman available for three counties and the ambulances from twelve states; psycho Christmas in the city. I had to flash some creds to get within a mile of the fucking building. Took me more than 20 minutes to find Frenchy.

He looked much worse for the wear.

"Fuck, what *happened*, man?"

He was pinching some snuff, his face was red on the left side and shining with a burn gel, there was blood in his hair. I looked around, saw a lot of people in similar distress.

"The fire alarms went off about an hour ago." There's a glazed look about him, he's dealing in middle distance and vacant stares. Then he shook his head.

"There was a muffled boom, I think . . . the whole fucking building shook . . . then in seconds . . . seconds . . . fuck . . . and smoke came from everywhere . . . we all stood up . . . then this— Jesus Christ, son . . . a rolling fucking fireball came tumbling down the corridor from the direction of the elevators . . . man, fuck . . . *fuck*."

"Everybody okay?"

He didn't answer for a moment. He was very pale. Tucked the tobacco with his tongue, sucked and spat.

"Yeah, yeah, I think so, son—I mean, at least nobody got bad hurt." We both looked up at the building with its fingers of smoke.

Firemen on ladders, firemen on foot (looking like some kind of weird undersea divers), firemen in windows, firemen in doors.

"I think we . . . all that fucking *work*, son."

"What?"

"The fire, son . . . shit, and the firemen I asked for a status report on our floor—it's fucked up there, son . . . we're going to be way behind . . . *way* behind."

"Our evidence, our files?"

"Uh, huh . . . There's only your personal files left."

"Only my personal files?"

"The computers, the computer banks, the files."

"But they're fireproof cabinets, right?"

"Fuck no, man, some of them maybe—but that's only if they're locked and sealed—there's shit spread all over that place, right now, son . . . the fire captain took a video for me . . . you want to see it?"

"Only my personal files?"

"The ones you left with your friend, yes."

I almost laughed. Believe me, I very nearly almost did. But I thought that I would cry if I did. I must have turned a lighter shade of pale, because Frenchy reached out and touched my arm.

"You okay, son?"

"Hmm?"

"You okay?"

"Just thinking, man, just thinking . . . look man, I'm going to desert you a minute . . . you staying right here?"

"Yeah . . . I hurt like a son of a bitch right now . . . I'll just sit here . . . you okay? Where you going?"

"I'm fine, fine, yeah, don't worry—I'll be right back."

I KNEW how it would happen next; there will be a call from the Feds, the F.B.I.; they would have received a tip—that possible terrorist action may have been involved . . . the ATF and military specialists will be called in to take over the investigation, to go over the building. They will lock it down tight and proceed with the investigation. That fucking station and everything in it was about to become a crime scene, closed to the public.

The "letter writer" case was as of this moment about to become inoperable: at least six months to rework all the evidence spread over—what, eight states, nine states? . . . redo all the interviews and lab reports, the trail would be nice and cold by then, like as in fucking *ice*.

And I had the only set of files. I could only laugh . . . nervously.

" . . . *You don't know what we can see, why don't you tell your dreams to me . . . close your eyes girl, look inside girl, let the sun take you away . . . you don't know what we can find, why don't you come with me little girl on a magic carpet ride . . .*" Me and Steppenwolf on the fucking trip of a lifetime . . . I might as well have taken some bad fucking acid.

PEACH FUZZ in a pale strawberry. She looked more statuesque today, that being possible? Valerie in a long blue overcoat.

Claud, blue eyes magnetic, sauntered up the hill. From here they could see the smoke in the distance.

"Fire fire burning bright, in the forests of the night."

"I was supposed to be here yesterday."

"Yes, darling, you were . . . god, you are tall, my lady." She smiled.

"Statuesque, positively." Claud continued. "Do you like my handiwork?" He waved a hand to indicate the smoke in the distance. "I got a rolling fireball going, I understand."

"You truly are talented, no . . . I am very sorry that I missed it fully . . . what is our story, have you been briefed?"

"Yes . . . one of the federals sat with me this morning."

"And?"

"They believe that Neathersole has gone under in Florida . . . they are running association checks—at least they were when I last saw them . . . what are the orders?"

"We are on the clean-up . . . Neathersole, and . . . well, perhaps others."

"Your friend the detective, perhaps?"

"Perhaps . . . his girlfriend maybe?"

"I saw her file . . . ah, would you look at that smoke . . . a bloody masterpiece eh? Darling, shall we go."

"Where are the others?"

"Setting up for us."

I AM, I would say in a word, panicked. I cannot find my Claire—I am freaked, things seem to be happening fast now.

I am at the edge of the crowd, smoking. It is Leeman who finds me; his left hand is bandaged in still white gauze and his pants are all soiled in the front. He smells not too sweetly. His eyes are very red.

"Hey."

"Yes."

"You doing okay?"

"Yes."

"What's up?"

"I just am getting away . . . you did miss de fun, man . . . I never get de number on yu friend . . . sorry."

"I'll get it, don't worry . . . what else?"

"Frenchy going 'ome—he did want to make sure you was all right."

"I'm cool . . . cool . . . staying close to a phone, that's all."

"Good . . . I be going home too."

"Yes."

When he was gone I tried the phone again. No Claire. So I dialed a number in Boca, a friend, a police friend . . . he would do a search for me on Humpty . . . I explained a little of the situation, he asked me to give him an hour.

I would go and get comfortably numb. I bought a "Q" and went back to my hotel. The room was dark and cool, I was white and hot, dusty and tired. I poured a tall rum and dialed the phone.

"I hate this fucking machine . . . puss, I am at the hotel, must talk to you . . . you've got the room number."

I light another cigarette, sitting back in the dark; let the demons roam where they will. I feel an urge to be on the beach, within the sound of the surf. Do you really wanna hurt me . . . my demons are here in the dark with me, but I am not afraid of them, they are mine . . . it is the demons that are unclear that worry me. I finger my turtle shell and smoke heavily, chase it down with a cold shot of rum.

I put my bag on the bed. I remove the two guns, I remove my shirt . . . the .38, I check the cylinder, check the load of the rounds; Glazier, hollow point, hollow, glazier, hollow, hollow. The .380 and two magazine clips. I chamber a round, slip the weapon back into its holster.

I try Bugsy's number. "Hello." Miles away and she sounding so very close.

"Bugsy?"

"*C'est moi . . .*" I warm instantly, the demons retreat into the shadows. " . . . Ohhh, it's you, how are you, sweetie? . . . Oh god, I miss you already, Thomas . . . are you okay?"

"Lost . . . I . . . well, me and my demons are sitting here in the dark, we're doin' some drinking and smoking . . . I'm . . . lonely . . . I . . . Have you seen Claire today?"

"She had like a meeting or something to go to in town . . . are you okay, really? . . . you sound . . . well, you sound kinda fucked up, you know."

I didn't need to tell her, so I didn't. "Aaahh, just a little sadly that's all . . . that's all . . . where's your mom tonight?" I chase the rum. Pour another.

"She left for Washington, this morning . . . she's got a, an NAACP banquet, I think . . . when are you coming back?" I hear the warmth in her voice and it drags me under. Sometimes people just make a connection, yeah and then what, what do you do, what do you say? Do they feel it too, is it the same feeling? It feels so nice you don't want to take the chance that it's just lust. The feeling is so . . . so aerated.

I wanted to dive down the line between us, to see into her eyes, warm myself by the glow of her soul. My pores opened wide and I could feel each particle of the air on my flesh, I became one large gland, smelt every changing odor in the air, tasted the flavors of the night. Blood pumped my heart into my ears. I am alive in liquor.

"Do you love Claire?"

"Yes." I didn't hesitate. "Yes."

"Will you come here soon? She wants this . . . she loves you too . . . I—I'd like it . . . come, just tell her you're coming and come . . . she wants you to come, I want you to come . . . can you handle it?"

"I always thought that it might matter, but it doesn't in the end . . . I just want to be happy. . . happy . . . I'm getting drunk."

"Drinking alone."

"It's been a fuck of a day."

"You want to tell me about it?"

"Not really, I want . . . I want to forget it ever fucking happened . . . have you heard from Claire at all?" There is ice in the glass, I suck a cube, spit it back. It rattles around the crystal.

"Something is worrying you, isn't it."

"Yes."

"What?"

"Premonitions, you can call it . . . I just want to know that she's all right—I . . ." I didn't know what else to say.

"I don't like the sound of this . . . are you going to tell me?"

"It wouldn't make any sense, I couldn't explain . . . really, just a feeling . . . nothing more than that."

"True?"

"True." *Lie!* I have paced the floor, phone in hand. I'm standing looking down on my least favorite chair.

It is shortly after that Frenchy calls. He doesn't sound much better. "Son . . . I uh, the guys from . . . from, fuck—do we still have an investigation going, son, *do* we?"

"Sort of . . . It's been a hell of a day; take it easy on yourself, man, do it slowly."

"Yeah . . . anyhow . . . ah—oh yeah, the guys from Congaree, from Eastover, they called, they flashed around them . . . them pictures of our stiffs, and sure 'nuff son, we got an ID . . . you were right, and they was both seen eating at the diner with a man, a bald man."

"A bald man . . . a lot of bald men in my day."

"What?"

"No . . . nothing really; you sound tired."

"I'm exhausted . . . dead tired . . ." I wasn't ready to tell him, besides he needed the rest . . . I needed the rest.

I had already fallen asleep when Claire called.

"Mmmm."

"You asleep, sweets?"

"Hmm . . . Claire?"

"Yeah, babes . . . how you doing? I miss you."

"Me too . . . are you okay?" My voice was a slow nasal gravel.

"Yeah."

"Where you been?" Sleep still fogging my brain . . . aargh.

"Publishers, then I had some things to research . . . you going to wake up?"

"Trying . . . trying . . . Claire . . . I think we have a problem."

"With what?"

"Our case . . . Atlanta had . . . had a fire today . . . I—a lot of stuff got burned . . . I have the only set of complete files, Claire."

"Do they know that?" Her voice broke.

"Do who?"

"The government."

"You know?"

"I guessed last night—you?"

"This morning . . . I've been trying to reach you ever since— Don't you have a beeper?"

"No."

"God . . . yak, my mouth tastes like shit . . . I got drunk to-night . . . I—I was worried about you . . . I think they know, Claire, I think they know . . . but they're probably not sure where . . . who did you call?"

"An old friend . . . three actually . . . what did you come up with? Fuck! I can't believe they burned the station . . . What?"

"Terrorist action, you know . . . then the F.B.I. will seal the building and begin an investigation."

"Yeah, and your case is at an end . . . except . . ."

"Uh huh, except for my files . . . I have a complete set of files, I have the case."

"I think I have a witness."

"I have a lot of bald people."

"What?"

"I have a lot of bald pros wandering arou—oh, shit, the girl, the fucking bald girl?"

"What girl?"

"Twice, this fucking bald—this tall, bald woman, once in . . . once in Atlanta, once in Ft. Lauderdale . . . she just *appeared*—twice." I shivered . . . I cold shook shivered, down to the core of my fucking bones.

"Fuck."

"They know . . . they *know*, then."

"They know, Claire . . . they . . . she knows, I could feel her—now I know . . . shit, babes, can you go somewhere? With Bugsy maybe?"

"You think they know about me?"

"I don't know . . . I—I don't know anything . . . *anything*." I wanted to cry out. "I love you, babes . . . god. Did you say you had a witness? . . . I've got to find Neathersole, Claire . . . Claire—I haven't told Frenchy . . . I—if we don't get hold of this . . ."

If I didn't get hold of this.

"Claire—they'll kill us . . . oh, god." The fucking fear was there—crystal sensation.

THE SAC Atlanta always drove the same way home, up Cheshire Bridge Road to Lenox and into Buckhead, where he lived on an oak-shaded lane in a white-on-wood little house with black shutters and a red brick fireplace set on a manicured green lawn fronted by beds of blooming perennials and a trellis entered path . . . A "Prep" fantasy in Technicolor truth; where the neighbors were all white and friendly, with cold fish hand shakes and salesmen smiles; wives with flat asses and aerobicized thighs, vegetarian diets, adventure holidays, rollerblading, mountain biking and pent-up libidos.

A tidy fucking life in need of a shakeup.

His name is Clifford. Clifford drives an old Volvo. His wife takes the convertible Saab. She likes to have her pussy sucked in the front seat by her 15-year-old son's best friend, Edward; "Edward silver tongue", she calls him. She is 42. It is the cold leather on her naked ass that really butters her twat.

Clifford doesn't take notice of the semi-trailer truck cresting the hill, traveling a little fast. The car in front of him seems to have stalled. He reaches out to tune the radio and then the truck fills his vision.

CLAUD AND Valerie sitting in a car, d r i v i n g.

Phone rings.

"Where's the subject?" It's on the hands-free phone."Do you have the subject in sight?"

"Yes."

"We are in his office . . . certain papers are . . . seem to be unaccounted for . . . we, we need to know where these papers are."

"You need to know, as in you wish to ask him . . . is that it, mate?" He looks at Valerie, makes a shrug, attaches a smile.

"In a word yes."

"No, in a word, Late! . . . if you need to talk to him you'll have to do it through god . . . he's little bits of flesh in the tread of a rather large tire right now." Claud breaks the transmission. "Asshole. I could smoke a cigar now . . . shall we go for a cigar, dahlink?"

IT WAS an hour later and Claire and I were still on the phone; we had drifted from one conversation to another . . . God how I crave to be near her; her absence is palpable, it is a bad taste on my tongue, talking to her alleviates but doesn't really satisfy. I want this woman and I realize that all avoidances aside, I have always, from the moment I met her, wanted to be near her. The further I ran away the more I wanted to get closer.

Who the fuck knows how we choose one another in our lives, fate or circumstance . . . I don't know if you call it instant love, instant rapport maybe, but you get a feel for that person the minute you breathe in that first fragrance of their being. That first time that I stood next to Claire, looked at her sideways, out the corner of my eye, I knew something was up. The second time I saw her, heard her laugh, saw her smile, the odor of her breath, the pliant feel of her flesh when I touched her hand.

I went to find her the next day . . . to see her again . . . you know, you always remember the first time you meet someone who strikes you, but in all the years Claire and I have known one another I can clearly recall every time I laid eyes on her . . . the first, the second, the third . . . god, how I crave her . . . if, I weren't such an asshole . . . *if* is a big word.

"I want to be with you."

"Are you still drunk?"

"I'm within the sound of your voice . . . I want to be in reach of your lips . . . shit . . . I'm sitting here running the slide show of our time together; I remember it all so clearly . . . I, I don't know what to do . . . I am so, so very, very . . . unsure of some of it—Christ I love you—what the fuck am I saying?   I don't know, I'm going crazy all of a sudden, talking fucking gibberish, god, all I know is that since I've been away it's been hell . . . *hell.*"

I ran away with myself there for a moment.   Take a deep breath, light a cigarette. I felt on the edge of welling passion. I inhaled deeply, draw that fucking smoke in, boy.

"God . . . Claire . . . what the fuck am I going to do . . . shit, will you marry me?"

"What?"

"Fuck, when this is all over with will you marry me—will you be with me will you love me care for me be with me, Jesus . . . will you marry me, Claire, it is archaic I know . . . *passé, non plus,* but it's the ultimate gift of love . . . giving of yourself—it's the ultimate . . . god, is this heavy or what, but shit, I just *want* you."

"Holy shit." And suddenly I realized that she was crying.

That in this fucking world of complete and total madness, where we were as close to being dead as two people can be without actually being slaughtered, that something nice had just happened, something soft, sweet, kind, gentle . . . love had occurred, blatant and furious, full of all the passion and vibrance that life could muster.

"Holy shit . . . god, look at me, I'm crying my fucking eyes out . . . yes, you miserable shit . . . oh fuck . . . yes, Christ *yes*— I'll marry you. . . I—I, no, I never thought that I would hear you say those words to me, I thought—I thought that I was going to have to do it all . . . I thought, oh shit —I don't know what I thought—yes, god, why aren't you *here* so I could kiss you—I want to *kiss* you, I'm crying all over myself, oh *Christ*."

And suddenly I realized that I was crying too. That it was all worthwhile.

Whatever sacrifice I made now would be more than worth it.

That god did indeed love me.

That I did indeed love Claire.

That Claire loved me.

Fuck them all, I thought, I am fucking happy now, fuck them, fuck them *fuck them* FUCK THEM! I lit another cigarette.

I WOULD have to call Frenchy and tell him; I would have to call Boom Boom and tell him; I would have to find Neathersole and get what he had. Claire would contact her sources; we would build a screen that they couldn't get through. A fucking steel screen behind which we'd all be safe.

"I love you babes . . . babes, I want you to go to somewhere, away from the house, okay . . . go and I will find you tomorrow, I think we have enough to hold them off of us for a moment, maybe, but take the things and go now—go *now* and . . . and tomorrow we . . . tomorrow, I'll come for you . . . can you do that? . . . I think we have some time."

"Are they listening on your line?"

"Probably . . . probably they are . . . but I don't know. Call your Fed friend, puss . . . we need that inside line. God, I can't think like this, all the fuck I want to do is come to you, I'm a mess, Jesus Christ . . . I'm a total fucking mess . . . I have to call Frenchy . . . I have to get him on line . . . clue him in. Are you going to be okay?"

"I'm going to be okay . . . you watch yourself, now that I've finally caught you . . . Jesus, Tommy, we're going to be happy. . ."

"Baby, we're going to be fucking ecstatic, live a life filled with all the possible joy that the world can hold, I will call your name out to everyone I meet and tell them how fucking wonderful my wife is." I laughed a little laugh. She is my joy, even now she is my joy.

She is my joy—and that is the really important factor here. I have known too much pain, I think, seen too much agony. Perhaps . . . not perhaps, truly, I have loved a time or two, badly . . . I have loved badly. Or love has left me badly . . . From the very first time that it really truly madly deeply happened.

THE FIRST time that it truly madly deeply happened, sitting on a hillside of bright white limestone, in a less than romantic locale. The two of us close enough to have been one. I told her how I felt, called her by the name of love, my longings screamed through my brain and out my mouth.

Her face was coffee perfect in its youthfulness, god she was beautiful in all that sunlight. We had grown together and I was older than her. At 15 she spoke to me like a woman would; I was 18 and sad. Her hair was black, her eyes were dark, her mouth was pink sex.

When eventually I had to leave her I nearly died of a broken heart.

THE LAST time . . . shit, the last time, you often wonder if you're not supposed to get used to it all . . . get used to the pain. It took me a long time after the first time to do it again. But I still carried the scars. I carry the scars of the last one like badges; my boy scout survival patches.

The last time.

I loved on an island once and she left me. My life has been full of leaving; leaving until my senses left me. I loved on a limestone mountain first, and on a deserting island last, hardly in between and never since.

Till now, and I let this love grow out of a friendship.

CLAIRE, Claire, every time I call your name . . . every time I call your name I hear god whisper it back to me on gentle breath.

IT WAS THE middle of another night, on which I couldn't sleep . . . there was nothing for it . . . love, fear, pain, confusion all bouncing around my head. I was living somewhere between doubt and indecision. So I went out and drank bad coffee and smoked strong cigarettes till the sun came up.

Daylight is an assault. I have forgotten my dark glasses. I am shuffle and squint as I walk the street. I call Frenchy's cell phone.

"What, what, we got work today son, what the fuck we gonna work on today? . . . I want sleep."

"Frenchy, Frenchy, listen to me, are you awake, are you awake? . . . The Feds done it . . . the killings, the *Feds done it*." It kind of blurted out.

"The Feds . . . are you nuts?" He sounded a little more awake.

"Yes . . . yes, look—I've confirmed it . . . Frenchy, I'm going back to the sources now . . . the fucking Feds did it, I'm sure, I don't know why yet . . . well that's kind of a lie, I think I know why."

"Wait, wait, wait let me get my thinking cap on, son, this, this is too fucking much too quick . . . hold it, okay . . . I need to piss, I need to wash my face . . . I need—shit, you sound like shit, by the way—just wait . . . okay?"

"I've been up all night." But he was gone by then. I adjusted the gun in my ankle holster, unused to it; it bothered me.

And then he was back. "Sorry, son, but I couldn't think . . . I . . . man, relief . . . okay, okay, so you said the Feds did it, right? Right, and you think you know why . . . so why, why?"

"Spies, I think . . . I think that they were spies, Frenchy . . . look, their diversity, the fact that they were all so completely dissimilar and the fact that the Feds did them . . . it's the only fucking solution . . . the only solution."

"Dissimilar . . . big words so early in the morning . . . my burns hurt, shit my head hurts . . . spies? Isn't the cold war over, son?" He still was unsure of my mind.

"Yes . . . that means that there are leftovers to take care of— you ever see a movie called, ahm, ahm, what was it . . ." fiddle the fingers, they're tied to the brain. "Ahm, yes, 'Telefon' . . . with—Charles Bronson. Deep cover, trigger agents, Russians . . . and this, this recent shit with the American deep-cover agents in Russia, discovered and executed . . . well, let's just suppose that there's been a transfer of information . . . Deep covers that cannot be recalled . . . so they have to be eliminated . . . shit, I don't know, I don't know . . . I just don't fucking know, but they are most definitely spies. I bet."

"Where are you? You're making me nervous . . . you are fucking making me nervous, son. I want to take this with a fucking grain of salt, but you're making it sound real time."

"Frenchy, it is real time, man . . . we're waiting on an affirmative from more than one source."

"Shitshitshit . . . fuck, look, where are you, son? I'm going to get dressed now—dressed, yes, not going to bathe, just dress, where can I meet you?"

"Just meet me by the MARTA in downtown, we'll go out to Fort McPherson . . . I have a call to make . . . Frenchy, start your car carefully."

"You been watching too many movies, son. Oh, yeah, I got something for you, man, your friend Humpty Dumpty, you want me to fax this to you?"

"No . . . no office, remember? Just read it to me, I'll write it down." The gun was on the inside of my left ankle, chafing my skin.

There was no one at Humpty's . . . no answering machine, just a ringing fucking phone. A ringing in my ear.

Frenchy called out, "Yo." He looked pale.

I set down the pay phone. "No bomb."

"No bomb . . . I made some calls . . . get in, get in, I made some calls, guess who showed up dead this morning . . . don't try to guess, the SAC Atlanta, F.B.I.'s top man in town, he wasn't one of your sources, was he?" Like he had a secret to tell, animated now.

"Fuck . . ."

"Yeah fuck, the Feds also sealed off our station, terrorist activity suspected . . . Terrorists, in Atlanta . . . man, we are in too deep, so what have we got that we can carry to the top? We have to have something . . . something."

"You haven't told anyone, then?"

"Not yet . . . should I, you think?"

"Yes . . . call Leeman, tell him, put it on the fucking wire, what we're looking for, we're looking for a possible ring of Soviet assassins, who may have come into the country to clean up some cold war leftovers . . . we should contact Interpol and give them the descriptions of the woman you and I met, the descriptions we're going to get from my friend at the Fort . . . where's Leeman working out of?"

"Wait, wait, wait . . . Interpol, Russians? I thought our guys were doing this, isn't that what you said, son?"

"Yes . . . and you want to open your mouth wide and say those words . . . out loud? Huh, how long do you think we would all live free and prosper . . . no, my friend, we have to let them know that we know, but give them a way out, a back door. . ."

"So who do we bust . . . who pays?"

"We feed them to themselves, we prove it and we feed the fuckers to themselves, let them clean shop and blame it on who- ever they want, that's the only way that it's going to happen ."

"Your way or the highway . . . I dig what you mean, son . . . fuck, give me one of those cigarettes . . . can we stop for coffee, I'll call Leeman . . . he's working out of Midtown, the whole team's moving in there today . . . F.B.I.'s got our files, what's left of them . . . hey, but you got your files."

"I'm going to Charleston."

"Do you think they know, son?"

"Fuck—I hope not man, I fucking hope not." The cigarette was nuclear hot in my lips. "So they've wiped out their own Special Agent, huh . . . House cleaning, the fucks . . . you've never been there, have ya, French? . . . You'd better call Leeman now . . . tell him to make a splash about the search, let 'em know what we're thinking . . . it'll get the COINTELPRO boys feeling good and they may even help us into the right direction, they'll probably give up the names and description of our perps, the wet team."

"Wet team —COINTELPRO, that what you all call killers?"

"That's what the Agency calls their 00 boys, their James Bonds . . . The COINTELPRO is information dissimilation, counter intelligence, tactical and propaganda espionage . . . Do I look as lousy as I feel? I need a wash up . . . fuck, I am tired . . . damn, this gun is killing me."

"You're carrying, son? . . . You are wearing a *gun*?"

"Two."

"*Fuck* . . . can I have a cigarette now? . . . this coffee is awful. You're carrying? . . . We're fucking *dead* . . . was it you who chose Denny's for coffee?" I smoke, Frenchy smokes, anything to cut the taste of the coffee. I need a shave, my face itches.

"No, it was you, put a lot of milk in it . . . god, my eyes feel like they're full of sand . . . are you going to call Leeman? It's nearly 8:30."

"Jesus . . . I can't believe you're carrying . . . shitshit*shit*."

31

Another dead body and not a soul in sight.

If you don't run faster, you'll get left behind . . . and then who'll tidy up my death?

You've been absolute darlings.

TaTa, write soon. Pardon the mess, but this one bled rather profusely.

—GBM #12

WELL WE ALL need some one we can bleed on, and if you want to baby, you can bleed on me . . .", Mick the lips, "Lean on me", a new mix on the radio, sounding more Southern Delta than ever before. The cruise control was on and I was only half awake; I would have to stop soon. Charleston had never seemed quite so far away.

" . . . *Solamente para mi, un besito para mi . . .*" Salsa, hot, live, *vivo*, del Nuevo Palladium, en Hialeah . . . Los Hermanos Rosaro. Miami airport—and I had Bugsy and Claire with me; Michael had gone to his mother. Jesus was the name of the taxi driver. Fuck Charleston, it just wouldn't have been safe. Jesus hailed from the Dominican Republic. On the move, throw the scent, if they were looking for one; Bugsy had booked the tickets —we were not untraceable, just a little harder to find. Jesus spoke little good English, my Spanish was sadly rudimentary. I had the files with us; this had been a snap decision . . . the minute Claire had told me that the dead Clifford was her waiting-in-the-wings witness. If they killed Clifford they'd kill us—no problem.

Jesus had been born in a small coastal town called Enriquillo, on the south coast of Hispaniola. He had fished off Isla Beata in his youth many a time, he said.

That was where I had caught my first marlin, just to the south. Not overly large, but blue and beautiful, around 200 pounds. I was . . . I was about 12, I think . . . some things I don't recall, but I'll never forget the feel of the strike, and how my heart raced away from me in its disbelief. I will dream forever about the first leap, when he broke the shining surface of the sea and danced a samba on his tail, the silver and blue of his flesh was lure-like, looking clearly unreal. I will remember the absolute deadness of the beast when we hung him from the scale; my pride didn't take notice, but later my conscience cried out its anguish. And I felt sad.

Felt sad, much as I do now; and I shouldn't, sandwiched as I am between—between joy and lust, Claire and Bugsy. They both turn to look at me and smile. We are 15th-Street bound, northeast; a friend has an apartment; I cannot go north to home, that would be unsafe.

Clifford had mentioned Miami to Claire; Neathersole was here somewhere, he had chosen to go under here for a reason. It wasn't Atlanta. The climate was safer. The weather better. Do I need to give any more reasons why I came? If it was going to happen it was going to happen here. I was wearing the .380 Browning . . . I had special permits to carry on the airplane.

I remember that we ate marlin for weeks after my catch; smoked, barbecued, battered and fried in cubes. We were fishing out of Montego Bay, Jamaica at the time . . . it was beautiful in those days . . . lush, secluded, peaceful . . . today it is a cesspool, its previous charm lost to pursuit of the nocuous. We all stayed in a low Spanish tiled house, with wide-shaded verandahs, and airy rooms on Brandon hill, overlooking the harbor over the tin roofs of the town. Reading was visible on the point. The house had belonged to a man that Grandpa knew . . . the man's family had hailed from Portugal in some time long forgotten. We always holidayed in groups of friends, staying together.

I had left a message on the jungle telegraph for Neathersole; they would let him know I was coming.

"SOMEBODY ran a locate on a man by the name of Humpty Dumpty Herman . . ." Blue eyed Claud was holding the phone just above the hook, an unlit cigar in the fingers of his right hand. He set down the phone and ran a hand up the back of his head. "He's an associate of Neathersole's . . . He's in Miami."

"Neathersole?"

"That is what they believe."

The F.B.I. has some talents that are truly remarkable. That they can turn the seemingly innocuous into the useful; that they can turn a charred piece of metal into a Ryder van rented by terrorists from New Jersey in just short days; that they can take an obscure computer-driven trace on a guy in Florida and turn it into the fugitive of their desires . . . the knowledge and com- puter-generated power that they have at their disposal, and the ability to monitor and decipher it all, is absolutely incredible. They are at their basest a brilliant feat of human endeavor; that they fuck themselves in the mire of their own government-ness is the only pity.

"Have they found the girl . . . the woman, Claire?"

"No . . . and he's gone too, your friend."

"You think she has the missing paperwork?"

"They think that she might."

"It would be better if they just did that sanction in Miami and walked away fast . . . Christ, this becomes a mess, no?"

"Can I smoke this?" He held up the cigar.

"It won't kill me . . . we're leaving soon anyway, no? He will be there, too, I think; we'll find my friend in Miami."

"Yes . . . yes, I am quite sure that we will; he will go to Neathersole . . ."

"You think Neathersole has found us?"

"Quite probably, he ran rather suddenly—anyhow, they have an interdiction team getting ready to move in, we'll lock them all down shortly, tidy up and go back home . . . are you packed yet?"

"Standing by."

"They have a plane for us at Hartsfield."

FRENCHY AND Dixie were stuck in Atlanta, where the weather had gone to shit. Today they were working with the sketch artists; it wasn't like in the old days—you did it by computer, no sketches. Laser disc high definition picture images of thousands of possible facial parts, head shapes, eye color and type, hair, ears, mouths—all photographic quality. The computer's coalitive conception of the various parts was held in an inset box in the corner of the screen, to be viewed as a continuous process. When the whole image was combined it could then be fine-tuned as a unit, as you looked at a real image. The result was a picture postcard, far superior to the pen and ink amalgams that used to pass for witness-generated perp sketches. Modern technology makes my dick hard.

The lady is a lesbian, Melissa, she said she had introduced our Number Nine to a tall and oh-so-elegant bald woman: Frenchy's and my woman, Valerie of the long leg—whom she had met a week earlier at a local club. She gave a good description; my memory of her was clouded by sexual imagery; Frenchy had a clear grasp.

Boom Boom had been reluctant; we offered to keep his participation out of it. I had explained our situation, my predicament . . . we needed his descriptions. He gave them finally, and a name to go with one: The name was Doug.

The word went down the line with the pictures to the F.B.I., Interpol, M.I.5, Surete and others . . . Atlanta was looking for Spy vs. Spy . . . possible Soviet agents running rampant.

"LET ME SEE, let me see, come on, Claud . . . god, I am going to frame this—Christ, it *does* really look like me." Valerie snatched the picture from Claud: A Ted Turner-colorized version of herself. They had received the computer color copies in flight. They had also received confirmation that Atlanta was searching for Soviets . . . spies, maximum security, top level, eyes only, not for general release.

"Your friend is good . . . man, would you look at this picture of Douglas . . . computers are absolutely amazing . . . absolutely; they have Douglas' name, they will do an associate search, I am sure that M.I.6 has him on file . . . your friend is good, darling." Claud held out the other photos for Valerie as they got to the top of the plane's steps.

"We'll have to tell her . . ." She being the cat's mother, of course. "She'll probably do Number 12 anyhow, but maybe we'd better move up the schedule."

"Amazing . . . amazing." And then he stopped in his tracks in front of a long large elongated turtle-shaped Chevy Caprice Classic. "I am not driving *that*—hello, excuse me, agent . . . what is your name, mate?"

"You may call me Frank, sir."

"Well, Frank, can I be frank with you . . . is *this* our car?" "This" was venom spat at the young man.

"This is your car, sir, yes."

"No, no; this is *your* car, Frank . . . now you run along and find me something I can really drive . . . fuck off now, and hurry—we have work to do . . . something German, Frank . . . something *German*."

THE MEANING of it all, like those Menier stones arranged in their three neat rows by people some 4000 years ago on the island of Corsica, is a mystery to me. I walk out onto the small balcony which overlooks the Miami Herald building and a piece of Biscayne Bay at the Venetian Causeway. It would be a nice view but for the radio tower. Modernity can be so obtrusively grotesque. I can see the cruise ship port. Evening is rushing in on us. I am lost on what to do next. So I smoke; the cigarette is to soothe.

"You want a drink?"

Bugsy stands in the doorway looking tired. She had not wanted to stay alone in Folly. She is askew and yet lovely to look at.   I raised my arm and she came under it; I hugged her close to me, she pressed her face to my chest, then looked up at my face.

"You look worried."

"Tired," with a large sigh. "I wish it would all end . . . I need to call Frenchy . . . you know, that drink would be a marvelous idea . . . Claire, what ya doing?"

"Fixing a snack. You two look lovely, we should go to the beach tomorrow, people always look so much better with sun . . . kiss her, kiss her."

Bugsy's lips were soft and warm, her breath tasted of cheese. Her fingers ran up through the back of my hair, cold electricity followed her touch. It wasn't long or deep, just soft and wet. Her eyes were moist when she opened them.

32

THOMAS IS soft on the system, easy on the eyes. Long and slim; he smokes like a chimney. A foggy haze seems to follow him through life. Yet I have seen him run three miles. He likes khaki pants and large cotton shirts. Sometimes he is so handsome, his long hair swept back, his shirt open and his chest all tanned. His bare feet are perfect . . . god, I can laugh at myself for my perceptions . . . his feet actually excite me almost as much as the turn of his hands.

He speaks often of his past; there is a longing for the life he left behind. Thomas, born of the islands. I think perhaps he would prefer to be sailing along on a sweet breeze over a sea of Caribbean blue, no destination in mind. But he has chosen to work at a complete opposite to his nature. The challenge is for his mind.

A mind can be a beautiful thing. He spoke to me the other day of life and love; the strength of his voice, the quickness of his mind, the hands gesticulating a point . . .

I am an avid listener, anxious to hear him say the word . . . cock.

MORNING IS broken, barely. It is just a hint of gray on the six o'clock horizon. The air conditioning is on. I open the sliding doors, feel the real thing. The day is yet fresh; Florida is perfect at this time of year. Half in, half out, half dressed. My chest is naked.

" . . . *Making love in the afternoon, with Cecilia up in my bedroom, I got up to wash my face, I come back, someone's taken my place . . . Jubilation, she loves me again, I fall on the floor and I'm laughing.*" The kettle is boiling; Simon and Garfunkel are on the radio. The girls are sleeping. I love mornings. I open the bedroom door to look at them. Bugsy is splayed out on her stomach, Claire is curled on her side, a hand resting outstretched on Bugsy's back.

It is a "triple play" day and Simon and Garfunkel follow Simon and Garfunkel on the radio. " . . . *and I'm laying out my winter clothes and wishing I were warm . . . In the clearing stands a boxer and a fighter by his trade . . . I am leaving I am leaving, but the fighter still remains . . . Li li li, li li li lala la liii . . . .*" They are both so peaceful, beautiful. I pull the door softly closed, go to settle the kettle, brew the coffee.

The apartment is not large, but well-appointed; a one-bedroom, one-and-a-half bath, a large enough kitchen for its size; bathroom is luxurious, with Jacuzzi tub and separate shower, marble everywhere. From the patio you overlook the pool and the bay; there's a table out there, wrought iron and inlaid glass. It had come from Trinidad . . . it is a beautiful spot for breakfast. The dining table is round mahogany, it had belonged to Mark's grandmother. Mark . . . we had known one another from childhood, it was he and I who had sailed up the Bahamas in—1959, was it? I think so, yes . . . Mark still lives on the farm at home, has a wife, four children, six dogs, two cats and enough cows to feed the land. He has a string of beautiful horses and plays a flat stick game of polo. At 52, he may well be close to the top of his form, playing at a five-goal international handicap. I have missed his handsome face framed in waves of dull blond locks.

Friends are such a precious commodity. . . the most substantial thing that you can say about yourself is the quality of the friends that keep you company through this fucking life. He has the most wonderful blue eyes, just like his mother had.

The kitchen is immaculate and filled with glistening technology. The maid still comes in once a week to clean and water the plants. The apartment kept at ready. "*. . . Just the way her* *hair fell down around her face and I recall my fall from grace, oh yeah another time, another place."* If Mark Knopfler can play a guitar! Dire Straits. And I stand over the bed looking down at them sleeping. I envy them their peace.

I have no peace; I am not sure that I ever have. No—that's not true, there was that time once when I was really happy, but it didn't last.

I think I am happy now.

At least I will be if I live through this.

If I live through this I don't think anything will make me sad again. I have seen too much death this trip. Leaning on the railing I drop the cigarette; I've already replaced it with another. My fingernails need cutting; I have bruised a knuckle and don't remember how. I've often wondered what a professional manicure would feel like . . . but being a real man, I have never had one.

The coffee cup has an old lithograph print of elongated horses and misshapen men playing a chukker. I am unbalanced still . . . the lade of my burden, heavy and akilter . . . my mind moves so fast from one thing to another that I am dizzy and cannot think.

I am in love.

I am in pain.

I am in confusion.

The coffee is not as good as Claire's, but still . . .

". . . Lovestruck Romeo . . . when you exploded into my heart . . . and I dream your dream for you . . . when are you gonna realize that it was just that the time was wrong . . ."

The time was wrong. I remember old lovers, a parade of indistinct faces, I want to compare them to Claire . . . and yes, perhaps to Bugsy too, but I can no longer remember them properly. Even the few that have left their indelible marks on my entelechy are lost in a haze of past time. Their love is unclear, the reasons for my passion long lost. When I think in pink now, only this love comes to mind. It is hard to tell the difference between the weight of sadness and the pressure of love. I want to go back to the bed with them both.

"Morning." Claire, and she is naked. Her hair is on end, her face made up girlishly, her flesh covered in bed marks. "I missed you . . . what are you doing up so early?" We hugged warmly, she sat on my knee. "I'm tired."

"You're naked."

And then she smiled tiredly. Her flesh is warm. "Yes . . . yes . . . you like?"

"Yes I like, very much."

She kisses my forehead, pushing my hair back, her small breast is eye level. I kiss it. "Thank you . . . I need to brush my teeth . . . and pee . . . can I go pee?"

"Please do . . . I'll be right here . . . you want some juice? It's fresh squeezed."

"I know, I squeezed it . . . I feel like I'm on vacation . . . I'd love some." She scratches the back of her head, pauses to stretch, loudly, as she goes. She is my joy.

She says vacation, I say holiday, she says line, I say queue, she says deposit, I still say lodgement . . . I'm going to go make a lodgement at the bank . . . I'll go pour the juice now.

Bugsy is on her back arms out, eyes only part open. Her breasts are full, round, olive. She raises a hand for a little wave, smiles for me.

"Morning."

"Already."

"You want some juice too? It's fresh squeezed."

"Hmmm."

"That sounds like a yes."

"Hmmm," and she laughs for me.

SO THE LASCIVIOUS amongst you cry out, go deh dude! Get in— Get it on! But we have all just slept together, no sex, no penetration, no pussy for dr. dick. I am in need of getting used to. This is not my fantasy, even if it is yours. That I love these two women is evident to me; that that love manifests itself in different ways is clear; that they love me is true; that the situation is perhaps peculiar, is a possibility that really hasn't been dealt with. That the two of them care deeply about one another is sure. That we enjoy each other as much singularly as we do together I cannot deny . . . we are seemingly the perfect couple, tripled, if we look at it geometrically. So I pour Bugsy's juice.

I go to find Frenchy. I make the call from a pay phone at Bayside Marketplace. Sitting, I overlook the little harbor filled with sightseeing boats and floating garbage . . . the new Hard Rock Cafe looks empty across the way. I am on hold.

"Son, you have surfaced . . . why didn't y'all call me last night? . . . fuck . . . everything okay?"

"Everything's cool, French . . . cool . . ." I can feel the weight of the .38 on my ankle. "What's your story?"

"The computer sketches came out excellent— so good, in fact, that we sent them out yesterday morning to Interpol and got back a reply already . . . we got a positive on, on your girl-friend, uh, Valerie something . . . shit—where is that file, I know it's here somewhere . . . anyway, anyway, yeah and we got back a confirmation on the guy Doug that your buddy from the . . . that your buddy gave us.—*where* is that damn file? I swear, sometimes, son, I just don't know. Anyhow they're running it through associations, and the F.B.I. and Immigration here are working overtime on it—" A little laugh. "We're on a roll now son, on a roll, we got those cocksuckers looking for themselves— you think we'll catch these guys?"

"You think it really matters, Frenchy? . . . All we've got to do is prove they *exist* . . . there's shit else we *can* do . . . but if we prove they exist, and that they may well have done the crimes, then we can walk away . . . we can't catch them, French, we can't convict them . . . fuck, man, we can't even bring them down, probably . . . It's the government, French, if it's important enough they'll walk . . . it's you, me and our friends that are im-portant, Frenchy—you want to live past tomorrow, right? . . . I mean, man, right now you're okay, you've fed them what they want to hear . . . me . . . and Claire . . . we're out here in the cold still . . . with the files."

"Files . . . files, oh shit . . . my fucking head's up my ass— freaked to the max, son . . . these guys . . . I wanna *catch* these fucks, Tommy, I don't give a fuck what you say, I wanna catch these fucks and make them suffer, fuck, *fuck*—fuck, files, shit . . .

fucks and make them suffer, fuck, *fuck*—fuck, files, shit . . . sorry, anyhow, I'm just fucking angry, I can't believe you said what you said, son . . . these guys are going to fucking kill again, you know that, right, kill some poor fuck horribly just because they want to cover up the purpose of their actions . . . fuck, man, that is sick, they deserve to fucking fry—you help me to fry them, Tommy . . . fuck knows, we gotta do this son, we *gotta* do this."

"Cool man, cool—I understand, French, I understand, man, but we gotta survive this shit first . . . they're half looking for me right now, you can bet . . ." I am smoking my third cigarette in a row.

" . . . A target of opportunity, they'll call me, French. Maybe, maybe they're concentrating on Claire, and probably Neathersole, he wouldn't have gone under otherwise . . . he's got something and they're going to want to make sure that he doesn't give it up; if they killed the SAC then they know about his conversation with Claire."

"Stop, stop—before I go off again . . . files, son, files—look, I was over at the other station yesterday . . . It was probably for my benefit, but I overheard some Feebies talking, they're tying the SAC to this so-called terrorist action . . . he's a mole, I guess—anyhow, they also said that some files are missing from his office, Blue cover files . . . it could be just a ruse, a herring, but but, well, a lie told with a touch of truth is always the best way, right? . . . .You get where I'm coming from, right, son? I mean, you called me before you left Charleston and told me that this Clifford was going to give Claire something concrete, right? The files son, the files—so where are the files?"

"Fuck!" Clifford had prepared himself for Claire. He had stolen files, shit, shit, we were free . . . we were safe . . . where were the fucking files? Claire would know . . . wouldn't she?

33

THEY WERE both on the patio. I could smell fresh croissants, god, I love fresh croissants, coffee and jam. Just look at them both.

I am suddenly the happiest man on earth; my heart feels like it is pressing against the confines of its home, wanting to break free, to roam the possibilities of loves. One is dark and pale, the other is light and tan . . . one slim and muscled, the other full of her womanness. They turn and smile at me; Claire's head is tilted just so as she looks at me. There is moisture in her eyes. They are backlit, both, by early day.

"I have news—I have good news—reality invades, yes, but in a good way." I twirl the dark glasses.

"Vacation over?"

"Yes . . . Clifford stole some files; the Feebies are looking for them, they probably presume you've got them, they're probably right, but you just don't know it yet."

"Clifford sent me files? Clifford—poor Cliff . . . standard procedure, right, when you're out in the cold, right? Send it to an associate, not a friend, an associate that your recipient has contact with, right? Oh, Cliffy . . . shit . . . My publisher, he'd send it to my publisher . . . He'd send it to Jane."

"Jane the publisher—call Jane . . . call her, but not from here—We'll call her from the outside."

"What are you guys rambling on about? . . . the mind just boggles . . . It's like Spy vs. Spy in here . . . shoot," and then she laughed, Bugsy brown-eyed and beautiful, so full of life.

We look at her blankly, not realizing what she finds so funny. "Sorry, sorry . . . it's just that it's like an episode from Scarecrow and Mrs. King."

We are being compared to bad television.

"We are not amused." I make a face, all the tension of our situation is gone, it is like we are . . . on yes, holiday, and we laugh together. We are safe.

I think.

CLAIRE is in the shower, Bugsy is on the toilet, singing to something on the radio.

"Ow—that's cold . . ."

"Pass me the lotion."

"Okay."

"Are you two fighting?" I come to the door. Actually, they kiss quickly, a lip smacking. They are having fun.

"Claire dripped water on me, the bitch."

She sets down the Elle magazine, unfurling toilet paper . . . wipe front to back . . . not once but twice.

" . . . *I get so lost sometimes . . . and the emptiness fills my heart . . . but whichever way I look I come back to the place where you are . . . in your eyes, the light the heat, I am complete . . . I see the doorway to a thousand churches . . . the resolution of all the fruitless searches . . .*" Peter Gabriel plays.

I reach out . . . for the volume on the radio. It is a mini-rack system. It is built into the bathroom wall; Mark always appreciated his music. I have come to realize that although I really love music, I can only hear its beauty and don't distinguish its subtleties . . . I may have told you that already . . . you get old, you tend to forget shit —talking of which, where's my watch?

"You owe me a shave, babes." Claire calls over the rainfall of the shower.

"I love this song." Bugsy stands and flushes. This is Florida; the water in the shower does not lose its acclimation.

" . . . *Love, I don't like to see so much pain . . . so much wasted, and this moment keeps slipping away . . . I look to my time with you to keep me awake and alive . . . and all my instincts they return . . . without a noise—without my pride—I reach out from the inside . . . In your eyes . . .*" The song . . . it is perfect—my emotions are afferent, welling, every fucking time I hear it.

"You're buttoning badly . . . look—you missed one, wait." Naked on legs of tan she walks to me. Her pubis is golden, a shade darker than the hair on her head, the color of corn tassels. "You're a mess, aren't you." She buttons me. Then on tiptoe she kisses my cheek.

" . . . *In your eyes, the light the heat, I am complete . . . I see the doorway to a thousand churches . . . the resolution of all the fruitless searches . . .*"

I take her face. I touch it between my hands, I feel its warmth, its pliancy, its life . . . I can feel the life breathing through it. And I kiss her lips softly. I close my eyes as I do. You only watch when it's rude; when it's love, you close your eyes. Her hands circle my back and we turn to face ourselves. We kiss. Her hands touch the flesh of my back. We kiss. I feel her hair, soft, fragrant. We kiss.

There are other hands on my back. I turn. It is Claire. She is wet. She is naked on legs of freckled cream. My fingers touch Bugsy's cheek, contact. I turn to kiss Claire. Claire who is so . . . she is the resolution of all my fruitless searches. Her eyes are full of her mind. We kiss and she touches my soul, Bugsy touches my stomach. Claire touches my neck. We kiss.

Christ, I shall go mad . . . I know that I shall; they shall find my bones shattered; broken and scattered across some barren fucking wasteland, bleached white and drying in the sun. I am love walking in the shape of a man, and it is something I had never thought to be again . . . to feel so deeply . . . god, I am happy, god I am sad . . . I am a jactitating love walking in the shape of a man. And we kiss.

34

"*IN TIMES of trouble, mother Mary comes to me . . . Let it be.*"
Jane has received a file in blue for Claire; it has the F.B.I. seal on
the outside cover, yes; Claire asks her to courier it to us, by
bonded service . . . not via one of the giants . . . we should get it
by tomorrow, "Hold for pickup at the Miami office." No point in
taking extra chances.

Bayside Marketplace is the Miami version of supposed sea-
side quaint . . . like Granville Island in Vancouver, 5th Street
Seaport in Seattle, Inner Harbor in Baltimore . . . ahm, what's the
name of the one in New York . . . ahm, Southpoint Seaport or
something, anyhow you get the drift; you know, full of restau-
rants, small shops, booths and vendors. There's marinas and
boats, a boardwalk along the water, there's music and entertainment. It is surrounded by Bayfront Park. Famous Flagler
street is spitting distance.

The girls want to go on a sightseeing boat . . . I don't. They
go . . . I stay. I wave to them from the dock. They look like tourists. Both are wearing hats. They smile widely, wave vigorously.
In your eyes, the light the heat.

I will look for Neathersole. I make my calls. There is a message in Hialeah. I am given a number to call.

"Hello . . . I'm looking for Arnold Ten Toes."

"Mr. Toes ain't in right now, can ya leave a name and a
number where he can get back to youse." The voice is full of
New York . . . I picture a large-jowled man, with dark greasy
hair, gray at the temples, fat and in need of a shave; probably,
too, in need of a bath, his pants are baggy, his shirt too tight . . .
and, and he has one of those wallets on a chain, like bikers carry.

"I'm at a pay phone." I tell him, he shrugs it off and asks for the number. I give it to him and hang up.

"**TOOK** you long enough to get here, man." Neathersole blurts out as I pick up the phone.

"Sole, shit—I've been here for fucking days . . . Christ, man, you scared the shit out of me . . . where the hell you *been*?"

"Hah, I scared the shit out of you! Do you have any fucking *idea* what you got me mixed up in—*do* ya? . . . scared? Man, you wanna know about scared, shit . . . I been hiding, man, where you think?"

"Oh, I know, my friend, I know . . . the government . . ."

"Yeah, the government . . . but do you know *why*, man?"

"No . . . no not really, I can guess, maybe."

"Well don't, don't . . . fuck . . . Are you doing okay?"

"No man . . . I'm on the hide like you . . . we pushed it out already that we're looking for spies . . . I know that we're really looking for our own guys . . . but . . . tried to cover our asses a little, buy time . . . but . . ."

"Yeah, 'but' is right, amigo—look, I'll give ya a little break-down, best I can: The Russkies fed our boys the names of some agents, see . . . well, look, them former Warsaw Pact guys, some of them were very active, especially like the Ukrainian GRU, most of the—most of your bodies are gonna belong to Ukrainian agents, uh, the rest are mostly East German . . . they were offered up as a swap . . . for what happened to those 16 American agents that were exposed, remember . . . a peace offering, so to speak, man . . . They're being killed as much for example as anything else; everybody else thinks its a serial job, but those who are supposed to know do . . . its a warning, pull your spies out or else. Or else."

"What do you have, man, you got any proof?"

"I've got a bad case of heartburn . . . I got Herman hiding out and complaining all day . . . there's a fucking interdiction team at Herman's house, camped out, waiting on my face so they can fucking blow me away . . . god, I love my fucking life— this is happy times. You?"

"I've got some proof, yes, maybe . . . They killed their Special Agent in Charge of Atlanta; he was about to pass us proof. We found the proof today; can we meet?"

"I'm not sure I want to leave my little security behind, my friend . . . it's fucking scary out there for one blind man and a fat old queer."

"Herman try to fuck you yet?"

"He wishes, the old fag . . . he says hi . . ."

"So who's the control on this . . . F.B.I. —and by the way, where you getting this info?"

"Where do you think killers come from, man? The best ones come out of government service, ex-mil, ex-intelligence, ex-IRS—joke; remember I grew up with these killers, we were over-seas together, wet work—fuck, remember France . . . I was stuffing fucking French civilians into fucking body bags, slant eyes and occidentals, man, no conscience, white and yellow alike, money boys . . ." I heard his pause . . . knew he was re-membering . . . badly.

"The NSA is really heading this up, I suppose—Baxter seems to be the top dog . . ." He continued, the phone line had a tinny sound to it. ". . . But all operations are running out of SIOC in Washington . . . F.B.I.'s providing the manpower, the hardware and the counter-intelligence . . . the wet work is being done by imports . . . CIA boys and girls and people from the other side, stone fucking killers, sanctioned, which leaves us in a bit of a fucking situation, I mean in case you haven't figured it yet."

"What, how?"

"The killers . . . you thought you were buying time with that spy shit, right? . . . well, you gave the F.B.I. a way out, but not the wet boys . . . they're fucked, they're compromised, and if they live past their last sanction, it'll only be because you and me are stone fucking dead and all the proof is burned . . . else, else the fucking Feds are going to feed them to the lions as the bad guys . . . Russian agents on the rampage—they gotta come after us . . . you dig, amigo?"

"Shit . . . the proof, though, if we get the proof we'll be safe?"

"Yeah, sure, maybe, if you make it public knowledge, maybe . . . they might just kill you for spite . . . you been there, man, you know, you *know*."

I know . . . I know shit anymore. I know he's right, though. They are going to come after us, after him, after Claire . . . after me—it's the only way out. The cops are a bureaucracy, they can be manipulated. Us, we're just fucking citizens, citizens can be killed, ex-fucking-pendable. I sigh heavily, pat my pocket for a cigarette. I am out. I need a smoke.

There is a man smoking over there; I could ask him.

"What are you going to do, Sole?"

"Hey man, I was only just waiting for you, hanging out long enough to talk to ya is all, my friend . . . now, shit now, I am fucking outta here . . . shuffle my blind ass off till all this blows over . . . Man . . . man, you wouldn't fucking believe how I, how I felt—I mean, man, you asked me to look into killers for ya, right, so I make a couple of calls, put the word on the street. And boom! two guys call me back, within the hour . . . anxious.

"They tell me to take the fucking walk, exactly that one guy say to me, he says 'Sole, my man, take the fucking walk, man, and take it fast and long . . . take the fucking walk and call me later when you're safe and I'll tell you all about it.' Shit . . . shit, you have any fucking idea what it's like to be a blind man surrounded by fucking *killers*? You can't see shit, you can't protect yourself . . . *Fuck*." He is drinking something, I can hear its liquidity, the ice in the glass, the motion of his throat. It is tequila, I am sure . . . Tequila sunrises.

"Ah, that's better . . . Herman makes a killer fucking Sunrise." Pay me up, I am a winner on that bet. "And what are *you* gonna do, T.?"

"Sole . . . what you told me, can you get me anything solid—you know, like two guys on tape saying it's so; a name, a number? I *need* this, man . . . where the fuck can I go, Sole, where can I go?"

"Fuck, my friend, fuck . . . yeah, yeah—I can get you some names, something . . . but—I mean, I don't know, man . . . who you gonna go to, who?"

"I don't know . . . CNN, CBS . . . there's this great woman, ahm, wha—Connie Bruck, at the New Yorker . . . Journalist; she could write this."

"Who?"

"Connie Bruck . . . at the New Yorker, she helped bring down opinion on Michael Milken."

"Never heard of her . . . you don't have time, man—where's Claire?"

"She's . . . she's here . . ." A little laugh. "She's gone on a sightseeing boat . . . with a friend."

"You guys are traveling light—you brought a friend along?"

"Sort of . . . long story."

"Crazy, man, crazy. Look, my advice, just take Claire and blow . . . you really want something more solid I'll get it for you . . . you want to feed it to CNN, CBS, whoever, you do it, but get the fuck out of this world first . . . they will *kill* you, man, and you fucking *know* that I am right."

A moment of silence.

Then he continued. "You know how to reach me, right? . . . same place, same way . . . five days and you'll have something; I'll be gone by then, though."

"I can't see ya?"

"No man no . . . fuck . . . I am gonna take Herman on a little trip . . . five days, okay? but if I were you I wouldn't wait. I *wouldn't*."

I was beginning to believe that I wouldn't either.

35

I BUM A CIGARETTE from the smoking man. There is sun. I have found cigarettes, they are Dunhills, which I have not smoked in years. They are good. Inhale deeply, feel the burn, be the smoke.

A fruit smoothie to rinse the palate. Reggae music plays somewhere in the periphery of my hearing. Jimmy Cliff, I would swear. God, how I love this music . . . it is so much home. I sit in the sun to warm my blood. I am tan. I am tired.

What do you do in between running and hiding? Hah, you smoke and listen to reggae music.

"Do you mind if I join you?"

She stands over me, from nowhere she has appeared; tall tall tall and not nearly as bald as the last time. Her eyes are penetrating. her smile seems genuine. Valerie. I am surprised.

A moment.

And then the moment passes. I stand and smile.

"Ah, my coincidence—how do we keep finding the time?"

"You are a funny man . . . and always a pleasant coincidence . . . but . . . I do believe that we have some business to discuss, eh?"

I look around, eyeing for backup.

"You don't have to worry—I came alone." She is looking at me through predator's eyes. I feel like dinner: *Over her brocaded robe/ She wore a plain and simple dress.* It is applicable, but it is not what Confucius meant to imply. There is evil in this woman. I feel the weight of my gun and realize that I want to kill this bitch. I want to draw my gun and shoot her right between those fucking eyes. I want to pump bullets into that fucking cunt that fascinates me. She is playing in the back of her hair. Her other hand is behind her, under her jacket. I'm quite sure that she is armed . . . with teeth.

"We can go now, if you'd like."

"Not really, but there's coffee over there; I'd like a cup, you?"

"It makes me . . . edgy." She is tall.

"We wouldn't want that at all." I smile. If I bent to tie my shoelace . . . could I get the gun out fast enough? . . . I could kick her in the stomach. Coffee, I need coffee and another fucking cigarette.

"Am I making you nervous?"

"Very."

"That really was not to be my intention . . . I just wanted to talk to you."

"How did you find me?"

"The F.B.I. has many resources, and you . . . well, you and your friends are top priority, eh?" Her smile I imagined to be fanged, but really it was . . . perfect . . . it was beautiful . . . I could fuck this woman. "Do you think, perhaps, Tom—can I call you Tom?"

"Might as well . . ." I pay for my *cafe con leche* without actually looking at the woman who hands it to me.

"Can we walk? The world is full of ears."

"Where are the Feds?"

"Probably close, but they don't know that you are here, I mean right here . . . this was my deduction."

"Where are you from?" The smoke dribbles out of my nose and mouth.

"I'm sure that you've seen my file."

"Actually, no . . . but it'll be here tomorrow; the suspense, though, is fucking killing me." I have some balls at the moment.

"I was born in Monaco; my mother is French, my father Italian, I've spent many years in Germany though . . . east Germany. You are from the Caribbean, it is very nice there . . . actually it suits you . . . the accent, I mean . . . I really do not wish to have to kill you, Tom."

It was added so matter-of-factly that had it not been my death she was mentioning I might have let it slip on by.

"Not my choice either. Look, this bugs the shit out of me, really it does . . . it does . . . why the fuck are you hassling me? Fucking hell, man, fuck . . . you people are fucking sick . . . this is no joke, you've just killed 11 people, for what? In the name of national security, as an example to Soviets of all kinds? . . . Shit, this isn't wartime . . ."

"Ah, but it *is* wartime, that's what you forget . . . you believe that newspaper crap that you read, the cold war is over and the Americans win. Come now, you don't believe that." We had walked to the end of the mall. The sunlight, on emerging, was bright. The Hard Rock was on our left, the bay in front of us. We walked down to the water and turned right. I put on my dark glasses, she didn't.

"The war goes on . . . the Americans see a chance, a superiority; the Russians feel threatened by their . . . their predicament, it is very dangerous. I will have to kill you if you continue."

"I don't want to die."

"No, I don't suppose that you do." She stepped past me and stopped, facing me. "There's also your friends to consider."

"Yes, yes, there's always that—but the police already have the information."

"They don't have the blue file . . . Clifford's file . . . we killed Clifford."

"I gather . . . so you want the file."

"Oh, yes . . . and I believe that perhaps your friend Neathersole has something to give you."

"I haven't been able to find him."

"I truly do doubt that."

"I could kill you right now." I say it. I smoke.

Her mouth is open. She isn't saying anything.

"I . . . I have—you are taking this rather well, eh?"

"I'm very tired, *very* . . . how long do I have to decide?"

"Tomorrow . . . I expect that you'll have all the information you're waiting for by tomorrow."

"Hmm . . . I'll have to talk it over with my friends."

"Do that . . . please. I am, I'm very sorry that it comes to this, I've really enjoyed our meetings."

"How did you find me?"

"I knew you'd be here . . . that you'd stay where you felt safe, safe, uh . . . where is safe for people like you and me? Home is safe, you'd stay in a place like home . . . so I had the computer run a check of your friends and their assets . . . Mark has rather a lot of assets."

Oddly, we walked then, like friends, along the waterline and talked a few bars; the rhythm of our accents syncopating the Queen's English. She was of interest to me.

She laughed. "Look at this . . . you are talking to me of Monaco . . . of times and pleasures . . . and tomorrow I am going to have to kill you." Reality intrudes, and rather rudely.

"You keep bringing that up."

"It is there."

"Yes . . . yes, it is there . . . but you don't *want* to kill me, do you? No, actually what you want is to walk the fuck away, that's why you're here; you have a job to do, right? . . . a killing to make. Listen to this shit . . . I have a proposition, tell me if I am wrong: You have tapes of everything, of the killings, of the meetings, of everything, video and audio . . . it would be your life if you didn't."

"You have a hell of a head, Tom . . . you think too much, eh?"

"Often . . . but you offered me a proposition, I'll offer you one. Give me the tapes; you walk, you and your friends walk . . . take the next flight to Timbuktu . . . I'll get who I really want anyhow . . . besides, who could like those hypocritical fucks, eh? Right now you're just after me 'cause you know it'll save your ass if I'm dead or taken care of." The world is alive in glorious sunshine. I just want to live. Pitch the sale, man, pitch that fucking sale.

"They'd kill you just as soon as have you walking around with all this information . . . governments are fucks . . . *fucks* . . . they feel themselves above reproach, they're doing it for the greater good, they say . . . bullshit—they're doing it to perpetuate themselves and a few hundred other fucks just like them at the top of some imaginary fucking ladder . . . the super elite, the powerful . . . I'm rambling, aren't I? . . . sorry, I'm angry . . . I'm scared, and angry."

"Yes . . . where are your friends, are they shopping?"

"No. So what do you say?"

"I hear what you say . . . but we have a contract to fulfill, you understand . . . mind you, what you have said is, well, it has validity. Validity, that is a good word, no . . . can I bother you for one of your cigarettes?"

"Oh, yes, sorry—I didn't realize that you smoked."

"I don't really, just the rare occasion . . . it is a passion that one just must enjoy sometimes . . . like heroin."

I nearly choked on the analogy, and my smoke.

"Heroin?"

"Yes . . . have you not tried it?"

"No . . ."

"Ah, you have missed something then . . . I have an opportunity once every few years . . . I take it in good company; please, habit in anything is not good, restraint, no? But there are pleasures in life that . . . well, life would not be complete without experience . . . flavor."

She makes perfect sense to me. I realize that I could be friends with this woman.

"Are we going to have to fight this out?"

"I have given you a suggestion, you have given me one; we will talk to our friends tonight and decide tomorrow what must be done. You will go back to your apartment?"

"Will it be safe?"

"Yes." She is not lying to me. It is a weird fuck world that we live in.

"Your friends will be looking for you."

"Yes."

"It has been interesting . . . I enjoyed the day with the planes very much; we can do it again sometime maybe, eh . . ."

The dice of God are always loaded . . . If the good is there, so is the evil; if the affinity, so the repulsion . . . I think in Emersonisms as I watch her walk away. The light shining through the loose linen of cream trousers; voluminous, so that I can see the shape of her legs, the curve of her ass. She has taken off her jacket and wears a sleeveless shirt, white white white. She is spring breeze, I can smell her fragrance lingering. Her hair shines, its touch of redness luminescent. She turns her head to look over her shoulder. I can see her smile from here; I can remember the pout of her mouth. I think the color of her eyes. A slight twist of the waist and she waves. Arms long, delicate, muscled. Hands, fingers, long, sensuous.

I can see the gun in the hollow of her back.

SHE IS DRESSED in a red that matches perfectly the dot in the middle of her forehead. Her features are that sharp East Indian lovely; age does not show on her flawless flesh. She sits quietly stroking the fur of a cat. It is the cat from New Orleans, she has brought it with her, become attached; actually she has brought the both of them. There is only the chair she sits on in the doorway of an otherwise empty room. The room smells vaguely of incense.

She sets down the cat and walks to the picture window. Outside, Doug is finishing the packing of the RV. Soon he will drive it to a remote spot and burn it to the ground. Claud has gone to keep the Feds occupied; Bertrand has gone to do the killing. She doesn't know where Valerie has gotten to. The fucking African genius and what's-her-face are cleaning up. With any luck at all they will be ready within the hour. They'll slip off into the night, clean the last few loose ends and be gone in two days . . . before the Fed realizes what exactly has happened. It is 5:12 p.m.

The cat rubs up against her leg, passing around one ankle and then the other in a figure eight.

The victim drives a nice car; he sells nice cars, that's his job. The victim . . . Mr. body . . . hole in the head. Hole in the head.

BERTRAND walked up to him that evening as he stepped out of his nice car in the parking spot of his nice townhome and shot him in the forehead . . . once. He slammed back hard against the car, slumped back into the doorway, didn't quite make the seat. His head lolled forward, his tongue hung out. There was a sound of flatulence and his bowels voided.

Killer flinched a little at the smell. Fuck! then fired two rounds more, one to the chest, one to the throat. There was a little stream of blood that trickled from the wound in the head. The body looked oddly deflated. Killer laid a note on the seat, dropped the gun on the floor of the car and turning walked casually away. Hole in the head had on a nice suit.

DARK OF A night, coffee close at hand . . . be the cigarette, be the smoke, deep inhale . . . aahhh. Bare feet up, night cool and fresh on my exposed chest, shirt unbuttoned. Claire and Bugsy have gone to the Omni to shop. I have neglected to tell her about my little meeting . . . let them have peace in their security. I wonder if the F.B.I. will trace us . . . no, no—I think that Valerie the not-so-bald will keep us safe . . . at least till tomorrow. There is the sound of traffic below.

That sound of distant traffic brings back past times; the sound of distant traffic always reminds me of London, of a hotel where we used to stay. The old-fashioned family kind of hotel, where people lived and people came to stay . . . you asked for a room with its own bath, if you wanted one; a telly was an option; it was not America.   In the evenings people gathered in the sitting room to watch television together, over a drink or a cup of tea . . . communal. London, W.9. I mostly remember the grays and browns of the world around me and I remember the butcher shops filled with "bangers".

I remember Edinburgh in the spring, green and gray with black cliffs rising above the commons. The castle so prominent lauding over the city. I remember Oxford in the summer, the smell of hay fresh-mowed and of silage decomposing; wide open fields and church bells and the wreck of an old tractor with steel wheels. I remember the Sussex coast, Tumbridge Wells with its little apple trees, the Three Counties Fair; Worcester, Hertfordshire and Devonshire . . .

. . . I remember a girl who was blonde and elsewise indistinct, who loved me for a too-short summer.

I liked England, I got very well laid there once, and by many an English woman since. There was a dancer once who I met on holiday. She did ballet, among other really quite terrific things with her body . . . absolutely amazing. God, what was her name . . . the wings of time are black and white . . . who said that? She was fantastic in the sack, but left me with a scorching case of the clap. Christ, I can laugh at it now, but when the doctor stuck that cold probe up my urethra . . . if I could remember the bitch's name I would call it out right now. The cigarette goes down good.

I am oddly relaxed.

" . . . *Planet Queen, perchance to dream . . . well it's all right, love is what you want . . . flying saucer take me away, gimme your daughter . . .*". T-Rex.

I look for stars in the sky.

SOME KIDS, out drinking in the fields, found the still-smoking hull of the RV. The police came.

They found five bodies amongst the ashes . . . well, seven, actually, but two of them were cats.

36

I COULDN'T sleep. It's all supposed to be all right, but I can't sleep. I can drink, though, and I pour a nice rum on the rocks. I can smoke—I am becoming very used to the Dunhills, but do have a craving for dark Turkish tobacco. It is raining a light drizzle. The Weather Channel is on inside, muted, but emitting light . . . Paris is mostly cloudy and 50, Frankfurt is not doing quite as well.

There's the sound of distant sirens. I fondle the cold of the gun on the table. I don't like the thought of having to carry the fucking thing. I want morning to come and for it all to be over. Just moments away from freedom, eh? I feel like that has been the story of my life; the carrot dangling just out of reach; the golden bowl . . . and then the phone rings —shit.

"Hello."

"Yes . . . it is your friend." And I know who it is.

"Walk outside and turn left, onto the bridge . . . I will meet you there."

The Venetian Causeway, an Art Deco series of white railed humpback bridges that island-hop across Biscayne Bay to Miami Beach. Valerie is there, leaning in the glow of modernity on an otherwise dark night. She looks dirty. When I get closer I realize that she is.

"You're limping," she says.

"Banged into the coffee table trying to get to the phone," I say. "You're—what happened to you?" I say.

"A long story " says she; perhaps, I think, she will tell it. "They hit us," she continues. "We were dumping the RV . . . the operations unit that we've used, and they hit us."

"The Feds." It really wasn't a question.

"Yes." She coughs.

"You're not hit?"

She laughs loudly. "Fuck no, I smelled them coming—took four of them on my way out the door . . ." The laugh, less heavy. "Claud is a bad man . . . he's my partner . . . he covered me . . . the others are dead—so is Claud, now . . . I left him in the car." Her eyes drifted, and on the road under a streetlight by the Herald building was a Mercedes. "The tapes are in the trunk." She seemed glazed over, battle weary; I had seen men walk out of jungles and house raids looking just the same: adrenaline dead.

"Jesus Christ—he was a good friend, a good man—ummm." A grunt and she shook her head. "You were right . . . they'll be after you now."

"Yes; I suppose they'll want the blue file."

"Oh yes, oh yes, they will—are you going to give it to them?"

"What are you going to do?"

"I don't know . . . I don't know . . . I could use a bath."

"You can have one upstairs."

"Yes yes, that would be nice . . . that would be nice . . . let me just make sure that Claud is all right." It was, perhaps, a strange thing to say about a dead man.

I woke the girls. Introduced the situation. Bugsy sleep-walked to the kitchen to make tea.

Claire became alive, got towels and fresh clothes . . . a bee-hive, veritably. Our enemy has become our friend.

You ever have one of those fights when you were a kid, beat somebody up and then they become your best friend for the rest of your life? Like that fight is the catalyst for common ground, the tie that binds you to another's life . . . Mark is a friend like that: the first time we met we fought, and have been together as friends since the very next day, when our mothers made us apologize.

What is that Japanese saying; "If you sit by the river long enough, sooner or later you will see the body of your enemy float by." Knowing the Japanese, it is probably more spare, but I think that I've achieved the gist.

Claire was in the bathroom with Valerie; the door was open, Claire looked up at me with sad eyes. I gave a question look. She made a sad face with a shrug . . . telepathic communication.

The evil killer was yet human.

WE ARE DEATH warmed over and strung the fuck out on too much caffeine. The four of us have spent the night on the patio, solving the problems of the world, and dawn is coming like a freight train toward day.

It is then that I make the call to Frenchy. I tell him that we are coming in, all of us.

I tell him we need cover to come in.

"French—you'll have to put out the troops; you gather up the boys and get here . . . I'm not walking out of this fucking place until the troops get here . . . we've got the tapes, we've got the files, we've got the F.B.I. weekly reports, the blue file . . . we've got a witness, we got witness big fucking time, *big* time— you know, French, I hope those fucks are listening on the line— fuck them, they are toast, stick a fork in them they are *done*, man . . . Frenchy, their ass belongs to us. —How soon can you be here?"

He estimates several hours, it is six a.m. now . . . noon till he walks in.

I instruct him to meet us in front of Las Tapas restaurant at Bayside . . . public property . . . 12:00 noon.

"French, bring the fucking backup, man, they're not gonna want to let us walk . . . they're not gonna want us to get away."

He made me promise to stay alive, no matter what, no matter how; he wanted them badly. We were going to bring the fucking world down around their fucking ears. I promised, I promised—crossed my heart and hoped not to die.

So, now, we needed to get out of here. We needed to take the walk. I needed a friend. So I called one.

He called from the lobby 20 minutes later; how he got here that fast, I still cannot fathom.

He looked different, as he did almost every time I saw him. Sylvester. His hair was long and ponytailed, gray and chestnut, a beard, bushy and much the same; he had dropped a few pounds. Dressed in jeans, tight at the ankle, and a Hawaiian shirt. He hadn't taken off the aviator sunglasses or his happy smile. There were three guys with him.

"I brought the guys."

"You look different." I nodded to the guys, exchanged half smiles.

"Yes . . . good, don't want anyone finding me . . . you like the hair color?"

"No . . . but the beard hides enough of your face . . . come in, huh?"

"Doesn't sound like it's really safe in here . . . why don't we go now."

"Okay . . . we're just waiting on the girls."

"Hey, you're a bad man, huh, go on the lam and carry chicks with y—" he couldn't fit the words around his tongue when Valerie appeared, followed by Claire and then Bugsy . . . "Fuck!" was all he could manage.

"Sylvester, this is Valerie the tall, behind her is Claire the considerate and last, oh but not least, Bugsy the beautiful."

"Wow ladies, it is a pleasure . . . oh, these gentlemen are Frank, Bobby and John . . . John and Bobby are brothers, they are gonna be your friends for the day; Rory is downstairs in the car. He isn't related either. —Now, anything, anything you want removed from your life today, you tell these boys, they are here to serve and protect." He smiled ever so nicely. "Tommy, I always thought that you were way cool, but, my man, this just proves it . . . these are three of the most beautiful women I could imagine . . . ladies, shall we walk." Always the salesman.

Frank and Bobby took lead. They were indistinct characters, nothing striking about them but the movement of their eyes. They were neither short nor tall, young nor old, big or small . . . you couldn't quite get a grasp on them. John was handsome, but his eyes were dead. They were hazel. He waited against the wall while we walked, then followed.

When the elevator came they stopped it and called another. When the second elevator arrived John and I took one and the rest the other; us first, them to follow. We were lucky—ours didn't stop.

Theirs did . . . I felt my fucking heart sink.

I must have counted to a hundred standing there in the lobby, my hands sweating.

Then the doors opened and Frank and Bobby were filling the doorway, one standing, one kneeling. I closed my eyes and let out my breath. Sylvester patted my shoulder as he passed. Claire took my hand, Bugsy kissed my cheek. Valerie smiled a dim hello.

John took the point this time and we walked into the lobby.

He crossed the lobby to the escalators on our right and positioned himself; it was the weak spot . . . Frank took the left flank . . . Bobby crossed the lobby with purpose.

Rory had the van against the curb, the doors open. He was somewhere in the parking lobby, but I hadn't fixed him yet. We were military patrol precision.

"Syl, there's a Mercedes across the street." I handed him the keys, "there's a body in the front and some tapes in the back."

"You kill him?"

"No . . . but he's a friend of Valerie's . . . the tapes are what we need . . . but if you can arrange something for him . . . don't want him to start rotting, eh?"

"I'll make a call." He had some interesting silver rings on his fingers. He was the real hippie. The last time he had looked— like Wall Street. Sylvester, slim and wiry, small as he was at 5'9," was a bad man . . . a very bad man . . . and a drug dealer in the big leagues. Sylvester moved poundage. A *bad* bad man.

He pulled out the cellular and placed his call. We paused at the door.

"Okay, go get in the van . . . Bobby, there's a Mercedes across the road; in the trunk is a box of tapes, bring it . . . Bob, there's a stiff in the front, ignore it, huh?"

"Sure." Like it was an everyday occurrence.

"Valerie . . . a friend of mine will be coming to pick up the car and take your friend to a funeral home . . . do you have anything special that you want done? Sorry if this is a bit morbid." Businesslike, efficient.

"No, no, not at all . . . I've seen a lot—no, no . . . you could arrange that his ashes go somewhere nice . . . he would like England." As if she knew it would be arranged, but then she understood people like Sylvester.

"I'll make it happen." I think perhaps that that should be Sylvester's motto, or his epitaph maybe. It is the key to his being; "I'll make it happen".

We were in the van. Plush in blue velour. At the back was a couch and table, two captain's chairs facing it. Up front there were four more captain's chairs. A TV-VCR setup was on the left (you facing forward), on the right, stereo; a fridge under one, a bar under the other. Stove and sink on the left. It was big and blue. I had no doubt that the windows were armored.

Our friends filled the four chairs at the front. Sylvester sat between Bugsy and Valerie on the couch.

I held Claire's hand.

I think Bugsy found this all very exciting.

Valerie was the walking wounded.

"So you gonna tell me the story?" See, Sylvester had come without a question. I had said that I was unsafe and needed to move. He had packed the goon squad and come to rescue. It is good to have friends.

I can tell you about Sylvester. We were born together only farms apart, in the same year, to grandparents who had always been friends. I spent a lifetime in his playpen, he was often stuck in mine. At age ten his father died and his mother married an American. They moved to Miami. He's been here ever since, except for trips home to my house.

I tell you, when your life comes to a close, if you can look back fondly on the quality of the friendships you have had, then your life has been worthwhile. I think that I can be happy with mine. I squeeze Claire's hand.

They are there. Frenchy, Leeman, Santi, others, six in all, waiting . . . surrounded, by suits, camouflaged, yet they stand out like sore thumbs, the suits. Sylvester looks out the window of the van.

"Would you fucking look at that—shit, Fed city; your friends dump on you?"

"No . . . no, I doubt it . . . Bobby, you find the marksmen yet?"

"There's four across the street, two different buildings . . . my guess is that there's probably one on the Miami Center tower too, but that's a wild shot . . . they're just covering with that one—no, those four across the street will have all kinds of angles on ya."

"Christ . . . Syl, why can't I smoke . . . huh, huh?"

"You know how I *hate* that shit . . . so, you going out?"

"Out there? fuck, I look like a nut to you? . . . *fuck* no . . . how many Feds you count, Bobby?"

"Eight in the open—there's probably a van in the back full of SWATs . . . I'll go."

"No . . . no, I'll go, I'll go . . . woof, I need a cigarette anyhow—stand by for me."

I put on my dark glasses. Stop a moment to light the cigarette, then slide that fucking door open and step into the light.

There seems to be a touch of surprise all around.

John and Bobby step down too, one breaks right, the other left. They do a flanking motion to cover.

The pathway is cobbled, perennials bloom in concrete as a border. Las Tapas is on my left . . . some outfitters' store on my right, J. Chisum, I think, I don't look; my eyes are on the Feds, who have instinctively begun to close the net. A large ficus shades the courtyard, umbiferous. It is the long walk.

I can see that Frenchy looks nervous, he has a hand on his gun; they have backed up against one another.

Then there is the sound of sirens.

I suck on that smoke.

Cops.

Frenchy smiles. His hand hasn't left his gun; mine is on mine too, at my waist, I know that I can pop the fuck on my right, maybe two of them. But I know the sniper has me, I can feel the crosshairs.

I don't look back for the cops. But Frenchy is smiling, so he obviously feels good.

"Your friend Dixie . . . he has a lot of friends."

"Oh, is that him making all that noise behind me?"

"Yes that's him . . . I'm nervous, son, how about you?"

"Scared shitless—look at these fucks . . . they don't know whether to shit or die . . . hi, guys . . . yeah, what the fuck you gonna do now?" A crowd is gathering.

"Shoot one of them, French, just for the hell of it." I am cold between my shoulder blades, yet sweat pours from me. I want another cigarette.

"You got everything?"

"I got everything, and some copies . . . they're delivering the shit to the Herald right now . . . it's good to have friends, French . . . Dixie, you back there?" I yell it out.

"I'm back here, boy . . . hey, don't these Fed fuckers look sweaty now, shee-*it!* We got us a party . . . so, you think we can go in now?"

"I fucking hope so man, I fucking *hope* so . . . I am so tired . . . I need a good pot of coffee, a pack of strong cigarettes and about 24 hours to myself by the beach."

The Feebies are the edge of the crowd, waiting for their instructions, still. As we were gathered together, a screen of blue for us. I hugged Frenchy, shook Dixie's hand, we were smiles and pats on the back.

I looked up and found Claire standing in the doorway of the van. God, she looked frightened. God, she looked beautiful. She seemed haloed in a haze of light. I smiled, she smiled, and I walked to her.

37

IT IS SUNNY and warm. Christmas in the tropics. The house is grayed wood in a natural surround, up on stilts, a scattered haphazard construction rambling around the expanse of the lot . . . the garden is sea grape, sand and palm trees. I am sitting on the top of four steps that lead down onto the sand. The sea is blue gloss.

THERE ARE two things I have read that I want you to hear:

" . . . *And so whoever has the legislative or supreme power of any commonwealth is bound to govern by established stand-ing laws . . . And all this to be directed to no other end but the peace, safety and public good of the people.*"

And: " . . . *A state which dwarfs its men in order that they may be more docile instruments in its hands, even for beneficial purposes, will find that with small men no great thing can really be accomplished; and that the perfection of the machinery to which it has sacrificed everything will in the end avail it nothing . . .*"

The first is by John Locke; the second by John Stuart Mill. Both men political philosophers who provided some of the thought that helped launch us into the political arena with which we are now all familiar. Their minds engineered the pos-sibilities of contentious government.

Our case is all over the television these days, Congressional hearings, oversight committees, Senate special sessions, media blitzes . . . CNN even has an update logo designated to the cover-up. The president is denying involvement . . . the vice president swears he was in fucking China while the key meetings were taking place. Rogue elements are being blamed, sacrificial lambs being chosen.

And I am a million miles away, drinking too much rum and smoking too many cigarettes. By the way, you owe me some congratulations; I got married last week.

The coffee is better here, the cigarettes have more flavor. The greens are more verdant, the colors truly vibrant. Odors have pungence, tastes are more piquant.

I am alive.

"Babes, you want more coffee?" Claire from over my shoulder. "Bugsy will bring it if you want . . . oops, no, here comes Valerie."

Valerie: the hair on her head has grown back in, but her pussy is pedophilic still.

I am a happy man.

I am at peace.

Printed in the United States
3484